D0290753

PRAISE FOR
SUNSET EMPIRE

"Another clever collision between history and what might have been, but this time with the USA's misadventures in East Asia and Indochina swept into the geopolitical storm."

—Ian R MacLeod, Sidewise Award–winning author of *Wake Up and Dream*

"To my delight, this book surpassed *Beat the Devils. Sunset Empire* kept me guessing, and I enjoyed all of the story's twists and turns... Although it's a work of fiction, *Sunset Empire* is very prescient as to what's currently happening in the world. I'm ready for more Morris Baker stories!"

—Michael Kronenberg, artist and graphic designer, Film Noir Foundation/*NOIR CITY* Magazine

"Bright, terrifying, alternate fiction that could be fact. Detective Morris Baker returns full force to the scene of a brand new crime. Pick up *Sunset Empire*, and you won't put it down until the very last word."

—Paul Lally, author of the *Amerika* and *Rise Again* trilogies

"Josh's writing is beautifully visual, with characters so perfectly realized that his melding of real history and fiction takes on a poignancy that transcends the 'what if?' genre and makes you worry 'what if again?' I can't wait for another Morris Baker case!"

—Ben Parker, writer/director of *Burial* and *The Chamber*

SUNSET EMPIRE

Also by Josh Weiss

Beat the Devils

SUNSET EMPIRE

A Morris Baker Mystery

JOSH WEISS

NEW YORK BOSTON

This book is a work of historical fiction. In order to give a sense of the times, some names or real people or places have been included in the book. However, the events depicted in this book are imaginary, and the names of nonhistorical persons or events are the product of the author's imagination or are used fictitiously. Any resemblance of such nonhistorical persons or events to actual ones is purely coincidental.

Grand Central Publishing
Hachette Book Group
1290 Avenue of the Americas, New York, NY 10104
grandcentralpublishing.com
twitter.com/grandcentralpub

First Edition: March 2023

Grand Central Publishing is a division of Hachette Book Group, Inc. The Grand Central Publishing name and logo is a trademark of Hachette Book Group, Inc.

The publisher is not responsible for websites (or their content) that are not owned by the publisher.

The Hachette Speakers Bureau provides a wide range of authors for speaking events. To find out more, go to www.hachettespeakersbureau.com or call (866) 376-6591.

Print book interior design by Marie Mundaca.

Library of Congress Cataloging-in-Publication Data
Names: Weiss, Josh, author.
Title: Sunset empire / by Josh Weiss.
Description: First Edition. | New York; Boston: GCP, 2023. | Series: A
Identifiers: LCCN 2022047953 | ISBN 9781538719473 (hardcover) | ISBN 9781538719466 (ebook)
Classification: LCC PS3623.E45537 S86 2023 | DDC 813/.6—dc23
LC record available at https://lccn.loc.gov/2022047953

ISBNs: 978-1-5387-1947-3 (hardcover), 978-1-5387-1946-6 (ebook)

Printed in the United States of America

LSC-C

Printing 1, 2023

To my unbelievably incredible wife, Leora:
You are my biggest fan and my harshest critic
I'd be lost without your guidance
Still not sure how a regular schmo like me ended up
with a swell gal like you
Love you to the moon and back!

SUNSET EMPIRE

PROLOGUE

> I will defend Korea as I would my own country—just as I would California.
>
> —*General Douglas MacArthur*

> We're gonna nuke each other up, boys, 'til old Satan stands impressed.
>
> —*Matt Maltese*

December 1, 1959

They called him "The Tiger" because of his ravenous devotion to the cause. He approved of the moniker, but not for the reasons *they* provided. He approved of the title because it reminded him of the bedtime stories his mother would often recite to him as a boy.

Korean fairy tales always began not with "Once upon a time..." but with "Back when tigers smoked..." Tigers did not smoke, of course. The traditional opening signified the start of a fantastical journey—one that could never take place in the real world.

The memory of his mother's voice enveloped him, soft and comforting like a beloved childhood blanket.

His true name was... wait, what was his real name...? William! Yes, William Yang. That's right. How could he have forgotten? William Yang, a near-lifelong native of Los Angeles and a... wait, what did he do for a living? Where was he? A pleading, panicked voice that seemed to come out of nowhere screamed: "*Wake up, William! Wake up!*"

The Tiger shook his head. His mind was just a tad foggy, but that was to be expected with the momentous job sitting before him. A job that was mere moments away from being carried out.

Nothing else mattered, except the cause.

Soft Christmas music brought him back to the hustle and bustle of the department store. "*Chestnuts roasting on an open fire...Jack Frost nipping at your nose...*" crooned Nat King Cole in a tender, fireside tone. Men and women, accompanied by giggling children, cast murderous, side-eyed glances in his direction as they went about their early holiday shopping.

He was the enemy to *them*.

It made no difference that he'd been raised in this country—had spoken its language, observed its customs, and fought for its values. The shape of his eyes was reason enough in their minds to loathe him, to lump him in with those fighting a conflict an ocean away.

He walked freely among them, and yet he was not free. Not when his very rights as an American were under attack. Not when people who looked like him were ripped from their beds and taken away, never to be seen again. It was why he'd traveled across that vast ocean to his ancestral homeland, where he had found glorious enlightenment. Those few months spent on the training grounds just outside Pyongyang—*Pyongyang? Do you hear yourself? You've never been to Pyongyang! Wake up!*—had imbued him with a profound, unshakable sense of purpose. Meaning had finally emerged from the infinite void of chaos.

He plunged his hands into the deep pockets of his heavy overcoat, pretending to innocently browse a display of neckties. An uncharacteristic chill had recently settled over the city of Los Angeles, and as such, his winter wear would not appear out of place to any casual observer. Fortune had smiled upon him in the form of steely clouds and swirling mists.

Thumbing the hidden detonator within his pocket, The Tiger experienced a rush of excitement at the thought of plunging it down in just a few minutes' time. The fifty pounds of plastic explosive strapped to his chest felt light as a feather.

The instructors in Pyongyang had taught him why it was necessary to strike before their culture was completely wiped from existence. And from there, the training began—from morning until night. *What did that training entail exactly, William? What were the names of your instructors? Can you even remember? No, you can't! Wake up!*

He didn't need to recall details of his training to grasp his ultimate purpose. All he knew was that they'd pushed him to his absolute limits and then farther still until there was no doubt of his loyalty to the cause. That he was indeed worthy of being called "The Tiger."

And when it became clear that his yearning for action was insatiable, they chose him for a mission that would change everything. They taught him the rudimentary mechanics of homemade explosives and, when the time was right, smuggled him back into the United States to do what was necessary. Nothing else mattered, except the cause.

"They know that Santa's on his way... bringing lots of toys and goodies on his sleigh..."

These people knew nothing of suffering; what it was like to have your homeland defiled by a viral interloper. How he hated them. They went about their pathetic little lives as if thousands of others weren't being starved and slaughtered in their name. They bought suits and brassieres, draped holly and tinsel over Christmas trees, while their own soldiers razed towns, raped innocent women, and haphazardly dropped firebombs of skin-melting napalm. Children screaming, their flesh dripping like wax sculptures under heat lamps.

Every American was complicit in the sacking of Korea—a bloody conflict that refused to end for eight long years. A string of Pyrrhic victories eroding American morale and bolstering Korean resolve.

Through a refusal to yield, to acknowledge when they were licked, President McCarthy and General MacArthur had unintentionally unified most Koreans under the banner of Communism. The concept of North versus South no longer mattered. Bickering over economic ideologies became immaterial in the face of an invading force too stubborn to leave.

Still, The Tiger thought to himself, *McCarthy isn't as foolhardy as he once appeared.* Despite the president's constant threats of exercising "the nuclear option," he had yet to provide the go-ahead—perhaps afraid of what dominoes he might knock over by eradicating a good chunk of East Asia. No, McCarthy was being sensible. But how long would that sense last? How high would the body toll need to rise until the president decided to play the most devastating ace in the deck?

If something wasn't done to stem the flow soon, the poison of war, of bigotry—and yes, radiation—would bleed across the generations, perpetuating an endless cycle of death and violence. And not just in Korea, but in Indochina as well. Emboldened by America's recalcitrance to yield to the inevitable, France continued its own unlawful occupation of Vietnam, Cambodia, and Laos. It mattered not how many soldiers were lost to the guerrilla fighters, who had nothing left to lose and everything to gain. Pride superseded bloodshed.

The United States was the illness, and The Tiger was the fever that would bring clarity once it broke. He would be the guiding light, the great liberator, the only person gifted with sight in a world that would rather gouge out its own eyes than see things for what they were. They would throw parades in his honor all over the homeland—from Pyongyang to Busan.

"Tiny tots with their eyes all aglow... will find it hard to sleep tonight..."

A young boy and girl suddenly emerged from a rack of maroon dinner jackets, playing a harmless game of tag. Staring after them, The Tiger was reminded of his youth. He had once played a similar game with a girl called Evelyn, but for some reason, he could not ascribe meaning to the name. Who was she? Yet again, the strange voice resurfaced inside his head: "*Please, William! This isn't you! You need to snap out of it before you do something you regret! You need to call Evelyn! Tell her everything! It's not too late!*"

Tears that didn't feel like his own raced down his cheeks. He felt strangely torn and almost gave in to the faint voice, almost took his finger off the hidden trigger and walked away. Almost. The hesitation was painful and tiring, like trying to swim against a raging tide in the middle of a storm.

And now there was a second voice—one wholly disconnected from his own. "*Go ahead, William,*" it said, cutting through his brain tissue with the ease of a white-hot kitchen knife. "*Do what we trained you to do. You will be doing your homeland a great service, ja? These people are the enemy, remember? Go ahead... Do it... Do it... Do it...*"

Szell... Szell... Szell... went his mind in monotonous, meaningless repetition. Instinctive word association turned it into a pun on capitalism: *Buy... Buy... Buy...*

"*It's a lie!*" bleated that other William Yang. "*You're an American, William! You of all people know what this will do to Evelyn, to our parents, to all our friends! Everyone that looks like us! For fuck's sake, WAKE UP!*"

"Enough of this," The Tiger muttered, unaware that he was cradling his pounding head in his hands. Slowly, he walked to the middle of the crowded showroom, spreading his arms out wide. The anguished version of William weeping inside his head belted one last futile scream—"*NOOO!*"—while that *other* voice happily exclaimed in a language he did not speak.

"DEATH TO AMERICA! LONG LIVE KOREA!" The Tiger boomed. He beheld a sea of confused faces before depressing a thumb down on the bomb's detonator.

Twenty-six people, including twelve children, were blown to pieces in an instant.

"Although it's been said many times, many ways... Merry Christmas to youuuu..."

PART I

December 25, 1959

McCarthyism is Americanism with its sleeves rolled.

—*Senator Joseph McCarthy (R-OH)*

Don't it make you angry the way war is dragging on?

Well, I hope the president knows what he's into, I don't know.

Oooh, I just don't know...

—*Chicago*

I can no longer keep my blinds drawn

And I can't keep myself from talkin'.

—*The Mamas and the Papas*

CHAPTER 1

She walked into his office with a swagger that suggested an easy payday.

Until the door opened with a gentle creak, he'd been enjoying a friendly game of chicken with a bottle of peach schnapps sitting atop the desk, waiting to see who would blink first. The bottle was on the verge of pulling out another spectacular victory (with only half its sloshing contents left, it'd been winning a lot lately), but it wouldn't have a chance to gloat this time.

The bottle was shoved into the bottom desk drawer—with a speed that suggested he'd done this many times—before the woman could even notice she was about to engage the services of a struggling alcoholic. That little chestnut usually turned potential customers away. *Ha! Chestnut. God bless us, everyone*, he thought to himself, wondering what could make a person desperate enough to come see him on the merriest day of the year.

Her sultry voice was like a mug of hot chocolate spiked with whiskey. Or a bit of schnapps. "You are Morris Baker?" she asked. "The private detective?"

"That's what it says on the door, ma'am," Baker responded, steepling his fingers together. "If not, then I'm probably in the wrong office."

He pointed to the door, whose frosted glass proclaimed: MORRIS E. BAKER, PRIVATE INVESTIGATIONS. The little joke was meant to put clients at ease, but it didn't seem to work on this one. Morris Baker had learned to read body language as a cop and saw an almost imperceptible twitch as the woman's muscles tensed with... what? Nerves? Indignation? Sure, many patrons came in here begrudgingly, furious that a *Jew* was the last avenue left to them. But sometimes, it was only when you were out of choices that you realized why they're called the Chosen People.

"They say you're the person to see when you've got nowhere else to go," said the woman.

"So I've been told," he said, abruptly seized by a violent coughing fit. "Sorry," he said, dabbing at his lips with a handkerchief. "Just a slight cold, is all. Please, sit..."

The woman did not comply, took an apprehensive step backward. "They say there's some sort of flu going around," she whispered as though it were a juicy piece of hair salon gossip. "From that Yang terrorist, you know? He brought it over here as a"—she screwed up her face in concentration, obviously trying to remember something—"a biological weapon. That's it."

"I wouldn't know anything about that," Baker lied, knuckles curling behind the desk. He tried to keep a smile against the ugly piece of HUAC propaganda she'd swallowed like a gluttonous trout. "Please sit, Miss...?"

"It's Mrs.," she corrected him, sitting down in the uncomfortable wooden chair reserved for optionless schlimazels and lifting a silken veil from her young and pretty face. Baker couldn't help but notice a poorly concealed shiner under the woman's left eye. "Mrs. Ann Kissinger," she said.

"My apologies," said Baker. "How can I help you today, Mrs. Kissinger?"

"It's my husband, Henry. He's gone missing."

"I see." Baker coughed again and opened his notebook to a fresh page, grabbing a fountain pen off the inkwell. "And your last name, that's with two *s*'s?" Ann nodded and he scribbled the name *Henry Kissinger* at the top of the page. "Now," Baker said, looking up, "I'm going to ask you a question, Mrs. Kissinger, and I don't want you to be offended in any way. It's something I ask all potential clients."

"Go ahead, Mr. Baker. Ask your question."

"Well, like you said upon your arrival, I've got a certain reputation for taking on hopeless cases. I'm curious what makes finding your husband worth my time. Why, for instance, have you not gone to the police?"

He held his breath, desperately hoping she wouldn't get up and walk out in a huff. Baker couldn't afford to lose this one. The cases weren't exactly pouring in like they used to, and his meager savings (critically damaged by the forfeiture of an LAPD pension) were alarmingly close to drying up like a sun-baked watering hole. That stack of overdue bills at his apartment was starting to become a problem he couldn't ignore for much longer.

"Isn't it obvious?" Ann asked. She pulled out a cigarette and Baker leaned over the desk to light it for her with a quickly struck match. He sat back, chair creaking, and pulled out his own pack of Kools. They both took in lungfuls of smoke before Ann continued, "Tell me, Mr. Baker—do you have all of your potential clients frisked as they walk in the door?"

"Mr. Greenbaum is simply here for...a little added security," he said. "One can never be too careful these days."

No need to mention that he'd seriously pissed off a cabal of former Nazi scientists the previous year by driving a switchblade into their leader's back (the knife in question had been taken from a dead Huey, which he now kept as a talisman of good luck). Baker hated looking over his shoulder all the time, but if the Black Symphony was out for revenge—and that seemed more of a *when* than an *if*—he didn't want to be caught with his pants down. He wouldn't roll over for those Kraut pricks ever again.

Hershel Greenbaum guarded the office during business hours, and when he wasn't around...well, Baker's snub-nosed .44 Magnum was never too far away from his hip. Acquiring gun and PI licenses might've been a lot harder for another Yid hoping to get into the gumshoe business, but Baker was lucky enough to still have a friend in William Parker, the influential chief of the Los Angeles Police Department.

"Well, there you are," puffed Mrs. Kissinger, exhaling a perfect smoke ring from between her lips. "My husband and I are Jewish just like you, Mr. Baker. And last I checked, we aren't exactly the most popular kids on the playground these days."

"I understand," said Baker, smiling wanly.

Most, if not all, of his clients were people who had been antagonized and discarded by the McCarthy administration: Jews, gays, Koreans, Chinese, and the worst of them all—Communists. Morris Ephraim Baker was the man to visit when you didn't want to risk involving the ruthless inspectors of the House Un-American Activities Committee, who regularly liked to wipe their asses with the Bill of Rights.

"In any event, I'd be happy to take on your case, Mrs. Kissinger," Baker continued, and Ann nodded her silent appreciation. "May I ask where you saw your husband last?"

"At home. Before he left."

"And home would be...?"

"Washington, DC."

"So you're not local?" Baker asked, putting pen to paper again.

"No," said Ann. "Henry works as a consultant for the State Department."

Baker dropped his pen and looked up in surprise. "Sorry for asking, but your husband is a Jewish man working in the State Department? I mean to say it's not something you hear in today's...uh...climate."

"An astute observation, Mr. Baker," Ann said. "Yes, it is highly unusual, but Henry is good friends with the vice president and that kept him immune from McCarthy's purge."

Baker picked up his pen. "I see. And what does he do for the State Department?"

"Advises on policy relating to East Asia," she said. "I can tell you he's had his hands full after what that young man did, blowing himself up like that."

Ann Kissinger shuddered dramatically.

"Yes, it was quite horrible," Baker replied, not wishing to dwell on the round-the-clock HUAC roundups of Korean-Americans that had been taking place nearly every day since William Yang decided to go kablooey in a department store. He pressed on: "If your husband is close with Nixon, then why not ask for the vice president's help in finding him? Surely the government has better resources than I do."

Ann looked past Baker and out the office window. The dreary, overcast weather had not changed once in three weeks—not since Yang. "I tried that already," she said softly. "Richard told me not to worry. That was a little over a week ago. You see, Mr. Baker, my husband may be valued for his intellect, but he's still not good enough in their eyes. He grew up in Germany and escaped a few years after the Nazis came to power. It broke his heart when McCarthy was elected. He never thought he'd see history like that repeat itself here."

"I understand," said Baker, experiencing a slight feeling of distaste for the missing Henry. If the man had seen the rise of Hitler first-hand, why would he willingly work for an administration that owed so much of its vile policies to the Third Reich? If he was being honest with himself, though, Baker knew the answer to that question; knew exactly what it was like to partake in a system that actively called for your destruction. Who in the hell was he to judge Kissinger?

An oven of scorching flames threatened to burn down the thin veil that separated him from the haunted past. A past filled with burning corpses, shoveled ashes, lips stained blue.

Feeling like he might be on the verge of a seizure, Baker reached into a trouser pocket and pulled out a bottle containing a severely dwindling pile of round white pills. Phenobarbital. He hated the stuff (it made him lethargic and his mind hazy), but it was the only thing that kept him from an embarrassing collapse, foaming at the mouth, and a potentially bitten-off tongue.

As much as he wanted to chase the pill down with some schnapps, he forced himself to get up and walk over to a small side table his secretary, Joanna, had insisted on placing inside the room.

Personally, Baker didn't want his office to feel too cozy, lest a client overstay their welcome. The faster he could get them in and out of the spartan space, preferably with their billfolds a little lighter, the better. And since his own apartment was a complete mess, he figured it'd be harder to become disorganized with less furnishings.

He picked up the pitcher of water sitting on the table and poured himself a full glass. "Would you like some?" he asked Mrs. Kissinger.

"No, thank you," she said, taking another drag on her cigarette and gazing back out the window. Her face took on a blank expression and her lips began to move absentmindedly.

Baker nodded, slightly confused, and surreptitiously popped one of the pills onto his tongue. He tried not to grimace at the bitterness of the medicine, immediately chasing it with the entire glass of water. "Medicine" might not have been the best word for it since the tablets hadn't exactly been prescribed by an actual physician.

"Sorry for the interruption," he said, striding back to the desk and sitting down.

"Wha...?" said a dazed Ann Kissinger, who looked away from the swirling clouds of late December mist. "Oh, not at all. Nothing to be ashamed of, Mr. Baker. I took a Barbie before coming over."

"Excuse me?" Baker inquired. "You're talking about that doll that just came out? I hear it's a popular Christmas item."

"No, silly," Ann Kissinger responded airily, sounding like a young child correcting their parents' arithmetic on a simple math problem. "Barbiturates. 'Barbies' for short! Get it? They're all the rage these days. Calm the nerves right down. You just took one, didn't you?"

Baker cleared his throat in lieu of answering. "Where were we...?" he said. "Oh yes, you said you lived in DC. Quite the journey from Los Angeles. Do you have any particular reason to suspect that your husband is here in California?"

"Did I not mention it? Henry was here for the goodwill tour. You know, with the Japs?"

"I am aware."

How could he not be aware? It'd been all over the radio and television for weeks. The government wanted every man, woman, and child in California to know about the collection of speeches on American-Japanese relations that Prime Minister Nobusuke Kishi would deliver in the run-up to New Year's Day. Since California was Nixon's home turf, the vice president and his wife, Pat, would be making special appearances along the way.

"Henry was asked to come out here earlier this month to prepare for the Japanese delegation's arrival," Ann explained. "He would call me every day from his hotel until the calls just...stopped."

"When was that?"

Ann thought it over for a moment before answering, "A little over a week ago, around the fifteenth. I called the front desk of the hotel that evening because he didn't check in and they told me he hadn't returned since leaving that morning."

"And what hotel would that be?"

"Chateau Marmont, on Sunset Boulevard."

"Swanky."

Mrs. Kissinger shrugged. "If the government's paying for it, why not?"

"Got a room number?"

"Six-C."

"Any idea where he was supposed to be the day he went missing?"

"According to his official agenda, he was in Santa Monica, overseeing preparations for the speech on the twenty-eighth."

"Very good," said Baker. "I'll start with the hotel and go from there. Would you happen to have a recent picture of your husband on hand?"

Ann produced a small black-and-white photograph of a slightly pudgy man in thick-framed glasses and a corona-like poof of hair set far back on his head. The man's eyes were unreadable, but there was a knowing smile on his lips.

"You may keep that," she told Baker. "It was taken last year, and aside from a little weight loss, Henry's face hasn't changed much."

"The weight loss," Baker said. "Was that caused by anything in particular?"

"Just your run-of-the-mill stress," she replied. "As you can imagine, it's a lot of pressure, trying to find a solution to the war in Korea."

"This is incredibly helpful, thank you," Baker said. "The only thing that remains is the matter of my fee. I charge twenty-five dollars a day, plus expenses. Now, there are financing options availab—"

Before he could finish the usual spiel, Mrs. Kissinger reached into her purse and brought out six crisp fifty-dollar bills. She carefully slid them over the desk to Baker, who raised his eyebrows in surprise. "Say what you will about the government, Mr. Baker, but they sure do pay well. I believe this should be sufficient for the next week or so."

"Um, yes, quite sufficient," said a nonplussed Baker, hardly believing his luck as he scooped up his largest payday in months. "I'll be sure to provide regular updates on my investigation. Where can I reach you, Mrs. Kissinger?"

She dove back into her purse to retrieve a piece of paper containing a hastily scribbled phone number. "Call that and ask for me by name."

Baker accepted the paper and made a show of gently tucking it into the breast pocket of his suit.

"Unless there's anything else, I think that should do it."

"Thank you," Ann said, her eyes now overly bright. "I didn't know where else to turn."

Baker considered getting up to comfort the woman but decided against it. Instead, he offered up hollow words of consolation: "It's going to be all right. We'll get your husband home in one piece."

While he'd been in this business for a little over a year, he still found it difficult to cheer up despondent clients. He could get photographs of a cheating spouse, find someone who owed you money, but ask Morris Baker for emotional reassurance and his mind would stall like an engine with a bad alternator.

Before he could pass over a handkerchief, Ann stood up. She was halfway out the door when he decided to pose the one question still nagging him. "Uh, one more thing, Mrs. Kissinger. If you don't mind?"

"Yes?" she asked, turning around.

"Was everything okay at home before your husband went missing? I mean to say... well, I couldn't help but notice..." He trailed off and pointed to the pocket of skin underneath his own eye.

Mrs. Kissinger smiled knowingly. "This bruise is not from Henry's fists, if that's what you're asking. I foolishly walked into a door after getting up in the middle of the night to use the facilities. Everything was just fine at home before Henry's disappearance."

"I see," said Baker. He wasn't swayed by the curtness of her reply, which felt rehearsed, but he decided not to pry further in case she changed her mind and asked for the down payment back. "I'll be in touch and, uh, a merry Christmas to you, Mrs. Kissinger."

"I think you mean happy Hanukkah in our case, Mr. Baker," Ann said, turning around again.

"That's right," Baker said, remembering the first night of Hanukkah was that evening. "*Chag Sameach* and all that."

Mrs. Kissinger didn't seem to hear him as she left the office, closing the door with a snap that made the cheap frosted glass wobble in its frame.

CHAPTER 2

Once he was certain Ann had gone, Baker extracted the schnapps he'd been staring at before her arrival and took a generous swig straight from the bottle. Schnapps: 1; Baker: 0. Another pothole on the road to sobriety. Trying to stay on a wagon that felt more like a bucking bull.

The drink warmed him up as he swiveled around in his chair to stare through the office's Venetian blinds, gazing out at the mist strangling Los Angeles. For once, the city was not choked by smog, though an abnormal cold spell wasn't much of a consolation prize. Not acclimated to such a chill, Angelenos walked the streets with a subdued hunch. Even the ubiquitous palm trees lining every street seemed to droop in the sudden absence of the usual desert heat.

He saw Mrs. Kissinger leave the building, pull her coat tightly around herself, and disappear into the light drizzle. Sick of looking at the steely gray oilcloth that was the sky, Baker turned back to his desk and reached for the phone atop its surface, began to dial. He took another long pull from the bottle while he waited for the call to connect. After a minute of clicks and whirs, the slippery voice he was hoping to hear came on the line.

"*Los Angeles Times* news desk, this is Andrew Sullivan."

"Andy, it's Baker."

"Baker!" Sullivan exclaimed, clearly delighted. "Glad to see I ain't the only one who's having to work on the holiday. I was starting to feel a little left out."

Once upon a time, Baker would never have entertained the idea of reaching out to Andy Sullivan of his own volition. He had detested the nosy reporter during his eight years on the force. It was just the way things worked: Cops didn't open their mouths to muckrakers, especially greasy ones like Andy Sullivan, who'd sell his own mother to a pack of hungry cannibals for an exclusive.

But times had changed. Now that he was in business for himself, Baker tolerated a cautious symbiosis with Andy, who provided him with information in exchange for a few shekels and the right of first refusal on any juicy story Baker might stumble upon.

It also helped that Andy had dialed down some of his more obnoxious tendencies after securing a full-time reporting position with the *Times*. He could be a real pain in the ass sometimes, but no one could deny the man's ruthless determination as a journalist.

"So what can I do you for on this merriest of holidays, Baker?"

"I need whatever intel you can give me on a State Department consultant by the name of Henry Kissinger. Apparently he's in town for the peace tour."

"Roger." Baker heard a shuffling of papers on the other end of the phone. He used the lull to light a cigarette, which prompted another coughing fit. "You all right, Baker?"

Funny, Andy actually sounded concerned.

"Just the sniffles from all this cold weather. I'll be fine."

"I'd bring ya a bowl of chicken noodle with some matzo balls in it, but I'm manning the desk all day. You people like matzo balls, right?"

"I said I'm fine," Baker replied curtly. He wasn't really in the mood for Andy's casual anti-Semitism today. "Just tell me what you've got on Kissinger."

"Oh, right—sorry. I'm looking through the press packet the feds sent to the office, and it's mostly boilerplate stuff. Not much on the guy. Says here he's part of Nixon's entourage and an advisor on East Asian affairs, who—and I quote—'has been instrumental in shaping policy that helps maintain stability in the region.'"

Stability in the region? Baker thought to himself. *That's a laugh.* "Thanks, Andy. Let me know if you find anything else."

"Will do, Baker. You got a big fish on the line? My senses are a-tinglin'.

"We'll see. Have a good one."

"Talk soon, Baker."

"'*If the fates allow*,'" Baker replied in a piss-poor impression of Sinatra.

He placed the receiver back into its cradle, satisfied that Mrs. Kissinger wasn't blowing smoke up his ass. Jew-baiters would often crank-call him with phony sob stories and get a cheap laugh out of sending him on a wild-goose chase. Stubbing out his barely smoked cigarette into a crystalline ashtray, he stood up and let out a sigh of relief as his back cracked pleasurably. The phenobarbital dissolving into his bloodstream was beginning to make him feel tired, but there was no time for a nap on the hidden Murphy bed he had installed in the office for late nights.

He put the schnapps back into its drawer and crossed the office, opening the door that led to the cramped reception area, where Joanna was shrugging on her coat.

"Oh good," she said. "You just saved me the trouble of knocking."

Baker smiled and leaned against the frame, watching his secretary wrap a festive red-and-green scarf around her neck. "Didn't realize I had given you the rest of the day off."

"We went over this last week," said Joanna, now affixing a dark green beret atop her sleek blond hair. "I guess it must have been the schnapps talking."

He frowned and decided to lie rather than admit his inability to remain abstinent. "I remembered. Just having a little holiday fun. Speaking of..." He jogged back into his office and reemerged with a bottle of red wine. "For you and... what's his name again?"

"Stanley," said Joanna, accepting the bottle with a warm grin of appreciation.

"Ah yes!" Baker exclaimed in mock astonishment, pretending the name had been on the tip of his tongue all along. "Who could ever forget the famous Stanley? How long have you two been seeing each other now?"

"It'll be six months in February." She placed the wine down next to her typewriter and reached for the maroon purse draped across her chair. "We're having Christmas dinner with his family tonight."

"Good luck. Families can be... interesting."

"Thanks, Morris. And thank you so much for the wine. I feel a little guilty now. I didn't get you anything."

She crossed the desk and gave him a small peck on the cheek, causing him to blush.

"Huh," he said, making a big show of glancing up at the ceiling. "And no mistletoe in sight."

Joanna laughed. "Really, I am sorry. Things have just been so hectic with all the added security at the department stores and tutoring—and Stanley, of course. Things are getting pretty serious between us."

"Think nothing of it," he said, feeling a small pang of jealousy. He also had someone to go home to, but the thought of Shira did not bring much comfort. "You came into the office on Christmas Day. That's enough of a gift for me. Now, go enjoy yourself and tell that young man of yours that I say hello."

"You are a sweet one. Do you have anywhere to be tonight?"

"Shira roped me into a little potluck at Ohev Shalom. First night of Hanukkah and all that. We've been tasked with bringing the borsht and sour cream." He puffed up his chest in mock pride. "A very important job."

"That should be fun," said Joanna. "I remember my father used to make us light the menorah every year. But the tradition sort of petered out after... well..."

An awkward silence ensued. Joanna's father, Maurice Rapf, had once been a talented and respected screenwriter in Hollywood before he was blacklisted for his ties to the Communist Party. He refused to renounce his political views and tragically took his own life before HUAC agents could drag him away.

"Well," Joanna said, breaking the tension, "I'd best be off. Before I forget, though, Valentina called to wish you a happy holiday and asked that you stop by the Red Sword for a drink when you have some free time."

"Noted," Baker said. "And has there been any word from"—he lowered his voice—"our mutual friend?"

Joanna shook her head gravely. She understood that by "mutual friend," Baker meant Edward R. Murrow, the disgraced ex-journalist who had faked his own death in order to create a semiclandestine organization known as the Liberty Boys, whose sole purpose was to resist McCarthy and HUAC. Joanna, who advised Murrow on matters relating to nuclear physics, was now the organization's senior operative in Los Angeles (with Baker serving as her right-hand man).

When she wasn't running Baker's private investigations office, she was either helping to build out the Liberty Boys' network of informants in Southern California or tutoring graduate students at UCLA. If Baker recalled correctly, Stanley had been one of those students.

"Not a peep," she replied. "The last coded message I got was just before the Yang incident and it's been total silence since then. There haven't even been any radio broadcasts, either, as I'm sure you've noticed. I think he's gone to ground. The president wants to look tough after what happened, and it'd be a huge win for the administration if our friend was captured."

Her reasoning was sound, and Baker said as much. It would've been nice to have regular updates on the Symphony's whereabouts and intentions from the man who'd once managed to infiltrate the shadowy organization. But even when coded messages came in on a regular basis, Murrow kept turning up empty-handed when it came to fresh intel on the federation of cunning Nazis recruited by the US government via Operation Paperclip. They'd vanished into thin air.

"That's actually part of the reason why I'm heading out now," Joanna continued. "I've got a rendezvous with a file clerk who works at the Office of Hebraic Affairs over in Encino. Hoping to get a report on which members of the Jewish community HUAC is currently monitoring."

"Need backup?" Baker asked. "I can ask Hersh to—"

"No need," she said. "This one's a real pushover. But it's like pulling teeth lately. Edward isn't the only one who's spooked by the Yang affair."

"I can imagine," Baker said. "As our friend would say, 'Good night and good luck.' Now, go on—before I schmooze you to death."

She bestowed another kiss on Baker's cheek and left the PI alone with his own blurred cognizance. Similar to his stance on Andy Sullivan, Baker's view of Joanna had also changed over the last year and a half. Prior to learning her true identity, Baker thought of Joanna as a pretty and kindhearted member of the LAPD typing pool (simply a cover story so she could keep an eye on him for Murrow). These days, he felt a sense of paternal responsibility toward her but also grasped the foolishness behind that sentiment. Baker needed Joanna more than Joanna needed him. She was the only reason his professional life had not yet collapsed in on itself like a dying star.

Unable to stand the silence left by the secretary's departure, Baker grabbed his trench coat and fedora off a chipped wooden coat rack and left the office, locking the door behind him.

CHAPTER 3

"Oof!" An absentminded Baker had completely forgotten about Hersh until he collided with the towering bodyguard standing just outside the office door.

"Well, you seem to be in a hurry," said Hersh, righting Baker, who'd been knocked off balance, with hands the size of large skillets.

Tall and broad-shouldered, Hershel Greenbaum was a member of Ohev Shalom, a local synagogue frequented by European survivors of the war. Like a good portion of the congregation—Baker included—Hersh had lost his entire family to the Nazis. The man's impressive stature and strength meant he was worth more to the Germans than a wasted bullet or a few extra pellets of Zyklon B.

Hersh had lived out the entirety of the war moving stones of granite in a quarry at Mauthausen. Most of his fellow workers dropped dead from overwork, but not him. By the time the Americans liberated the camp in the spring of 1945, Hershel was one of the few quarrymen still left alive. Filled with pent-up rage and more lifting power than ever before, he smashed a German guard's head into a splattered mess of brains and eyestalks with an immense stone block while the GIs pretended not to notice.

He had been introduced to Baker by Ohev Shalom's rabbi, Jacob Kahn, and the two immediately got along like a house on fire. Their first meeting occurred at a fortuitous juncture in both of their lives—Hersh had just lost his job as a bank security guard (owing to the fact that the bank's new manager didn't much care for Jews) and Baker was in need of someone to watch his back for revenge-driven followers of the Third Reich. Hersh, who shared Baker's distaste for the so-called Master Race, was only too happy to take the gig.

"Sorry, Hersh," Baker said, adjusting his ruffled coat. "Forgot you were here. I was just about to take a trip over to the pits. Clear my head a little."

"Want me to come with?"

"No, that's okay," said Baker. "I'll see you at the potluck later." He reached into his pocket, extracting a bill from Mrs. Kissinger's down payment.

"Morris, that's not necessary," he said, "I can wait another week or two..."

"Let me worry about the money problems, Hersh. Besides, you're going to have another mouth to feed soon. Consider this a holiday bonus. Thanks for coming in today."

"Nu?" Hersh said, accepting the fifty with a grin. "What else am I gonna do on Christmas?"

"Judging by your size," Baker began, "I'd say dress up in a red coat and deliver toys to all the good little girls and boys."

Hersh boomed with laughter and slapped Baker on the shoulder, causing his knees to buckle. "That's a good one," he roared. "I'll have to remember to tell that to Mindy when I get home. Let me walk you out at least."

"Oy, would you look at that?" breathed Hersh once they were outside and making their way along the sidewalk. "Such a shanda. Of all the places, never thought I'd see this shit here."

They'd spotted a long line of downtrodden Korean-Americans being led to a HUAC processing center down the street. From here, they'd be loaded onto trucks and driven to reopened internment camps out in the desert. (Manzanar—ironically located in Independence, California—was said to be the largest and most frightening of them all.)

Just an average day in McCarthy's America.

Baker had read some of the published excerpts from Yang's manifesto, which called for his fellow Koreans to follow his example and "rise up against the oppressive US regime." It was all the pretext the government needed to repeat its own ugly history with the camps. Men, women, and children were ripped from their homes, forced to hastily pack whatever they could carry in a bag or two. All of them paying for a young man's tragic mistake.

Baker didn't realize he was moving toward the crowd until Hersh called after him through gritted teeth. "Morris!" he hissed. "Where the hell are you going? *You nuts?*"

He didn't stop until spotting a tired-looking boy of about six or seven with puffy red eyes—a look with which Baker was all too familiar. He'd seen it countless times on all the children he helped shepherd off the cattle cars during his time as a member of the Sonderkommando. That blank and haunted stare of a person who has lost their innocence too soon.

That expression never left their faces, not even when Baker went to remove their fragile bodies from the gas chambers. They continued to stare up at him, eyes wide and puffy, mouths agape and stained blue with Zyklon. After a while, he stopped shutting their eyelids. There were just too many to close.

The kid in line was holding on to his father's trouser leg, a helpless expression contorting his face. Making sure there were no Hueys moving along the line, Baker bent down, knees cracking. Under the cover of pretending to tie his shoe, he produced two unopened packs of cigarettes and held them out to the boy, who stared at him. The boy's parents were too busy talking in hushed tones to take notice.

"Take these," Baker whispered. "You can trade them for whatever you might need once you get to... well, when you get to where you're going." Slowly, the boy accepted the smokes without a word. "Keep them hidden, all right?" Baker added. "It'll be our little secret." The kid nodded his understanding.

Baker flashed a smile and a wink before standing and walking back up the sidewalk.

"You're crazier than you look, you know that?" said Hersh, clearly impressed, when Baker had rejoined him.

"Nothing crazy about wanting to do the right thing. I'll see you later, Hersh."

"Yeah, sure. See you later. And do me favor, Morris... try not to fall into the tar, eh?"

"You're just looking out for your wallet."

Hersh shrugged, not denying the claim. "What can I say? You pay *too* well."

The heat from the bubbling tar pits littered throughout Hancock Park was a wonderful buffer against the perverse cold. Baker didn't have to tighten the belt on his coat as he stood on the lip of the steep bank, transfixed by the jet-black goop said to contain the remains of an entire menagerie of prehistoric creatures: massive lizards with gaping maws caked in rotting flesh; shaggy elephants with shattered, blood-soaked tusks; and mean tigers the size of Baker's own light green Lincoln Continental with the noisy engine. It was almost too much to believe that such beasts had once walked the earth, but the bones that had been dredged out of this scalding muck didn't lie.

Not for the first time in his life, Baker questioned the biblical stories he was taught as a child—stories about Noah, a righteous man who, acting on instructions from God Himself, built a massive ark and saved every single animal, two-by-two, from a great flood. Maybe the dinosaurs preferred to take their chances with the rain or maybe they just got the time wrong and missed the boat.

History was full of beings who couldn't get out of the way in time. The danger always caught up with you in the end. It consumed you like scalding, viscous tar until there was nothing left but a few bones and a distant memory of what once was.

Baker, who was coughing again, flicked his cigarette into the morass and watched it fizzle out. His office was a stone's throw from the park and he often came here to think with only the faint *gloop... gloop... gloop...* of tar pits to keep him company. They were mesmerizing, a reminder of how cruel and chaotic the world could sometimes be.

People went missing without a trace. People like Henry Kissinger. Was everything okay between Ann and her husband, or had she lied to save face? It was very possible Henry had started shacking up with a secretary and was now avoiding his spouse. The peace talks were the perfect cover for an extramarital affair. But if that were the case, why didn't Henry just tell Ann he was too busy to continue checking in? Why cut off communication entirely?

The phenobarbital fog blanketing his mind started to wear off and he could finally think clearly again. Excitement over the fresh investigation laid out before him, the anticipation of the chase, bubbled in him like hot tar. Usually, he was content to stand here, watching the antediluvian cauldron, until it got dark. Not today, though. Today, he'd have to get a move on if he and Shira were going to make it to the potluck on time. The sky was quickly losing light, and a ferocious gale had just kicked up.

Even the ancient thermal warmth of the tar pits had its limits. Checking the banged-up IWC on his wrist, Baker smiled. There was just enough time to bother an old friend.

CHAPTER 4

It took Baker less than half an hour to reach Downey. The city streets, so often clogged with bumper-to-bumper traffic, were almost completely devoid of cars thanks to the holiday. He saw an unbroken succession of Christmas wreathes as he pulled onto Pangborn Avenue, the street alight with decorations that ranged from blinking red and green bulbs to elaborate manger scenes. Some families had even gone the extra mile of sprinkling fake snow across their lawns and roofs. An eerie winter wonderland straight out of *The Nutcracker*. The only thing straining the illusion was the chorus line of palm trees dotting the horizon.

Baker parked the Continental next to the curb of 10046 and got out, rubbing his frigid hands together in an effort to warm them up. He regretted his procrastination when it came to getting the car's heater fixed. What he really needed was a new vehicle altogether but he couldn't bear the thought of parting ways with the trusty Continental, which had provided him with several quick getaways over the years. For someone who didn't like to think of himself as superstitious, Baker sure had a nasty habit for holding on to worthless items ascribed with bullshit sentimentality.

Without warning, Baker's brain spun back to his upbringing in Czechoslovakia before the war; to when his grandfather, a frightening man obsessed with Jewish mysticism, told a young Morris about the shedim. Malevolent spirits with the feet of a chicken that could be glimpsed only by way of an archaic cabalistic ritual that involved burning the placenta of a black cat.

Baker's mother chastised Zayde Leopold for scaring the children, but it was already too late. Morris couldn't sleep soundly for a month after hearing the story, convinced he was being watched at night by a pair of glowing red eyes hovering above his bed. He would sometimes walk outside and scream at the sight of chicken footprints in the dirt, temporarily forgetting the fact that his family kept a coop in the backyard for fresh eggs and meat.

Baker reached into the Continental's glove compartment and pulled out his emergency bottle of schnapps. The alcohol warmed him up and also prepared him for the verbal beating he knew was about to take from the patriarch of 10046 Pangborn.

He took one last look around, noticing how curtains twitched open to reveal brief glimpses of magnificent Christmas trees decorated with baubles and tinsel, and topped with the mandatory twinkling star. Several pairs of mistrustful eyes followed him up the drive, but he paid them no heed as he rapped his knuckles on the door.

The door was opened by a distracted, red-haired man in a knit brown cardigan. "Margaret, stop flinging mashed potatoes at your sister!" he called over his shoulder. "Damn kids," he added under his breath with a fatherly smile. That grin disappeared when his gaze landed on Baker.

"Oh Christ," said the man, immediately genuflecting. "To what do I owe this pleasure?"

"And a merry Christmas to you, too," said Baker to his former partner on the LAPD, Brogan Abraham Connolly. "I see you decided to shave off those ridiculous muttonchops. You almost look like a regular member of society now."

Connolly's smile returned and he pulled Baker into a crushing bear hug. "How are you, ya no-good Sheenie? Been wondering about you lately. No calls, no nothing."

"Sorry, Brogan. Been busy," Baker wheezed. "I also didn't want to get squeezed to death by a Mick bastard."

At last, Brogan let go, looking past Baker. Curious, Baker turned around to see one of the neighbors still glancing out their window. Brogan flipped them the bird and shouted, "Ah, go kiss a reindeer, Frank! And mind your own damned business!" The curtain twitched back into place. "Come on in," Connolly said, moving aside. "We'll have a drink, and you can tell me why you decided to ruin my Christmas."

It was delightfully warm inside the Connolly household, a one-story ranch whose entranceway branched off into a living area. A roaring fire crackled merrily next to the tree, torn wrapping paper strewn around its base, and Baker could hear the clink of knives and forks, as well as the laughter of Connolly's two young daughters, coming from the kitchen down the hall.

"Honey! Fix another plate!" Connolly shouted, closing the door. "We've got an unexpected guest."

"No need," Baker said. "I won't stay long."

"I'm not taking 'no' for an answer," Connolly said. "You haven't lived until you've tried Maeve's roast turkey!" Then he lowered his voice conspiratorially. "No matter how dry it is, just smile and keep chewing until it goes down. If it gets stuck, ask Jesus to go easy on my wife when you see him."

Maeve Connolly came rushing down the hallway, wiping her hands on a flowery apron. "Oh, Morris!" she exclaimed. "How lovely to see you. Merry Christmas!"

"Merry Christmas," said Baker, returning her salutation with a smile.

"We were wondering when you'd stop by," she said, bestowing him with a delicate hug and kiss on the cheek. She was the polar opposite of her large and abrasive husband, but she could keep the man in line better than anyone Morris Baker had ever met during his years as a cop. "Brogan's been so lonely at the office since you left. Please, come in and have some food. We've got plenty."

"I really don't want to be a bother," Baker said. "Just need a quick word with your charming husband here."

"If you're sure," Maeve said, looking Baker up and down as though she wanted to comment on how thin he looked. "Well, I'll give you some mince pies to take home, shall I?"

Connolly gave Baker a look that said, *Don't you dare refuse this one or she'll have both our necks.*

"I'd be delighted. Thank you, Maeve," Baker said with a small bow in her direction.

Looking satisfied, Connolly's wife bustled back into the kitchen, where she shouted: "Margaret! What did your father just tell you about flinging potatoes? Give me that fork, young lady!"

"Over here," Connolly said, guiding Baker into the living room. "Take a seat and sorry about the mess. Had to get my girls those damn

Barbie dolls everyone's been clamoring for. Was nearly trampled before I even got in the store."

"I should be the one apologizing," Baker replied, sinking into the sofa near the hearth, turning his hands back and forth against the flames.

"Whiskey okay?" Connolly asked.

"Please."

Connolly walked over to a small wet bar set into the opposite wall and poured out two healthy measures of whiskey into glass tumblers. "You know," he began, "I guess I shouldn't be getting on your case for not calling. Phone's wrecked anyway."

"Pardon?"

Connolly pointed to a spot near Baker's foot where a pile of shattered plastic and jumbled wiring sat in a tired heap. Had it not been for the handset and numbered rotary, Baker would have never known he was looking at the decimated corpse of a telephone.

"Hueys keep trying to install those fucking bugs in the house," Connolly explained. "Whenever they do, I just destroy the phone and blame it on one of the girls. Not sure how many more times I can keep getting away with it, though. We're on our fifth phone and HUAC is recommending that my daughters be committed to the nearest mental asylum. They're sending someone over tomorrow to put in another one. Like clockwork."

"I keep wondering when they'll come for me," Baker said. "Remember what Lonergan said at the diner?"

"'This isn't over,'" supplied Connolly in a buffoonish imitation of the HUAC inspector who headed up the main Los Angeles branch in Echo Park. "They've got their hands full these days, I can tell you. Forgotten all about you, I'm sure. In fact, they probably feel like they owe you a debt of gratitude."

"How do you m—?"

"Anywho, what are we drinking to?" Connolly asked, steamrolling over the question. "How about the good old days?"

He walked over and handed Baker a glass, clinking it with his own.

"If you say so," Baker said. "Why are the Hueys installing bugs? Not attending any Communist meetings, now are you?"

This drew a hearty laugh from his ex-partner and they both took large gulps of the amber liquid. Connolly let out a large belch, plopped into the overstuffed corduroy armchair opposite the sofa, and placed his feet on a matching ottoman.

"So," Connolly began, grunting with relaxation, "what brings you to my doorstep on the birthday of our lord and savior?"

"*Your* lord and savior," Baker corrected him, taking another sip of whiskey. "We disowned him a few centuries back, remember?" He angled his glass toward the agonized Jesus effigy carved into a large wooden crucifix hanging on the wall. "He's all yours."

"Don't get me started on you Christ Killers."

Connolly narrowed his eyes and Baker returned the look in kind. There was a moment of silence when the fire crackled, and Connolly's daughters could be heard screaming at each other in the kitchen. Then both men burst out laughing, falling back into their old rhythm of trying to get a rise out of each other like a pair of immature schoolboys.

"I really have missed this," Connolly said, leaning forward to clink glasses with Baker again. "The office just isn't the same without a Yid lurking about. And how I do miss the chase."

"Cushy desk job and pay raise not all it's cracked up to be, Sergeant Connolly?"

"Maeve likes that I'm no longer tracking dangerous murderers, and the hours are better. But I tell ya, sitting in one place all day long, pushing pencils, is more boring than staring at cow shit. Remember when we took down Mencken and Parker shouted himself hoarse? What a day that was! The most action I see nowadays is putting in a weekly order for typewriter ink or threatening to fire Hanscom if he doesn't stop snorting that Guatemalan shit up his nose."

"Where's Parker in all of this?"

"Parker's slowly been losing his autonomy after the little stunt you pulled with Lonergan at Merv's last summer. The Hueys blame the chief for what they saw as a miniature revolution among the city's 'criminal' elements. That's the whole reason McCarthy's tolerated Parker's big mouth for so long. He was supposed to be keeping the Beaners, Chinks, and Blacks in their 'rightful place.' Away from the rest of us, that is. He's been cracking down hard on minority communities since you left."

"I've noticed an influx of patrol cars over in my neck of the woods," Baker said, referring to his apartment in the heart of Chinatown. "That's what you meant by them owing me 'debt of gratitude'?"

"You proved their propaganda about Jews was right, Morris. Not that they needed it, but your behavior gave the Hueys a blank check to point to you and say, 'We told you so.'"

"So...what? They're keeping me alive in the hopes that I prove them right again?"

Connolly let out a jarring "*Quack! Quack!* You're the golden goose."

"I can't imagine Parker is too happy about all this."

Connolly let out a defeated sigh. "I know how close you and Parker were. But since you're no longer with us, I don't have to hold my tongue anymore. The chief may like to think of himself as high-minded, but if it weren't for his apathy towards Communism, he'd probably make for an exemplary Huey. I don't think he's hired a new Negro or Hispanic officer since he took office. Despite all of that, he still failed in HUAC's eyes. They've slowly been chipping away at Parker since the diner fiasco, and after that business with the kamikaze Korean kid, well...they had all the pretense they needed to absorb us."

"I haven't heard about any of this," Baker said. "Sullivan would've told me, surely."

"They've kept a tight lid on it, all right," answered Connolly. "They keep promising it'll only be temporary—that it's in the interest of Los Angeles security, the usual crock. I'm not so inclined to take McCarthy's Boys at their word. There's rumblings of a larger plan to consolidate all of the country's police forces under the president and HUAC."

"McCarthy's trying to form his own goddamned SS?" sputtered Baker, choking on his whiskey.

"Bingo. Make way for the American Gestapo! Here they come, goose-stepping by Pennsylvania Avenue!"

"Christ—no wonder they're bugging you," Baker said. It spoke to the severity of the subject matter that Connolly didn't object to Baker's blaspheming. "I'd say I'm shocked, but I'm all out of voltage. Remember his election campaign when he riled up crowds everywhere he went?"

"Do *I* remember?" Brogan asked, indignant. "Must've been... what? 'Fifty-one? 'Fifty-two? I was barely off my rookie days when he rolled into town with those goddamned Brownshirts of his. No better word for it. Thugs, the whole lot of them."

"McCarthy's Minutemen," Baker supplied, the alliteration leaving behind an acrid taste in his mouth. Nearly all of those men had gone on to become the first Hueys.

"Exactly," Brogan answered grimly, his eyes misting over with unpleasant memories.

Ol' Joe would get folks all hot and bothered with one of his fiery speeches about 'Communists this' and 'Communists that.' And once the crowd was nice and softened up, the Minutemen would cause a commotion and all hell would break loose. McCarthy then got to claim that the country was devolving into chaos and he was the only one who could set things right again—all while failing to mention that *he* was the one causing it all.

"Stevenson didn't stand a snowball's chance in Hell," Brogan added. "Thought Ike might've had him licked by contesting the votes, but that heart attack came out of nowhere."

"Oh, come on, Brogan," Baker snorted in derision. "You don't actually believe that's what happened, do you?"

If the old war hero's death really was a random event, it couldn't have come at a better time, when rumors of stuffed ballot boxes were running rampant in the papers. Eisenhower, who had thrown his support behind Adlai Stevenson after losing out on the Republican nomination to McCarthy, was found slumped over his desk at Columbia University just two days after publicly calling the 1952 election results into question.

"Would it kill ya to just let me pretend that we live in a just world for five goddamned minutes?" Brogan asked. "I'm trying not to remember those days. They were dark times."

"*Were?*" prompted Baker. "I'm still waiting for the sun to rise over here."

"I'll lend you a flashlight," quipped Brogan. "To brighter days ahead, eh?" They clinked glasses again. "Anyway, I'm surprised you haven't already heard about the HUAC merger," Brogan added, lowering his voice. "You know... from Murrow."

"He's MIA," Baker admitted. "Joanna thinks he's in hiding, letting the Yang business blow over. And you should be careful what you say about your new bosses, Brogan."

"Ah, fuck 'em. I should be fine, so long as I don't try to seize the means of production. I tell you, Morris, you got out of that corrupt cesspool at just the right time. If you didn't resign, you'd have been forced out by now. They're cracking down harder than ever. But you're free, aren't you? You don't answer to anyone!"

"I wouldn't go that far. Being a Jew isn't exactly a walk in the park these days."

"I meant relatively speaking."

"The grass is always greener, my friend."

"Yeah, I suppose. Oh, while we're on the subject of Jew-haters, how was your trip to Germany? I didn't get a single postcard! You help get one of those Schmeissers the death sentence?"

"I'll tell you all about it some other time," said Baker. He wasn't exactly keen to recount what it was like to testify against a concentration camp guard who had tortured him during the war.

"Sure, sure. So anyway, what do you need from me? And don't say money."

"No." Baker chuckled, draining his glass. "Wanted to see if you had any information on a guy by the name of Henry Kissinger. Big-shot advisor for the State Department who works under Nixon. Apparently went missing in the last week or so. Ring any bells?"

Connolly got up to pour himself another drink. "The one who's here for the Kishi tour?"

"Yes!" Baker exclaimed, gratefully accepting a refill of his own. "Here," he added, handing over the photograph given to him by Ann.

"That's him," Connolly said, studying the photo. "His wife reported him missing at the end of November. I only remember because we were working with the feds on extra security for the events. His name kept crossing my desk, him being associated with Nixon and all. And when he disappeared, the case was given top priority. But like I say, that was about a month ago."

"Well, that's very interesting..."

"What is?"

"His wife came to see me at my office this morning. Said he only went missing in the last week and asked *me* to find him. Didn't say a single word about the LAPD being involved."

"Well, I don't blame her for looking elsewhere. My guys can find neither hide nor hair of the guy. The investigation is still ongoing, but the odds get slimmer every day."

"So why didn't she tell me she'd already gone to the police?"

"Maybe she thought you'd think it a waste of your time if the trail was already colder than my plate of turkey in the other room."

"Yeah, maybe," said Baker, grateful to have input from the man with whom he'd closed many homicide cases. "Were there any leads at all?"

"None," Connolly said, his voice now a little slurred from the drink. "The man simply left his hotel one morning and never came back."

"Who were the officers you assigned to the case?"

"Bletchley and Pistone. You remember them, don't you?"

"Sure I do. You trust them?"

"Hell no," said Connolly without missing a beat. "I don't trust anyone outside of myself, but of all the options left to me, Bletchley and Pistone are pretty reliable. What? You think there's foul play involved with Kissinger?"

"That's what I'm being handsomely paid to find out."

Maeve came into the room at that moment, carrying a checkered cloth napkin bulging with homemade mince pies. She handed Baker the care package with another peck on the cheek.

"Are you seeing anyone these days, Morris?" she asked.

"Maeve..." Brogan said warningly.

"It's okay," Baker told him. "Yeah, I am. As a matter of fact. Her name's Shira." He looked down at his watch, "In fact, I need to go pick her up now. I'm running a bit late. Thank you for the pies, Maeve. And thanks for the drink, Brogan. My apologies for intruding on your dinner."

"Not at all," Maeve answered. "Do bring this mystery girl around for a meal sometime."

"And just let me know if you have any other questions," Connolly said, standing up to shake his hand. "Oh, and a happy Hanukkah to you." Baker looked shocked, prompting Connolly to let out a wet bray of laughter. "Didn't expect that from me, did ya?

Don't worry, I ain't converting to your side anytime soon. Heaven forbid."

"So how'd you know it's Hanukkah tonight? I'm on the edge of my seat."

"Our new butcher's a kike! Really knows his way around a ham."

"You know us Jews, Brogan," Baker said, slurping down the last of his whiskey. "We're just full of surprises."

CHAPTER 5

The sky had darkened into a shroud of inky blackness when he pulled up to Shira's apartment building in Pico-Robertson at six o'clock on the dot. Shira stood on the curb, a large pot of cold borsht held in her gloved hands and an equally frosty look of anger on her face.

He got out of the car and ran around to open the passenger door.

"M'lady," he said. Shira got in without saying a word. "Okay, I know I'm late," he added. "I took on a new case this afternoon, needed to look into a few things, and lost track of time." Still no answer. Slumping his shoulders in defeat, he slammed the door and walked back the driver's side. He sat with his hands on the wheel for a moment. "I know you're angry," he said, "but let's not bring it to the potluck, okay? If you've got something to say, Shira, just say it."

Shira Abramovitch looked over at him with those piercingly hazel eyes he'd initially fallen for at Ohev Shalom two summers ago. Like him, she didn't enjoy talking about her experiences during the war, though he often wondered if those ravishing and vaguely hypnotic eyes had helped her survive the horrors of Auschwitz, where she'd worked as a seamstress for Commandant Rudolf Höss.

"I've been waiting outside for the last hour," she said with a thick Slavic intonation that recalled her Belarusian homeland.

She sounded calm, but the sloshing borsht in her lap betrayed the fact that her knees were shaking—a sign of suppressed rage or a by-product of the cold. Most likely a combination of both. He stared at her, slack-jacked and aware that a fight was brewing. It wasn't their first and it would most certainly not be their last.

"Well, that was stupid," he said without thinking. "Why not just wait inside?"

"Because if I did, Mrs. Maisel would've talked my ear off until Mashiach came."

Now it was his turn to remain silent. Shira did have a valid point—Mrs. Maisel, an elderly tenant of the building—had a penchant for droning conversations that qualified as "cruel and unusual punishment" under the terms of the US Constitution.

"It is now six o' clock," Shira continued. "Do you remember what time you promised to pick me up at?"

"Five thirty," he mumbled.

"What was that?"

"*Five!*" he bellowed. "Damnit, Shira! I told you I was working a new case. I'm sorry! What else do you want from me? I have to make a living, *don't* I?"

"I don't want an apology!" she shouted back. "How many times have we been over this? I want you to communicate with me! Pick up the phone for once. And even when you *are* with me, your mind seems to be somewhere else. I don't think I can handle being the second most important thing in your life for much longer."

"Of course you're important to me!" He tried to run a hand through Shira's dark brown hair and she jerked away.

"You have a funny way of showing it, Morris. If you just laid off the booze once in a while."

"What did you just—?"

"That's right, I can smell it on your breath. The entire car smells like a distillery. You promised me you'd stop."

Another valid point. He did promise, and for a while there, things seemed to be going pretty well, didn't they? He'd cut back on the drink and tried his hardest to be a standup boyfriend and member of the community. So where had it all gone wrong? At what point did Morris Baker revert to the old fuck-up role he excelled at playing? It was hard to say.

A string of late nights and frustrating dead ends working a case had the power to drive a man back to the bottle faster than a fly sensing a fresh pile of turds pinched out of a dog's rear end.

But it was more than that. He'd gone into business for himself with the naive idea of tearing down the bureaucratic red tape like a bunch of Christmas wrapping paper and doing some good in the world. *Genuine good.* The kind of sentimental schmaltz that was said to warm your heart right up.

There was only one drawback: People didn't much want to be helped. They continued to lie, cheat, murder, steal, abandon their spouses, and dodge your calls—not giving two shits whether you were a shamus or a private dick. All Baker had done was opt for a measly title change.

Maybe it wasn't so hard to say after all. He could have spoken this aloud and apologized. It might've ended the trouble right then and there.

"How many times are we going to have this fight, Shira? *Huh?*" exploded Baker. Now his anger was getting the best of him and he gripped the steering wheel until the tips of his fingers turned white. "I'm trying to help people in this town who've got nowhere left to turn. We of all people know what it's like to be thrown overboard without a life jacket. What we saw and did during the war? All of that shit is happening again right here, right now—and I'm done turning a blind eye to it all. People are scared, and you're asking for a measly fucking phone call?"

He felt disgusted with himself as soon as the diatribe left his lips. Shira felt neglected—and rightly so—and here he was, blaming her for his own emotional inadequacies.

"Forget it," Shira muttered. "We're late as it is. Oh damn!"

"What is it?"

"I forgot the sour cream."

"I can wait while you—"

"No, I can't risk a run-in with Mrs. Maisel. Let's just go. And can you turn the heat on? It's freezing in here." She wrapped her arms around her midsection, revealing the blue, tattooed numbers inked into the pale flesh of her left forearm.

"It's broken."

"Typical. You know, Isaac says—"

"Oh great! Here we go again! Let's hear what the great Isaac Kremnitzer has to say! You really should just fuck him at this point and be done with it, Shira."

That did it. Looking as though he'd just slapped her across the face, she turned away. It was times like these when Baker pined for the days of his last girlfriend, Elizabeth Short, who didn't mind his erratic hours and emotional distance. Liz might have been a bissel crazy for reporting him to HUAC that one time, but she had certainly been less of a handful than Shira was.

He uttered a curse in his native tongue and started the engine, which was beginning to sound a lot like his own coughing fits of late. *Mock me, too, will you?* Baker thought as he peeled away. *Keep it up, maybe I will get a new car after all. Those nuclear-powered models I keep hearing so much about sound nice...*

Located on South Robertson Boulevard, Ohev Shalom was a large stone building that brought to mind the grand Gothic churches of old Europe. While a number of synagogues across the city did inhabit the guts of old Christian structures, Ohev Shalom was always intended to be a Jewish house of worship from the moment it first broke ground in the middle of the last century under the leadership of Rabbi Ernst Lemlin—a native of Prague who harbored a febrile obsession with the golem that was said to have been created there.

After the construction of Ohev Shalom was completed in 1861, the same year the United States would be torn in half by the Civil War, Lemlin sailed back to Europe to search for Judah ben Loew's docile clay protector, only to disappear under mysterious circumstances. Some congregants liked to claim that Lemlin had succeeded in smuggling the golem onto American shores at the turn of the century, burying the behemoth deep beneath the building's foundation.

These days, much of the shul's architectural majesty was obscured by a ten-foot-high brick wall reinforced with sandbags and festooned with barbed wire. The place looked more like a London storefront during the Blitz than it did a synagogue, and it was no mystery as to why.

In the years since McCarthy had taken office, dozens of synagogues around the country became common targets of vandalism and arson. Once it dawned on the Jewish population that the president's constant insinuations (and sometimes overt statements) about a link between

Communism and Judaism would come to define his entire administration, American Jews either hightailed it up to Canada or decided to defend themselves by any means necessary.

Baker, who'd willingly excommunicated himself from the Jewish nation for nearly fifteen years, knew things were bad for his people. Until joining Rabbi Kahn's congregation, however, he didn't realize the full extent of the shitstorm that mirrored the years following Hitler's ascent to power two decades before. The wall and sandbags were recent additions, but when part of your synagogue burns down in an act of blatant arson, you've got no other choice than to put up deterrents to anti-Semitic assholes.

It was nothing short of a miracle that Ohev Shalom had gone unscathed for so long. Rabbi Kahn's initial decision to install a number of reinforced doors throughout the building as a precaution seemed almost laughably unnecessary until the attack. It was as though God had decided to pass over this humble parish—like he did all those centuries ago in Egypt—giving it special treatment in deference to Kahn's piousness.

In the end, all protections, divine or otherwise, expired, just like old milk.

Hersh, tightly buttoned up against the cold, stood in front of the heavy steel door built into the bricks.

"Geez, Morris, thought you guys wouldn't make it," he said, bending down to peer inside the car. His eyes roved to the back seat, looking for any uninvited party crashers. "I was just about to lock us all in for the evening. They're going to start the lighting in a few minutes. Hi, Shira!"

"Chag Sameach, Hersh," replied Shira, looking happy for the first time since Baker picked her up.

"And to you, maideleh," said Hersh, adjusting his tweed cap and fuzzy earmuffs with a pair of enormous, gloved hands. "Head on in. I just have to close the gate and I'll be right behind y—"

An egg exploded on the side of Hersh's head.

"Merry Christmas, Jews!" a slurred voice called over the roar of the engine. "Thought you might want some eggnog, hold the nog!"

"Go back to Commie Land, ya kikes!" yelled another.

"Christ Killers!" howled a third.

Baker looked out the passenger window to behold a trio of men leaning on one another as they drunkenly swayed from side to side.

The pogroms always started this way. First came the booze, next came the broken glass and dead Jews. The one in the middle held the carton of eggs while the other two clutched green glass bottles. Baker initially mistook them for wine bottles until he spotted the filthy rags sticking out of their long necks.

"Shira," Baker said firmly. "Go inside. Now."

"Morris..." she began.

"Now!" he repeated, no longer angry at her. "Go!"

Shira opened her door and ran past Hersh, the pot of borsht sloshing in her hands, toward the synagogue entrance just as the man on the far right produced a lighter.

"Hersh, cover your ears," Baker said.

"Already there, my friend," Hersh said, tapping his earmuffs. "Do it."

Baker shifted over to the passenger window, extracted his gun from its holster. He aimed the muzzle toward the group of men, who, even through their inebriation, knew a firearm when they saw one. "Oh shit!" they screamed in unison and Baker was pleased to see a dark stain spreading over the crotch of the pudgy, red-faced man holding the eggs.

Baker angled the gun up to the sky and fired a warning shot into the air. "Next one goes into one of your heads!" he roared. This effectively scattered the hecklers. The egg man dropped his carton, which landed upside down in a yellow pool of broken yolks. Another member of the group abandoned his Molotov cocktail. It exploded on the pavement, creating a small blanket of fire that was quickly extinguished by a strong gust of wind.

The third man, however, turned back around and took aim. "And a partridge in a fuckin' pear tree!" he shouted, letting the bottle fly.

"Time to go!" Hersh shouted.

Baker scooted back to the wheel, put the car in drive, and drove it through the door. Hersh followed, putting all his weight against the reinforced steel, which slammed shut just as the homemade incendiary device hit the metal with a loud *Woomph!* of detonating flames.

Baker got out of the Continental, reholstering his gun. "You okay?" he asked.

"I'm fine," Hersh said, wiping yolk residue from his head. "Those gentile meshuggeners. May they all go take a shit in the ocean," he added in Yiddish. "How are you doing?"

"Peachy."

"Ha! Just like those schnapps you're always guzzling down! Nice work, by the way."

Baker cracked a smile. "What's a holiday without some fireworks?"

CHAPTER 6

Baker and Hersh leaned against the Continental for a few minutes, sharing Baker's bottle of schnapps and allowing the adrenaline of their recent encounter to subside.

"We were lucky there were only three of them," Hersh said, wiping his sleeve across his lips after taking a generous sip.

"And that they decided to use eggs instead of bullets," Baker replied, accepting the bottle and tilting it toward his own mouth like a man dying of thirst in the desert. "You should've seen the crowd that attacked Chinatown after the PLA launched the Seollal Offensive in '56. Twelve people killed and half the storefronts destroyed once the sun rose. I'll never forget all the broken glass. Took us three whole days to sweep it all up."

He went to take another pull and started coughing again.

"Whoa! Easy there, boychik," Hersh said, slapping him on the back with enough force to cause the schnapps bottle to fly out of his hand and shatter on the pavement. "Oops! Sorry about that, Morris. I'll get you a new one."

"Don't worry about," heaved Baker. "I've had enough."

"You see Dr. Ehrlich about that cough yet?" Hersh asked. "Doesn't sound very good."

"Just a cold," Baker said, expelling a nasty ball of phlegm onto the spilled schnapps. "I'm fine, really. We better get inside for the lighting."

Shira was talking animatedly with Hersh's wife, Mindy, when they entered. The chapel's usual aromas of varnished wood and musty carpeting now mingled with the mouthwatering scents of potluck items: potato latkes, jelly donuts, beef brisket, freshly churned applesauce, sweet lokshen kugel, and more. Under all that lingered the odor of burnt wood and masonry from the destroyed part of the synagogue currently undergoing renovations.

The wooden pews were packed with chatting congregants. Baker could see Rabbi Kahn affixing fat waxy candles to a large menorah near the front of the room with some help from his young son, David. As per usual, the left sleeve of Kahn's jacket was pinned up, concealing a horrifically scarred stump of flesh where an arm had once comfortably resided until it was hacked off by an irate concentration camp commandant.

Baker and Hersh slid into the pew behind Shira and Mindy, allowing the women to continue their conversation about how big Mindy's belly was getting with her first child.

"Dr. Ehrlich says I'll be ready to pop by mid-February!" Mindy exclaimed, clearly not registering the thinly veiled look of jealously on Shira's face. "There's still so much to do!"

"Well, you just let Morris and me know if we can help in any way," Shira said, patting Mindy's hand.

"Just don't ask me to change any diapers," Baker added, leaning forward between the two women. Mindy chuckled and Shira put on a forced smile. The crinkle of her nose told him she smelled the latest slug of schnapps on his breath.

"Oh, Morris! Hersh!" Mindy exclaimed. "Shira was just telling me about what happened outside. Are you two all right?"

"Never been better," Hersh said, leaning forward to give his pregnant wife a kiss. "Morris actually made one of those kadokhes wet his pants. I bet I'd be able to fry one of those eggs on his face now."

"The borsht make it in once piece?" Baker asked Shira.

"A few drops were spilled, but otherwise, no harm done. To the soup, I mean."

Baker laughed, grabbed her hand, and gave it a reassuring squeeze. Shira reciprocated, albeit half-heartedly. Baker turned around to take in his favorite part of the chapel: a stained-glass mosaic of a burning bush, its colorful shards dully reflecting the boxy chandeliers running in a straight line down the center of the aisle.

"Ladies and gentlemen," announced Rabbi Kahn from the front of the room. "Welcome and Chag Sameach. It is so great to see such a lovely turnout this evening. With the sun now fully set, we can begin the mitzvah of lighting the menorah. Normally, the act involves publicizing the act for the whole world to see, but if I did that, you'd probably never hear from me again after tonight."

This drew a bout of raucous laughter from the crowd. Kahn possessed a very special talent for putting people at ease. Maybe it was his soft, understanding voice or the almost stooped, unassuming way in which he held himself. The man was well liked by all, especially by Baker, who admired Kahn's continued ability to believe in God after living through a parade of unending atrocities at Theresienstadt. Fellow survivors of the war and the camps were attracted to him like moths to a lightbulb.

Patient and wise beyond his years, Kahn was a modern-day Solomon, though everyone knew he was too humble to accept such a comparison.

"*Psst*," whispered Hersh out the corner of his mouth. "Need one of these?" He held a pair of large black yarmulkes.

"Thanks," Baker said, taking one and placing it atop his curly brown hair. "What? No bobby pins?"

Hersh snickered, affixing the other yarmulke to his own head.

"And now," Kahn continued, "I will light the first candle and then we can get to the good part: eating." More laughter. Kahn took a match and struck it on his heel to many "oohs" and "ahhs" from the congregants. He walked up to the menorah and lit the candle on the highest bracket known as the shamash. "Feel free to join in if you know the blessing," he said, extracting the shamash and bringing it to the wick of the lone candle on the far right.

Most of the congregation began to sing the ancient words together in a low, melodic tone:

Baruch ata Adonai Eloheinu, melech ha'olam, asher kid'shanu b'mitzvotav v'tzivanu l'hadlik ner shel Hanukkah.

Baruch atah Adonai Eloheinu Melech ha'olam, she'asah nisim la'avoteinu ba'yamim ha'heim ba-z'man ha'zeh.

Baker followed along as best he could, but didn't get far when the coughing set in again.

"*When are you going to get that checked out?*" hissed Shira.

"*I'm working on it!*" he whispered back. "*You think I like hacking up a lung?*"

"Lastly," said Kahn after the first night's candle was officially lit. "We close out with the Shehecheyanu, a blessing we say when performing a mitzvah we haven't welcomed into our lives for quite some time."

Baruch atah Adonai Eloheinu Melech ha'olam, shehecheyanu v'ki'y'manu v'higianu la-z'man ha'zeh.

"Excellent!" declared Kahn, scooping young David up with his good, strong arm. "I now declare the buffet open. Bitei-avon, everyone. A good appetite!"

"About time, too," Hersh said, rubbing his stomach as everyone filed into the foyer, where the food was set up on long wooden tables. "I'm starving."

"Well, you know what they say, Hershel?" said a genial Kahn, walking up to them.

"And what's that, Rabbi?"

"That every Jewish holiday can be summed up in nine simple words."

Baker and Hersh looked inquiringly at each other.

Kahn chuckled. "They tried to kill us. We won. Let's eat!"

"Technically, Rabbi," Baker said, "that's ten words."

After coming here regularly for a little over year, Baker was acquainted with nearly all of the synagogue's members. While making his way down the scrumptious buffet, his plate piled high with latkes, pickled cucumbers, and kugel, Harvey Klein caught up with him.

"Hey, Morris, how's tricks?" asked the wiry dressmaker.

"Same drek, different day, Harvey," said Baker. "You know how it is."

"I hear that. Listen, someone's looking for you."

Baker lost his grip on a jelly donut, which rolled away, leaving skid marks of powdered sugar in its wake. "What do you mean, looking for me?"

"Just as I say," Harvey answered, carefully choosing a sufganiyah of his own and taking a large bite out of its side. With his free hand, he started to dollop healthy amounts of herring and sour cream onto his plate. "Young kid came into the shop yesterday, asking for you by name."

"Did you tell him where to find me?"

"Do I look meshugge?" Harvey said, sounding affronted as he sprayed donut crumbs and gobs of jelly filling everywhere. "A stranger asking suspicious questions about a Jew? Anyone who falls for that one again is a shmendrik of the highest order. Didn't trust him from the off. I asked why he was interested in you, but he wouldn't say and then he left."

"What'd he look like?"

"The opposite of me," Harvey said with a laugh. "Young and strapping. He also had a bissel accent. Now I think on it, he might've been Israeli."

"What's an Israeli doing all the way over here? I thought they couldn't spare any men in that war of theirs."

The Jewish state was still managing to cling on to its precarious existence despite a bloody conflict against a number of hostile enemy nations. No one thought they'd last a month after McCarthy cut off foreign aid six years ago, but here they were—still alive and kicking, much to the chagrin of the Jordanians, Egyptians, Syrians, Lebanese, and Iraqis.

"Just telling you what I heard," Harvey said, now distracted by a fresh plate of steaming latkes that had just arrived at the table. "I didn't give you up, Morris."

"You're a credit to our people, Harvey."

No longer feeling hungry, Baker left the table, strategically avoiding pockets of giggling children playing dreidel or else hungrily unwrapping chocolate coins covered in gold foil. After a minute or two of moving through the shmoozing crowd, he found Shira, Hersh, and Mindy talking near the chapel doors.

"Morris," Shira said. "Did you get me a bowl of borsht? I haven't had a chance to try it yet."

"Uh... no," he said sheepishly. "I forgot. I'll go get that now. Here, have some latkes in the meantime."

He handed her the plate of food, and started back toward the food when Kahn stopped him. The rabbi was now holding his five-year-old daughter, Shoshana, whose lips and fingers were coated in melted chocolate. "Morris! Happy Hanukkah."

"Happy Hanukkah, Rabbi," Morris said. "Glad to be here."

"I heard you and Hershel had a little trouble with some, uh, merrymakers before the lighting."

"Nothing we couldn't handle," Baker said. "Showed those, uh..." He didn't want to swear in front of the clergyman or his daughter. "Well, we showed those fellas we meant business."

"Yes, I suppose you did," Kahn said, his face drooping a little. "And how's business? Good?"

"Booming," Baker lied. "Just got a case this afternoon, as a matter of fact."

"Excellent, excellent. Any updates on the Boaz Friedman front, by the way? Tzipora's been asking about the get."

"I'm working on it. Is he here now?"

"No, he's been banned from the shul until he agrees to grant Tzipora a divorce."

"I still don't get this whole *get* thing, Rabbi. I mean, if Boaz's being stubborn about giving her the document, why can't Tzipora just move on with her life?"

Kahn smiled. "Jewish law is a lot like chewed-up bubble gum that gets caught in your hair. The more you try to untangle it, the more convoluted and stuck it becomes."

"Meaning...?"

Kahn laughed heartily, well aware that Baker was the only person here who was unafraid to call the rabbi on his nonanswer bullshit. He placed Shoshana down on the floor with a soft "Down you go, maidele. Go to your mother." He shooed Shoshana toward his wife, Abigail, who was in the midst of a chat with old Edith Landsman. "Come with me, Morris. We'll have a small side party of our own."

CHAPTER 7

They stopped by Kahn's office, where the rabbi pulled a dusty bottle of Slivovitz and two glasses out of his desk. He and Baker then proceeded to the abandoned kiddish room/social hall currently under renovation, separated from the rest of the building by opaque plastic curtains. It reeked of smoke in there, and there was a chilly draft coming in through burn holes that dotted the rafters like advanced leprosy.

"Here," said Kahn, sitting down on a pile of lumber. "This should help warm us up." He set the glasses down, uncorked the plum brandy with his teeth, and poured out two healthy measures. "It's taking forever to get this room restored. The city is withholding our permits."

"No surprise there," Baker said, sitting down and lifting one of the glasses. "From what I hear, the Hueys are running the entire show now, including the LAPD. Maybe things will change after next year's election."

"You really think that young man has a chance to secure the Republican nomination away from McCarthy? All the young ladies seem to be smitten with him."

"His chances aren't great. But schmucks like us can dream. I hear they gave him Bogart's old position as UAP mascot and now he's looking to leverage that into a political career. Someone recently suggested he go for the governorship of California first, build up his credibility more, and he laughed in their face. He wants the top prize, thinks weeding out Reds as president of the Screen Actors Guild makes him worthy of running the country. The guy is ambitious, I'll give him that."

"Shall we drink to a Reagan victory in 1960, then?" Kahn said, holding up his glass.

"Don't see why not," Baker said, clinking his cup against Kahn's.

The two men drank deeply. Baker sputtered at the harshness of the spirit while the rabbi smacked his lips in appreciation. "Delicious," he said, already pouring himself more. "Nothing like a taste of the homeland. I've been holding on to this bottle for quite some time now. It's almost impossible to get your hands on Slivovitz anymore. The producers who make it are all behind the Iron Curtain, I'm afraid."

"How old is that bottle?" Baker asked, eyes watering.

"You probably wouldn't believe me if I told you. Would you like some more?"

"Don't have much of a choice," said Baker, wistfully remembering how his schnapps were currently soaking into the parking lot. "Let her rip."

Kahn refilled their glasses and took a more cautious sip of his second helping. "And so, to business. Time to see if you completed your homework. Did you read the story I recommended when last we spoke?"

Baker grinned. He was one of very few congregants who knew of Kahn's infatuation with science fiction. The rabbi loved reading the works of Bradbury, Asimov, Le Guin, and Heinlein, whom he often described as modern Talmudic sages.

"I did as a matter of fact," Baker answered, thinking back to the short story he'd read over a half-hour period the previous week. "Didn't see that twist coming. A cookbook!"

"Simple, yet elegantly devastating. A sucker punch to the reader's mental gut," Kahn said. "What is the phrase the Americans like to say? 'There is no such thing as a free lunch'?"

"'Everything comes with a price.'"

"Precisely. Are you familiar with Abraham's purchase of Ma'arat HaMachpela?"

"Abraham, I know. But what's the second thing you just said?"

Kahn guffawed, the sound a forlorn ghost in the burnt and empty space. The laughter was not cruel or condescending, but more akin to the reaction of a father who has just been told a dirty joke by his underage son. Kahn and Baker were about the same age, but the former seemed older somehow—wiser, more comfortable in his own skin.

He and Baker would often chat about sci-fi stories, with the discussion almost always tying back into a lesson derived from Jewish tradition. Baker didn't much care for Torah study, but it was inarguably more palatable when wrapped up in exciting tales of the weird and unusual.

"Abraham, our very first forefather," the rabbi explained. "When his wife, Sarah, died, he wanted to bury her in a very special cave with a connection to the Garden of Eden. That cave was known as Ma'arat HaMachpela. The only problem? The cave was located on the land owned by a man by the name of Ephron." Kahn took another sip of brandy, continued, "Ephron was as shrewd a businessman as they come, and mind you, this was in the days before free market capitalism."

"All hail the invisible hand," Baker said in mock toast.

"Initially, Ephron offered the cave to Abraham, free of charge, no strings attached."

"Just like the Kanamit and their miraculous gifts of alien technology."

"Glad to see you're paying attention," Kahn said. "So Ephron offers up the cave at no charge. But Abraham, instantly recognizing the man's shrewdness, makes an offer anyway. He wisely knows that if he takes Ephron up on his generous offer, there will almost certainly be ownership disputes down the line once both of them are dead and buried. He wants to pay for the cave fair and square, and he also wants a receipt. A proof of sale. But even then, Ephron won't accept Abraham's offer. He continues to obfuscate, dancing around the issue and making a seemingly unrelated aside about how much *he* values the land."

"And that's Abraham's 'it's a cookbook' moment," cut in Baker.

"Indeed. He's decoded the Kanamit language, as it were. And what's more, he's decoded it before accepting a single acre of property from a cunning individual like Ephron. He's sized the man up and fully understands who he is dealing with. Abraham knows that almost nothing in this world comes for free. He could go for instant gratification, bury his wife, and be done with it. But he's thinking several steps ahead—or rather, several generations."

"If it's too good to be true, then it probably is," Baker said.

"You've got it," Kahn said encouragingly. "Taking a person at their word or accepting a free gift isn't always hazardous. It may not seem like it these days, but there are kind men and women out there who expect nothing in return for their generosity. But Abraham, unlike the humans in Mr. Knight's excellent story, teaches us that if something you really want is being handed to you on a silver platter, then there very well could be an ulterior motive behind it. Even if the person or people—or aliens—seem trustworthy, you should always strive to discover if there is some sort of quid pro quo. Only then can you have true peace of mind about the transaction. The Torah doesn't say it outright, but the takeaway is this: Always get it in writing."

Baker gave a small clap. "You never fail to impress, Rabb—" He stopped mid-sentence when he saw tears cascading down Kahn's cheeks and into the man's salt-and-pepper beard. "Rabbi, what is it? What's wrong?"

"It's getting worse out there, Morris," he said croakily. "After everything we went through in the war, I cannot believe it's happening again. I didn't want to believe, and yet, here I am bearing witness to the harsh reality every day. And the worst part is I'm powerless to do anything."

Similar to his interaction with Ann Kissinger earlier that day, Baker felt wrong-footed, unsure of how to best comfort the distraught individual before him. He decided to call on his skills as a detective in an effort to assuage Kahn's emotional pain. Getting to the bottom of the pain was essential to its alleviation.

"We've known what that putz McCarthy has done to this country for years now, Rabbi," he said. "What's bringing this all on now?"

"I foolishly thought we could simply weather the storm, wait for it all to pass over us," Kahn said. "The verbal abuse, the propaganda, the attacks on our synagogues, homes, and businesses. Those were all things I was willing to accept—or tolerate at the very least. Stinging words and shattered glass can be swept away and forgotten. Crowds of innocent souls rounded up and carted off in broad daylight do not fade so easily."

Baker had no answer to this, no grand solution to the helplessness Kahn was feeling. Perhaps the best course of action was to let the rabbi say his piece and, in doing so, exorcise a modicum of pain. That pit of despair was a place Baker knew incredibly well. He'd languished at the bottom of it for many years until the rabbi had lowered a hand down with the promise of pulling him up and into the light. What could you even say to someone you thought had all the answers?

"Every day I watch, sick to my stomach, as Koreans are forced from their homes and taken to God knows where to face horrors unknown,"

Kahn said. "Every day I watch and want to tear my clothes and scream myself hoarse until somebody jerks me awake from this unending nightmare. Every day I watch and wish and do nothing. Because I am afraid—not just for myself, but for my family, for my congregation. I am a selfish coward, no better than the Germans who stood by and gave Hitler free rein because it was more convenient to do nothing than to risk everything."

"How can you say that?" Baker demanded, now looking up, offended on Kahn's behalf. "How can you even—?"

"Because it is the truth, Morris," said the rabbi. "And when they come for one group, they invariably start to come for another."

"What do you mean?" Baker asked.

Kahn dabbed at his eyes with a handkerchief. "Several members of the community have gone missing," he said.

"Who?"

"Abner Greenspan, Netanel Horowitz, Noah Levinson, Yehuda Mandelbaum, and Eliyahu Margules. You know them, all close friends and thick as thieves. They organized the Purim spiel last spring. Do you remember?"

"I remember," Baker said, recalling the group's comedic doo-wop performance. "Any idea where they were all last seen?"

"From what their wives told me, they all met up for drinks after work two weeks ago and never came home."

"You suspect HUAC?"

"Who else?"

"Why didn't their wives come straight to me?" Baker asked. "This is what I do. I find the missing people that no one else cares to look for."

"I advised them to do just that as soon as I heard."

"So why is this the first I'm hearing of it, Rabbi?"

Kahn looked up, eyes still full of sadness. "I do not engage in idle gossip, Morris. You know that."

"They refused to come to me for some reason. It's okay, Rabbi. I'll take the aveira on this one."

Kahn looked up and Baker was happy to see the corners of the rabbi's lips twitch upward. "So you have done some studying beyond the sci-fi?"

"I dabble. Now, out with it. The sin is on me. God can add it to my tab. I'll probably never pay it off at this point."

"I'm sorry, Morris. It's lashon hara. I will not repeat negative falsities if I can help it. Our president does that enough as it is. Needless to say, I told them you were the best man for the job."

"So what are they doing?"

"Working with the police, but if what you say about HUAC taking them over is true, no one is actually searching for those poor men."

"I am," said Baker before he could stop himself. He felt angry that members of his own congregation would refuse to come see him in their time of need. But he wanted to do something that would remove the mortal agony from Kahn's face. "I'm now on the case," he added. "As a favor to you, Rabbi. Free of charge. And don't try to make me an offer like Abraham."

Kahn laughed croakily this time, a very good sign. "Morris, I cannot ask you to take this on. I am sure your current caseload is—"

"I won't hear another word against it," Baker said forcefully. "I'm on it, whether their wives like it or not. Now, come on." He practically lifted the dejected Kahn off the lumber pile. "Let's get back to the potluck. I think there are still a few latkes left with my name on them."

CHAPTER 8

Contrary to his claim, Baker did not eat anything. Any appetite he might have had was gone. He walked back into the lobby, deposited Kahn with his wife, wished them both a happy holiday, and went to seek out Shira. It was just his luck that she'd be deep in conversation with Netanel Horowitz's spouse, Shelly.

"Let's go," he said bluntly, breaking up their chatter without a single word of apology.

"What?" asked Shira, shocked by the abruptness.

"We're going. I've got a stomachache."

"Well, I'm not ready to leave," she replied through gritted teeth, trying to avoid a scene.

"So stay then!" Baker shouted, causing eyes to move in their direction. "See if I care!" He gave a curt nod to Shelly that represented only a fraction of the animus he felt toward the woman. He turned on his heel and walked out the front doors into the frigid parking lot. Hersh was outside, enjoying a cigarette.

"Leaving so soon?" he called after the retreating Baker.

"Just open the gate, Hersh."

Baker was unlocking the Continental when Shira caught up with him, grabbed his arm. "What is *wrong* with you?" she demanded.

He jabbed a finger at his own chest. "What's wrong with me, Shira? I don't know—why don't you enlighten me? Clearly Shelly seems to know since she and her friends never came to see me when their husbands went missing two weeks ago!" Shira's eyes went wide, and she took a step back, confirming his suspicion that she'd been in on it. "So tell me, what is *so* wrong with Morris Baker that his so-called friends won't come to him in a pinch when he's probably the only fucking person in this town who can actually help them? Tell me, Shira. What's wrong?"

"*Everything!*" she tossed back at him, her voice cracking with the strain. "Everything is wrong with you, Morris. You're cold and distant, and when you're not working every hour of the day, you're drinking yourself half to death with those fucking schnapps. You've become an absolute stranger to me. To all of us!"

"Now, Shira"—Hersh was standing a few feet away—"you don't really mean that."

"No, Hersh," Baker snarled. "Let's get it all out in the open. Go ahead, Shira."

"You really have no idea, *do* you?" Shira bellowed, and now Baker could see people poking their heads out of the synagogue doors to see what all the fuss was about. "You have no clue why people don't want to be around you, do you? Why I don't even want to be around you? Look at Hersh and Mindy! Married with a child on the way. Where are we, Morris? I can barely get you to remember when to pick me up on time!"

She didn't wait for answer, was already headed back inside.

"If that's how you and the rest of them feel..." he called after her, slightly embarrassed to see Rabbi Kahn among the throng of people growing near the entrance. "Then that's fine with me!"

He rounded on Hersh. "Open the gate."

"Morris," he said calmly. "Let's just—"

"I said open the fucking gate!"

"No," said Hersh, firmly standing his ground, well aware of his advantage in the categories of both height and weight. "You're drunk."

"You too, huh? Fine." Baker reached into his pocket, feeling around for his bottle of schnapps, which had shattered all over the parking lot an hour or so before. "Motherfucker!"

"*Me?*" inquired Hersh, looking offended.

"No, not you—my fucking schnapps!"

Baker stormed back into the shul, pushing the onlookers aside with careless abandon. Even those who had not peered outside knew that something was off—the entire mood of the potluck had taken a nosedive. Shira, Mindy, and Shelly were nowhere to be found, though

Baker suspected they were now in the restroom, besmirching whatever was left of his good name.

Refusing to make eye contact with anyone, including Harvey Klein (by the look of the man's renewed presence at the buffet table, he didn't have a clue what was going on), he plowed forward and into the burned-out dining hall, where the bottle of Slivovitz continued to rest on the pile of awaiting lumber. Whatever qualms Baker might've had about drinking the rabbi's prized liquor were immediately stamped out by his own fury at everyone in the building. They wanted absolutely nothing to do with him? Fine. He'd make sure they regretted the day they ever met him.

Baker posted up in a corner of the lobby, glaring at them all between sips of the horrific plum brandy. After fifteen minutes of hypothermic awkwardness, the tension finally cracked like a frozen lake at the onset of spring. Harvey accidentally dropped his plate; the ceramic shattered, someone jokingly yelled "Mazel tov!" and the atmosphere returned to its comfortable status quo.

Shira, Mindy, and Shelly reappeared. They spoke in a quarterback's huddle for a few moments before Isaac Kremnitzer, Ohev Shalom's bottom-feeding putz-in-chief, showed up to ask Shira for a word. She broke away from the group, and before long, Baker's girlfriend was laughing and playfully touching Kremnitzer's arm.

"Enjoy it, Isaac!" Baker shouted over the din as he polished off the last of the booze. "Easiest pussy you'll ever get!"

Kremnitzer paid no heed to the remark but leaned forward to whisper something in Shira's ear. She nodded and the two started to make their way toward the exit. Somehow, Shira had forgotten all about her pot of soup. Baker followed, but was soon stymied by Mrs. Landsman.

"Morris, there you are!" she wheezed. "I've been having a dispute with my landlord and was wondering if you might be able to lend an old woman a hand."

"That's great, Mrs. Landsman."

"There's nothing great about it, young man. They're trying to evict me."

"Lovely," Baker said. "Be sure to call my secretary and I'll get right on it."

He brushed Mrs. Landsman aside, quickened his pace. By the time he broke through the doors, however, Kremnizter's light blue Thunderbird was already cruising through the open steel door separating the shul from the rest of Los Angeles. Baker chucked the empty Slivovitz bottle after the light blue vehicle to no avail. It shattered just below the taillights and made Hersh, who was holding the door open with a groan of effort, yell in surprise.

"Oy! I'm about to be a father, Morris!" he thundered. "I don't need the added stress of glass shards lodged in my tuchus."

"Just keep the door open, Hersh!"

"Morris..."

"I said keep it open, goddamnit!"

Baker hopped into the Continental, peeled out of the parking spot with an earsplitting screech of tires, and drunkenly steered onto South Robertson Boulevard.

CHAPTER 9

The plan was to follow Shira and Kremnitzer, but since the Thunderbird was already long gone, Baker decided to pick up a fresh bottle of schnapps and drive around aimlessly before his stomach started to growl with hunger. His fury at Shira and the rest of the congregation had begun to morph into an unpleasant combination of self-pity and despair.

How foolish he was to think those people were his friends—almost a surrogate family. They didn't trust him, were frightened of him even, and had therefore decided to cast him out. Turn him into another pariah. Baker was used to such things, but had never expected it from his own people. People who had been considered outsiders for five millennia.

You've become an absolute stranger to me. To all of us!

Shira's words rang in his head like a death knell. For the briefest moment, Morris Baker had been a hero to the congregation and the wider disenfranchised communities of Los Angeles. His struggle against the Black Symphony, broadcast to the masses by Edward R. Murrow with all the excitement of a pre-television radio drama, was the stuff of legend. People wanted to shake his hand; have him over for dinner; hear his story; be his friend.

What had he done in turn? What Morris Baker did best, of course—he pushed them all away, citing work and headaches and whatever else popped into his mind. Because it was easier to be alone than to work at something real. Easier to already be the disappointment others suspected you to be. And over time, the praise and well-wishes and dinner invitations began to peter out along with the heroic legend of Morris Baker. All of it replaced with quiet, apprehensive whispers of whether any of it was actually true. The people wanted a hero, a savior, a pseudo-messianic figure to look up to for some spark of hope in their darkest hour. What they got was a schnapps-swilling schlimazel. No wonder the work had begun to dry up.

Still, who were *they* to judge him? To deem him lesser? His entire private investigation business was built around the promise of bringing hope to the hopeless. And yet the wives of those men would rather take their chances with the police than come to someone who fully understood their plight. It spoke more volumes than a direct insult to the face ever could. The worst part of it all was that Shira knew. The entire shul had conspired against him by keeping this secret about the missing men. Men who had most likely been arrested for the simple crime of being Jewish.

Baker couldn't help but laugh at the utter hypocrisy of it all.

What did Rabbi Kahn tell him over the summer during the annual festival of Tisha B'Av? That both Temples in Jerusalem had been destroyed not from the result of idolatry or hedonism, but from sinat chinam, the baseless hatred the Jewish people had for one another. Well, at least history was consistent. Same drek, different day. If they wanted to hate and avoid him, that was A-OK with Morris Baker. The rest of Ohev Shalom could burn to the ground for all he cared. It was what they deserved.

Deep down he knew that wasn't entirely true. Rabbi Kahn was still a decent man and didn't deserve to have his house of worship destroyed because of the bad eggs among his flock. But Kahn's refusal to tell him the truth—even if it was to spare them both heartache—had arguably made things worse. The rabbi's reaction had been one of inaction.

At what point did piety cross over into iniquity? *Stop it*, Baker chastised himself. *You shouldn't be thinking like that.* The outcome would have been the same, whether the rabbi was up front with him or not. Everything in life had a natural unavoidable progression. Chad gadya.

His stomach rumbled again, and he decided it was time to pay a visit to his favorite late-night eatery in Chinatown. If he couldn't have latkes, then he'd fill up on Peking duck.

———

The Golden Fowl was packed when Baker stepped into the restaurant half an hour later, expecting to nab his favorite corner table.

Sadly, it was occupied, forcing him to settle for a cramped one-seater right next to the open kitchen, where a team of sweaty cooks in grease-stained aprons and squashed paper caps shouted in unintelligible dialects of Mandarin, while expertly manning the gas pedals of their various wok stations. Every so often, Baker would see bits of meat and vegetables briefly suspended in midair as ingredients were tossed and sauces added.

Being so close to the action meant Baker quickly warmed up via wafts of piping hot steam carrying the scents of chili, anise, cardamom, garlic, orange peel, and numbing Szechuan peppercorns. As he waited for someone to take his order, Baker occupied himself by stirring up the deeply crimson chili oil in the condiment pot on the table. Overhead, he could just make out the Bobbettes cheerfully singing "Mr. Lee" on an endless loop from mounted speakers.

"Ah, Baker!" exclaimed a familiar, bubbly voice. "So good to see you!" Hollis Li, owner and operator of the Golden Fowl, strode up to Baker's table, adjusting his favorite teal bow tie. "Sorry about your usual table. Busy night. Everyone seems to want Chinese food on Christmas!"

"Not a problem, Hollis," Baker said, shaking the man's hand with vigor and jerking a thumb toward the kitchen. "Any duck left back there?"

"For my favorite customer? Always!" Hollis suddenly leaned over the table and called out to his cooks. None of them looked up from their stations, but Hollis seemed satisfied. "Mind if I join you? Been on my feet most of the day. First round of baijiu is on me."

"You're on," Baker said, happy to drown out thoughts of Shira and Rabbi Kahn in the powerful spirit Hollis brewed illegally in the bathtub of his apartment above the restaurant.

Hollis snapped his fingers and a purple-jacketed waiter instantly appeared with another chair. He set it down, ducked under a low-hanging paper lantern, and disappeared back into the sea of crowded tables. Hollis plopped into the chair and sighed with immense pleasure. "That's better."

A moment later, one of the cooks appeared with a steaming plate of

Peking duck and scallion pancakes, a small tureen of hoisin sauce, and two shallow cups of the clear baijiu.

"Chī hǎo hē hǎo," said the cook, backing away.

"Just what you need in the middle of a long dinner rush like this," Hollis said, cradling one of the cups in his palm. The rim was nearly to his lips when another waiter turned up, seemingly out of nowhere, to whisper something in the proprietor's ear. Hollis's face drained of its color and he muttered something back. The waiter nodded gravely in response.

"What is it?" asked Baker, quickly polishing off his first assembled duck pancake and chasing it down with the liquor. "Run out of soy sauce or something?"

Hollis placed his cup down on the table. It was very odd to see the usually exuberant restaurateur without a wide grin spread across his face. "Morris, you must come with me now."

"I just started eating, Hollis. Can it wait?"

"I'm afraid not," Hollis replied sternly. "Don't worry, my staff will keep your table free until we're done."

"Done with what exactly?"

Hollis stood up, smoothing out the wrinkles on his brown suit. "Come, they don't like to be kept waiting."

"Who is 'they'?"

In lieu of an answer, Hollis turned and strode off into the kitchen. Baker jumped out of his seat and followed like an obedient canine. He'd never been in the kitchen of the Golden Fowl before and he wasn't sure he would ever like to repeat the experience. The cooks immediately parted for their boss, but refused to do the same for Baker. They barked what he could only assume were Mandarin obscenities while brandishing sharp cleavers and fat florets of broccoli.

"Uh...Hollis?" Baker called out, barely dodging a young man plucking feathers off a chicken carcass the color of charcoal into a waste bin. "What's this all about, huh? If you wanted to give me a tour of the place, you could've just said so."

He flattened himself against the wall as another prep cook came barreling through with a bucket filled to the brim with hopping spot prawns. Hollis did not speak until they'd reached the far end of the kitchen, where a saltwater tank containing fresh crabs and lobsters stood, gurgling lazily.

"Once we get in there, let me do all the talking," Hollis said, adjusting his bow tie again. "Do not speak unless spoken to—is that understood?"

"How can I understand anything when you haven't told me who the hell we're meeting with?"

Hollis, who was now extracting a fat ring of keys, looked up, a harried look stretching his features. "The leaders of the other Los Angeles tongs are here," he said. "And they want to meet with you."

CHAPTER 10

While Baker knew that Hollis was the head of a local tong, he never asked too many questions about what the role entailed. During his tenure as a cop, he preferred to maintain his friendship with the man without the awkwardness of having to arrest him. Over the years, it was implicitly understood that the topic of illegal activities was taboo during their many late-night drinking sessions. Now that Baker was off the force, however, he had no problem posing a few queries about it.

"The tong leaders?" he repeated. "What do they want with me?"

"Relax," Hollis said, tugging open the door to the kitchen's massive walk-in refrigerator and stepping inside. "You're not in trouble."

"Well, that's comforting," Baker said, following Hollis into the frigid space. "Still doesn't answer my question," he added, accidentally knocking over a box of mushrooms.

"They just want to talk," Hollis answered, choosing a sharp-looking silver key off the ring. "Do as I say, and you'll probably be fine."

"Probably?"

"I promise you'll live long enough to eat the rest of your duck. On that, you have my word."

"Are we all going to meet in here?" Baker asked. "Might be a bit cramped. Is there reserved seating? Does anyone have a claim to that crate of bok choy over there? Looks comfy."

"Get out all the sarcasm now," Hollis said, striding over to black rubber strips dangling from the back wall. He pushed them aside to reveal another door into whose lock he inserted the silver key. "Because I warn you that these people don't have much patience for flippancy."

He turned the key, and the tumbler gave way with a loud *ka-chunk!* "Here we go. Ready?"

"As I'll ever be," Baker said.

Hollis pulled the door inward and Baker got his first glimpse of a dark parlor room full of cigarette smoke. Through the heavy curtain of tobacco vapor, he could just make out eight to ten shadowy figures sitting in high-backed armchairs arranged in a semicircle formation. The harsh fluorescent light filtering in from the kitchen made it impossible to discern any specific features about the people or even of the room itself.

"*Go on*," Hollis whispered. Baker took two steps forward onto the Persian rug. Hollis followed, closing the refrigerator door and locking it behind him. He then stepped in front of Baker, bowed respectfully to the other tong leaders, and began to speak in Mandarin. While Baker didn't speak a lick of Chinese, he did catch his name amid what was almost certainly a short introduction.

Now that the door was closed, Baker's eyes slowly adjusted to the room's weak illumination, which came from a dying fire in the very back of the room. The undulating orange glow hinted at the presence of a tall grandfather clock; a handsome bookcase packed with massive, leather-bound tomes; and a collection of watercolor paintings of junk ships.

It was stiflingly hot in here and the air was thick—not only with tobacco smoke, but also with the overwhelming scents of cinnamon and sandalwood. On a small wooden table near the hidden entrance, a number of incense sticks smoldered down to their tips.

"Thank you for coming, Mr. Baker," said a deep and measured voice emanating from one of the dark armchairs closest to him. "Your reputation is rather impressive, if it is to be believed at all."

"And what's that supposed to mean?" Baker demanded.

"It means we have need of your services," said a curt voice from another chair. "I believe it is time for Hollis to call in a favor you owe him."

"And you fellas are...?"

"Our names are not important," rasped a third.

"Hi, Not Important. That Scandinavian? It's a real pleasure," said Baker, exasperated after an evening that had already strained his patience to the breaking point. "Hollis, come on. These jokers can't be serious."

"The less you know about us, the better," Hollis answered, stone-faced. His expression was more severe than ever as if to say, *What the fuck did I just tell you about getting wise with these people?* "A little over a year ago," he continued, "I helped prevent those HUAC inspectors from arresting you at Merv's Diner. I pulled important guards away from their posts on very short notice. Moreover, our little standoff has brought more scrutiny upon our community, as I am sure you have noticed."

"Yeah, I have."

"HUAC and the LAPD are making arrests left and right, Morris."

"On what charges?"

"Being Chinese. Our mutual friends over at the Red Sword have a similar story to tell. We paid a great price in coming to your aid that night. Now I am asking you to return the gesture."

"Well, sure, Hollis," Baker said, suitably chastened.

To be quite frank, he had barely spoken with any of the people who had helped him out on that fateful evening in early July 1958. If he had stayed in close contact, he'd probably know about all the trouble his actions had caused them. But as always, he'd decided to cut himself off from the world, diving into a fathomless crater of work, schnapps, and self-pity.

"I didn't mean any disrespect," Baker added, staring beyond the tong members and into the crackling fire. "I've just had a rough day, is all. Of course, I'm happy to help. What do you need?"

Hollis nodded gratefully. "One of our number has gone missing."

"Seems to be going around a lot lately," said an unsurprised Baker, pulling out his cigarettes. "Let me guess, you want me to track them down?"

"Correct," answered one of the adumbral tong leaders.

"And why," said Baker, putting out his match in the nearby tray of incense, "do you even want them found? I was under the impression that you all hated each other."

"That was true for many years," said Hollis, his face gloomily illuminated by the decaying flames. "But once McCarthy took office and began maligning us and our homeland, it became very clear that we all had—"

"Similar interests," finished another member of the group. Baker was surprised to hear the delicate voice of a young woman. A *very* young woman by the sound of it.

"Yes," continued Hollis. "We put aside the senseless warring amongst ourselves for the betterment and protection of the greater community. Han is no exception."

"Who?" asked Baker.

"Han Zhao, the missing man we'd like you to locate for us," Hollis said.

"Any other details I should be aware of?"

"Only that he is a crucial member of our organization."

"Gonna need more than that to go on, Hollis. A picture, last known location—whatever you can give me. Otherwise, I'll just be groping around in the dark."

Baker stared at one of the junk ship paintings and could almost see the depicted vessel moving against the choppy seas in which it had been depicted. The flickering hearth played tricks on the eyes.

"Here is a picture."

It was the voice of the young woman again. This time, she stood up and walked to the front of the parlor. Sporting a brushed-under bob hairstyle, she couldn't have been older than sixteen, but there was a look of fierce determination in her dark and watery brown eyes that suggested she knew how to handle herself among all these powerful, irascible men.

She held out a sepia photograph, which Baker accepted. It showed a laughing man with prematurely gray hair in fishing waders and a little girl sitting atop his shoulders. Her wide grin displayed a number of missing baby teeth. Baker raised his head to get a better look at the person who had just handed him the photograph and there could be no doubt as to her identity.

"So Han is your . . . ?"

"My father, yes," she said softly. "My name is Mingmei Zhao. I have taken over his responsibilities toward the collective in his absence. I am hoping that it does not become a permanent arrangement. Please find my father and bring him back to us, Mr. Baker. Hollis speaks very highly of you and your skills as a detective."

"I'll do my best, Miss Zhao," Baker said solemnly, shocked at Mingmei's eloquence and maturity. Most girls her age were preoccupied with makeup and what boy might ask them to the year-end dance. "If I may, do you know where your father was last seen?"

"We have a warehouse in San Pedro, near the port. My father was there last week, taking care of some business, and never came home."

"Are you able to provide me with an address of the warehouse?"

"San Pedro, Mr. Baker," said the raspy tong leader. "That is where you will start looking."

Baker nodded his understanding and turned back to Mingmei. He knew that attempting to wheedle more information out of these people would be an exercise in futility. And besides, Hollis might ban him from the Golden Fowl for life if he disrespected them again.

"Thank you for the photograph, Miss Zhao. I promise to return it in the same condition in which it was given to me." He gave the girl a curt bow and she did the same before returning to her armchair.

"We expect regular updates on your progress," said the deep-voiced man who had first spoken when Baker entered the room a few minutes ago. "In terms of compensation—"

"That won't be necessary," said Baker. "Like you say, I owe Hollis a favor." He probably wouldn't have been so magnanimous had Ann Kissinger not paid him so handsomely earlier that day.

"Very well, then. Good luck, Mr. Baker. You will keep Hollis apprised of your progress, and in turn, he shall pass that information along to us."

The tong leaders turned away from him and began conferring among themselves in muttered tones. This was clearly an exit cue because Hollis unlocked the hidden door back into the refrigerator and ushered Baker through it.

"Thank you, Morris," he said after he had locked the door again. "I really mean it."

"Don't mention it," Baker said. "What're friends for, right?"

Hollis steered him back into the noisy kitchen and the man's veteran smile returned in full force, as though they hadn't just entered a smoky back room of restless gang leaders. "And now," said the restaurateur, undoing his bow tie with apparent relief. "Let's get you fed."

Baker, who didn't have much of an appetite anymore, was more than happy to continue drinking with Hollis, who ended up eating most of the duck. At the end of the meal, one of the waiters brought over a small plate of two fortune cookies surrounded by a ring of orange segments.

"Ah," Hollis said, his eyes a little out of focus. "You have to try these oranges, Morris. They're from Lamotte Farms. Best in the state!"

"Think I'll pass," slurred Baker as Hollis began sucking on one of the wedges. "I will, however, take one of these." He picked up one of the fortune cookies and pocketed it. "Could always use a little more good fortune in my life."

When he stumbled out of the Golden Fowl around one in the morning, he was so full of concentrated baijiu that he wouldn't have been surprised if his piss was flammable. Clutched in his left hand was a bulging oyster pail printed with a bright red pagoda. (Like a good Jewish mother, Hollis had insisted he take home some leftovers.)

Even with copious amounts of Hollis's homemade libation coursing through his system, Baker still had room left for schnapps. There was *always* room for schnapps. He sat in his car on Hollywood Boulevard, allowing the twinkling lights of the public Christmas trees adorning the street to lull him into a drunken stupor somewhere between sleep and consciousness.

The storefronts, usually full of whimsical holiday displays, were plastered with flamboyant posters of William Yang's face that warned passersby to BEWARE THE YELLOW PERIL!, and below that, REPORT ANY SUSPECTED SUBVERSIVE ACTIVITY AMONG THE KOREAN AND CHINESE COMMUNITIES TO YOUR LOCAL HUAC OFFICE.

A second poster below that showed the image of a person wearing a cloth mask over their mouth and nose. IF YOU FEEL SICK, IT MAY BE THE YANG FLU, read the caption. PROTECT YOURSELF AND OTHERS: WEAR A MASK. STOP THE SPREAD!

Baker didn't want to go home just yet. His apartment in Chinatown held numerous reminders of Shira (an extra cardigan in the dresser, a second toothbrush in the bathroom, a picture of the two of them riding the Ferris wheel on the Santa Monica Pier), and he wasn't quite ready to let go of his resentment toward her.

Still, he needed to rest his eyes, which could barely stay open under the thought of all the work lying ahead of him. Several people had decided to pull disappearing acts and it was now Baker's job to find them—pro bono on two counts. With thoughts of Henry Kissinger, Han Zhao, and the missing Ohev Shalom congregants swirling around his booze-befuddled brain, he slipped away.

CHAPTER 11

Blood poured from between his fingers like a gushing fountain and there was nothing he could do to stop it. Nothing at all as the hot crimson liquid stretched across the smooth marble floor of the Griffith Observatory's planetarium, filling the entire room with the visceral stink of heated copper. He tried exerting more pressure on the wound, only making things worse. Blood spurted out of the woman's mouth with the horrendous gurgling of a clogged sump pump.

"Try not to speak. You really saved the day," he said to Sophia Vikhrov, the woman who, in just a few seconds from now, would be dead. Gone forever. Her face had almost no color left in it. Hard to believe how rosy those cheeks had been just moments ago.

And now she'll say: "After messing it up in the first place. I'm so sorry about how things turned out. I just wish we'd gotten to know each other under better circumstances."

She'll say it, just you wait and see, an anticipatory voice whispered out of the shadows, where a group of strangers sat underneath the massive observatory dome, watching in objective silence. *Just wait, she'll say it right now. Any moment now.*

Sophia always repeated her last words, no matter how many times Morris relived the moment of her death nearly every night since it had occurred two summers before.

Except this time, she didn't. This time, she went off script.

"Why didn't you save me, Morris?"

Sophia Vikhrov looked up at Morris Baker with intense hatred. The broiling life force pouring out of her chest froze. "Why didn't you save me?" she spat, drops of blood flecking across his face like paint off a brush.

"I...I...I..." he stammered back. "I couldn't. There was nothing I could have done. Nothing."

And now she was sitting up, as though it had all been a knockout performance on opening night. Blackened, coagulated blood rabidly oozed at the corners of her mouth like molten tar.

"You could have saved me, Morris, but you didn't. You could have saved *all* of us."

Sophia gestured to the shadows, where the people were getting to their feet. They stepped into the early evening light and Baker screamed in silent horror. These were not members of the Black Symphony—they were children in striped uniforms that were at least three sizes too big for them. Their eyes were the clouded milky white of a rotting fish, and the cracked flesh around their lips was stained a deep, profound blue. A shade of blue only Zyklon B pellets could create.

"Why didn't you save us?" they asked, their prepubescent voices forming a macabre youth choir of accusation. "You led us into the gas chambers, Morris. Told us everything would be okay. Told us we'd see our parents again soon. Listened to us choke and die. Loaded our bodies onto wheelbarrows. Shoved us into the ovens. Scattered our ashes to the winds..."

"No. No. No." Baker got up and lost his footing on the marble floor still slick with blood. "Please. I didn't want to do it. They made me. I was—"

"Just following orders," proclaimed a new voice. A man's voice. Wernher von Braun shambled out of the darkness, his head the wrong way around. With a horrible cracking noise, the rocket scientist wrenched the switchblade out of his spine and licked the blade with relish. "You were just following orders, Herr Baker. Like the rest of us. You are no better than I or the Black Symphony. You helped us. You helped the Führer. Why don't you just admit it and tell them what you did?" The dead rocket scientist spread his arms across the advancing children with a monstrous leer of triumph.

"*No!*" and this time Baker did manage to scream. "Sophia, you said bearing witness to evil after the fact is just as important as fighting it head on, remember? *Remember?* I'm here to speak out for those who didn't get a chance! You said that! *Remember?*"

Sophia let out a high, cruel cackle that reverberated around the hall.

"And you *believed* me?" She giggled. "I was your foil, remember? Tailor-made for you, and you alone. I told you everything you ever wanted to hear. You are a traitor to your own people, Morris Baker. You are a cold-blooded murderer who deserves to be ostracized. Shira and the rest of them are right. How could anyone ever love a man like you?"

And now the crowd was upon him. They backed him into a corner and began swiping at his flesh with long yellow nails, jagged like barbed fishing hooks. They dug into his arms and legs, gaining purchase by ripping muscle and splitting bone. Blood and marrow trickled to the floor and some of the dead-eyed children gave up the assault to hungrily lap it up.

Others probed deeper still until the group could lift him up above their heads and give him a perfect view of a fiery pit that had opened up in the center of the planetarium floor. They slowly shuffled toward it, reciting a ghoulish verse from parshat Korach over and over in ancient Hebrew: "*And the earth opened its mouth and swallowed them up. And the earth opened its mouth and swallowed them up. And the earth opened its mouth and swallowed them up.*"

"And the earth opened its mouth and swallowed *Morris Baker up-up-up-up-up*!" von Braun chanted, loudest of them all, laughing with the intensity of a madman who has lost all touch with reality. Part of his spinal column jutted out of his twisted neck like stalagmites in a dank cavern deep within the earth.

One of the children, an insane grin plastered across their cerulean lips, hopped from foot to foot, beating a tribal drum made of leathery human skin. Jewish skin.

Baker could not escape the intense heat emanating from the flames, which looked impossibly elated to see him. They were old friends, after all. The fire reached out for a loving embrace and this parade of the dead was only too happy to cast its burden into the hellish pit.

His own personal Tartarus that led back to the crematoria and a glowing hunk of fissile uranium.

CHAPTER 12

N*ooooo!"*

Baker snapped awake, drenched in sweat. He was back on Hollywood Boulevard. Safe and sound...but no. Someone was still beating that ceremonial drum of tanned flesh directly into his left ear. He turned and was surprised to see a woman with makeup caked on her face rapping her knuckles on the window.

"You all right, honey?" she asked. She sounded genuinely concerned.

He rolled down the glass. "I'm fine," he said, closing his eyes and taking in a breath of cold night air. Mildew and raw sewage. It wasn't exactly fresh, but it beat the pants off the terrified musk inside the Continental.

"You sure?" she said, now leaning on the open window and primping her curly blond hair. "You were shaking and screaming in there."

"Just nodded off for a second and had a little nightmare. Too much eggnog, I suppose."

"Got any left?" the woman asked hopefully. "I've been out here all night and didn't get to celebrate. I'd kill for a glass of eggnog right about now."

"I've got some peach schnapps," Baker said. He handed over the bottle, unsure why he was engaging her. The woman downed it in one go with a quick hum of thanks.

With the window open, he could see that the makeup made her look older than she actually was. She had to be somewhere in her early to mid-twenties. A baby by all accounts, but there was definitely something in her posture. A sensual confidence that came only from working these streets as a prostitute.

She leaned in closer, and Baker caught the mingled aromas of schnapps and Wrigley's chewing gum on her breath. "You looking for a good time, mister?"

Baker had never solicited sex before and wasn't interested in starting now. However, the thought of going back to his empty apartment alone, of closing his eyes and falling right back into the nightmare he'd just awoken from, terrified him beyond words.

Without thinking, he procured two of the fifty-dollar bills given to him by Ann Kissinger. "How long will this get me?" he asked, holding out the cash.

The girl's eyes widened with disbelief. "Mister," she exclaimed, already snatching the bills out of his hand and stowing them down the front of her dress, "for money like that, you can have me for the whole week!"

The sex was perfunctory—just something to keep his mind off bitter memories of the war and Sophia. It was the kind of emotionless lovemaking he'd once enjoyed with Liz. She, too, had been a kind of respite from the dark and slimy crevasse where Baker had spent most of his days since 1945. There was also the uncomfortable thought of being unfaithful to Shira, muffled somewhere under a thick cork of baijiu and schnapps. After the fight they'd had, their little romantic experiment was most likely at an end—her exit with Kremnitzer dealing the final knockout blow. And even if the relationship could be salvaged, things would never be the same between them.

"You know," said the young prostitute—her name turned out to be Debbie Milner, a natural brunette, it transpired—when they were both lying naked in Baker's bed in the wee hours of the morning of December twenty-sixth. "You're a pretty lucky fella. You just fucked a bit of a starlet."

"That's nice," Baker said, his mind slipping in and out of focus. He was trying to decide on what missing persons case he'd tackle first and settled on the one he was actually being compensated for. Before he knew it, Debbie was gently snoring against his chest.

She eventually rolled over, pulling most of the blanket with her, when he started coughing again.

"Should see a doctor 'bout that," she murmured, briefly awake.

"Yeah," Baker said, tentatively closing his eyes and praying the nightmare from earlier wouldn't make a recurrence. "Guess I should."

The following is a snippet from the manifesto of the Korean insurgent and terrorist known as William Stuart Yang. The incredibly troubling document was discovered by HUAC inspectors at a motel in Venice Beach shortly after Yang's unprovoked attack on innocent American citizens at a department store in Oakwood...

When I was a little boy, my mother would often regale my sister and me with tales of the inmyeonjo—a great bird with the face of a human. According to Korean mythology, this majestic creature was the bridge between Heaven and Earth and would only descend upon the land when there was lasting harmony among all peoples. She grew up in a small village in the North Chungcheong Province on the outskirts of a thick bamboo forest, from which the locals would often hear strange calls they sometimes ascribed to the winged entity.

(I now wonder if it was simply a flock of red-crowned cranes, whose unnerving calls suggest a herd of angry, stampeding elephants.)

In any case, the benign cultural significance of the inmyeonjo never made much of an impression upon my young mind, which was thoroughly preoccupied by the visual of a great-taloned raptor leering down at me with impeccably straight human incisors. I could barely sleep after hearing the legend. Constantly falling into nightmares where I was torn apart by the bird, or else carried away to its ravenous newly hatched young, which—understandably—had the faces of the boys who would often bully me at school for the color of my skin and the shape of my eyes.

One thing all parents share in common, I think, is the special talent for unintentionally scaring their children. Adults are ignorantly unaware of how much a young mind is able process at once. Kids tend to save the chaff and throw away the wheat, if you will. That is to say they usually remember the first thing you say rather than the last. Had my mother led with the bit about peace and prosperity, the recurring vision of a human-faced bird may have faded with time, relegated to the cobwebbed corners of memory we leave behind after hitting maturity.

But, as I say, the reverse occurred. The inmyeonjo continued to haunt my dreams and I am not ashamed to admit that the mental image of it caused me to lose control of my bladder on more than one occasion. On others, my parents were forced to let me crawl into their bed with them as I cried myself softly to sleep.

And, when my father left us without a word, my mother never protested again when I came into her room, blubbering on about my latest night terror. Truth be told, I think she enjoyed the company on those lonely nights. We kept each other safe—one of us haunted by nightmares, the other heartbroken and terrified at the prospect of raising two young children on her own. It was this mutual feeling of abandonment, of facing the unknown, that drew us together. My mother held me close and before long, the bad dreams stopped. They melted back into the ephemeral place where all dreams are taken out to pasture when they lose their potency.

Every child encounters their own personal boogeyman at one point or another. Mine just so happened to be derived from my Southeast Asian heritage. I am sure my Jewish and Slavic brethren can say the same thing about the dybbuk or the Baba Yaga or the shedim.

I now know that the fear was irrational, of course. Silly, even. I have nothing more to fear from the inmyeonjo than the average person has to fear from the ideology of Communism.

Age brings crystal clear perspective as well as brittle bones and crippling arthritis. Knowledge, as Adam and Eve learned in the Garden of Eden, is cursed. Perhaps our bodies' sudden decline represents an adverse reaction to the vast wealth of wisdom we are granted over the years.

Ignorance is bliss, but it may also be healthy for you.

Which brings me back to the once dreaded inmyeonjo, who I did not fear, as it turns out. The insatiable raptor I saw in my nightmares as a boy was not the bird with a human face that joins Heaven and Earth—the bird of peace and prosperity. No. The entity that so often wanted to rip flesh from bone was none other than the Bald Eagle, the symbol of American freedom.

I have come to understand that the democratic republic in which I was raised wants to strip me of my identity and swallow me whole. Wants to peck out my eyes, so I shall not bear witness to the atrocities committed in the name of democracy and capitalism. Wants to peck out my tongue, so I that I may not speak up in favor of my brothers and sisters currently being murdered by a sadistic, occupying force.

The United States has made the same grievous error as a five-year-old William Yang. It has conflated Communism with unspeakable terrors when, in reality, there is no bloodthirsty creature waiting in the depths of that apocryphal red shadow. The American people have been told a myth that has festered in their minds like an untreated, malignant fungus. They have allowed it to take root and without proper action, it will continue to deepen its hold in the psychological soil.

Uprooting such an entrenched infestation would be painful and maybe even fatal. When that day comes, when we lay down our sharpened spears of paranoia and join together in peace and understanding, the inmyeonjo will—at long last—be free to descend upon this world.

And only then can I tell it how sorry I am.

PART II

December 26, 1959

I happened to glance over at my side, and I saw this strange sight. It looked like a mannequin that had been cut in half and was separated and was lying there. I didn't glance at it too long because I had my little girl with me... The thought of a dead person did not enter my mind.

—*Betty Bersinger (Black Dahlia witness)*

CHAPTER 13

Baker couldn't quite understand why he felt so lousy when he opened his eyes at a quarter to eleven the next morning. The throbbing hangover was nothing new, so what exactly was making him feel this way? The answer to that question rolled over on the bed and started moving her hand down his abdomen, toward his crotch.

"Morning, sleepy head," cooed Debbie. "Was wondering when you'd get up. Why don't we have some fun?"

"No, thank you," Baker said, sitting up a little too quickly.

Trying to ignore the spinning room, he swung his legs over the side of the bed and cradled his face in his hands. How could this have happened? What was he going to tell Shira? And that's when their row from the night before came back to him along with the gut-wrenching vision of Isaac Kremnitzer guiding her out of the shul and into that stupid blue Thunderbird. Savage pleasure overtook remorse as Baker remembered the sex with Debbie.

"You don't gotta worry about keeping me overtime, mister," Debbie said. "Like I told you last night, you've got me for the whole week, if ya like."

"No, thanks," Baker repeated. "That's okay, Debbie. Thanks for... well, thanks. You can go... and keep the money," he said.

"Well, if you're sure," Debbie said, pulling on the curly blond wig that hid her naturally brown locks. "You know where to find me if you change your mind. I'm on the Boulevard most days when I'm not on set."

"On set?" Baker asked.

"Yeah," said Debbie cheerfully, slipping into her frilly red panties and reaching for the matching brassiere. "I do nudie films on the side with my roommate! They're actually quite good."

"Oy vey." Baker put his face back into his hands, hoping she hadn't passed on some sort of venereal disease. The Coasters began to sing inside his aching head: "*Poison Iiivvvyyy...*"

"Don't worry," she said, as if reading his thoughts. "I've got all my shots! By the way, ever thought of a hiring a maid? It's a little messy in here." She was getting just a little too comfortable for Baker's liking. "What are these?" she asked, inspecting a pair of black boxes attached to matching leather straps.

"Phylacteries," Baker said.

"They don't look like any factories I ever saw."

"Not 'factories.' Phy-lac-te-ries," he responded, slowly sounding out the word. "Jewish people put them on every morning for prayer."

The pair of tefillin had been a birthday present from Rabbi Kahn, who had also shown Baker, who had not owned or worn a pair since his bar mitzvah at the age of thirteen, how to properly wrap them around his arm and head.

"I'm not into any of that bondage stuff," Debbie said, shimmying into her tight leather skirt. "But I bet these'd add quite a bit of excitement to the bedroom. Any idea where I can pick some up?"

"Just...go, Debbie," he said into his hands. "Please."

"If you say so." She finished dressing and walked to the door. "A happy New Year to you, mister."

"Uh-huh."

Debbie left, closing the door behind her, and Baker waited for the sounds of her high heels to recede down the hall until fully extricating himself from the mattress. Walking over to the window, he saw another thick shroud of dreary mist swirling at ground level. It swallowed up the display of anti-McCarthy graffiti scrawled onto the brick wall of the abandoned seafood restaurant across the street.

Not looking forward to another day of frosty weather, Baker forced himself into the shower. The jet of warm water made him feel a little less dirty about what he'd done. Not by much, though. As he was wrapping a towel around his waist, the phone began to ring. He thought it might be Shira and all the guilt of infidelity he had tried to repress with alcohol clawed its way to the surface. He didn't much fancy engaging in a string of awkward pleasantries that was sure to devolve into a shouting match of accusations—followed soon thereafter by a mutual agreement over the statement *I never want to see you again*.

It was only Hersh, who sounded nervous.

"Uh... hey, Morris," he said.

This was enough to sever the fury in Baker's chest. The memory of making a complete dumkopf out of himself in front of the entire shul was more sobering than a pair of Tylenol tablets chased with a mug of strong coffee.

"Let's not beat around the bush on this, Hersh," Baker said, wanting to dispel any trace of embarrassment from the conversation. "I fucked up last night."

"I wouldn't say that."

"What'd I just say?"

"Well, maybe you fucked up a little."

Baker laughed, cradling the phone against his shoulder as he reached for a pack of Kools on the kitchen counter. "That's more like it. I'm sorry I yelled at you, Hersh. You're about the only person at the shul who doesn't think I'm nuts. Well, maybe you do now after last night."

"Oh, you're nuts all right," said Hersh, and Baker could tell the man was back to his usual genial self. "You're one roasted almond short of a bar snack, but that's why Mindy and I love you."

"Guessing you realized things are pretty much over with Shira?" Hersh didn't answer, though Baker could hear his husky breathing on the other end. "I'll take that as a 'yes.'"

"What would you like me to say, Morris?"

"That Kremnitzer's a putz!"

"Kremnitzer's a putz," Hersh said in a calming voice one might use while trying to coax a child out of a temper tantrum. "I just think he gave her a ride home is all."

"More like a ride on his c—"

"You really should consider washing your mouth out," Hersh interjected. "She was terribly upset. I'm not saying what Isaac did was right, but he saw an opportunity and he took it. All he had to do was compliment her on her borsht recipe."

"*Vulture*," hissed Baker.

"That's not why I called, Morris," Hersh said. "I'm not entirely sure how to say this..."

"What?" Baker prompted. "Did Kahn ban me from the shul or something?"

"Not Kahn..." Hersh said cautiously.

"You gotta be fucking kidding."

"The shul board held an emergency meeting once the potluck was over and decided to temporarily bar you from entering the building."

"For how long?"

"Indefinitely."

"They can't do that! Rabbi Kahn should be able to—"

"The board strong-armed him into going along with it, Morris," Hersh said. "Shelly Horowitz led the charge. There was nothing he could do. They pay his salary."

Baker felt gutted, hollow. After so many years of being alone—of feeling like he didn't belong anywhere—he was once again tossed to the curb by a group of people he had come to see as a proto-family. Even his fellow Jews didn't want to be associated with him anymore. And Kahn, seemingly the most righteous man Baker had ever met, had failed to do the right thing.

"Thanks for letting me know, Hersh. You can tell them they won't have to worry about me showing up ever again."

"Morris, come on. We both know it's just a lot of meshugas."

"Sinat chinam, Hersh. We're our own worst enemy. No wonder we keep getting the shit kicked out of us every few decades. We choose to destroy ourselves rather than put up a united front."

"You're not wrong, Morris. I'm just saying don't leave the congregation over a good-for-nothing yenta like Shelly Horowitz. And you shouldn't leave Shira, either, come to think of it."

"You heard what she said, Hersh. She's bought into the propaganda about me. Besides, she shtupped Kremnitzer."

"We don't know that."

"I know it," Baker insisted.

"People do terrible things they don't mean when they're angry," Hersh added. "You shouldn't let one fight ruin your entire relationship."

Baker didn't answer, and Hersh, as his friend, knew not to pry further and changed the topic. "I also wanted to call and see if you needed me at the office today."

"Office?" For a moment, Baker had no idea what he was talking about. "Oh! The office. No. I'll be out all day, working on that case I took on yesterday. Enjoy the day off. And Hersh?"

"Yeah?"

"Thanks for sticking by me."

"You kidding? I didn't survive the camps just to turn my back on a fellow Yid. Am Yisrael Chai, right?"

"Amen v'amen. Send my love to Mindy."

"She sends hers right back."

Baker hung up the phone and stood there, damp towel still wrapped around his waist. He looked down to see mangled cigarettes tightly grasped in a clenched fist. "Fuck," he said to no one in particular. "Fuck. Fuck. Fuck."

Despite the copious amount of investigative work lying before him, he felt directionless and unmotivated. Well, one thing was for sure—he would no longer be keeping his word to Kahn about looking for those missing men. If this was how their wives treated him, then they deserved to be ignored by the police, who, for all intents and purposes, were now Hueys.

Mining a vindictive happiness out of letting those women continue to grieve without a shred of solace, Baker began to dress himself. He didn't get far when the phone rang again.

"Yeah?" he said, not caring to downplay the annoyance in his voice.

"Morris?" It was Rabbi Kahn, notably anxious. "Morris . . . I'm—" But the rabbi didn't get to finish. Baker slammed the receiver into its cradle and went back to dressing.

He started removing items from the pockets of his pants worn the day before and discovered a pile of egg-yellow crumbs inside one of them.

Confused, he brought the debris to his nose and realized it was the fortune cookie he'd taken from the Golden Fowl. He dug deeper, finally extracting a small piece of paper. He held it up to his eyes, which struggled to read the minuscule message printed upon it in faded blue ink:

About time I got out of that cookie.

CHAPTER 14

India Street could be found about a mile and a half from the Silver Lake Reservoir, which now served as the site of the local nuclear power plant, operated under McCarthy's Grant Chute Energy Corporation. People got power and the president got rich. On a normal day, the body of water glittered like a freshly excavated diamond mine under the penetrating rays of the California sun. Today, however, the reservoir took on the appearance of a dreary European loch as light droplets of icy rain cascaded upon its steely and foreboding surface. The concave cooling towers of the power station rose out of the gloom, resembling a pair of poisonous toadstools.

While Silver Lake was an hour away from the first stop on his Kissinger investigation, Baker knew he wouldn't be able to get down to work until he made this particular house call.

He knocked on the door of the modest two-story home at 3325, admiring a magnificent wreath of red (and slightly wilted) Christmas roses hung upon it. A Negro housekeeper in a blue apron answered.

"Good afternoon. May I help you?" she asked, wiping her hands on the apron.

"Good afternoon," Baker repeated. "Yes, you may. Is William home?"

"He is, though he's enjoying his lunch right now. Is it urgent?"

"Can you please tell him that Morris Baker is here to see him?"

Her eyes widened a little at the mention of his name, but if it meant something to her, the housekeeper kept it to herself. "One moment, sir," she said, retreating back inside.

Baker took this opportunity of momentary isolation to lean against the doorframe and let loose with another deep-bellied cough. When the housekeeper returned a moment later, she was accompanied by William H. Parker, the big-eared and jowly chief of the LAPD.

"Baker, m'boy!" he exclaimed happily, pushing his thick-framed glasses back up the bridge of his nose. "This is a surprise." He turned to his housekeeper. "Thank you for letting me know, Glenda."

The housekeeper nodded and walked away. "Well, Baker," Parker continued, "don't just stand out there, freezing half to death. Can I interest you in a spot of lunch? All we have are Christmas leftovers, but Helen's honey-baked ham is even better after a night in the icebox."

"Uh, no, thanks," Baker said. "I'm okay on the ham front. Though a cup of coffee would be nice."

"Coming right up! Glenda here makes the best cup of Joe this side of the LA River."

The kitchen was small but cozy, a brick-and-tile affair populated by lime green appliances. Parker's wife, Helen, sat at the white table in the center of the room, cutting thick slices off a brown-pink ham studded with cloves and rings of pineapple. When she saw Baker, she grimaced, dropped the carving knife, and stalked out of the room.

"Don't mind her," Parker said, striding over to the table and picking up a particularly large slice of ham.

Forgoing a single word of explanation, he brought it over to the sink, stuffed it down the drain, and flicked on the garbage disposal. The sounds of sharp metal blades cutting through the pork were deafening and Baker instantly understood: the chief's house was also being bugged by the Hueys. This seemed to be a normal occurrence in the Parker household because Glenda did not react to the din when she brought Baker a cup of coffee on a metal tray with cream and sugar.

Tucking back into his loaded plate of ham, mashed potatoes, string beans, and gravy, Parker called above the disposal racket: "I'm sorry about Helen! She's a little fed up with recent events at the department!"

"Connolly told me all about it yesterday," Baker shouted, stirring a splash of cream into his coffee. "That's actually why I'm here—to say I'm sorry for all the trouble. Sounds like I really messed things up with that little stunt I pulled at Merv's. I assume that's why your wife was so happy to see me?"

"Oh, don't let them put this on your conscience," Parker said, gesticulating with his fork and accidentally sending a lump of potato into Baker's mug. "I blame those upstart Wetbacks from the wild tribes of Mexico. And the Orientals, of course. If any Darkies had been present, you'd have hit the trifecta."

Baker furrowed his brow. "I *asked* them to back me up, sir. They're good people."

"You were one of the best detectives to ever have worked for me and I don't say that lightly," the chief continued, failing to register Baker's consternation. "Those damp rags over at HUAC were always on my ass to get rid of you. They'd have come for me sooner or later; I guarantee you that. Just have to be grateful they didn't drag me out of bed in the middle of the night. I keep telling Helen that, but she won't listen. She thinks we're under house arrest."

"Well, aren't you?" Baker asked. He pointed in the direction of the sink, where the disposal seemed to be ripping through a particularly fatty piece of gristle.

"Ha! That's a good one!" Parker said, cutting up a cluster of green beans and dipping them in the silky puddle of gravy. "I wouldn't describe a few listening devices as 'house arrest.' A minor inconvenience, that's all. No different than being at the office. Helen is none too pleased. Those bastards came in here to search the place—and without a warrant, mind you. Didn't even care that we could see them installing the bugs at the same time. They don't care if we know where the devices are; they just want us afraid in our own home. The balls they've got on them never cease to amaze me. What's the word your people have for it, Baker?"

"Chutzpah, sir," Baker answered.

"That's the one," Parker said, repeating the word as "Hootz-paw." He reached across the table for another thick slice of ham and got up to feed the disposal again. "And none of this 'sir' nonsense," he said when he sat back down. "You're no longer my subordinate, Baker."

"Yes, sir," Baker said, and he started to laugh at the look of indignation on Parker's face. "Only kidding, William. Couldn't resist."

"Where were we?" asked Parker.

"The bugs in your house."

"Ah, yes. Well, like I say, it doesn't bother me much. If those bastards want to listen to Helen and me sharing the pleasures of our marital bed a few nights a week, they're more than welcome to it. What's really getting on my nerves is the fact that I'm barely able to do my job anymore."

He grabbed a dinner roll from a wicker basket, ripped it open, and started to butter the interior with more vigor than was necessary. "I've become the bloody Queen of England. It's my job to smile and wave and play with the fucking dogs while HUAC runs the show, training my men up as lawless thugs. They have zero interest in catching genuine criminals—all they want are Communists, Communists, Communists."

"Why not resign then?" asked Baker. "Tell them to stick their puppet police department where the sun doesn't shine."

"Come now, Baker. Use those deductive skills that kept you on the city's payroll all those years. The president still needs me—whether he wants to admit it or not. He and his toadies were furious about you getting off with all that bomb business. I didn't hear the end of it for a year after the fact. As you well know, they blamed me for that little militia at the diner. HUAC seemed to think I was giving you a long leash that allowed you to forge criminal connections right under my nose."

"That's ridiculous!" sputtered Baker, no longer interested in his coffee. His sudden outburst caused another coughing fit. When Parker made to pat him on the back, Baker held up a hand that said, *I'm fine.*

"Of course it's ridiculous! It's hogwash, rubbish, a load of hooey, complete and utter horse shit. Whatever phrase in the thesaurus catches your fancy. You didn't have any other choice, so you turned to the city's most disreputable elements for help. Using them to your advantage. Smart thinking, Baker."

"That's not exactly—"

"I don't blame you for taking matters into your own hands once the Hueys came to arrest you on some trumped-up charge. I'd have done the same thing, had I been in your shoes. Helen knows it, too. You know how women are—they have to be right about everything until they're not."

"She has every right to be angry with me. I didn't want to involve you with any of this."

"That's why I'm grateful! You could have come to me at any time when HUAC was on your tail for that bomb malarky, but you didn't. You decided to keep me out of it, even though you know I'd have been on your side in an instant. You kept Helen and me safe—not only from HUAC, but from those Symphony Krauts as well."

Baker's head snapped up. He looked at his former boss in amazement. "You listen to . . . ?"

"On occasion," Parker said, now grinning paternally. "Any port in a storm, right? I've noticed he's been off the air for a while, though. Hope he's doing all right." Baker opened his mouth to answer, but Parker forestalled him with a flat palm. "The less I know, the better."

Baker nodded, and this time, he obliged to stuff some pork down the sink drain.

"So," he began, returning to the table, "what were you saying about not being able to resign?"

"Well, it's like I say. McCarthy needs me. Plain and simple. If you'll allow me to toot my own horn for a moment, I've built up quite a reputation in this town. People respect me, which means they also listen to me."

"I assume there's been some pushback about the American Schutzstaffel plan?"

"Ha!" Parker laughed, spraying more potato in Baker's direction. "Haven't heard it called that yet! As good a description as any, I suppose. But yes, you are correct. Not everyone wants to be a HUAC inspector, believe it or not. Oh, don't get me wrong, some have taken to it like ducks to water. Dashiell Hanscom, for instance, has a real knack for the job."

"Why am I not surprised?" Baker asked sarcastically. "Does his nose still look like an overripened tomato?"

"Try a pomegranate," answered Parker. "Anyway, not everyone is so willing to join the McCarthy cheer squad. That's where I come in. I'm meant to lead by example—to keep the flock under control, as it were."

"And if you don't?" Baker queried. The police chief raised his eyebrows in a *Surely you don't really need to ask, do you?* kind of way. "Sorry, dumb question."

"I am—as the timeworn expression goes—between a rock and a

hard place," Parker continued. "Still, it's better than being sent up to Manzanar."

Baker couldn't help but feel a little disheartened at what he was hearing. To hear Rabbi Kahn (a Jew who would get the snot beaten out of him for looking at a Huey the wrong way) discuss his feelings of helplessness was one thing. But Parker? The police chief was a man of influence, who commanded the respect and loyalty of his underlings. If he told his men to jump, they'd simply respond with: "How high?"

Baker leaned forward, said, "You fought in the war, William. That's exactly how the Germans saw things. Follow orders, keep your head down. So long as it's not me, who cares?"

Parker put down his fork and knife. Baker could not recall a time when the man had looked so abashed.

"You think that hasn't occurred to me? If it were just me, I'd go up to that Lonergan prick today and tell him to go take a long walk off the Santa Monica Pier. But Helen and Glenda depend on me. And so does everyone at the department. My men have wives and children. Many of them are innocent bystanders in this, and if I stepped out of line, they'd be forced to pay the price, too."

"All it takes is for good men like you to do nothing," Baker said, anger bubbling up to the surface. "You tell yourself you're doing the best you can, make yourself helpless, because it's so much easier than actual resis—"

"I'm racking my brain, looking for a way out, goddamnit!" Parker suddenly thundered over the roar of the disposal, which was starting to quiet down again. "You think it's easy going along with their way of thinking? It makes me sick to my stomach. But I'm fast running out of hope, Morris. As someone who saw combat in Normandy, I can say with absolute certainty that no one is coming to storm the beaches. No one is coming to rescue us."

The disposal had chewed through its latest piece of pork, and a frosty silence hung in the air.

"I used to look up to you, Parker, did you know that? I really thought you were different."

"Excuse me?"

"You talk about standing up to the Hueys, yet you discuss the downtrodden peoples of this city like they're nothing more than dogshit on the sole of your shoe."

"Baker, what are you on about?"

"The 'Wetbacks.' The 'Orientals.' The 'Darkies.' That's what I'm on about. Those 'disreputable elements'—as you call them—were the only human beings I could rely on to come to my aid when our government wanted to flay me alive for the crime of being me."

Glenda, who was at the sink drying a salad bowl, stopped dead.

"Now, Baker—"

"You don't give a damn about them or their well-being. The president doesn't just need you to help keep your officers in line. McCarthy also relies on you to enforce the old ways of thinking that were around long before he came along. If they don't look like us, fuck 'em, right? It was never about preventing a citywide revolution for McCarthy's sake—it was always about a mutual appreciation for discrimination."

"I...well...I...you're not looking at the whole picture, m'boy. Look no further than Yang, blowing himself up like that. These people aren't deserving of—"

"Of what? Compassion? Kindness? Respect? It's that same line of thinking that got us into this mess, William! I came here today, hoping you'd prove me wrong, but you didn't. For years, I turned a blind eye to all of it because you showed me a little bit of decency. I felt a sense of loyalty to you, but now my eyes are open. I can't help but wonder...would you have been as kind had my skin been of a different color? Would you have hired me if my eyes were shaped differently or my last name was *Lopez*? Taking pity on a single Jew doesn't give you the right to—"

"You need to leave."

Both men turned around. Parker's wife had reentered the kitchen, her face full of a detached fury Baker had seen many times during the war. It was the kind of look that made a person feel subhuman; the look one might give a many-legged pest that has just crawled out through a hole in the wall.

"You need to leave," Helen repeated when Baker did not respond. "Now!"

"Helen..." Parker said warningly.

"No, William," Baker said, putting his hands up in mock defeat.

"It's okay. I was just on my way out." He took a final sip of coffee and made to stand when he remembered something.

"Say," he said, plopping back into his chair and drawing a groan from Helen. Baker leaned in close, lowering his voice now that there was no ham left to drown out their conversation. "Would you possibly have any updates on a missing person by the name of Henry Kissinger?"

"Nixon's man?" Parker asked, raising his eyebrows. He seemed relieved at the abrupt change in conversation. "How do you—?"

"Doesn't matter how I know," Baker replied. "The less you know, the better. Have there been any breaks in the case?"

"Not that I've heard," Parker said. "But that doesn't surprise me. I'm not kept in the loop anymore. All I know is he was in town for the Kishi tour. He stopped by the station once or twice with the Japanese embassy officials to look over parade routes and security measures. Nothing out of the ordinary, especially after Yang."

"I thought he was just a policymaker," said Baker. "What was he doing weighing in on parade routes for the Japanese prime minister?"

"Didn't seem like a small cog in the machine," Parker replied.

"How so?"

"Well, the Hueys had no trouble shutting me up when I asked to make a suggestion, but they didn't dare make a peep when this Kissinger was talking. Looked a little scared of him by the size of it."

"Anything else about him stand out to you?" Baker continued.

Parker thought for a moment. At last, he whispered back, "Had a bit of a Kraut accent, if I recall correctly. Was kind and courteous. Asked a few questions here and there, but otherwise, I wouldn't be able to pick the guy out of a lineup, to tell the truth."

"That it?" Baker pressed his former boss.

"Now that you mention it, I did see him charming a few of the secretaries during his visits. Struck me as a bit of a Casanova. I only remember because I had to shoo him away from the ladies and get them back to their typing. But there's nothing wrong with chasing a skirt or two, is there?"

"I suppose not. Thanks for the coffee."

CHAPTER 15

Constructed in the late 1920s, Chateau Marmont was famous not only for its lavish accommodations, but also for its former reputation as a haven for unruly studio icons in preregulated Hollywood. Once McCarthy took office and brought nearly all of the competing studios under the umbrella of United American Pictures, misbehavior among the celebrity crowd was strictly forbidden.

Any actor or actress found guilty of airing their dirty laundry at the hotel—be it an extramarital or a homosexual affair, a nasty drug habit, or a predilection for underage sexual partners—was immediately terminated without a second thought. This was specified in every performer's contract, leading some to refer to the proviso as the "Chateau Clause."

Of course, there were ways of getting around the ban. Instead of checking into a prestigious establishment, UAP stars simply opted to retreat into the privacy of their gated communities, getting up to all sorts of debaucherous activities within their Beverly Hills and Bel-Air mansions.

Out of sight, out of mind.

It was nearing three o'clock in the afternoon when Baker pulled onto Sunset Boulevard and glimpsed the Chateau—Henry Kissinger's last-known location. Boxed off from the rest of the street by a lush collection of trees and bushes, the hotel, with its gabled roof and triangular turret, normally resembled an open book standing up on its side. But like every other notable Los Angeles landmark in this weather, it was almost completely shrouded by mist and fog, giving off the creepy impression of a crumbling Transylvanian castle in an old vampire movie.

Aliens and UFOs were all the rage on the big screen these days, but if a person really wanted to take in a banned film that had been produced in the days before UAP's endless parade of anti-Communist slop, all they had to do was attend one of the seedier theaters in town. There, they could see everything from classics like *Dracula* to more recent offerings like *12 Horny Dames*.

Baker was a little ashamed to admit he'd seen the latter—a pornographic film about a group of female jurists whose disagreements over a nuanced murder case devolves into an orgy—but the direction, cinematography, and even the acting had been quite exemplary. In fact, most of the naughty pictures he'd taken in over the last few years were surprisingly better than almost anything the government had been able to come out with.

He parked the Continental on Haverhurst Drive and walked the remaining half mile, his head turned down against the bitter wind. While his hangover was gone, he still felt lousy.

Visiting Parker was meant to leave him with a clear conscience, but it had done nothing to alleviate the guilt—percolating like freshly brewed coffee inside his skull—over all the trouble he'd caused to friends like Connolly, Hollis, and Valentina by saving his own skin. Or perhaps it had something to do with his foolish idolization of a man whose claim of disliking the Hueys extended only as far as their treatment of upstanding white folks. The chief and his wife deserved all that was coming their way, but the look of pure loathing on Helen's face kept bubbling to the surface of his mind's eye. Why should it bother him so?

No matter where Baker went, an imperceptible cloud of negative emotions hung over him. No matter how much he tried to atone for the sins of the past, it never seemed to be enough, and new offenses were being piled on every day.

His ledger was still in the red and the loan sharks were out for blood. Every move, no matter how calculated, put him further into debt.

It was like feeding an abandoned dog. Once you showed it even the slightest bit of affection, the damn thing never left you alone. Except the dog currently nipping at Baker's heels was rabid and mean and rotting from the inside out. An aggressive beast whose stomach-turning appearance warned others to remain at a safe distance.

Knowing that it would help numb the mental anguish, if only for a little while, Baker popped one of his last phenobarbital tablets under his tongue, allowing it to dissolve into an unpleasant, chalky powder.

Before long, he had reached the hotel, cheeks raw with cold, hands deep in their respective trench coat pockets. It was quite the relief to duck into the heated lobby.

The place was filled with narrow couches and chairs upholstered in paisley and maroon fabrics. Two-person tables topped with fake flower arrangements lined the walls closest to the windows, and several spade-shaped archways led off into smaller sitting areas that put Baker in mind of a hookah den in the back alley of a sweltering Arab souk.

A lazy and comforting air hung about the lobby, which was virtually empty, save for a pair of old geezers playing a game of chess across an oval-shaped table closest to the front door. The lack of people was not surprising in the slightest. Everyone was still enjoying the Christmas vacation. People either left town or, if they were visiting from somewhere else, stayed with family.

One of the chess-playing seniors, a fragile-looking specimen, looked up at Baker, blinking through spectacles that magnified his eyes to four times their size.

"Good day," rasped the man in a heavy British accent, moving one of his rooks and overtaking his opponent's final bishop.

"Uh, yeah," Baker mumbled, rubbing his hands together. "Good day."

"Do you *mind*?" snapped the first man's companion, an American, his gnarled fingers dangling above a knight. "I'm trying to concentrate here. I've got five bucks riding on this match."

Noticing his companion's distraction, the man in the magnifying glasses strategically switched a few pieces around the board, fast as a cricket evading a hungry toad.

The incensed player looked back from his reprimand of Baker and moved his knight three spaces. "Check," he said, sitting back and smugly crossing his arms.

The British player took one look at the board, scratched his head of wispy white hair, feigning confusion, and then moved his queen a number of spaces across the board toward the other fellow's king. "Checkmate," he said. "How many wins is that for me, Cyrus? Seven? Eight?"

"Ahhh, phooey! I've had enough of this, Archie. I'm going to take a nap!"

Archie gave Baker a tiny wink.

Cyrus swore under his breath and dug inside his pocket for a five-spot, threw it down, and stalked off. Archie, it seemed, was no dope. He was as good a hustler as Baker had ever seen, and he'd come across a lot of them during his tenure as a cop. As a private investigator, he sometimes called upon their sleazy demeanors to slip in and out of places, undetected.

Something that worked equally well, if not better, was acting like you belonged in a place when you clearly didn't. No need to charm the concierge or bribe the bellhops. All you had to do was walk like you owned the place and no one thought twice about it, especially if you adopted the haughty strut of a HUAC inspector that said: *Look at me funny, and I'll murder your entire bloodline.*

Except that strategy might not work in this case, for Baker had just spotted a pair of surly Japanese men sitting at a foldout table to the right of the concierge desk. Dressed in immaculate double-breasted pinstripe suits, their legs severely crossed, the two men did not take their eyes off him. A guy didn't have to be a world-class detective to figure who they were: security for the Japanese delegation of Kishi's peace tour.

Thinking quickly, he plopped into the chair vacated by the irate Cyrus and started resetting the chess board. Archie confusedly blinked at him, eyes bug-like through those ridiculous spectacles.

"How would you like to go from ripping off Cyrus to making some real money?" Baker whispered, pulling out his cigarettes and patting around for a lighter.

"The basket behind you," Archie said, raising an arthritic digit toward a wicker basket full of matchbooks.

Baker plucked one out, lit his cigarette. "So are you interested?"

"Well, that depends," Archie responded, placing Cyrus's captured pieces back onto their respective squares. "What would I need to do? I'm no poof, sonny."

"It's not like that," said Baker. "I just need to get up to the sixth floor. Are you staying here?"

"Course I am. Can't stay with my son, can I? That wife of his will only have me over for meals, she will. I'm a complete nonentity with my grandchildren. Not entirely sure why I agreed to fly across the pond in the first place! She's a nurse, you see. Treated my son during the war and they fell in love, they did. She brought him back to this piss pot and I've hardly seen my Kevin since."

"Look," Baker continued, not the slightest bit interested in Archie's familial woes. "I'll pay you fifty dollars if you get me past those charming Japanese bodyguards over there," Baker said. "What do you say?"

"I say it beats an afternoon with my bloody daughter-in-law."

"So you're in?"

"Haven't I just said I am?"

"Perfect. Shall we begin?"

"Lead the way, sonny."

Baker got up, walked over to Archie's chair, and helped the wizened man to his feet. "Well, Dad!" he announced. "Are you ready for your pre-supper nap?"

"Humbug," growled Archie, allowing Baker to grip his arm. "I don't need a ruddy nap, son! I feel quite awake, thanks." But as he said this, the old codger's eyes began to droop behind their lenses.

"Up you get," said Baker, tightening his grip on Archie—who felt surprisingly muscular for his advanced age—and ushering him past the concierge and Japanese guards. One of them stood up and Baker swore internally.

"Excuse me," he said, pointing at Baker. "I have not seen you in here before. I'll need to see some identification."

"And who the ruddy hell are you?" asked an incensed Archie.

"I," said the man, "am Akihiro Takagi of Japan's National Public Safety Commission."

"Guessing you're the reason why it was so hard to get a reservation, then," said Archie, causing Takagi to scowl. "Now, if you don't mind..."

"I must insist on identification from your *son*, sir," Takagi reiterated.

Archie eyed the guard with contempt. "Are you taking the piss?" he asked. "My son here only just arrived in town this morning. He's been across on the country on business and was forced to miss Christmas with his old man. Now, he's too polite to say it, but my colon hasn't been the same since around the time the Americans dropped the big ones on you Japs."

"There's no need for that kind of—" sputtered Takagi, but he was cut off by Archie, who really seemed to be enjoying this little charade now.

"I haven't had a regular shite in over a decade, boy-o. So, unless you want to clean up an old man's mess on this very spot, I suggest you let us pass."

Takagi looked equal parts furious and embarrassed. "Very well," he said at last, stepping aside to let them continue on to the bank of elevators. "But I'll still need to check your identification on the way out," he added to Baker.

Baker nodded his understanding and for good measure mouthed the words *So sorry about him* to Takagi, who looked mollified for the time being.

Once they were out of earshot of the Japanese watchmen, Archie broke free of Baker's grip and gave a theatrical bow.

"I do believe that is the most fun I have had in quite some time. You can hold your applause, sonny. That fifty quid will suffice. If ever you find yourself in need of my services, dear boy, I will be here until the third of January. I hope you will not hesitate in calling on Archibald Christopher Hicks."

"I'll keep that in mind," said Baker as he paid Archie his money. The old Limey hobbled away, jabbing a gnarled finger onto the elevator button while whistling "God Save the Queen."

CHAPTER 16

Never much one for the claustrophobia of elevators (the hours spent inside a packed cattle car had put him off the prospect of tight spaces for life), Baker proceeded up the stairs, taking them two at a time, lest Takagi decided to change his mind about letting him pass without an ID check. He was out of breath and coughing terribly by the time he reached the sixth floor.

He sank onto the final step, sitting there for nearly ten minutes before his breathing returned to normal. Able to stand again, he vacated the stairwell into a hallway of Herati-patterned carpet, black wooden doors, and ornate golden ceiling fixtures, whose pallid illumination imbued the space with a sickly hue. It didn't take very long to find room 6C in the silent corridor and he knocked, lightly rapping his knuckles upon the black wood in "shave and a haircut" fashion.

There was no answer, so he did it again, this time a little louder. When no one came calling, Baker reached into his pocket to retrieve a leather pouch of lock-picking tools given to him by a petty thief and bail jumper named Joel Cairo near the start of Baker's career as a private investigator.

He had tracked the scared and sniveling little man to a flea-ridden motel on the outskirts of Encino, and in exchange for another day's head start, Cairo provided his pursuer with the lock-breaking tools and a crash course on how to use them. Joel probably would have gotten that head start, too, had he not tried to nick Baker's wallet in the middle of the lesson.

Since then, Baker had practiced on his own office and apartment doors, filing down his personal time with each attempt.

Tongue sticking between his teeth, he knelt down and set to work, carefully inserting two of the small metal rods into the narrow keyhole and jiggling them back and forth until the tumbler clicked open. Glancing both ways again, he turned the knob and slipped inside Kissinger's hotel room unnoticed, locking it behind him. It was deathly quiet, discounting an incessant clicking noise Baker ascribed to the hotel's antiquated heating system.

The accommodations looked expensive. A queen-size bed draped in smooth Egyptian cotton took up a good portion of the room. Next to it sat a cherrywood nightstand topped with a lamp, its marble base carved into the shape of a regal elephant. A taller lamp with less impressive nickel plating stood closest to the window beside a personal walnut writing desk embellished with complimentary Chateau Marmont stationery.

The place looked immaculate, completely unoccupied, and Baker guessed it had been cleaned since Kissinger's early checkout. There was probably no need to check for fingerprints, but he did it anyway, exercising the cover-all-your-bases philosophy instilled in him by the LAPD.

He reached into a coat pocket and pulled out a pair of sheepskin gloves he probably should have worn during his half-mile walk to the hotel and proceeded to dust all the flat surfaces. No prints.

"All right, Henry, old chap," Baker muttered, mimicking Archie's thick British inflection. "Your wife is paying me good money to find out where you are. Give me something here."

He began his thorough search in the front closet and worked his way through the room, including the lavish bathroom, which contained a capacious porcelain bathtub standing on clawed brass feet. The inspection turned up a disappointing assortment of everyday items: wire hangers in the closet, two stray tablets of aspirin in the medicine cabinet, a pamphlet called *How to Recognize a Communist in Ten Easy Steps* in the nightstand, and a lethally sharp letter opener in the drawer of the writing desk.

Baker also made sure to lift up the mattress and pull out the nightstand drawers, probing all the usual hiding spots. Either the room had already been searched—by whom, he could not begin to guess—or Kissinger had simply left with all his possessions, allowing the maids to tidy up the place as usual. The latter outcome seemed more likely, given Parker's recollection of Kissinger giving off the aura of a lothario. If the man had run off with another woman, there would be nothing to leave behind.

Planning to call Ann with an update, he was halfway to the door when that soft clicking reasserted itself. Sure enough, the noise could be traced to the aeration vent. Now that his ear was flush with the grate, Baker reckoned this was not the sound of an old heating system. It sounded more like an old baseball card stuck between the spokes of a bicycle. Cupping his hands around his eyes for a better look, he peered through the tight horizontal slots and could just make out a thick paper object no longer than four inches across. It was lodged in such a way that it could be agitated by the constant flow of air without falling into the room or being sucked farther into the vent.

"*Damnit!*" He had not brought along a screwdriver, and the lock-picking rods were not nearly strong enough to pry the vent's screws loose. That's when he remembered the letter opener. Baker procured it from the desk drawer and gingerly worked it under several layers of paint entombing the screws in their respective holes.

After five minutes of chipping away, he got a good grip and pried the vent slightly ajar. The opening was just big enough for Baker to run three fingers along the inside of the grate toward the *click-click-clicking* item. Thinking it to be a playing card that had somehow ended up inside the vent, he tugged it out.

Not an ace, jack, king, or queen—but a lacquered and cream-colored business card for Lamotte Exports. Founded and run by charismatic millionaire Orson Lamotte, it was the biggest import-export business in California. In addition to the man's looming presence at the Port of Los Angeles—massive freighters bearing the Lamotte Exports name were always seen coming and going—Lamotte also owned nearly every orange grove in this part of the state.

The card is probably a holdover from some business conference, Baker guessed, not entirely convinced of this initial hypothesis. He turned it over to reveal a string of unknown characters—Chinese? Japanese?—that had clearly not been printed on the original paper. Baker pocketed the card and flattened the vent cover back into place.

He returned the letter opener to the desk drawer, taking extra care to make sure it fell perfectly within the original dust outline.

With everything back in its rightful place, Baker crept out of the room and straight into a pretty Asian maid with a cart of freshly laundered towels. Even with the woman's shockingly black hair done up in a tight bun, Baker could still make out a few streaks of premature silver locks running across the length of her scalp.

"Sorry," he grumbled.

"Oh!" exclaimed the maid, whose English didn't seem to be too good. She slapped a hand to her mouth and giggled. "So sorry. So sorry. Did not know someone here. Come back later."

"Not a problem," said Baker. "Have a nice day."

He walked back down the hall without a true destination in mind. At last, he rounded a corner and located a fire exit that would take him down to an emergency door, far away from the suspicions of Akihiro Takagi.

CHAPTER 17

The drive to his office on Wilshire took only around fifteen minutes. Night was falling fast.

Thinking longingly of the schnapps bottle waiting inside his office, Baker planned on renewing his drunkard's subscription before giving Ann Kissinger a call. He'd also put in a call to Hollis. Perhaps the restauranteur would be able to translate the letters found on the back of the business card.

He pulled into the parking lot when he noticed a familiar 1957 Eldorado stationed near the entrance. The car's equally familiar owner, Brogan Connolly, leaned against the hood, smoking a cigarette and looking concerned. When he saw Baker, he flicked away the smoke and tapped on the Continental's passenger window. Baker leaned over and rolled it down, smiling.

"To what do I owe the pleasure of your ugly Irish mug?"

To his great surprise, Connolly did not smile back. He didn't even crack an anti-Semitic retort. He simply took his hat off and held it against his chest.

"Morris," he said in a deeply somber tone Baker had never heard the man use before. "I need you to come with me right now."

"What is it?" Baker asked. "Is it Maeve? The kids? Are they okay?"

"They're all fine, Morris. It's just that... well, something has happened, and you need to come with me now. We can take my car."

Without another word, Baker rolled the window back up and parked in his usual spot. What could reduce Brogan Abraham Connolly—one of the toughest bastards Baker knew—to a melancholic shell of his former self? Nothing good, that was for damn certain.

"Not under arrest, am I?" he asked after settling into the Eldorado's passenger seat.

"No," replied Connolly, turning the key in its ignition. "You're not in trouble, Morris."

"So what's this all about, then, huh?"

His ex-partner remained silent. He made a three-point turn and left the parking lot.

Connolly drove in silence for close to an hour, chain-smoking Pall Malls and not offering a single one to Baker—not that he wanted one. He was beginning to feel genuinely frightened and was about to ask where they were headed when he noticed a sign for Redondo Junction, an industrial area where a last-minute decision from locomotive engineer Frank Parrish had saved a lot of lives from a potential train wreck three years earlier.

Few ventured out here, particularly in this weather. Had Connolly been forced to deliver his old Jewish partner out into the middle of nowhere by his new Huey masters? Were they planning a quiet execution for Morris Baker, who'd stuck his toe over the line just one too many times?

"Here we are," Connolly said, his voice hoarse from disuse.

Baker looked out the window to see that they had arrived on the thick concrete bridge suspended over the drained LA River.

Several squad cars, lights flashing, were already there. More relieved than he cared to admit, Baker didn't see a single Cadillac V-16, the Hueys' vehicle of choice.

Connolly got out. Baker followed, nearly slipping on the wet concrete. Uniformed officers milled about, chatting or else setting up bright crime scene spotlights. They illuminated the collection of power lines that ran the length of the empty, manmade river—transforming the metal towers into misshapen gargoyles.

"Brogan," he began—you knew shit was serious when he started to use Connolly's first name—"can you please tell me what the hell this is all about?"

Connolly stood near the railing, looking off into the distance as he lit another cigarette. "We need you to identify the body."

"The *what*?" All the spit in Baker's mouth dried up. He knew what Connolly had said, but his brain was taking its sweet time catching up. What he needed at this very moment was a few healthy glugs of schnapps.

"The body," Connolly repeated somberly.

"Who is it, Brogan?"

"Come with me."

"Who *is* it, goddamnit?" Baker shouted at Connolly's retreating form. He started to run and almost slipped again. "*Fuck,*" he hissed, drawing dirty looks from the other cops on the scene. But he did not care as he drew level with Connolly, who had left the bridge and was cautiously making his way down the smooth embankment. The river basin was empty most of the time, but a few scant inches of water had collected from all the rain and mist.

More crime scene lights were set up here, their beams pointed at a plain white tarp, the sight of which raised the hairs on the back of Baker's neck. Crouching over the obscured corpse was Thomas Noguchi, the head medical examiner for Los Angeles County, who had inherited the macabre position from the late Charles Fitzpatrick Ward.

Noguchi turned around and his face fell. The medical examiner stood up, began approaching Baker and Connolly.

"Morris," he said, trying to place a gloved hand on Baker's shoulder. "Thank you for coming. I am very sorry. We need you to..."

Baker wasn't listening. He marched straight past Noguchi, bent down, and yanked the tarp to one side—immediately wishing he hadn't.

"No," was all he managed to say as bile rose in his throat. Turning away, he retched, but mastered the biological instinct to be sick. All was numb.

It was Elizabeth Short. Naked, dead, and alabaster white. Not just dead. Cleanly bifurcated at the waist, with viscera trailing out the lower half like an improperly kept garden hose. Leaning in closer, Baker noted the slashed labia and skinned right breast. Liz's face was nearly unrecognizable with deep slashes from ear to ear that left her with a final ghastly smile.

It was a miracle he could identify her at all. Thankfully, her eyes were closed. Whether this was the case upon her death or if Noguchi had had the good sense to close the lids prior to their arrival, Baker did not know.

The mutilation was not what bothered him—it was the sight of his ex-girlfriend, a woman Baker had admittedly cared for very much, reduced to such a sickening display. Tears started to leak out of his eyes of their own accord, and though he was no longer a homicide detective, some instinct of the old job possessed him to step back, so his own DNA would not soil the evidence. Noguchi walked over and tenderly drew the tarp back over Liz's body.

"I am truly sorry," Connolly said. "If there was any other way… You were the only person I know who would be able to identify her outside of myself."

"How—" Baker's voice cracked a little. He tried again. "How did you find her?"

"Couple of teenage drag racers. Called it in a few hours ago."

"How"—he held back a painful sob—"how did you know it was Liz?"

"A purse with her driver's license was found a half mile from here. I went by your apartment, but you weren't there. I know you don't really enjoy leisure time, so I went by your office, and sure enough, you turned up. Where were you, by the way?"

The question was asked innocently enough, but Baker knew better than to treat it as such. Cheeks wet with rain and grief, he looked Connolly full in the face. "You think I had something to do with this? I haven't seen or spoken to Liz since we broke up almost two years ago."

"Of course I don't think that, Morris," said Brogan, who sounded truly affronted. "I know how much Liz meant to you. But it's still my job to follow up every lead. You of all people know that."

"You want my whole day's itinerary? Fine." He knew Connolly was right, but he needed to direct this typhoon of emotion somewhere. Anywhere. "Let's start at the very beginning. I woke up hungover and next to a prostitute."

"What about Shira…?"

"May I continue?"

"Be my guest."

"I got up, showered, got a call from a friend, Hershel Greenbaum. I can give you his number and address if you like. He'll corroborate that part of my alibi. Then I went to see Parker. Dug into him pretty good, but he'll back me up, too, if necessary. After that, I went to Chateau Marmont for the case I took on yesterday. An old bloke staying there by the name of Archie saw me. Hell, he helped me out of a pinch. He's staying there until January third in case you'd like to question him as well."

Connolly was feverishly marking all of this down in a small notebook. "And you can roughly account for the times and durations for each location?"

"Sure."

"Excellent. Then you have absolutely nothing to worry about, Morris. The Hueys may want to kick up a fuss about how you dated her for a decade, but I won't let them. And that's only if they hear about it. I'll do my best to try and keep it under wraps for the time being, but some of my men have big mouths. Think you're up to giving a formal statement down at the station?"

"Whatever you need," said Baker, not really listening. He looked out into the distance where the crime scene spotlights could not reach.

Standing on the slick aqueduct in this blackness gave one the horrible feeling of being inside the digestive tract of some great beast. Baker recalled the biblical story of Jonah, a man swallowed whole by a massive sea creature known as the Leviathan.

Only when Jonah agreed to heed the word of God and warn an iniquitous town to cease its wicked ways did the monster spit him back onto dry land. Baker felt a lot like Jonah, cramped and scared inside the literal belly of the beast. Except this Leviathan would not cough him up, despite Baker's willing commitment to call the sinners out on their bullshit. He was forever trapped in here with only a few soggy matches left to guide the way.

Connolly made to shepherd him back to the car, but Baker resisted.

"I'd like to see her one more time."

"Morris, come on. What good will come from—?"

"Brogan, please."

"All right. Thomas, let him see."

Noguchi pulled the tarp away from Liz's severed remains. The medical examiner then took a step back, allowing Baker to get close again. He knew he couldn't hold her hand, but he muttered a swift Kaddish for her soul, even though Elizabeth Short was not Jewish.

Yitgadal v'yitkadash sh'mei raba...

He then reached up, untucked his shirt, and ripped an inch of fabric, a traditional act of Jewish mourning known as kevurah. When he was done, he started to replace the sheet over Liz's segmented form but stopped himself. He'd only just noticed Liz's fingernails.

Unable to help himself, he turned to Noguchi. "There's caked dirt under the nails, but this entire area is pretty much made up of concrete. Any idea why?"

"I noticed that, too," answered the medical examiner. "I'll send some samples off to the lab as soon as I'm finished with the autopsy tonight. Didn't want to move her until we got a positive ID."

Baker nodded his understanding. "Sorry, Thomas." He took one last look down at Liz and added, "The old ways die hard." With that, he allowed Connolly to lead him up the embankment, across the bridge, and back to the car.

"Any idea who did it?" Baker asked, thirty minutes into the ride back. He didn't really feel like talking, but could tell the full gravity of Liz's murder would crash down upon him like a tsunami of grief if he didn't focus on the procedural elements.

"No," Connolly replied brusquely. "But I promise you, Morris—I'm going to get to the bottom of this. You have my word on that." Another five minutes of silence. "Do you...have any theories...?" Connolly asked apprehensively.

"Theories on what? Who did it?"

"Yeah. Was there a jealous boyfriend or something? Known enemies?"

"Couldn't tell you," said Baker, thinking that aside from selling him out to the Hueys that one time, she'd been harmless and sweet. Liz was a doll, not really the "enemies" type. Unless she was trying to ruin your life, but that was only once every ten years or so. "I don't think anyone could have hated her. And yes, I'm aware that her ratting me out to HUAC is a very good motive for homicide. But if that were true, why would I wait almost two years to do it?"

"It would take the suspicion off of yourself, I suppose," said Connolly, now sounding more like his old self. "You break up with Liz, bide your time until she stops talking about you to her friends and family. The dust settles a bit, you become a faded memory, and then..."

He looked over at Baker's reproving expression and chuckled a bit.

"Her mother. Phoebe," Baker said. "Does she know yet?"

"No, not yet. Where does she live?"

"Boston, unless anything's changed. It's been a while."

"It's late back East. We'll let her have one more peaceful night before dumping this shit pile on her doorstep. I'll personally make the call myself first thing tomorrow morning."

Baker lit a Kool with trembling fingers. "I'll write down her number once you drop me off. Just do me one favor, Brogan. When you do speak with Phoebe, try not to go into too much detail."

"Wouldn't dream of it."

CHAPTER 18

There was a small brown package waiting for Baker against the apartment door when he returned home. He gingerly picked up the delivery and read the message written directly onto the butcher paper:

Hoping this brings some light into your life —RJK

Baker tore off the wrapping of a small copper menorah and a pack of candles. Caught up in all the day's excitement, he'd completely forgotten: It was now the second night of Hanukkah. Smiling at Kahn's present and feeling a twinge of guilt at hanging up on the rabbi earlier, Baker placed the menorah on the kitchen counter and stuck two candles into the brackets on the far-right side.

He lit the shamash and recited the blessings as he moved it across the two wicks—right to left, starting with the new candle first.

Baruch ata Adonai Eloheinu, melech ha'olam, asher kid'shanu b'mitzvotav v'tzivanu l'hadlik ner shel Hanukkah.

Baruch atah Adonai Eloheinu Melech ha'olam, she'asah nisim la'avoteinu ba'yamim ha'heim ba-z'man ha'zeh.

He affixed the shamash to the highest bracket and stood back. The menorah candles flickered for only a moment—creating the shadow of a great, nine-headed hydra—before settling down into a regular burn.

Sleep did not come easily that night. It took a bottle and a half of schnapps and the last two tablets of phenobarbital just to round out the razor-sharp agony slashing its way through his insides. He lay awake for a long time, blankly staring up at the ceiling as a light rain pattered against the windowpane and the candles melted down into waxy puddles. He wasn't sure why he didn't simply keep drinking until the world slipped away for good, but deep down he knew the answer. He was still a coward, clinging for dear life to the fraying ropes of corporeal existence.

When unconsciousness did arrive, it did not bring comfort or the numb embrace of pure nothingness.

Sophia, the gassed children, and von Braun came for him—now joined by Elizabeth Short. Just the upper half. She clawed her way along the floor with dirt-caked fingernails. The remaining portion of her spinal column whipped back and forth, leaving a trail of blood in its wake like some sort of ghoulish slug.

"History comes for us all," she hissed, trying to snatch at one of Baker's ankles. Her green eyes were fully open now, and the morbid gash on her face gave her the look of a poorly sewn rag doll. "Oh yes. Time marches on, and sooner or later, we are all consumed by it."

He woke up, covered in sweat and hacking worse than ever, an invisible weight pressing down on his lungs. He sat up in an effort to fill them with precious oxygen, remaining on the edge of the bed for what felt like hours, steadily drawing in breaths until the sun rose behind another sheet of gray clouds.

When he got up to use the bathroom around seven thirty, he grabbed a tissue from atop the toilet tank and coughed into it. Expecting to see a glob of oozing green mucus that signified a slightly ill—but otherwise healthy—respiratory system, he pulled it away from his mouth and nearly pissed right there on the floor. The tissue was covered in blood.

The following article was originally published in an April 1957 issue of the *Jewish Daily Forward* (a paper that has technically been banned in the United States of America for close to five years owing to its socialist ties). It has since been translated from its original Yiddish into English.

First-Time Film Director Elevates "Smut" into Rarified Air of Memorable Cinema

To call Sidney Lumet a visionary filmmaker may be a little presumptuous. After all, the 33-year-old director only has one feature under his belt as of this writing. But to say the Jewish New York native *isn't* a talent to watch would also be disingenuous.

In his feature-length debut, *12 Horny Dames* (now playing on an incredibly—and criminally—limited number of screens throughout the country), Lumet has done the impossible: transmogrified adult entertainment into bona fide cinema with genuine staying power.

One might be inclined to use the words "smut," "nudie films," or even "pornography" when it comes to a film like *Dames*, but in Lumet's hands, the genre of pure carnal desire becomes something else entirely.

"I've been fascinated with plays ever since I was a boy," says Lumet, whose father is a veteran performer of the Yiddish Theater in Manhattan's Lower East Side. "I wanted to take that intimate, almost claustrophobic atmosphere of the stage and transfer it onto celluloid if I could. It didn't matter that the script ended with an all-female orgy—I simply treated the material as seriously as I could."

Loosely based on a 1954 teleplay penned by Reginald Rose, *12 Horny Dames* follows a dozen female jurists deliberating the fate of an 18-year-old criminal defendant. The proceedings take an unexpected turn when the women—sequestered in a cramped and sweaty room—begin to squabble over the verdict. All too soon, their various turn-ons and kinks are brought to light in the face of "reasonable doubt," a phrase espoused by the unnamed jury foreman (Ann Austin).

As Lumet states above, the story climaxes—no pun intended—with a free-for-all of sexual pleasure between the female jurists. Before we get there, however, Lumet and his talented cinematographer, Boris Kaufman, turn the deliberation room into a veritable hot box of disagreement, shame, and most importantly, jump-to-conclusion mob mentality.

"I'd be lying if I said this picture isn't a slight commentary on the state of our country these days," says Lumet, referring to the deplorably draconian policies of President Joseph McCarthy that have resulted in a systematic and calculated purge of suspected Hollywood Communists, as well as the formation of a single, government-run studio (United American Pictures).

At the time of McCarthy's unprecedented crusade to nationalize the film industry, Lumet was directing episodes of *You Are There*, hosted by CBS journalist Walter Cronkite. One day, Lumet and several other crew members were told to leave the studio and never come back. The CBS program—created by fellow Jew Goodman Ace—was canceled not long after due to a blatant lack of anti-Communist messaging.

"The Jews found themselves out of work in an industry they helped build from the ground up!" exclaims the filmmaker. "UAP obviously wouldn't hire us, so after a while, we decided to stop feeling sorry for ourselves and get off our lazy tuchuses. We couldn't make the mainstream stuff anymore? Fine with us. We'd simply move into adjacent work that was considered to be 'lesser' and make it respectable. We had to start completely from scratch."

Nevertheless, it took a while for the public to take notice that the quality of X-rated "skin flicks" was slowly on the rise. These pictures aren't exactly honored at the Academy Awards, least of all screened in federally mandated movie houses. There is still a thick layer of grime coating the reputation of silver screen erotica that doesn't simply wash off overnight.

"It's going to take some elbow grease," Lumet admits. "But we're already starting to see some promising returns at the box office, which means bigger and bigger budgets in future. People are taking notice and frequenting those underground theaters they once gave a wide berth. They want something new and unexpected and subversive. Something that goes against the tedious UAP narrative. They say to cut a steak against the grain if you want it to be tender. The same principle applies here."

Lumet remains mum on the names of his fellow pornographic collaborators, lest HUAC take an interest in their work, but he insists that these explicit films have more in common with "pure art" than anything the government has made in the last four years.

There is certainly no denying that the up-and-coming director is at the forefront of a brand-new epoch of American filmmaking—a wave carried forth by a tide of once-naughty exhibitionism. With rigorous studio oversight a thing of the past (at least for Jewish and Communist storytellers), the creative cuffs are off. As we speak, Lumet is entering production on his next feature, *Stage Shtup*, the story of a woman willing to do anything to become a Broadway star.

And we mean *anything*.

"Give a man a camera, a vision, and cast of actors willing to do... well, just about anything, and the skies truly are the limit," Lumet declares with a knowing smile. But how does he feel about making a living off what many would characterize as indecency?

At this, the down-to-earth filmmaker shrugs and throws up his hands. "What can I say?" he concludes. "Sex sells. Don't like it? Go join a monastery!"

PART III

December 27, 1959

Stars don't make movies. Movies make stars.

—Darryl F. Zanuck, studio executive/film producer/ cofounder of 20th Century Fox

CHAPTER 19

Joanna? Yeah, it's Morris. Listen, I need you to schedule an appointment with Dr. Ehrlich for me soon as you're able. What's wrong? Just fancied a checkup, is all. Okay, thank you. I'll be into the office later. Bye."

Baker hung up the phone and slumped back onto the bed. This cough wasn't something he could put off any longer. That bloodstained tissue settled the matter once and for all. Morris Baker had been wary of seeing physicians ever since Herr Doktor Professor Adolf Lang of the SS subjected him to radiation poisoning and removed a tumor the size of a grapefruit from his arm without the use of an anesthetic. An experience like that usually turned a guy off to the world of medicine for life.

Even after his bout with the Hueys and the Black Symphony left him a little worse for wear in '58, he still refused to go to a hospital. He allowed the LAPD medics to patch him up best they could and endured a month and a half of painful discomfort—eased with plenty of schnapps and phenobarbital, of course—until his bruises and fractured bones healed of their own accord. He also agreed to lie down in a dentist's chair, only for the sake of replacing teeth that would not be able to regenerate on their own.

Ehrlich was a kindly old congregant of Ohev Shalom for whom Baker had done some pro bono investigative work the previous August. It didn't take long to deduce that the doc's thirteen-year-old nephew, Nathan, was the one pilfering vials of morphine from the storeroom under the guise of volunteering around the office.

Baker set the boy straight, promising not to involve Nathan's uncle or parents if he promised to put the stealing in his rearview mirror.

The kid agreed and the vials stopped disappearing. Dr. Ehrlich was so grateful that he promised Baker a free checkup the next time he needed one. Baker never expected to be taking the doctor up on his offer.

HUAC and Nazi-related injuries notwithstanding, Baker had been incredibly lucky up to this point. He couldn't even remember the last time he was bedridden with a serious illness. It was just a matter of time, really. And that's when the nightmare, what Liz said as she squirmed across the Observatory floor, came back to him: *History comes for us all.*

Liz! The bloody tissue had completely removed the thought of her from his mind. A hot avalanche of shame threatened to smother him. Liz had been murdered, sliced in half like a flank of beef, and here he was, worrying about himself. Shira was right; he always put his needs first.

Hoping to receive an update on the case—not that there'd be anything to report so soon after the discovery of Liz's body—he called Connolly's home number.

"Oh, Morris!" answered Maeve. "I am so sorry for your loss. If there's anything I can do for you, anything at all, you just say the word."

"Thanks, Maeve. Really, I mean that. Is Brogan there?"

"You're in luck. He was just about to head out." There was a shuffle on the other end as she handed the phone off to her husband.

"Morris, how are you?" inquired Connolly.

"Barely slept, but it's the least of my worries. How'd the call with Liz's mother go?"

"A lot of crying. I didn't mention *how* Liz died, of course. I'll personally make sure Thomas has her all cleaned up before Mrs. Short arrives in town to claim the body."

"Thank you, Brogan."

"Don't mention it. This is my top priority. We'll find the son of a bitch who did it."

"*Brogan!*" came Maeve's chastising voice over the line.

"Sorry, dear."

"If you want me to look into anything, I can..."

"Morris," Connolly said sternly. "I know you want results, but you need to let the LAPD do its job."

"Ask Morris if he'd like a casserole or two."

"Maeve wants to know if you'd like—"

"No, thank you," Baker said. "You've got one hell of a woman over there, Connolly. Don't ever let her go."

"He says thanks, but no thanks," Connolly said to Maeve.

"Well, ask him if he wants—"

"Maeve!" He returned to the conversation. "Full service over here. Anything else we can get you, sir? A couple of chili bacon cheeseburgers maybe?"

"With a side of fries and an ice-cold Cherry Coke, please."

"Fuck yourself," Connolly said, incurring another bit of wrathful protest from Maeve, who, by the sound it, was hitting her husband with a dish rag. "I better get going before she grabs the frying pan."

"You two lovebirds have fun," Baker finished, hanging up the phone.

His third call was to Hersh, giving him the rest of the day off.

"Don't worry, you good-for-nothing schnorrer," Baker said. "I'll still pay you. I probably won't be in the office until late, so there's no sense in you watching the back of someone who's not even there."

"And what about Joanna?" Hersh asked.

"It's me the Symphony wants, not her. They kill an uppity Yid like me, no one bats an eye, but they kill a pretty young shiksa like Joanna, and there'll be hell to pay."

"If you say so."

"I do."

Baker hung up and made one final call.

"Yes? Hello, it's Baker. I'd very much like to renew my encyclopedia subscription."

CHAPTER 20

The Los Angeles Memorial Sports Arena had opened five months previously in a widely publicized ribbon-cutting ceremony hosted by Vice President Richard Nixon.

A televised bantamweight title match between José Becerra and Alphonse Halimi was supposed to serve as the inaugural event. The bout was unceremoniously canceled when Halimi—a proud French Jew—refused to swap out his favorite pair of shorts, which had a Star of David sewn into the fabric.

Halimi received a one-way ticket back to France and a lifelong ban from the United States. HUAC decided to break in the new arena with a political rally. The keynote speaker was the religious counsel to President McCarthy, Charles Edward Coughlin. The nearly seventy-year-old priest, whose orating career was once again on the up-and-up after so many years out of the public ear, took more than a few proverbial jabs at Halimi and his "noxious Jewishness."

The parking lot behind the oval-shaped arena was completely empty when Baker arrived twenty-five minutes later. He squinted through the swirling moisture, just able to make out the familiar 1953 Daimler and its red-nosed owner.

"Ah, there he is. The man of the hour!" sniffed Dashiell Hanscom.

"You got the stuff?" Baker asked, hoping to limit the interaction with one of his least favorite people in Los Angeles. Scratch that: He was one of Baker's least favorite people on the face of the earth. A bold statement given that most of the Black Symphony was still at large.

"Sure, I got it," answered Hanscom with a shit-eating grin that never failed to boil Baker's blood. "Wouldn't be here if I didn't. The question is, do you have my payment?"

"Of course I do." Baker retrieved the last of the fifty-dollar bills given to him by Ann Kissinger and held it out toward Hanscom, who kept his arms folded and shook his head.

"I'm afraid the price has gone up," he said.

"We agreed on fifty."

"And now I'm agreeing on a new price," Hanscom said, picking at his teeth with an overgrown pinky nail. "It'll be seventy-five if you want the pills. We'll call it a Sheeny surcharge."

Hanscom's smile widened, and Baker entertained the wonderful idea of simply shooting the corrupt detective and taking the phenobarbital he so desperately needed.

No, he'd have to resist that temptation for the time being. Dashiell might be a Jew-hating piece of shit with an awful cocaine habit, but the man was arguably one of the best narcotics traffickers in all of Los Angeles. His regular vice beat gave him access to all sorts of high-quality substances he could seize and then sell on the secondary market at wildly inflated prices.

"I've never met a bastard quite like you, Hanscom," said Baker, reaching into his wallet for the extra twenty-five bucks. "You really are perfect Huey material."

"Why, thank you." Hanscom snatched the money out of Baker's hand and tossed over a small plastic bottle filled with pills. "There, that should tide you over for a while."

"Hold on," Baker said, inspecting the bottle. "This is half the amount of last time."

"What's with you people always wanting to make sure you get your money's worth," said Hanscom. "Jews never can leave well enough alone, can they? It's called supply and demand, Baker. Our wonderful free market system at work. I have the supply, which means I also get to dictate the price of my choosing. The best part? There's not a single thing you can do about it."

"Fuck you."

"Watch it, Baker," Hanscom said. "Don't forget about who you're talking to." He proudly jabbed a thumb at the HUAC pin—a clenched fist embossed with the Stars and Stripes—on his lapel.

"I know who I'm speaking to, all right."

"Nice doing business with you, too. Until we meet again, Baker. Ta-ta."

Hanscom disappeared into his car, merrily whistling Vera Lynn's "We'll Meet Again."

"Parker was right!" Baker shouted as the Daimler vanished away into the mist. "Your nose does look like a fucking pomegranate!"

Hollis was unlocking the front door to the Golden Fowl when Baker pulled up to the curb.

"Hollis!"

The restaurant owner jumped a little at the sound of his name and turned around. "Oh, it's just you, Morris," he said, walking over to the Continental and leaning into the open window. "I take it you have an update on the case assigned to you by our mutual friends?"

Shit! Baker had totally forgotten about the missing tong member he was supposed to be looking for.

"Uh...no," he admitted sheepishly, not wanting to lie. Hollis frowned but did not speak. "I need your help in translating something." Baker pulled out the Lamotte Exports business card from the day before and handed it over. "Take a gander on the back there. Looks like Japanese or Chinese."

Hollis took one look at the stamp of characters and handed it back. "It's neither."

"It's not?"

"No, it's Korean." Hollis sounded none too pleased as he stood up and adjusted his bow tie.

"Well, how are your Korean translation skills then?"

Hollis raised an impatient eyebrow. "Morris, the people you met the other night are not to be trifled with. They expect immediate results, and so do I, for that matter. Han Zhao is a good man, and he needs to be returned to the organization right away."

"Still not going to tell me what he does for you guys?"

"That's none of your concern," replied Hollis coolly. "You are my friend, Morris, so I'm happy to give you a bit more slack than my associates would. But I must ask that you don't come here again until you have an update on Han's whereabouts."

Baker opened his mouth, but Hollis forestalled him in a slightly worried undertone. "They're always watching," he whispered frantically. "I'll make an excuse for you this time, but I won't be able to do it again. Good luck, Morris."

Los Angeles's famous traffic had returned with a vengeance now that the holiday was over and Kishi was embarking on his speaking tour. Dozens of men, women, and children lined the streets, waving American and Japanese flags with patriotic gusto. Not wanting to get stuck behind the upcoming parade, he honked at a bright red Bel-Air convertible that failed to move forward when the light turned green.

The commute from Chinatown to Hollywood Boulevard took close to an hour instead of the usual fifteen to twenty-five minutes. Off in the distance, that shining beacon of glamour, the Hollywood Sign, was totally hidden behind a dense layer of fog.

The squat and crummy-looking apartment building that sat behind the Florentine Gardens nightclub had not changed in the slightest. Its decently priced units were inhabited by the club's various singers, dancers, and waitstaff, whose meager salaries meant they couldn't afford to live in the swankier parts of town. Besides, who didn't want a short walk home after an exhausting night of catering to drunk patrons?

Liz had lived here while trying to make it as an actress. She was always "one audition away" from becoming UAP's next big starlet. Against his better judgment, Baker had fed Liz's ambition, running lines with her ad nauseam, even though her acting chops never got any better. To make ends meet, Liz worked as a server and cigarette girl at the club.

He didn't know why he wanted to see the place again. Who was to say Liz hadn't moved in the time since Baker broke her heart? Whatever the case, he parked in the empty nightclub lot and walked over to the shabby apartment building.

The door to the lobby was not locked. Baker walked right in and up the stairs to what had been Liz's apartment. It wasn't until he was standing in front of the door that he remembered bringing along his set of lock-picking tools.

Was he really about to break into the home of a dead woman? And for what purpose? Connolly had promised to personally lead the investigation. What good would Baker be doing himself by mucking up potential evidence? Before he could come to an acceptable conclusion, the door swung open and Baker's jaw dropped.

"*Debbie?*" he exclaimed.

"Hello, handsome," said the prostitute, now leaning against the frame and playing with the feathery pink boa draped around her neck. "Didn't think I'd be seeing you again so soon. If you went to the trouble of tracking down my address, you must really want it bad. I was just about to hit the Boulevard, but if you wanna book me for the day, I'd be happy to—"

"What the hell are you doing here?"

"What do you mean? I live here."

"Since when?"

"Coming up on two years, I think."

"You and Liz lived together?"

"How do you know about her?"

"We dated for almost a decade."

Debbie sized him up for a moment, then said, "So you're the fella who went and broke her heart? Liz always brings up the louse who ditched her, but never gives me a name. You were personata insalata with her."

"Persona non grata," Baker corrected her.

"Yeah, that. Anyways, what are you doing here? Come to beg her forgiveness? Sorry, pal, but she ain't here and even if she was, she wouldn't take you back if you were the last man on Earth."

A beat of silence passed before Baker posed his next question. "Weren't you concerned when Liz didn't come home last night?"

"Come home?" said a distracted Debbie, unsticking two feathers on her boa. "I haven't seen her in about a week. She comes and goes mostly. Probably been shackin' up with her new boyfriend. He treats her a lot better than you did, mister, I can tell you that."

"Debbie," Baker began, knowing full well he was treading through a field of emotional land mines, "I don't know how to tell you this... but Liz is dead."

"You really shouldn't joke like that."

"This isn't a joke, Debbie. She was murdered."

Debbie looked up from the boa, furor and confusion taking over. "No. No. That's not possible, mister. I just saw her yesterday morning. I saw her! She ain't dead! Quit your lying!"

"I wish I was," Baker said.

"No! No! No!" Debbie screamed through tears, beating his chest with a pair of dainty fists. "Liz can't be dead. She just can't be."

Baker pulled her into an embrace and allowed her to cry until the first wave of shock had passed. Debbie did not object or try to pull away—she simply bawled into his chest, repeating: "No. No. No. No."

"I'm so sorry, Debbie. I cared for Liz a lot, too."

"Yeah," she said, pulling away. "What a big man you are. Coming around here now that she's kicked the bucket. You must care a whole lot."

This stung to hear, but Baker knew it was only the pain talking. "Listen, I would never have wished harm on her. I just want to figure out who killed her."

"You a cop?"

"I was. Now I'm a PI. But I wouldn't be surprised if my former partner shows up here at any minute to ask you some questions."

Yet again, he wondered why he didn't just let Connolly handle it.

"Well, I don't know nothin'," Debbie sniffed, wiping at her running nose with the boa. "Like I said, I thought she was out with her boyfriend."

"Who is this boyfriend?"

"No idea. She wouldn't tell me. I think because he's married, you know? Also loaded. Real moneybags. Always buying her expensive gifts. Even got her a nice apartment out in Venice Beach. But Liz usually stays here with me. That fancy life was too much for her."

"She never mentioned a name to you? Not even once?"

"Nope."

"Damn."

"But I know someone who might know," said Debbie.

"Who?"

"Darryl."

"Who?"

"The adult film producer, Darryl Zanuck. You never heard of him? He's a darling."

Baker had forgotten all about what Debbie told him the morning prior: *I do nudie films on the side with my roommate!*

"Liz... was a nudie actress?" He couldn't believe it, but if her dream of getting signed by UAP never panned out, he reckoned the woman might just be desperate enough to do anything to get her face up on the big screen.

"*Was*," said Debbie, stressing the word. "Quit once she shacked up with Mr. Moneybags last year."

"But she might have confided in this Darryl?"

"Oh, sure. They were close. He offered to let Liz out of her contract early, but she saw it through to the end. One of the best. Really knew her way around a woman's body, if you know what I mean. Knew how to do things with her tongue I'd never—"

"Where is Darryl right now?" asked Baker, cutting off Debbie's sexual reminiscence. "Could you take me to him? I'll pay you for your time."

Her eyes lit up and Baker knew she was relieved at the thought of not having to stand in the cold and rain all day just to make a few bucks with some sleazy dirtbag looking for a good time. "I don't see why not. He's probably on set in the Valley and I'm sure he wouldn't mind talking about Liz. She was his favorite."

"Great. Do you want to get changed?"

"What's wrong with my outfit?" she asked, looking down at the low-cropped blouse, leather pencil skirt, and fishnets.

"Nothing," said Baker. "We'll take my car."

CHAPTER 21

"Debbie, do you mind?"

She'd been toggling with the Continental's radio dial for the last twenty minutes, trying to find a station she liked. The intermittent static was giving Baker a headache.

"Come on," said Debbie petulantly. "You're no fu—ooo..." Elvis Presley's "(Now and Then There's) A Fool Such as I" came over the speakers. She sat back in her seat. "You listen to Elvis? He's absolutely dreamy."

"Yeah, I guess," replied Baker, who was smoking a Kool against his better judgment. Cigarettes probably wouldn't help his little coughing-up-blood problem. "Where did you say we're headed again?"

"Parthenia Street in Panorama City."

"What's the address?"

"Uh," said Debbie, now finicking with her hair in the rearview mirror. "Not sure, but I'll know it when I see it. Can I get one of those?"

He handed her the box of Kools and the pack of matches he'd taken from the Chateau Marmont lobby. The origin of the matches was not lost on Miss Milner. "Ooo," she cooed again. "Fancy. I haven't been at a hotel in a *looooong* time. Not since I got to Los Angeles anyway. I'm from a small town in New Jersey right outside Philly. Can you believe it?"

Baker let Debbie drone on, often throwing in a vapid "that's nice" or "uh-huh" whenever the young prostitute stopped to draw breath. After an extra fifteen minutes, Debbie let out a shriek of delight and pointed her finger to a nondescript ranch house with an overgrown lawn of scrub oak, California lilac, and miniature palm trees.

"This is the place!"

"You sure?" Baker asked, trying to discern any movement from within the dead-looking front windows. "Doesn't look like much of a film set to me."

"Course it is. We don't have all the money in the world like the government does. Gotta make do with what we got. Most crew members offer up their houses for the shoots and we rotate to keep the Hueys on their toes. But I know this place is Darryl's favorite 'cause it doesn't draw a lot of attention."

"If you're sure..."

He parked several blocks away and the two of them got out of the car. Debbie shivered from the cold. Baker took off his suit jacket and offered it to her, which she accepted gratefully. While Debbie slipped it on, the sleeves drooping well below her hands, he slipped a phenobarbital tablet under his tongue.

They strolled up the weed-infested pathway. Baker noticed a number of earthworms wriggling between the red-brick tiles. The Los Angeles ground, usually so parched by the heat, was saturated enough to force the worms to seek out oxygen before they drowned.

"Okay," Debbie said quietly once they had reached the front door. She curled her fingers and rapped her knuckles in strange succession. At once, a small rectangular recess in the door slid open and a pair of probing brown eyes stared out at them.

"Deb?" came a muffled voice from within. "What are you doing here? You're not on the call sheet today."

"I know that, Eddie," replied Debbie, now businesslike. "But I've got some really, really bad news for Darryl. May we come in?"

"We?"

"I'll explain in a sec. Just open the door, please."

"You're lucky, Deb. We're in between shots right now. Rod and Herb are having another one of their famous script disagreements. If I had a dollar..."

Eddie's eyes flicked over to Baker for a moment and the recess slid back into place. Next came the sounds of bolts, chains, and locks being undone, and the door swung inward. A tall and slightly stooped balding man with an unshapely nose and a calculating gaze stood in the doorway. Despite some pudginess and a shocking mane of white hair, Eddie gave off a powerful aura that immediately told Baker this was not someone to fuck with.

Debbie smiled and flung herself into his arms. "Eddie dear, so great to see you. This is Morris Baker. He's a private investigator. Morris, this is Eddie Mannix. He's head of security for our little underground studio. You got a problem? Eddie is the guy you call to fix it."

"How do you do? 'Baker,' was it?" said Mannix, sticking out a beefy hand covered in wrinkles and spider veins. He did not break eye contact. "Not a Huey, are ya?"

"I applied to be one, but my circumcised schmekel was a dead giveaway," replied Baker, not sure why he was trying to crack a joke.

Mannix's hardened expression softened a little and he chuckled. "A Yid, eh? All right, come on in."

He shuffled aside, allowing them to cross the threshold into the merciful warmth of the house. Mannix closed the door and began to lock it.

Baker noticed a cane clutched in the man's right hand. Debbie must have seen him staring because she whispered, "Eddie's got a bad ticker. Just don't bring it up with him. Not unless you want your lights knocked out. Thinks he's Superman or something."

"So," Mannix said after sliding the last heavy bolt back into place, "what's this dire news you two soothsayers have come to deliver?"

"Liz is dead—murdered," Debbie said darkly. The smile disappeared from Mannix's mug.

"*Our* Liz? You're kidding."

"Wish I was, Eddie. Morris here is looking into the case, and Darryl might be able to help him find the killer."

"You should've said so sooner," said Mannix. "Darryl's either in his office or out back playing arbiter again."

"Thanks, Eddie."

She and Baker began to step away when Mannix grabbed Baker's upper arm, turned him back around. "Liz was like family to us. You find her killer because we won't accept any failure."

"Neither will I," said Baker. This statement drew a nod of respect from old Mannix, who now looked his age—weary and tired. Sure enough, he sank into a nearby chair and closed his eyes, resembling an ancient tortoise settling down for a snooze. Before long, he was snoring.

"He's *really* your head of security?" Baker asked as they walked into a vestibule lined with periwinkle blue carpet. Every square inch of wall was covered in foamy gray sheets of soundproofing material.

"Eddie may not look it, but he's the best in the business," answered Debbie. "Used to cover up all sorts of nasty stuff for the old-time studios. Abortions, affairs—you name it. He's still got all sorts of useful contacts across town, including connections with some of the folks who were able to make the transition over to UAP. They're loyal to Eddie... or scared of him."

"Why not just stay at UAP, then? Surely they offer better job security."

Debbie smiled. "Nudie films pay better. In here."

She led him to a living room, whose white-and-pink couches were occupied by the strangest assortment of equipment Baker had ever seen: lights, film reels, cartridges of fresh celluloid, racks of costumes, boxes of sex toys, and lubricant dispensers. The windows were covered in heavy black blankets, which, Baker realized, was the reason he could not discern any movement from inside the house when they first arrived. The two blinding klieg bulbs keeping the room alight made the place feel stuffy.

"Wait here and make yourself comfortable," said Debbie. "I'll go and find Darryl."

She left the room, and Baker sat on one of the couches—only after brushing aside a flesh-colored dildo resting on the cushions. He stayed there, legs crossed, for about five minutes, watching as harried crew members popped in every few seconds to grab this or that.

None of them paid him any mind.

The heat from the klieg lights started to become too much for the growing tightness in his chest. Loosening his tie, Baker stood up and decided to seek out a bit of fresh air.

He ventured down the cramped hall, avoiding a number of production personnel, who filed in and out of doors with makeup kits, tripods, and in one case, a palette of fake mustaches. Baker followed the sounds of friendly conversation all the way to a humble kitchen, where even more crew members chose from an assortment of muffins and beverages lining the counter.

No one gave Baker a second glance, which was fine with him. He'd just spotted a sliding door that he hoped would lead out to a back patio of some kind. Like the windows in the living room, the door was draped with a thick blanket of onyx material. He crossed the kitchen, wrenched the door open, and gasped.

The bombed-out vestiges of a city stared back at him, framed by sickly orange-and-red clouds drifting off into the infinite sky. Someone had detonated a hydrogen bomb in the backyard of this house—or at least that's how they wanted it to appear. Baker had been on a movie set only once before, but the experience left him with an ability to discern where reality ended and make-believe began.

Looking past the phony backdrop, he now understood why this house was optimal real estate for a clandestine pornography shoot. Tall and wild hedges kept the entire area boxed off from the outside world, creating a natural soundstage.

The irradiated set dressing circled a small patch of grass next to a swimming pool clogged with shrunken leaves. Emaciated palm trees dotted the perimeter, rising high above the hedges. Strategically placed spotlights really brought the tableau to life, though the bleak illusion of a post-apocalypse was somewhat marred by the two men arguing in the middle of the staged fallout.

"Herb, you've bastardized my script!" shouted the younger-looking of the two, a handsome man with a head of black hair in an almost-crew-cut style. He wore a crisp blue suit and there was a cigarette dangling between his tight knuckles. "Bemis is supposed to be alone after the bomb goes off. It doesn't make any narrative sense for a naked woman to be lying across the steps of the sex shop. We already have the main sex scene with the wife earlier in the story, which is another issue entirely, but we don't need *another one* right at the end. Let the story breathe, for God's sake!"

"Rod," said the older man. Clearly flustered, he adjusted his thick-framed glasses and ran a hand through a mane of equally thick white hair. "Need I remind you what we're making here? I know you want to be all high-minded with this stuff, but—"

"And what's wrong with that?" countered Rod. "Why can't we stimulate people's brains as well as their *loins*?"

"The people who pay to watch our pictures aren't exactly looking for a lesson in morality once they've cracked their nuts! Now, I've agreed to retain that mean-spirited ending of yours. Bemis can lose his glasses, okay? But now it's time to let your baby go. Can we please resume shooting?"

"*Mean-spirited ending?*" blustered Rod, and Herb rolled his eyes as if to say, *Here we go again.*

"Rod," he began, "I only meant—"

"We'll shoot it both ways!" This from a third gentleman, who had just appeared at Baker's side. He had severe, hawk-like eyes and an incredibly well-manicured mustache whose ends didn't quite meet at the philtrum. Despite the newcomer's stern cadence, he wore a kindly smile that seemed to imply he'd broken up quarrels like this many times before.

"*What?*" sputtered Herb.

"Just as I say," answered the third man, who could only be Darryl Zanuck. "We'll shoot it both ways. Your way and then Rod's way. We'll see which one works better in post."

"Darryl," Herb said, looking aghast. Rod, on the other hand, looked ecstatic. "You can't be serious. Do you know how much money that'll—?"

"You let me worry about that," said Zanuck, walking over and patting Herb on the shoulder. "Let's just get this show on the road. We're burning daylight here."

"Fine," said the rankled Herb. "All right, everyone!" he shouted to the cameramen and microphone operators, who were casually chatting and smoking during the altercation. Clearly, they were also accustomed to Rod and Herb's quarrels. "We'll be rolling in ten. Someone please get Midge out of makeup. Randy, on your mark, please. We'll go over your monologue once more."

Baker watched a stubby actor in a shabby, oversized suit and comedically owlish glasses step on set. The crew member cradling the palette of fake mustaches ran over and started gluing a wispy prosthetic to Randy's upper lip.

"Children. I'm dealing with children," whispered Darryl, back at his side. "You must be Morris Baker."

"Where's Debbie?"

"I left her in my office. Thought she had enough heartache for one day. Would you like a coffee?"

"No, thanks, I'm goo—"

"Nonsense. Have a coffee with me. Steven!"

A boy of about thirteen came running over. "Yes, Mr. Zanuck?" he asked eagerly.

"Steven, would you be so kind as to grab two coffees for Mr. Baker and myself? Four creams and three sugars for me. How do you take your coffee, Morris?"

"Splash of cream, no sugar."

"You heard the man, Steven. Now off with you."

The boy gave a sort of half salute and ran into the house.

"You think it wise to have a kid on a set like this?" Baker asked.

Darryl laughed and said, "Didn't have much of a choice, did I? That kid somehow got a bead on our erratic shooting schedule and snuck onto set one day. Took me about a little over a week to notice he didn't belong! Steven's pretty resourceful, holds himself like an adult. Came here all the way from Phoenix."

"What about his parents? Don't they miss him?"

"Might as well not be his parents. Divorced and distant. They're pretty much catatonic, the way Steven tells it. Couldn't take the stress of life under McCarthy and snapped. It's happening more and more from what I hear through the grapevine. That's no way for a boy to grow up. Steven wants be a filmmaker more than anything else in the world. Who am I to deny him that?"

"A pornographer, you mean."

"Happen to see one of our little pictures lately?"

Baker did not answer, which Darryl took as a resounding "*Yes!*"

"No need to be ashamed, Morris. No need to be ashamed at all. Yes, we make naughty films, no two ways about it. But I can assure you we are more creatively free than we've ever been. Unfettered from the MPAA, from the Hays Code, from whatever bullshit guidelines UAP's been following for the last five years. Do we need a bit of explicit content to sell our product? Sure. No theater would dare show it otherwise. But it's only a small part of what we do. This..."

He gestured to the dreary backyard like a carnival barker trying to lure in paying customers on a slow night, "This is the First Amendment at work. Freedom of expression in its purest form!"

Baker smiled. Zanuck's passion for the creative continuation of the industry reminded him of an ill-fated screenwriter. "You didn't happen to know Dalton Trumbo, did you?"

"*Know* him?" Zanuck said. "I revered him! That man had balls of steel to stay in Hollywood long after most of us had already called it quits. I could've kept at it, of course, but what was the point, really? Ah, thank you, Steven." The boy had returned with their coffees. "Why don't you go and see if Rod needs anything. He could fill an entire gallery with those woes of his."

"Sure thing, Mr. Zanuck!" Steven ran off again.

Darryl took a sip of coffee and smacked his lips in contentment. "Kid gets my order right every single time without fail."

"What do you mean, you could have stayed in the industry?" Baker asked, taking a sip of the hot coffee and accidentally burning his tongue. "Your name, Zanuck. Isn't it... well, Jewish?"

"You'd think that, wouldn't you?" Daryl replied with a knowing wink. "No, I'm Protestant, but I can tell you that damn near everyone in this town thought I was a Hebe when I first started in the industry. Got denied from every country and social club I applied to."

"So why'd you get kicked out by McCarthy then?"

"HUAC made the same error you did. They saw my name and assumed I was a Member of the Tribe. They don't really give a shit about the finer details. In any case, I had no desire to work for them. No, I've always been more comfortable calling the shots myself."

They stood in silence for a moment. "Ever heard of a picture called *Gentleman's Agreement*?" posited Zanuck. Baker shook his head. "Course you haven't," he said. "McCarthy probably had every single print destroyed once he took over. Ironically, it was directed by the very head of UAP, Elia Kazan. I won't bore you with too many plot details, but it's about a journalist who goes undercover as a Jew to expose anti-Semitism in America."

"They actually made movies like that?"

"Why, sure. And if you can believe it, several of your kinsmen—very influential men, mind you—tried to stop me from making the damn picture. They thought it might cause trouble for the Hebes over here. This was two years after we learned what the Krauts had been up to in those camps of theirs. Goes to show how fucked we were as a country even then. McCarthy didn't invent the current system, but he sure as hell found a way to make it accessible to everyone. In any case, the experience of making *Gentleman's Agreement* came back to me when ol' Joe took office. I realized that if the Jews weren't even willing to stand up for themselves, then there was no hope for the rest of us."

They stood in silence again, sipping their coffees and watching Randy rehearse a scene that required him to caress a large pile of nudie magazines on the stoop of a bombed-out sex shop.

"Poor Elizabeth," Zanuck said. "Sorry, Morris, I've been talking your ear off when all you wanted to do was deliver the news about this terrible murder. Walk with me." The producer led him over to the leaf-choked swimming pool. "I was incredibly shocked to hear the news from Debbie. Elizabeth Short was like family to us, and based on what Debbie's told me, you and her had a history as well."

"Yes," Baker said, swirling the dregs of his coffee in the Styrofoam cup. He suddenly found his throat tight with bereavement. It was hard to speak about Liz, but Zanuck's understanding air made him feel as though he could admit to just about anything at the moment.

"We... we dated for a while," Baker added.

"I see. Hey, now—it's all right, son. It's all right."

Baker had finally broken down in tears, the grief slicing its way through the phenobarbital haze with the swiftness of an executioner's axe.

"I should've made sure she was okay," Baker said, still not looking at Zanuck. "I should've checked up on her. This is on me, I know it."

"You mustn't think in those terms," Zanuck said. "You firmly go about blaming yourself for every tragedy that crosses your path, and you'll dig a hole you won't be able to climb out of. Debbie tells me you split up with her nearly two years ago, is that correct?" Baker nodded. "Then what were you supposed to do? Elizabeth was a grown woman who could make her own decisions. You couldn't hold her hand every step of the way."

"That's one way of looking at it."

"Then here's another: I don't believe Elizabeth would have joined our little troupe if she hadn't been so heartbroken and lonely once you called it quits. I think your cutting the cord, so to speak, may have convinced her to give up that silly dream of working for UAP and start making some real money."

Baker looked up. "So you saw it, too, then, huh?"

"Oh, let's not kid ourselves, Morris. I don't like to speak ill of the dead, but Elizabeth Short was—"

"Not very talented," Baker finished.

Zanuck smiled, eyes clouding with sadness. "You've hit the nail on the head. No, she was not, but you don't need much acting talent to do what we do here. So long as you've got decent looks, a deficit of self-consciousness, and a good sense of fun."

Baker did not answer.

"Ah—you must think me a callous old pervert for the way I talk. I apologize. Everyone, from the cameramen, to the actors, to the script supervisors are here of their own volition. I can assure you that no one has been coerced or blackmailed into what one might call 'showing off the goods.' This is a business like any other. Competitive, unfeeling, solely focused on chasing the almighty dollar. Capitalism, m'boy. People need to eat."

"So what are you saying? That Liz was just a dollar sign to you? I thought she was family?"

"Of course she was! Lit up every room she walked into. Elizabeth was more than just an employee. I cared deeply for her, the same way I care for my own children."

"Which means she told you who she was seeing before she died."

"Yes. I tried to talk her out of it. Told her dating a man like that would bring too much unwanted attention onto us. We try to keep a low-profile, as you can probably well imagine."

"Who was he?"

Zanuck finished off the last of his coffee before answering:

"It was Orson Lamotte."

CHAPTER 22

Orson Lamotte?" Baker could hardly believe it. "You're sure?"

"I don't see why Elizabeth would have any reason to lie."

"Do you think he had anything to do with her death?"

"Oh, no," Zanuck said. "He absolutely adored her. Orson was the reason she left this crazy business behind. He talked her into an early retirement."

"Was Lamotte going to leave his wife for Liz?"

"I do believe that was the eventual plan. Though I'm not sure the idea sat well with Elizabeth."

"Why is that?"

"Well, on more than one occasion she told me she felt guilty about tearing Orson's family apart. He's got two young children along with that wife of his."

"Could be a possible motive for Lamotte," Baker said, thinking out loud. "Maybe Liz got cold feet about the whole thing and planned on telling the wife. She tells Lamotte about what she plans to do and he kills her...or else hires someone to do the dirty work. I'd imagine paying for an assassination would barely put a dent in his wallet."

"Hmmm," said Zanuck contemplatively, and Baker felt like a student who had just answered a question incorrectly. "I don't think it likely. I never met the man personally, but from what I heard secondhand, he was deeply in love with Elizabeth. He would have done anything for her, and I'm not a man known for hyperbole."

"Well, I'll just have to pay a visit to Mr. Lamotte to be absolutely sure, won't I?" Baker asked rhetorically. "He's got a house out here in the Valley, right?"

"Yes, I do believe so. Somewhere between Woodland Hills and Tarzana."

"Got a street address?"

"I'm afraid not, but those orange trees of his shouldn't be hard to miss."

"Thank you for your time, Mr. Zanuck."

"My pleasure. I wish you the best of luck on your investigation and hope you're able to track down the sick fiend who took Elizabeth away from us before her time."

"I'll do my best. You said Debbie was in your offi—?"

For a moment, he thought the anti-seizure drug was causing him to hallucinate. Ann Kissinger, the woman who had hired him to track down her missing husband, was striding onto the set in a silken robe. "Who is that?" he asked Zanuck in a quavering voice.

"Wha—? Oh, that's Midge, one of our starlets. Is everything all right?"

"Yes. Everything's fine. Just feeling a little faint, is all."

"Maybe you'd like to sit down inside for a while. Stay as long as you like. Looks like they're about to start filming the next scene. If you'll excuse me, I need to supervise. Keep Rod and Herb from biting each other's heads off again."

"Yes," said Baker, his ears ringing. "Sit down. I'll go do that."

Ann disrobed. Her pale, naked body stood in stark contrast to the apocalyptic backdrop of deep reds and oranges. She sensually stroked the patch of brown hair on her pubis and knelt down, slowly reaching for the fly of Randy's baggy suit.

Baker made his way back inside, his desire to witness movie magic satisfied.

He sat on the couch for close to an hour, smoking one cigarette after another. The image of the bloody tissue had finally left his mind, effectively chased out with torches and pitchforks by the sight of Ann Kissinger about to perform fellatio in front of an entire film crew. His chest felt like it was crawling with red-hot fire ants, but he did not much care.

Ann, or whoever she was, had not been completely honest with him.

The memory of Sophia reared its ugly head, and Baker fought back nausea. Was Ann another agent of the Black Symphony? Were they coming to exact their revenge through the conduit of another actress with a phony sob story?

If Baker had an Achilles' heel, it was beautiful women in distress. He'd have to resist the impulse to offer help to another pretty face in future, but the $64,000 question still remained: Who would hire a nudie actress to pose as Henry Kissinger's wife and for what purposes? Why the hell would someone go to all that trouble when Kissinger's disappearance had already been reported to the LAPD a month earlier—presumably by his *actual* wife?

Isn't it obvious? he thought. *Someone else is looking for Kissinger and clearly doesn't want to involve the cops.* This gave rise to another query: How much progress had Officers Bletchley and Pistone made in their missing persons investigation? Baker made a mental note to track them both down at his earliest convenience and ask...

"There you are!" Debbie reentered the room, plopped down next to Baker, and helped herself to a cigarette. "Darryl said you looked ill. Everything okay?"

"Yeah. It's just my medication. Makes me loopy sometimes."

"You think you'll be up to driving me home? The last thing I need is you veering off the road and disfiguring me in some horrible accent. I mean, my face and body are all I've got."

"I'll be fine to drive, but first, we need to make a quick stop."

"For what?"

"Don't worry ab—"

"What?"

"Shhh!"

He had just heard Ann's voice from around the corner. It sounded bubbly and cheerful—a long ways away from the wounded doe shtick she'd pulled on him Christmas Day.

"Where are you going?" Debbie asked when Baker got up and crept toward the hall.

"I'll be right back," he whispered. "Stay there."

He snuck a look around and saw Ann talking to someone he could not see. "Thanks, Francis! Think I'll take a little cat nap in my dressing room before the next scene."

She retreated into a nearby room and closed the door. Baker followed and knocked surreptitiously. Ann opened the door with a large smile, which vanished as soon as she saw her gentleman caller.

Her eyes bulged and her mouth twisted into an O shape, about to let out a scream for help. Acting quickly, Baker cupped a palm over her lips, sidestepped into the room, closed the door, and locked it behind him. He did not immediately remove the hand from her mouth but raised his free pointer finger to his own lips.

"Quiet," he said calmly. "I'm not going to hurt you. Okay? Nod if you understand."

Ann complied, eyes still alight with terror, and he lifted his palm, keeping it close in case she tried to shout again. Her robe slipped a little, nearly dislodging the breasts within.

"What do you want from me?" she squeaked hoarsely.

"Let's just say a pretty face has played me for a sap before and I'm not looking to make a regular habit out of it," he said. "So talk. Who hired you to play Kissinger's wife?"

"I don't know who he was. He came up to me on the street a week ago and asked if I'd like to make a few hundred bucks for memorizing a few talking points. How could I say no?"

"You get a name off this mystery benefactor?"

"No. He said I wouldn't need it."

"Okay. Can you give me a description then?"

"Big. Like, *really* big. Looked like one of those giant sloths they have on display at the Natural History Museum. And he talked funny."

" 'Talked funny' how?" pressed Baker.

"Some sort of accent. A snooty one. French, maybe? Yeah, definitely French."

"Anything else?"

Ann shook her head.

"Did he give you that shiner?" Baker said, pointing to the bruise covered in makeup.

"What? No, one of my clients got a little too handsy. I also work the Boulevard sometimes."

"Don't lie to me. If I find out you're withholding information..."

"I swear, that's it."

"Fine. If anything else comes to mind, you know where my office is. If I'm not there, talk to my secretary, Joanna. Here..." Baker reached into his pocket, pulled out the bottle of phenobarbital, extracted a pill, snapped it in half, and held out one of the halves. "It's one of those 'Barbies' you like so much. Take it to calm down. I'm sorry for frightening you."

He forced the half pill into Midge's quivering palm and left the room in search of a phone. Joanna picked up on the third ring. She sounded annoyed.

"There you are! I've been trying to reach you all morning."

"Sorry, Joanna—figured I'd check in. What's the latest?"

"I wasn't sure what times worked for you, but Dr. Ehrlich said you can just stop by whenever you're free."

"Thanks. I'll head over there later."

"And Tzipora Friedman called about that writ of divorce thing. Any updates I can give her?"

"Not yet. Bigger fish to fry at the moment."

"All right. I'll stall again, but she's getting impatient."

"Then offer her a partial refund. That all?"

"No. There is someone coming to the office who wants to meet with you."

"Who?"

"He didn't provide a name, but said it was very important."

"All right. If they show up before I get there, start taking down their basic information. See if you can get a down payment out of them, too. By the way, how was Christmas with Stanley?"

"Very nice. He... well, he actually popped the question under the mistletoe."

"You're kidding! Mazel tov, Joanna! We'll have to celebrate soon."

"Thank you, Morris. I'm still processing. How was the rest of your holiday?"

"Fine," he lied. "Oh, by the way, how'd your other meeting go?"

"Total waste of time. Guy was a no-show. Like I said, everyone's spooked."

"Aren't we all..."

CHAPTER 23

Baker took Lindley Street all the way down to West Oxnard Street and pulled onto the ramp for the US 101 highway that would take them south. He wasn't entirely sure where they were going, but figured they'd start in Tarzana and work their way up to Woodland Hills. Lamotte's presumably palatial estate was sure to be somewhere along the route.

"Why do we have to go to Tarzana again?" asked Debbie, perusing a crumpled map extracted from the glove compartment.

"I already told you," he said. "I've got an important business meeting. Don't worry, it shouldn't take long. What does the map say?"

He was trying to see through the curtains of mist on either side of the road, hoping to detect a sudden flash of green and orange through all the gray.

"Looks like there's a large patch of green over here," said Debbie, jabbing a finger at the map and accidentally poking a hole through the thin paper. "Oops."

"It's fine. Where are you seeing that green?"

She scrutinized the map for a moment, then answered: "Oakdale Avenue. Where are we now?"

Baker slowed the Continental to look at the nearest street sign. "Wells Drive."

"We're less than two miles away. Continue on this road and we should be there in a coupla minutes. Why couldn't we just stop and ask for directions?"

"Because you're supposed to be directing me."

"Men are all the same. They'd rather drive around in circles for hours than admit they're lost."

"I'm trying to surprise my business associate. We're old friends."

But that wasn't true in the slightest. This was Lamotte's territory and Baker wasn't sure who the man had in his deep pockets. He didn't want to tip off the import-export mogul if he could help it; didn't want to give Lamotte time to rehearse his alibi. If he needed one, that is.

True to Debbie's word, it took only about ten minutes to reach Oakdale Avenue, which suddenly dipped into a sea of lush greenery planted along an unpaved and isolated dirt road.

The orange trees grew thicker and more numerous as he drove farther along, the Continental hitching and jerking every time the tires encountered pockets of gravel and stone. The ground was also incredibly wet, and twice Baker had to make sure the car did not skid through the loose soil and off the path.

They drove on for half a mile when a large manor house rose out of the trees like a slumbering giant. The entire grove seemed to bow in deference to the extravagant structure—an architectural mishmash of columns, pillars, balconies, and pergolas.

Baker was reminded of a prophetical dream chronicled in the Torah. Yosef wakes up one morning and decides to tell his brothers how he saw their bundles of wheat capitulating to his own bundle. Jealous of this vision—and of their father's overt favoritism shown toward Yosef—his siblings decide to sell him into slavery.

We really are our own worst enemy, Baker thought, parking the car under cover of a secluded copse of trees where oranges hung like cheerful tumors.

"Wait in here," he said, turning off the engine, which *tick-tick-ticked* as it cooled.

"But—"

"Do as I say, Debbie. Keep the doors locked and don't open them up for anybody unless they're me, got it?"

She frowned, crossed her arms, and threw herself back against the passenger seat. Baker got out of the car and unlocked the trunk, extricating a tall vinyl carrying case and clipboard from within.

Tightening his tie and smoothing out any wrinkles on his suit,

Baker heaved the case past a deep stone fountain and over to the front portico.

A gold lion knocker roared out of the front door, calling to mind the defunct MGM logo. Baker grabbed the ring looped through the lion's flared nostrils and rapped it against the thick white pine three times. It was opened without delay by a tired-looking maid, who held a feather duster in one hand and a pacifier in the other.

"Good afternoon, ma'am!" he exclaimed, reciting the oft-practiced spiel in his best American timbre before the maid could protest. "My name is Charlie Edmund Torrance of the Kirby Vacuum Company. Is there a"—he pretended to check the empty clipboard—"Mr. Lamotte home by any chance?"

"What's this all about?" asked the maid. She reached up, absent-mindedly, trying to dust the lintel with the pacifier.

"Well, like I say, ma'am, I am a representative of the Kirby Vacuum Company, and I am here to demonstrate the unparalleled cleaning power of our top-of-the-line model."

He bent down on the stoop, threw open the three clasps on the vinyl case, and pulled it apart to reveal a shining vacuum within. Truth be told, the vacuum was three years out of date, but no one ever seemed to be able to tell the difference.

"Our patented suction technology collects twenty-five percent more dust mites and pollen—the leading causes of asthma, mind you—than any of the vacuum models sold by our leading competitors. We guarantee it or your money back! If we hear you've gotten so much as a sniffle after using our product, the money will be returned to your account, no questions asked. And if you act now, we'll throw in an extra dust bag and our patented extension wand."

He reached into the case and pulled out a long plastic tube that reminded him of all the sex instruments he'd just seen at the pornographic house of operations. "I'd love to give Mr. Lamotte a live demonstration," he said. "Wouldn't take more than five minutes; such is the efficiency of Kirby."

"I'm sorry, but Mr. Lamotte is busy at the moment," said the maid.

"Is there a Mrs. Lamotte I could speak with then?"

"She is also indisposed."

"Well, how about you then, madam? I'd bet my bottom dollar

that your daily responsibilities would be cut in half by the power of Kirby."

The maid opened her mouth to answer when a disturbance made her look down. Baker followed her gaze to a naked toddler. He tugged at the maid's apron, thumb in his mouth, saying something that sounded like "Bawa."

"How many times do we have to go over this, Brooks? You are too old for your bottle. Here."

She knelt down and handed the boy the dusty pacifier. He stopped sucking his thumb and immediately got to work on the rubber teet. The maid wrinkled her nose a little and Baker could understand why. The boy stank of feces.

"Brooks, do you need to be cleaned up?" she asked.

"Rosy! Rosy!"

A young girl of about five, wearing a bright magenta dress, practically collided with the maid, holding her nose in an exaggerated fashion. "Brooks made a ca-ca in the playroom again!"

"*Again?*" Rosy seemed to have reached her breaking point for the day. Brooks simply looked up at her with big blue toddler eyes that did not yet understand the severity of his excrement-based actions. "Well, let's go clean it up, then, shall we?"

She lifted Brooks up from the armpits and held him at an arm's length. "I am sorry, Mr. Torrance. You'll have to come back another d—"

"Nonsense, Rosy, old girl!" Baker said. "I won't take no for an answer! You take care of young Brooks there. I'll just wait in here until you're finished. Trust me, you won't be sorry."

Rosy opened her mouth again, probably to say she didn't think that was a very good idea, but before she could get out another word or even slam the door in his face, he stepped over the threshold and into a lobby of marble opulence, lit by a crystal chandelier that probably cost more money than Baker could ever make in a single lifetime. He found a tufted bench that looked more decorative than practical and sat down with the vacuum case between his legs.

"You know," Rosy said. "You really shouldn't sit th—"

"I'll just sit tight while you clean up," Baker said genially.

Still holding Brooks at arm's reach, the defeated Rosy shrugged (she probably wasn't paid enough to argue with door-to-door salesmen who wouldn't take "no" for an answer), closed the front door with one foot, and walked away. The young girl who had informed the maid of Brooks's accident remained in the lobby, staring at Baker with birdlike curiosity.

"Who are you?" she asked, head cocked to one side.

"My name is Charlie Edmund Torrance of the Kirby Vacuum Company," he said with a grin. "And who might you be, young lady?"

"Ansley Lamotte, of course. My daddy does emports."

"You mean imports?"

"Yeah!"

"It's a real pleasure to meet you, Ansley," Baker said. The cavernous interior of the house resulted in a slight echo, and he lowered his voice a little. "Say, would your daddy or mommy happen to be home by any chance?"

"Daddy's in a meeting and Mommy's having her quiet time."

" 'Quiet time'?"

Ansley stretched her legs, started trying to touch her toes. "Yeah, quiet time. Mommy gets real sad sometimes, so she eats her special candy and then has quiet time."

"And who is your daddy in a meeting with?"

Ansley stopped trying to touch her toes and crossed her legs. "I'm not *opposed* to listen to Daddy when he's working. He says it's a big dis...dist..."

"Distraction?"

"Yeah! Rosy says I'm getting real good with the big words. She reads me lots of stories while Mommy has quiet time...She has quiet time *a lot*."

"You sure are getting good with those big words," Baker said encouragingly. "So you don't know who Daddy is talking to right now?"

"I didn't say that! I just said I'm not *opposed* to listen. I was getting my dolly out of her crib and heard him shouting at Arnold."

"Arnold?"

"Yeah, Arnold. You deaf or something, mister?"

"What was your daddy yelling at him about?"

Ansley screwed up her face in concentration. "Daddy called him a 'crazy son of a bitch frog.' But Arnold isn't a frog. He's not green like the ones in my picture books and I never heard him ribbit before."

"Ansley . . . what does Arnold look like?"

"Big and mean," the girl confided.

"Does he have an accent?"

"*Aggs-ent?*" Ansley repeated, stumbling over the word.

"Does he talk funny?"

"Oh . . . oh, yeah! He always calls me *my cherry* when he sees me. I'm not a cherry!"

"Hey, I've got an idea," Baker said, brightening up. He reached into his pocket and pulled out a Hershey's chocolate bar. "Do you like candy, Ansley?"

"I sure do!"

"Well, I just so happen to have an extra candy bar here. Would you like it?"

"Gee, that's mighty nice of you, mister." She accepted the candy, tore off the wrapping, and let it fall to the floor without hesitation. "Daddy doesn't really let me have candy. He says it's no good for my *glue-kiss*."

"Then it'll be our little secret, Ansley," Baker said, giving her a dramatic wink. "All I ask in return is that you give me directions to the bathroom. Can you do that?"

"Course I can," she said, her mouth now full of chocolate. "Do I look like I'm three?"

"Of course not. How silly of me."

"It's next to the big fish," she said, pointing a chocolate-coated finger down the vast hallway.

"Big fish?"

"Yeah! The big fish that lives on the wall."

"Much obliged, Ansley. I'll be right back, okay?"

Baker left the girl and vacuum behind, passing hand-carved vases, potted plants that seemed to grow right out of the walls, elegant paintings, and strange ornaments whose purpose he could only guess at.

What he didn't see were any family photographs of Brooks, Ansley, or Mr. and Mrs. Lamotte. The "big fish" turned out to be a mounted marlin (doomed to spend eternity as a signpost of the porcelain throne). The small gold plaque beneath proclaimed that the fish had been caught by Orson Chester Lamotte on a fishing trip in 1951.

He did not need to use the bathroom, of course, but started to do what he did best: snoop. In addition to branching off in a half-dozen different directions, the passageway also contained a multitude of doors. Some were storage closets—for coats, golf clubs, and children's toys—while others led to spare rooms larger than Baker's entire apartment. And this was just the first floor. He couldn't even imagine what awaited a person on the upper levels.

At the very end of the passageway was a set of oaken double doors resembling massive chocolate bars. They were slightly ajar, and Baker could hear gentle music from within. Quietly as he could, he crept inside a cozy drawing room decorated with the most magnificent Christmas tree he'd ever seen.

Lights of every color blinked on and off in lazy succession. Baubles the size of ostrich eggs stuck out from between thick layers of tinsel and holly. A glass star sat atop the tree, reflecting the illumination around the room in kaleidoscopic splendor. To top everything off, a model train ran around a track circling the base, letting out real puffs of smoke. It was a goyishe kid's wet dream.

Frank Sinatra warbled out of a large, Depression-era radio set, wishing the listener a merry little Christmas and promising that their troubles were, from now on, miles away. Baker was so blown away by the magnificence of the display that he almost failed to notice the motionless body on the chaise lounge under the window.

It was a young woman (in her late twenties or early thirties, Baker guessed), her eyes glassy and vacant.

"Um...hello," he said. "Sorry for interrupting."

The woman did not answer. Baker moved closer, taking in the dilated pupils and insipid smile.

"Miss, can you hear me?"

Still no answer. He bent down and listened for any sound of breathing. Hearing none, he took her wrist and felt for a pulse. His fingers detected a faint thump. Clutched in the woman's limp hand was an envelope from the Banc of California. He began reaching for it when a voice of restrained fury gave him pause.

"I do beg your pardon, but that's my wife you're examining."

Baker turned around to face the man he'd come here to see. A man he immediately recognized from the papers and television.

Orson Lamotte was tall and handsome with high cheekbones, impossibly straight eyebrows, and a full head of strawberry-blond hair neatly parted to the side. He looked every bit the suave businessman, though today he was dressed a little more casually, trading his usual double-breasted suits, designer shoes, and silver cigarette case for a green-and-black smoking jacket, loose-fitting pajama pants, fuzzy house slippers, and a Meerschaum pipe.

"What's wrong with her?" Baker asked, standing up. "She's barely got a pulse. Does she need a doctor?"

"No," Lamotte said with a grimace, his teeth tightening around the pipe. He walked over to the lounge chair, snatched the envelope out of the woman's hand, and stuffed it into his pocket. "She's fine. Please come away from her, sir."

"I am very sorry to barge in on you like this, Mr. Lamotte. But I'm—"

"The reason why my daughter's mouth is currently smeared with chocolate?"

"Well, yes. But—"

"Then I take it you are unaware that she is a Type-1 diabetic who would have died a horrible death just now, had I not given her an emergency injection of insulin?"

"Oh Christ. I had no idea that—"

"I also take it you are not a vacuum salesman as you so claimed to my maid?"

"No, but—"

"Then tell me why I should not be calling the police to arrest you at this very moment?"

"I'm here about Elizabeth Short."

Baker couldn't tell if Lamotte's eyes flashed with recognition at the mention of Liz's name or if it had simply been a trick of the blinking Christmas lights.

"I'm sorry. To whom are you referring?"

Baker looked over at Lamotte's wife before lowering his voice. "I don't mean to come into your home and call you a liar, Mr. Lamotte, but I know about you and Liz."

Lamotte removed the pipe from his mouth and seemed to size Baker up with an intense, probing gaze he probably used to intimidate competitors and underlings.

"Very well," Lamotte said after a moment's contemplation. "But let's have this conversation on the veranda, if you please."

Baker nodded and followed Lamotte out of the drawing room. The tycoon gave one last despondent look at his nonresponsive wife lying on the lounge chair and closed the doors.

CHAPTER 24

Lamotte led him through a kitchen of spotless chrome, where Rosy was fixing a ham and cheese sandwich for Ansley. The girl's fingers and mouth had been cleaned of chocolate. Baker gave Rosy a sheepish grin, which the maid returned with a glower. Brooks sat in a nearby high chair, blowing bubbles and turning his lunch of roast turkey and mushy peas into an arts and crafts project.

"Did you find the fish, mister?" Ansley asked eagerly, turning around on her stool to address Baker.

"I sure did," he said. "Thank you."

Lamotte paid his two children no mind, opening the door to a broad stone veranda that overlooked acres and acres of orange grove that ran behind the house.

"Have a seat," he said, gesturing to a wicker table, where an ornate metal tray of orange juice, coffee, and scones rested. "Help yourself. That orange juice was squeezed fresh this morning."

"Got anything stronger than OJ?"

"I can have Rosy bring out a selection of spirits if that is your pleasure."

Baker sat down while Lamotte moved over to the railing, resting his palms upon it. An embattled ruler surveying a tiny fraction of his magnificent kingdom.

"So what it is you want?" he asked. "Money, I presume? Name your price."

"No, it's nothing like that."

"If blackmail is not on the agenda, sir, then what is the purpose of your visit?"

"I'm not sure how to tell you this, Mr. Lamotte, but Elizabeth Short is dead."

"What?" The man's voice carried an unmistakable note of disbelief.

"I'm very sorry, Mr. Lamotte, but it's the truth," Baker continued. "The LAPD found her body in the river gully yesterday. She was murdered."

Lamotte turned around, his handsome face aghast.

"How can you be sure?"

"I saw the body myself," said Baker, making a calculated decision to withhold gruesome details of the mutilated corpse.

"I guess I'll be needing a stiff drink, too, then," Lamotte said. "Excuse me for a moment, please."

He disappeared inside the house and returned several minutes later with a decanter of amber liquid, two glasses, a seltzer dispenser, and a small bucket of ice.

"How do you take your whiskey, sir?"

"In a glass," said Baker.

"King's Ransom," said Lamotte, pouring a healthy measure into each cup. "Aptly named, given the cost, but only the finest if we'll be drinking to Lizzie's memory."

They clinked and drank deeply. The whiskey was smooth, offering a welcome internal warmth on the chilly veranda. Lamotte refilled their glasses, took a more reserved sip.

"And your name would be . . . ?"

"Morris Baker. I'm a PI."

Lamotte raised his eyebrows. "What was your connection to Lizzie?"

"To be quite frank, Mr. Lamotte, we used to see each other for the better part of a decade. But that might as well be ancient history. I take it she never mentioned me?"

"Not that I can recall, no."

"I don't blame her. Things didn't end all that great between us."

"You say she was murdered? Have the police apprehended any suspects?"

"Not yet. A good friend of mine is leading the case, but I'm conducting my own little side investigation just to cover all the bases. I don't think the LAPD knows about your affair with Liz. Not yet anyway."

"And how, pray tell, Mr. Baker, did you find out?"

Baker dodged the question with a sip of whiskey. The drink went down the wrong pipe and he started coughing. And once the coughing started these days, it was hard to stop. Lamotte leaned forward to give him a firm pat on the back. Baker brought a handkerchief to his lips, hastily wiping away the bloody residue.

"Easy now, old boy," said Lamotte. "Easy now. You quite all right?"

"Yes, my apologies. Look, Mr. Lamotte—I really didn't mean to barge in on you and your family like this, but I did care for Liz, even if she did write me off as a bad job. Do you have any idea of who might have wanted to hurt her?"

Lamotte's face seemed to darken at the question. He crossed his legs and said, "If I didn't know better, Mr. Baker, I'd say you are implying I had something to do with her death."

"Of course not. It's just that I was told you loved her very much. Loved her enough to leave your wife, in fact."

"I don't know with whom you have been speaking, but I can assure you I had no intention of leaving my wife."

"Is that so?"

"Indeed," said Lamotte, placing his glass down and reaching for his pipe. His hands were quite steady. "I won't deny that I enjoyed a small...fling, we'll call it, with Lizzie. But like the brightest candle, it only burned half as long. You see, it was not *I* who wanted me to leave my wife, it was Lizzie. I came to my senses and told her our arrangement could not continue. My wife is unwell, as you just saw for yourself, and it would have been unfair to continue harming her and my children."

"I imagine Liz didn't take that well?" Baker said.

"Not in the slightest," answered Lamotte, lighting the tobacco in his pipe and giving it a small puff. "'Hell hath no fury like a woman scorned,' as Congreve put it. Lizzie turned nasty at the end and threatened to expose our affair to my wife and the press."

"How did you respond?"

"How any man of my socioeconomic standing would. I offered a monetary settlement to keep her quiet."

"She's quiet now, all right."

"As you have just informed me."

"When's the last time you spoke with her?"

"Around mid-November."

"No disrespect meant, but her death would be the best outcome for someone in your position, Mr. Lamotte. The secret stays under wraps and you get to keep the money. Not a bad deal." Realizing he was thinking out loud, Baker quickly added, "Not that I'm accusing you of—"

"Ah, but there you go heavily insinuating again," Lamotte said with a rueful smile. "Take a walk with me."

Lamotte stood, prompting Baker to guzzle down the last of his whiskey and follow. They left the veranda down a set of winding set of stone steps and onto the soft, loamy soil of the orange grove below. Lamotte didn't seem to mind that his slippers were becoming saturated with dirt. A man of his—what did he call it?—"socioeconomic standing"? He probably had an endless supply of them in a bedroom closet the size of a small cathedral.

"This weather has been a right pain in the backside, I can tell you," Lamotte said, stopping by one of the trees and caressing some of its lower leaves. "Orange trees require tender love and care in the form of nitrogen-rich fertilizer, hammock soil, and a great deal of sunshine. I am not sure how much longer these trees will be able to hold out for if this blasted cold spell doesn't break."

"Good thing you have that little shipping business of yours to fall back on," said Baker, admiring a clump of nearby oranges. Up close, they looked pale and sickly.

"Ha!" Lamotte chuckled. "Very good, Mr. Baker. But agriculture and horticulture are in my blood. My ancestors tended some of the finest vineyards in the south of France before they came to this country. My father made his fortune buying up and reinvigorating farms in the Dust Bowl during the Great Depression. Worked with Roosevelt to alleviate rampant starvation. He made his way across the entire country until settling here."

Lamotte moved on, heading for a large greenhouse. They stepped inside and Baker immediately found it necessary to loosen his tie. It was stiflingly hot amid all the exotic flora in here. Sweat broke out on his forehead and under his armpits. Lamotte, on the other hand, seemed unbothered by the humidity. The man was in his element.

"Tell me about yourself, Mr. Baker," he said, lifting a nearby watering can and using it to quench the thirst of some violently purple orchids.

"Not much to tell," said Baker, removing his jacket and placing it over a chair whose spindly legs were wrapped up in the tendrils of some creeping plant.

"Oh, I very much doubt that," said Lamotte.

"I was a homicide detective with the LAPD until late 1958," Baker answered. "I quit before they could fire me for insubordination. I seem to have a knack for it."

"I always did myself," said Lamotte. "Never could quite follow the rules. And I couldn't help but notice your accent. You are not American?"

"Czechoslovakian."

"Jewish, too, if I may be so bold?"

"Right on the money, Mr. Lamotte. How'd you guess?"

"Why else would a man willingly leave behind a comfortable union job with a pension?"

"It's easier for a Yid to operate as a gumshoe these days—assuming he's able to get a license."

"You are a man who enjoys his own autonomy. I can respect that. Life is all about control—seizing it where you can and ceding it where you cannot," said Lamotte. "This greenhouse is a perfect example of that philosophy. I alone control the temperature and humidity at all times. These plants are at my mercy. Sadly, the same cannot be said for my beloved orange trees, which must bow to the meteorological whims of Mother Nature."

Lamotte moved over to a terra-cotta planter and let out a small exclamation of delight. He beckoned Baker over to view a number of plants whose petals resembled a pair of inflamed lips dotted with long, spiky frills along either side. Not a very pleasant thing to look at.

"Venus flytraps," Lamotte breathed. "Watch closely."

Both men leaned forward just in time to see a thimble-size housefly crawling across the surface of the petals. The insect beat its wings, ready for takeoff, when the lips of the plant snapped shut, sealing the fly's fate. Baker could just see the insect's tiny legs sticking out from between the toothy frills like a prisoner rattling a tin mug against the bars of his cell.

"Power and control," Lamotte said with a grin. He straightened back up and replaced the pipe between his teeth. "We are all the fly at one time or another, Mr. Baker. We aimlessly buzz around this world, hoping to land safely. Sometimes we do and other times . . . well, we find ourselves where we shouldn't be. Tragic, yet quite uncontrollable. Biology at its most ferocious and uncaring. Now, if you don't mind, I must be getting back—"

"One last question, Mr. Lamotte."

"Certainly."

Baker hesitated. He suddenly felt like the fly, a minuscule creature wandering across the open maw of a hungry predator much larger than himself. Hopefully he'd be able to buzz off before the jaw snapped shut.

"Does the name *Henry Kissinger* mean anything to you?"

Lamotte's smile faltered slightly, and not for the first time, Baker got the sense that the man had been caught off guard.

"No, I don't believe so. Should it?"

"He's a consultant for the State Department. Works with Nixon."

Lamotte shook his head. "I am afraid you still find me at a loss, sir."

"I just thought that maybe, given your line of work . . ."

"I don't work in politics, Mr. Baker."

"I meant that since your company operates all over the world . . ."

"Mr. Baker, I have entertained your little game for longer than I care to admit. If you dare come near me or my family again, brandishing outrageous accusations of infidelity and murder, I can promise that you will be hearing from my attorneys as well as HUAC. I'm sure you are aware that I can make life very difficult for someone of your . . . ethnic background."

Baker was at a momentary loss for words. Lamotte's demeanor had changed with the unnerving speed of a Venus flytrap detecting a juicy morsel.

"That won't be necessary," Baker said. "I'm sorry to have bothered you, Mr. Lamotte. Thank you for your time."

He retrieved his suit jacket off the chair and was nearly out of the greenhouse when another thought occurred to him.

"Before I go, I'd like to ask you about Arnold."

"Who?" Lamotte said, taken aback.

"The particularly large Frenchman in your employ."

"I don't have—"

"Don't bother denying that one, Mr. Lamotte. Your daughter spilled the beans when I got here. Said you were leaning into him pretty hard earlier."

"Fine. I'll admit as much. A man can scream in his own home if he so pleases. Or has the law changed?"

"Not that I'm aware of."

"Then what are you driving at?"

"The 'crazy son of a bitch Frog' Ansley mentioned. Does the man spend time around prostitutes?"

"You mean like the pretty little thing sitting in your car right now?" asked Lamotte, now adopting a self-satisfied smile.

"Top-notch surveillance you have around here," Baker said. "The woman in my car is none of your business, but I'll play along. Your man have a weakness for girls like her?"

"The leisure time activities of those in my employ is none of my concern, Mr. Baker. Now if you don't leave the property this very instant—"

"Thank you for your time, Mr. Lamotte."

The fresh, cold air filled his tight lungs, cleared his head a little. He walked back to the car among the dense cover of the dying orange trees, thinking.

With Ann Kissinger turning out to be a fraud, his obligation to track down Henry was no longer necessary. But someone had gone to all the trouble of hiring him to locate the man.

What was more: The person who had hired the counterfeit Ann was a burly Frenchman who, unless Baker was very much mistaken, was on the payroll of one Orson Lamotte.

That felt a little flimsy on its own, though. After all, he had not questioned this "Arnold," let alone met him. Baker might have been inclined to drop the whole thing, had it not been for the Lamotte Exports business card found in Kissinger's hotel room.

Pair that with the man's alarming reaction to the mere mention of Kissinger's name, and something definitely didn't sit right. Orson

Lamotte may not have had a hand in Liz's death—after all, the man's version of events jived with Baker's own memories of the woman—but the orange-growing mogul almost certainly had a connection to Henry Kissinger.

"How was your meeting?" Debbie asked once he was back behind the wheel. "Hope you had a grand old time. Me? I've been bored out of my mind here. No radio or anyth—hey, you okay?"

"Yeah, why?" Baker asked her.

"Do you not hear the way you're breathing right now? You sound like an old accordion."

Baker dropped Debbie off at home. He grabbed her arm before she could step out of the car.

"Be careful," he said.

"Of what?"

"I'm not entirely sure. But it's only a matter of time until someone learns you were roommates with Liz. The police may have already tried to stop by while we were out."

"So? I don't have anything to hide."

"You do now. When someone comes asking questions about Liz, don't mention my name or where we were today. Say you were out working the Boulevard and make sure you have a trusted friend or two who can corroborate you were there."

"Why?"

"Because if it gets back to the killer that people close to Liz are conducting their own investigation, then we're both in danger."

"I'm not conducting—"

"I know you're not. But the murderer won't give a shit. They'll only see you as another loose end."

"You tryna scare me?"

"I'm trying to put you on your guard," Baker said. "Promise you'll keep an eye out and call me if anything seems off."

"I promise, *Dad*."

"Debbie..."

"I said I would. Geez! What do you want? A sworn statement?"

"Couldn't hurt, but I'll settle on your word for now."

She tried to leave, tugging at his grasp, but he stayed her with another question.

"You gonna be okay? You must still be in shock. It's not fair to ask you to deal with this all by yourself. Would you like to stay at my apartment for a while? As my guest, of course—not as..."

"An easy lay?" offered Debbie.

"Are you going to be all right?"

"I don't think it's fully sunk in yet, to tell the truth," she said wearily. "But I don't think running away from the apartment I shared with her is going to do me any good, either. I just want to take a long bath and go to bed."

"Sounds like a good plan. I'm here if you need me. Don't hesitate to call if it becomes too much. Do you have my number?"

"I don't think so."

"Hold on."

He reached into the back seat and found the notebook of monogrammed stationery Joanna had given him when they first opened the private investigation business together. It was completely unused. Jotting down his number and home address under his own ornately printed initials, he tore out the page and handed it over to Debbie.

"Thanks," she said. "Take care of yourself, Morris."

"You, too."

Debbie got out of the car, slamming the door behind her.

CHAPTER 25

Hoping to put off his visit to Dr. Ehrlich for as long as possible, Baker stopped by Merv's Diner in Angelino Heights. Owned by the gruff, yet lovable military veteran, Merv Pachenko, the establishment had acquired a sort of religious status after Baker's miniature insurrection nearly two summers before. Avid listeners of Edward R. Murrow's Liberty Boys broadcasts made pilgrimages here from all over the state just to see where McCarthy's Boys had been forced to make a hasty retreat by the forgotten citizens of Los Angeles.

Others, mostly young kids looking to piss off their conservative parents, were drawn to the rebellious aura of the place. Since the summer of '58, Merv's had been considered the unofficial hangout spot for the city's teenagers—from preppy girls in poodle skirts to upstart greasers who tucked packs of cigarettes into the sleeves of their undershirts.

It was a modern-day Lexington and Concord, which suited Mr. Pachenko just fine. The unexpected uptick in business over the last seventeen months allowed the one-legged proprietor to expand the dining room and hire a battalion of roller-skating waitresses who delivered take-out orders to hungry customers on the go.

There was even buzz of a potential franchise.

Almost overnight, Merv's had gone from a sleepy neighborhood joint to the talk of the town. But as the crowds at the diner grew, Baker's interest in eating there waned. It had nothing to do with Merv's cooking, which remained as delicious as it ever was.

No, it came down to the fear that someone might recognize him and ask for an autograph, or a detailed account of the night Sophia died. That was still too painful to revisit, and besides, if he began running his mouth about the Black Symphony, he'd be putting innocent lives in danger. These were the same monsters who had murdered an eighteen-year-old boy named Oliver Shelton, whose only sin had been delivering a letter to Baker's front door.

Baker did not discuss the events of July 4, 1958, with anyone, except, of course, with those who had been directly involved like Merv and Joanna. He was a celebrity among the Liberty Boys crowd and made sure to give the places where they were known to congregate a wide berth.

The wild theories some of them came up with assured anyone within a 500-foot radius that they had to be nuttier than squirrel shit. Maybe that was why the Hueys allowed the hubbub to continue; they didn't consider the crazies worth their time. Or maybe Merv was simply paying HUAC protection money out of his entrepreneurial windfall.

Capitalism at work!

The anonymity afforded to him at the Golden Fowl and other eateries throughout Chinatown suited Baker just fine. With that said, he would need to risk his own privacy for a little chat with Merv.

The parking lot was packed with automobiles of every size, shape, color. Some had obviously been souped up with more powerful engines and other accoutrements by drivers who liked to race on the underground circuit for pink slips.

Hot rods were their most prized possessions and they rarely left the driver's seat, preferring to order burgers, sodas, fries, and shakes via the array of two-way intercoms Merv had installed throughout the blacktop. That's where the roller-skating waitresses came in; they popped in and out of the diner, affixing heaping trays of food to open car windows.

Japanese and American flags were stuck to every hood. Even the kids, usually so apathetic to the larger goings-on of the world around them, had clearly been caught up in the excitement of the Kishi visit. The deep red orb of the Japanese flag—so much like a setting sun on an airless summer evening—furled and unfurled dozens of times over, bending to the mercy of the frigid wind.

Baker squeezed the Continental in between a Ford Nucleon and a canary yellow 5-Window Coupe. Their owners—a broad-chested teen (come to think of it, the kid was probably in his twenties) wiping his hands with a grease-stained rag and a stockier boy in a plaid shirt—were deep in discussion about a girl, whom Plaid Shirt was describing as "the most perfect, dazzling creature" he'd ever seen.

"Dazzling, huh?" replied Grease-Stained Rag, admiring his reflection in the coupe's sleek paint job. "I think you're losing it, Curt."

Plaid Shirt countered that the girl in question had mouthed *I love you* through the window of her own car and accused his friend of having no soul.

"I don't know much about romance, Curt, but I can tell you that I've only got one soul mate and she's right here," said Grease-Stained Rag, gesturing to his car and swiping at an errant smudge on the hood.

"You really are something else, you know that?" said Plaid Shirt. "My future wife is out there and all you can think about is your precious ride?"

"Relax, would ya?" said his friend, lighting up a cigarette. "I'm sure she'll show up here at some point."

Baker left them to it and stepped onto the curb, where a large sign he initially mistook for a menu board gave him pause.

NO JEWS, KOREANS, CHINESE, or BLACKS
ALLOWED BEYOND THIS POINT
(JAPANESE WELCOME!)
All patrons must be ready to submit to a protractor
examination
Temperatures will also be taken to test for the Yang Flu

Below that was a handy reference chart on how to properly recognize "Asian eyes slants" (down to precise degrees of measurement), acceptable skin tones, and Jewish nose length.

Suddenly feeling ill, Baker passed the sign and walked into the crowded diner, alive with the sounds of music and youthful merriment. Teenagers still enjoying their Christmas vacation danced in time to the Penguins' "Earth Angel," which poured from the blinking jukebox like sewage from a busted pipe. The pretty girls clung to the jocks while the nerds and wimps watched enviously from the counter, letting their burgers grow cold as beads of perspiration rolled down their glasses of cherry cola.

He approached the counter, where a pretty waitress held a piping hot carafe full of black coffee. A genuine menu board sat against the wall, promising a number of tantalizing blue plate specials: chipped beef, chicken à la king, tuna noodle casserole, Swedish meatballs, and in honor of Kishi's visit, uni. Whatever that meant.

"Can I help you, hon?" asked the waitress.

"Yeah, you can," said Baker, leaning over the counter. "What the hell is uni?" The strange word came out as "uh-knee."

"*Oo-ni*," she corrected him. "It's sea urchin gonads."

"People really eat *that*?"

"I've heard the Japs do. We haven't sold a single order since I wrote it down on the board a week ago. Now what can I get you?"

"I'm here to see Merv. He working today?"

"When is he ever not?" The waitress turned around and called through the kitchen's service window. "Merv, honey! Someone here to see you!"

Merv Pachenko's sweaty and jowled face, covered in bristly five o'clock shadow, appeared.

"What is it, Norma?" She answered by sticking a finger out at Baker. "Morris!" the diner's proprietor exclaimed joyfully. "What a surprise."

"Hello, Merv," Baker said with a smile.

"Take a seat, I'll be right there. Norma, be sure to set him up with a cup of coffee and whatever else he wants."

Baker squeezed himself into a booth far away from the dancing teens. Norma poured him a steaming mug of joe and asked, "What else can I get ya, honey? Merv isn't usually so generous."

"Coffee's fine, thanks."

"If you're sure..."

Norma drifted off to take care of other customers. Merv stumped over two minutes later, wiping his beefy hands on an apron that might've been white once upon a time. His fake wooden leg, standing in for the appendage he'd lost to a land mine in Korea, had been replaced with a sturdy metal one.

"New leg?" Baker asked as Merv slid into the booth (not an easy feat with his large belly).

"Aluminum alloy," Merv said with a grunt, his voluminous bottom filling up the leather seat. "Same stuff they used on the rocket ship to the moon."

"I take it business is good then?"

"Booming."

Norma returned and slid a large plate with a bacon double cheeseburger and fries in front of Baker. She also put down a shallow bowl lined with what looked like squishy orange tongues.

"It's on the house," Merv said. "You look thin."

"You could've given my mother lessons," Baker said, munching on a fry and, realizing how hungry he was, attacked the cheeseburger with vigor. "What's in the bowl?"

"Uni," Merv said with a chuckle. "Norma said you asked about it."

"I'll stick with the burger," said Baker, and Merv shrugged.

"Don't care much for the stuff myself," he said, "but they say it's an aphrodisiac."

"A what?"

"A dish that puts the ram back in your rod, if you know what I mean."

"I'll take your word for it," said Baker, pushing the bowl of sea urchin gonads away from his plate. "By the way," he added, his mouth full of ground beef, cheese, and smoked pork belly, "real cute sign you got out front."

"Oh, that malarkey? Hueys made me put it up. Scout's honor. Gotta keep the bastards happy if I don't want them to shut me down. I don't even know what a fuckin' protractor is."

"I wondered how you were able to stay in business after what we did."

"They wanted to shut me down, let me tell you. But once word got out about what happened... well, even the dodos over at HUAC know a good business opportunity when they see it. Anyway, what can I do for you, Morris?"

"You can help translate this for me," Baker said, putting down the burger and extracting the Lamotte Exports card from his wallet. He flipped it over in one hand like a magician doing a spectacular card trick, displaying the string of Korean characters stamped there.

"Wow," said Merv, taking the card and holding it up to the light for a better look. "Haven't seen Korean in a good long while."

"Can you translate it?"

"I'm a bit rusty, but sure. I believe it says 'gumiho.'"

"Come again?"

"Gumiho," Merv repeated. "It means nine-tailed fox."

"Do those exist?"

"No—they're mythical. Said to be shape-shifters who take the form of a beautiful woman in order to lull gullible young men to their doom."

"Sounds like every woman I've ever dated."

Merv let out a hollow laugh, still gazing at the characters. "'Taint right what we're doing over there," he said, handing the card back to Baker.

"Where? In Korea?" Baker said, trying to coax some ketchup out of its bottle and onto his fries.

"Aye," said Merv, his eyes glistening with memory. Beyond the story of losing his leg, Baker had never heard the man speak of his combat experience in East Asia.

"The things I saw and did over there...we became monsters. Can you believe that? I think you can, Morris. You of all people know what we're capable of when reason melts away like butter on the flattop. Rape, murder, torture...all of it becomes fair game. Then *boom*!"

He slapped the table, causing the saltshaker to spill over.

"Your leg is blown off and it's like—I don't know—like a spell is broken or something. They send you home, give you a pat on the back, a flimsy piece of bronze for valor, and a nice chunk of change through the G.I. Bill. Then you're on your own. Don't let the door hit you on the way out. You wake up in your own bed, shaking and drenched with sweat, telling yourself over and over that it was all just a bad dream. That none of it was real. But you know deep down it weren't no dream. You're free from the carnage, but some other kid's taken your place. It's endless."

"I'm sorry, Merv," Baker said, putting the business card away. "I really didn't mean to reopen old wounds."

Merv, who still had that haunted, faraway look on his face, did not respond.

"The most fucked-up part is, you're never really free. That shit never washes off. I'd never admit this anyone else, but far as I'm concerned, that young man blowing himself up in the department store is us getting our just deserts. We deserve it and so much more."

The ensuing silence hung heavier than all the bacon fat in the air. A gaggle of greasers at a nearby table were swapping dirty jokes and braying with donkey-ish laughter. Baker heard one of them telling the rest of the group that he planned on hightailing his ass to Canada if his draft number came up. His friends laughed, though it felt impossible that anyone could be happy at a time like this. Not when Merv was spilling his guts like an eviscerated soldier on the battlefield.

Baker slid his plate away, no longer hungry. "Merv," he said, "I'm so sorry."

"Ji-Ho."

"What?"

"Her name was Ji-Ho."

"Who was?"

"The person who taught me about 'gumiho.' When my leg went kablooey, the mine attracted some nearby NoKos."

"NoKos?"

"Military slang for North Koreans. Some of the guys just referred to 'em as 'Nicole.' My unit sought refuge at a nearby village of friendly rice farmers. We couldn't go far because I was hemorrhaging pretty bad. We posted up there, laying low for a few weeks until I was well enough to be moved, and that's where I met her. The most wonderful woman I'd ever come across before or since. Ji-Ho was one of the few villagers who knew a bit of English and she would assist the medic, wiping the sweat off my brow and lulling me to sleep with Korean folk stories."

"Like gumiho," Baker said.

"Yep. By the time we were about to head out, I had fallen head over heels. Promised her I'd come back and make her my wife."

Baker had a sense of where the story was headed.

"And then, out of nowhere, my CO gets it in his head that the villagers are stashing weapons for the NoKos. I objected; put up one hell of a fight for someone in my condition, but the medic was ordered to give me morphine until I went quiet."

Merv's voice quavered, cracked. "Ji-Ho was lined up and shot with the others. The entire village was burned to the ground. That's the way it was told to me anyway. By the time I came to, the village was nothing but a heap of smoldering cinders. Turns out there were no weapons. The CO had just snapped. I tried to get the bastard court-martialed once I got stateside, but it was his word against that of a doped-up cripple."

"The dope didn't stop in Korea, did it?" asked Baker.

"No," said Merv, helping himself to one of Baker's French fries—not necessarily because he really wanted it, but because it was something to do. An excuse not to look at the other person while in such a vulnerable state.

"I used up a good chunk of my G.I. Bill on smack once I got back. Anything to numb the pain, you know? But chasing the high only got harder and harder."

"How'd you kick the habit?"

"I found my calling in hospitality. An old fella by the name of Johnston picked me up outta the gutter, got me clean, and put a spatula in my hand. I've never felt more comfortable than I have over a stove. He co-signed on the loan for this place once I was ready to strike out on my own. I owe that man everything. Never considered myself much of a religious man, but if angels ever walked among us, I'd reckon ol' Johnston was one of 'em."

"Merv," said Baker tenderly, "I never knew any of this."

"Ain't your fault. It's not something I usually prattle on about. But it feels good to talk about it with someone after all this time. To—"

"To admit that it actually happened," finished Baker.

"Knew you'd understand, Morris. Not all of us are so lucky to have a Johnston looking out for us, though. See that poor bastard over there?"

Merv leveled a finger at a table next to the restrooms (quite literally, the shittiest seat in the joint), where a haggard specimen in a shabby Army jacket sucked down a bowl of vegetable soup. The man's bloodshot eyes kept darting back and forth, as though he were expecting a sneak attack at any moment.

"Most of us end up like that," Merv continued.

"You try giving him a spatula?"

"Yes, actually. Said he didn't need my pity. We're sent off to fight in a war we've got nothing to do with until we're dead or outlive our usefulness. The only thing we're good for after that is a shelter. I gotta be honest with ya, Morris, I envy those who didn't make it out alive."

Baker could relate. He'd come to the United States because of its reputation for freedom and blind justice. It all sounded good on a piece of crumbling parchment, but those ideals seemed to mean nothing to the people entrusted to put them into practice. Personal freedoms could be violated, lives snuffed out, war criminals given safe haven—all in the name of security and freedom. But what was the definition of freedom anymore? It was whatever those in charge said it was. Up is down. Down is up. Better dead than red.

"Morris...? You still with me, pal?"

"Huh?" Baker looked up to see Merv eyeing him concernedly. "You say something?"

"I said I've got a good idea what that little business card of yours might mean."

"I'm listening."

"Now that I'm one of the most sought-after restauranteurs in town..." Baker mimicked the toot of a horn and Merv laughed. "Well, I've become aware of some of the other hot joints throughout the city. One of them recently opened up in Fairfax. Highly exclusive spot—Korean-themed and invitation only. They've had to keep a low-profile for...obvious reasons."

"What's the name of the place?"

"What else?" said Merv. "The Nine-Tailed Fox."

CHAPTER 26

Could just be a coincidence," Baker said.

"Don't think so," countered Merv. "Unless I'm very much mistaken, you've got yourself a ticket into that club."

"Who runs it?"

"No clue. I just hear bits and pieces through my delivery guys."

"Got an address at least?"

"Somewhere on Fairfax Avenue."

"Real precise, Merv. Think I'll find 'somewhere on Fairfax Avenue' in the phone book?"

"That's all I know! Scout's honor."

"Guess I'll just have to go door-to-door until I find it."

"Be careful. This place doesn't keep a low-profile for nothin'."

Baker thanked Merv for his help and the free meal and tried to hightail it out of the diner as quickly as he could. Sadly, he wasn't fast enough because the twitchy Korea vet abandoned his bowl of soup and stopped him at the front door.

"Eyyy!" said the man, blowing a puff of rank air into Baker's face. Merv didn't sell alcohol, but it smelled like this fella had thrown back an entire cask of beer. "I know you!" *Hic!* "You're Baker, right?"

"Uhhh," said Baker. "Not sure who you're talking about. Excuse m—"

"Come on!" the guy shouted, drawing the attention of more patrons, who spun around on their stools and booth seats with interest. "I know it's you. I heard ya talkin' with Merv. You're the"—*hic!*—"one that stopped the A-bomb from going off back in '58, right?"

"Sorry, don't know what you're talking about."

"Don't play dumb," said the man, closing his eyes and shaking his head. "I heard it on the radio. You stopped those aliens from detonating the bomb at the Observatory."

"*Aliens?*" Baker asked, not sure he had heard the man correctly. "I...uh...I heard it was Germans. Ex-Nazis employed by the United States."

"No, no," the man replied stubbornly. "It was aliens from outer space who just looked like Nazis. It's all a"—*hic!*—"misdirect."

"That's nonsense," said Baker, his anger rising. "Where did you even hear that?"

"Don't matter, but it's"—*hic!*—"true. They wanna take over the planet. Figure if they set off some A-bombs all over the place, it'll wipe us out and they can take over. Whoever's left will be brainwashed to do their bidding. It's already happening. McCarthy and Nixon are part of it. So's Khrushchev. Lizard men straight outta Area 51! They took my friends, abducted them right off the street! Been getting away with it for years!"

"You're nuts."

"What'd you just"—*hic!*—call me?"

"N-U-T-S," Baker said, spelling out the word. "Need me to go fetch one of the lizard men to simplify it for you?"

The drunk took a wild swing. Had he not been thoroughly inebriated, his fist might have actually landed on Baker's jaw. Baker sidestepped and the man lost his balance, toppling forward and knocking a nearby jock into his chocolate sundae. The kid—a towering linebacker of a specimen probably named "Moose"—pulled his face out of the cold, sludgy mess. The sprinkles and hot fudge coating his face gave off the impression of a rare skin disorder.

"Who. Did. That?" he demanded, snorting like a bull about to charge.

The diner had gone completely silent, excluding the jukebox, which belted out "Rubber Biscuit" by the Chips. Everyone—Baker included—pointed a finger at the would-be pugilist.

The ice cream–covered jock wiped his face with the sleeve of his varsity jacket, picked up what remained of the sundae, and brought it down on the drunk's head. Someone yelled "*Food fight!*" and the diner erupted into open, culinary warfare. Burgers, soda, onion rings, and more ice cream flew through the air.

"*What the hell is going on?*" shouted Merv, who had just limped into the middle of the chaos and received a face full of chipped beef for his troubles.

"Sorry, Merv!" Baker called, stepping over the limp form of the knocked-out veteran. The shattered remains of the ice cream dish twinkled bloodily in his hair. "Put it on my tab!"

Baker felt a little guilty for helping start the fight, but that man deserved it. During their first meeting together, Rabbi Kahn said something along the lines of "*The downtrodden people of this country now know they can count on you for help when they're in trouble.*"

This had led Baker to believe that people—at least those who tuned into Murrow's hijacking broadcasts—were a little more informed about what those in power could do when they thought no one was looking. Maybe some did subscribe to that way of thinking, but he couldn't help shaking the feeling that the belligerent man in the diner was not an outlier.

Without the existence of concrete proof, listeners would spin their own wild interpretations of what had occurred on that fateful night in July 1958. It made it that much easier for the government to discount Murrow's proclamations of truth as outlandish hogwash from an unhinged ham radio enthusiast in a rotting basement somewhere.

Baker did not remember much of the twenty-minute drive to Dr. Ehrlich's small office in Boyle Heights. Most of that mental haze was due to another tablet of phenobarbital washed down with a freshly opened bottle of peach schnapps. He must've been more out of it than he thought because he collapsed as soon as he stepped into the cozy waiting room.

The secretary yelped in fright and called for the nurse to come right away. Baker didn't mind; he was enjoying the ethereal numbness of pill and booze. When a nurse did crouch down to inspect him, he heard himself wheeze, barely able to draw breath.

"It's my chest. It's my goddamn chest."

The nurse looked up, calling out to someone. Baker did not catch their name. He had just fainted.

CHAPTER 27

Blue lips. Charred faces. Clawing hands.

"Morris... Morris... Morris..."

Baker's eyes fluttered opened and immediately contracted from the small penlight Dr. Ehrlich was shining into his pupils.

"Ah," said the stooped Hungarian. "Glad to see you're back with us, boychik. Was hoping I wouldn't have to call an ambulance, not that they'd come. My practice isn't exactly licensed by the state board anymore."

Ehrlich clicked off the light, placed it into a pocket of his white lab coat, and pulled out a pack of Chesterfields. He offered one to Baker, who declined.

"Where...?" he began, sitting up on an examination table covered in white butcher paper.

"Easy, boychik. Easy now."

Before the war, Ehrlich had been a well-respected family doctor in Budapest. When the Germans came, he was stripped of his medical license and gained what was supposed to be a one-way ticket to Auschwitz, where he worked in the infirmary alongside Josef Mengele.

Ehrlich's impressive medical work was the only thing that kept him and his younger sister from the gas chambers. When the camp was liberated in '45, they both immigrated to the United States. Ehrlich, whose frail wife was gassed upon arrival, never remarried, while Eva started a family of her own with a fellow survivor named Benjamin Politzer. Eva and Benjamin were the parents of the little shit who had been stealing vials of morphine from Ehrlich's storeroom.

"Sorry," said Baker, cradling his swimming head in his hands. "I've got epilepsy. Must've had a seizure when I stepped in."

"That was no seizure," Ehrlich said, gesticulating with his cigarette. "You said something about your chest just before you passed out. Once you were brought in here, I listened to your lungs."

"And...?"

"It sounds pretty farkakte in there! You didn't get in a fight with Kremnitzer the other night, did you?"

"No."

"Because the man is a former prizefighter. He could have really done a number on you."

"So you've heard about the potluck?"

"How am I not going to hear? It's all anyone wants to talk about when they come in."

"Someone should have told Einstein. Jewish gossip moves faster than the speed of light."

"How's your breathing been of late?"

"Lousy," Baker said. "Coughed up some blood this morning."

"Oy, really?"

"Really."

"Guess it's good you didn't take one of my cigarettes, then."

"What do you think is wrong?"

"I can't be sure until we get an X-ray. Come."

Ehrlich left the room and a swaying Baker followed him into a narrow hallway that reeked of rubbing alcohol and liquid iodine.

"Coughing up blood," Ehrlich muttered. "*Tsk-tsk.* Not good. Not good at all. In here, Morris."

They entered a slightly darker room occupied by a metal table and, hanging from the ceiling, what looked like a science fiction death ray.

"Take off your shirt and lie down," Ehrlich instructed, removing a lead-lined vest from a nearby hook and pulling it over his front. His hunched frame became more pronounced with the weight of the protective smock. Baker did as he was told, his mind springing back to full wakefulness as the bare skin of his back touched the icy metal of the examination table.

Ehrlich flicked a switch and the far wall buzzed to life. At first, Baker thought he was looking at a large television set, but the milky gray color of the screen disabused him of that notion. It was an X-ray viewing board through which the doctor would view the interior of his chest.

"Okay," Ehrlich said, the smoke of his Chesterfield unfurling against the ghostly illumination of the viewing board. "Let's see what we've got here."

Moving awkwardly in the cumbersome vest, the doctor reached up, grabbed the death ray device, and pointed it down. Baker flinched.

"No need to be nervous, boychik. I was doing this in Budapest long before you were born."

"What'd you say before about not being licensed?"

"The state medical board is refusing to renew my paperwork. They keep trying to blame it on bureaucratic meshugas, but I know better. Those HUAC putzes are singling out all the Jewish doctors in California. They're trying to squeeze us dr—oy vey..."

"What is it?" Baker thought he knew the answer.

"Sit up a little. Try not to move too much."

Baker got up on his elbows and gazed at the screen. He could just make out the rib cage, but everything else appeared as grayish-black blobs.

"Help me out here, Doc. I slept through most of biology class."

Ehrlich walked over to the screen and pointed to a spot that looked darker than the rest. "See that?" he said. "*That* should not be there."

"Is it...?"

"Cancer? Probably."

"What do you mean 'probably'?"

"I'll need to run some more tests, but in the meantime, I'd lay off the cigarettes for a while if I were y—hey!" Baker slid himself off the table, reaching for his shirt. "You can't leave, boychik!" Ehrlich exclaimed. "We need to discuss treatment methods. The IV bags for chemotherapy aren't cheap, but I can probably get them for you on the black market."

"Thanks, but no thanks, Doc."

Ehrlich stared at him, mouth agape. "You can't be serious, Morris. This is a good thing. The growth doesn't look too big. If we get you on an aggressive Mustargen drip right away, we might be able to stop the cancer before metastasis."

Baker clapped a hand on Ehrlich's lead-lined shoulder. "I really appreciate you seeing me on such short notice, but I've had enough poison inside of me for one lifetime."

"You're making a mistake," said the wizened doctor, now looking a little sick himself. "I can't allow you to...to kill yourself! I took an oath!"

"You're not allowing anything," Baker said, feeling strangely at ease. "It's my decision."

After all these years, the radioactive experiment in which the Nazis had forced him to take part during the war had caught up with him. Baker was the only surviving lab rat of Special Field Test Experimentation Number 665, and he had been forced to carry that burden—along with so many other lamentable things—for far too long.

He was, at last, getting what he so richly deserved: punishment. Punishment for letting countless people die so that he might live.

As he left the office and a stunned Dr. Ehrlich in his wake, those nightmarish words hissed by the top half of Elizabeth Short came back to him: *History comes for us all.*

"Whatever it is, Joanna, it can wait," said Baker as his secretary opened her mouth to speak the moment he stepped in the door. "I need a stiff drink first."

"Too late," Joanna said. "That man I told you about over the phone? He's here."

"Where?"

"Waiting in your office. He was quite insistent."

"You should've called Hersh to come in."

"I don't think this guy is a threat."

"Well, he sure as hell picked the wrong day to pull this crap," Baker said. He crossed the waiting area, hand poised near his gun, and barged into the office. "Look, buddy, I don't know who the hell you think you are, but this isn't a great time. I'll have to ask you to leave."

The man sitting in the wooden chair reserved for clients shot up. He was tall and powerfully built with a deeply lined face, sunken eyes, and a head of gray curly hair streaked with bolts of darkest brown. He did not respond, which wasn't the best thing for Baker's rising temper.

"You deaf, fella? I just told you to get lost. Scram!"

"I didn't want to get my hopes up," said the stranger, looking at Baker as though he'd just seen a ghost. "But there you are. Alive and well." He strode over to Baker in a pair of long strides and pulled him into a crushing hug. "I never thought I'd see this day."

Baker pushed the stranger away. "Get the hell off me. I don't know you!"

The man looked hurt. "You mean to tell me...that you don't recognize your own brother?"

CHAPTER 28

"You're mistaken," said Baker, moving over to his desk and wrenching open the drawer hiding the emergency bottle of schnapps. "My brother died during the war."

"And yet here I stand. Ze'ev Backenroth, in the flesh."

Baker stopped dead, hands trembling slightly, chest on fire. "Where did you hear that name?"

"It was the one given to me by our parents, Elias."

"My name is Morris. Morris Baker."

"Yes, I know," said the man in Yiddish. "That's why it's been so hard to find you."

"Your Yiddish is good, but I've heard the shtick before." Baker tried to pour himself a glass of schnapps. His hands shook so badly that he slopped the remaining contents all over the desk. The bottle rolled over the side and smashed.

"Who the fuck are you?" he murmured. "What do you want from me?"

"All I want is to reconnect with the brother I thought dead," said the man calmly. "Surely you want the same thing?"

"I already told you, my brother died during the war. The Nazis made him clear a field of land mines and—"

"Elias—"

"Stop calling me that!" Baker shrieked. "My name is Morris! Morris Baker!"

Joanna burst into the office. "Morris, is everything okay?"

"It's fine, Joanna. Everything's fine. Leave us." She reluctantly acquiesced. "I don't know who you think I am," Baker told the stranger, "but I ain't him."

"*I ain't him*," the stranger repeated in a teasing voice. "Listen to you, Elias. All tough and American. You've done a very good job of hiding your tracks."

"How many times do I have to tell you? My name is Morris. Or do you want your lights knocked out?"

"Of course. My apologies... Morris. May I sit?"

"Suit yourself," Baker said, now looking for a rag with which to sop up the spilled schnapps.

The cloying fumes of alcohol were fast going to his head, and when he couldn't locate a rag quickly enough, he went to open the window. When he turned back around, his trusty snub-nosed .44 Magnum was in his hand, pointed right at the stranger's midsection.

"Talk," Baker said. "Who sent you? Was it the Symphony?"

"Come now, Eli—Morris," replied the stranger. "You really think I'm a Nazi agent?"

"HUAC, then."

"No. I have not lied to you once since you stepped into this room. I am your brother, Ze'ev Backenroth."

"If that's the case, then why was I told my brother died clearing mines on the Eastern Front?"

"Because the story of my death was highly exaggerated. I'm grateful it caught on. Had it not, I would probably not be sitting here today."

"Explain."

"Can you please tell me... Momma, Papa, Magda, Ana, Ruth. What became of our parents and sisters?" he asked in Yiddish.

"Dead. All of them."

The man shut his eyes for a moment and Baker knew he was resisting the urge to break down. When the stranger looked back up to speak, his eyes were glistening, his expression one of reluctant acceptance. He'd known the answer long before asking the question.

"May I ask how they—?"

"I said talk!" Baker barked at the man. "Now!"

"Very well. When we were separated at the railway station all those years ago, I, along with a number of other fit young men, was selected for what can only be described as the complete opposite of the Einsatzgruppen. We walked ahead of the Wehrmacht soldiers, clearing any dangers that might be hidden along their path. Mines were the usual threat, but sometimes we'd come across a group of partisans lying in wait for an ambush. We took the hit so the Germans wouldn't have to."

"So...what? You just got lucky?"

"Didn't you?"

"Keep going. How did you survive?"

"In early 1942, the Nazis' hope of invading Russia was all but gone. Hitler didn't much care and ordered the battalion further into enemy territory. There was dissent among the ranks and many soldiers deserted their posts. Certain death awaited them on the other end of such a decision, but they knew their chances of staying alive were a little better if they ran."

"The confusion allowed you to escape?" Baker asked, sitting down, but never wavering in his aim. He was enthralled by what he was hearing, despite his apprehension.

"I wish," said the man. "Before they left, the soldiers decided to have a little fun with the surviving Jews. They took us to a nearby forest known to be littered with mines. I began walking, sure that these would be my final moments on earth. I started to recite the Shema when the soldiers dropped like flies."

"Was it the Russians?"

"Yes and no. The one who did the shooting was named Zus. He worked alongside the Soviets but fancied himself a partisan. He and his brothers ran a secret community of Jews deep within the forests of Belarus and offered to escort me there along with the others. I declined."

"Why?"

"I wanted to make sure no one would come looking for us. I took the coat, helmet, and gun of one of the dead Wehrmacht soldiers and walked until I came across the rest of the battalion. I told them my friends tried to desert, and when they refused to listen to reason, I followed and shot them for treason against the Führer. I added that the Jews were also dead. The blood on my coat completed the illusion nicely."

"And then what? You just lived among them after that?"

"It was the only way to give Zus and the others the head start they needed. Not long after, Berlin ordered its men to retreat, and I took every opportunity on the march back to loudly brag about the dead Jews who stupidly marched into the forest of mines. I repeated their names—mine included—as often as possible and allowed loose lips to handle the rest. I see the plan worked if the story made it all the way back to you in the camps."

Baker's eyes narrowed and his grip on the gun tightened. "So...what? I'm supposed to believe you made it back to Germany without arousing any suspicion onto yourself? That you lived happily ever after amongst our enemies until the war was over?"

"Hardly. I knew my cover wouldn't last forever. Someone was bound to double-check my identity at some point, so as soon as we reached the outskirts of Berlin, I jumped off the train and began making my way south. The authority of the stolen uniform helped pave the way, though there were plenty of near misses. I knew I had to get out of Europe, knew there was only one place where I'd be truly safe as a Jew."

"Where was that?"

"Where else?" asked the man with a shrug. "I went to Israel and saved as many poor souls as I could along the way. The group couldn't get too big, but it was about one hundred people strong by the end. It was slow going, but we managed to reach the port of Tel Aviv in early winter of 1943, and that's where I waited out the rest of the war. I became a citizen, learned Hebrew, and even got engaged."

"You're married?"

"I never said that. Once word came of Germany's unconditional surrender two years later, I was desperate for any news of our family. I was present for the arrival of *every* shipload of survivors from Europe, praying that just one of you would step off the boat. I pressed anyone I could for information, and at last, I came across Ruben Fleischer—do you remember him?"

"The butcher from our town. He was in the same camp as me."

"Yes. He was—"

"Another member of the Sonderkommando," finished Baker. He hadn't thought of Fleischer in years and the shock of the memory caused him to lower the gun.

"Exactly!" said the man, perking up. "He was eventually sent to Auschwitz in those final days but said he had witnessed your head injury and transport to the infirmary. He said that hardly anyone ever came back once they were placed under the care of Adolf Lang.

"Then a different kind of war came for us in '48 when Israel declared its independence. My fiancée, Maya, and I were drafted right away, and didn't hesitate. We'd learned the hard way of what happened when you didn't take a stand against those who wished to wipe you off the face of the earth. I made it out alive. Maya did not."

"I'm...sorry to hear that," Baker said, removing his finger from the trigger.

"Israel was free, but it no longer felt like home to me. Everywhere I went, it seemed, heartache followed. I stayed there for a few more years, teaching Czech and German at a school in Yafo, when I realized another conflict was brewing. The Rosenbergs had just been executed and McCarthy withdrew American support for Israel. We all knew what was about to happen and Ben-Gurion was calling in all the reserve troops. I left on one of the last boats headed for the US before the American borders were closed to Israelis for good."

"That would've been...what? Late '53? Early '54?"

"The latter. I settled in Brooklyn once I got here. I joined a shul and, after a fashion, became acquainted with the local Jewish community in New York by becoming a language tutor. That's when I began to hear stories of a wild man with long and curly brown hair who used to stand outside synagogues and drunkenly yell at the Jews who still believed in God. Do you know what that man was always said to be holding, Morris?"

Baker knew the answer, did not respond. Comprehension must have dawned in his eyes because the stranger smiled. "That's right, a bottle of peach schnapps. Now, I don't think I've ever met a person in this world with a taste for the stuff beyond our own father."

"That's absurd," Baker said with a snort of derision. "You immediately just assumed it was me?"

"Not immediately. The people who spoke of the man knew he was a survivor by the numbers tattooed on his arm. They pitied him and, therefore, did not have him arrested. I didn't dare get my hopes up, but I couldn't shake the feeling that my brother was alive after all. Call it intuition or Ruach HaKodesh or whatever you like. I knew the odds were one in six million, but I became a bit of a detective just like you are now. I tried to find this man who liked to indulge in peach schnapps, but my search was in vain. He seemed to have mysteriously disappeared from New York before I arrived there, and no one knew his name. It didn't sound like he had made a single friend or acquaintance. I was forced to give up hope yet again until—"

"Until you heard Lang's name mentioned over the radio," Baker said.

"Glad to see all the schnapps haven't slowed you down. Yes, those broadcasts are a source of hope and inspiration to a great many citizens of this country. I couldn't help but get swept up in the fervor shown toward the Liberty Boys. Well, you can imagine my shock when I hear this wild story of a Jewish LAPD detective thwarting a vast Nazi conspiracy involving one Adolf Lang, who had performed perverse medical experiments during the war. The name *Morris Baker* meant nothing to me, of course, but that hope of seeing my brother again instantly reignited."

"That was almost two years ago," Baker said. "Why are you only just showing up now?"

"I wasn't going to—what is the American expression?—chase gooses on some wild hunch. I needed to do more research, not to mention save up for a cross-country train ticket to Los Angeles. It's not cheap getting out here on a tutor's salary. But I have dreamt of this moment for the last seventeen months. I needed to see for myself and my hunch was right!"

"So you were the one asking about me at Harvey Klein's dress shop?"

"Harvey who?"

"A member of my shul. *Ex-shul*," Baker added hastily, remembering his indefinite ban, "told me someone with an Israeli accent had come by his dress shop the other day, asking questions about me."

"Wasn't me."

Baker furrowed his brow and let the matter drop. Hadn't Klein said the person looking for him was "young and strapping"? The man sitting before him wasn't exactly decrepit, but neither did he fit that description.

"Let's say for the sake of argument that you are my older brother. Where do you get the gall to walk back into my life after all these years?"

"It only took this long because you made it so hard! You think I didn't follow every single lead once the war over? I never stopped looking for members of our family, even when I knew the odds were slim. But I thought that if one or more of you were alive, they must be looking for me, too. It seems I was a fool to make that assumption."

"How dare you!" screamed Baker. He stood up so quickly that his chair toppled over backward, hitting the windowsill and causing the blinds to ripple back and forth.

"You have no idea what it was like! Having to see your loved ones die off one by one or else hear about it from people you hardly knew. To trick innocent men, women, and children into the gas chambers and to shovel their bodies into the ovens. You didn't have to see Magda's face after we arrived at the camp. She starved to death on the journey and there was nothing I could do about it. I was just a frightened boy, Ze'ev! Where was our older brother to take care of her? Of *us*?"

It was glorious to unload years of resentment onto the man sitting in front of him. To lay the blame at someone else's feet for a change and see how they liked it.

"You ask of Ana and Ruth. Allow me to enlighten you, Ze'ev. One was raped and thrown off a building—the other was forced to dig her own grave and shot in the back of the head. Our parents? Gassed as soon as they got to the camp. Where the fuck were *you*?"

"Elias..."

"Stop saying that name. It no longer holds any meaning for me. Elias Backenroth doesn't exist anymore. He died in that godforsaken camp along with so many others. Now get out of here. I don't ever want to see your face in here again. You come near me again, and I'll kill you."

Ze'ev sighed. He didn't look angry, or disappointed, or sad. Just exhausted beyond words.

"If that is what you wish, Morris," he answered solemnly. "I'll leave the address of my current accommodations with your secretary, should you change your mind." He turned to leave, making it all the way to the door when he swiveled back around.

"Chag Chanukah Sameach, brother."

The door closed. Ze'ev was gone.

CHAPTER 29

You okay, Morris?" Joanna had popped her head into the office.

"I'm fine," he said. "Everything's fine. Now please leave me. Take the rest of the day off."

"Who was that man?"

"Your boss just gave you a direct order. I said *leave*!"

Looking shocked and hurt, Joanna withdrew. Baker could hear her gathering up her things in the waiting room. He knew full well he'd regret snapping at her. For the moment, however, he was determined to keep everyone at bay, even if it meant shouting every expletive known to mankind in their general direction.

How could this have happened? How could Ze'ev just show up like this after all these years? After Baker had resigned himself to a lifetime of loneliness, like a monk taking on a vow of silence? It was unfair. Another twisted punch line in the never-ending cosmic joke that was his life.

Elias Backenroth was dead and buried—a relic of the infirmary where Lang had removed a uranium-birthed tumor from his arm with a dull scalpel. Backenroth perished and the man the Americans carried out of that building was someone new; someone who no longer believed in much of anything. If only Baker had had the courage to end things himself. Luckily, the cancer growing unchecked inside his lungs would do what cowardice could not.

He decided to hasten things up by lighting a cigarette. The first inhale of smoke led to another harsh coughing fit. The minuscule specks of blood on his suit sleeve gave him a profound sense of fiendish victory.

During their first meeting together, Rabbi Kahn had told him about the Jewish tradition of changing a person's name when they were close to leaving this world. Trying to trick the Angel of Death.

This hadn't occurred to Baker when he changed his own moniker upon arriving in the United States. It wasn't very hard to do so—all records pertaining to his previous life had been destroyed. He could be anyone he wanted. Start over from scratch. "Morris" had simply come out of a misunderstanding with the customs agent, who could not pronounce "Mordechai" while writing down his newly chosen name. And as for "Baker"... well, that one was easy: He never wanted to forget how he'd shoveled bodies in and out of ovens.

Ze'ev might think of Morris as his brother, but the feeling was not at all mutual. Morris Baker had no family. He was an orphan and single child with no past prior to May 1945. Everything up to that point had been sucked up the crematoria chimneys along with so much smoke and ash.

Elias Backenroth had reduced so many lives to charcoal, so it only stood to reason that his true identity, that genuine sense of self, would also join the blazing conflagration.

How could Ze'ev not see that? Why didn't he just keep to himself and leave Baker alone?

What was the true cause behind all of this anger? Deep down, he grasped the answer. That despite the insurmountable odds, Ze'ev had not lost hope. The man never gave up the belief—foolish though it was—that he might one day see a member of his family again. Baker had simply cut and run, never once entertaining the idea of reuniting with the people he once loved.

It was true, he didn't have much reason to hope for such an outcome. He had firsthand proof of his sister's death, and after everything he'd done and witnessed, what reason would there be to discount the anecdotal stories that came to him about his parents, brother, and two other sisters?

When the fighting ended and Jews could move freely throughout Europe—or as freely as one could move in a time when most of the continent still maintained the belief that the Nazis had had the right idea—Baker saw hundreds of people trudge in and out of his former concentration camp every day, looking for their own loved ones. He mocked them inwardly and outwardly whenever one of them tried to ask him a question about a person they longed to see.

"They're probably dead," he'd say with a snort of derision. "Just move on."

The wounded looks on their faces filled him with a dizzy happiness bordering on the grotesque. It was a feeling he'd never known before the war. He figured it must be the same ugly rush of euphoria the Germans derived from imprisoning and torturing those they deemed inferior.

There was no room for doubt or, worse, optimism. The dead would be left behind and those left standing would move on as best they could. Still, what would his life have been these last ten years or so had he just opened the door, however slightly, to hope?

He might have found Ze'ev earlier and the two could have helped each other through the pain.

The Americans had the perfect phrase for it:

Shoulda.

Coulda.

Woulda.

The ringing of his desk phone brought him back to reality. He picked up the receiver, which was nearly glued to the base from dried schnapps.

"Yeah?"

"Morris? It's Brogan."

"Yes?"

"We got the son of a bitch."

"Liz's killer?"

"Yup."

"That was quick. You sure?"

"Definitely our man. This guy was real sloppy. Truth be told, I think he wanted to be caught. He's being driven down to the station now for questioning. Meet me there in half an hour?"

"On my way."

CHAPTER 30

Connolly was waiting for him at the entrance to the station with a pair of handcuffs.

"Hands behind your back," he said, snapping open the silver bracelets.

"What the fuck, Connolly? I thought you said I wasn't under suspicion."

"You're not," he said. "But I can't just bring you inside without someone asking why you're here. It'll raise too many alarm bells with the Hueys."

"You called me from your desk phone. They must have already known I was coming."

"I actually called from a pay phone," answered Connolly. "Just play along, would ya?"

"Fine," said Baker, holding his wrists together behind his back. "I suppose booking a Jew will gain you some street cred with those pricks."

"That's the spirit."

Baker hadn't been to 150 North Los Angeles Street since turning in his resignation to Parker. The LAPD headquarters didn't seem to have changed very much over the last seventeen months beyond the removal of the Joseph L. Young mosaic in the lobby. Created by a Jew, the artwork had been ripped from the wall, which now sat bare and cracked like a poorly healed scar.

A palpable aura of tension and fear hung in the air. Not surprising if HUAC was officially running the place now—everyone needed to be on their best behavior.

Connolly lazily flashed his badge to the on-duty officer at the front desk.

"Mouthy Yid," he said, angling his head at Baker, who played along by fighting against Connolly's grasp. "Used to be one of us, if you can believe it."

"Get outta town!" said the desk man.

"Fuck your mother," Baker spat.

"See what I mean?" Connolly said and, without warning, slammed Baker's head into the desk. "We'll see how rude he is after a night in the drunk tank."

The on-duty officer's face broke out into a wicked smirk. He gave Connolly a knowing wink and waved them through.

"Thanks, Graham," Connolly said.

"Jesus, Connolly," whispered Baker, blinking stars from his eyes. "You could give a guy a warning. That fuckin' hurt."

"Sorry," Connolly hissed back. "Had to make it look convincing. Graham's got a pretty big mouth. He'll help spread the word, give us some cover."

Connolly led Baker into the area of the building that housed a number of interrogation rooms.

"Have you gotten anything out of him yet?" asked Baker.

"Not yet. He's requested a lawyer."

"How'd you pinch him?"

"Neighbor saw a bunch of bloody rags sticking out of his garbage bins. Perp's house is on Whittier Boulevard in Boyle Heights, less than two miles from where we found the body."

"Seems circumstantial."

"That's not all. We got a warrant and raided the house."

"Do I want to know what you found?"

"Not unless you've got a strong stomach."

"Try me."

"Well, you saw the body and . . . what was missing. We . . . uh . . . found the skin of her right breast in the guy's icebox. Clitoris, too."

"Jesus Christ," Baker said again.

"My thoughts exactly," said Connolly. "There were also a number of photographs of the body in various stages of the...procedure, let's call it."

"What's his explanation?"

"Claims he has no idea how any of that stuff got there."

"Think it could be a frame-up job?"

"Not likely. Thomas called it a hemico...hemicorp—oh hell! It's some sort of surgery that removes the lower half of the body in case of severe injury. This was no spur-of-the-moment homicide. It was precise and methodical. Not just anyone can cut a body perfectly in half like that. They had to have known what they doing. Our man fits the bill to a tee."

"The perp is a doctor?"

"A surgeon, yeah."

"Fucking doctors," Baker grunted, thinking of Lang.

"Name of Jasper Heo," Connolly continued. "Korean-American male, thirty-five years of age, and unmarried. Honors graduate of Keck Medical and now works at a small trauma center over in Lynwood. We're getting statements from his coworkers now."

"Does this guy have an alibi?"

"Yes, but it's thinner than a Communion wafer. Given the state of decomposition, Thomas estimates that the murder took place sometime between late evening on the twenty-fourth and early morning on the twenty-fifth."

Baker felt his stomach lurch. Had he been in the middle of sleeping with Liz's roommate while Liz was being sliced in two by a madman? "Nu? What's Heo's story?"

"That he's been on his back, sick as a dog, for the last few days, unable to keep anything solid down. Claimed he wasn't feeling well that night and went to bed early after leaving work."

"Can anyone corroborate that?"

"Not a soul. He lives alone. Speak of the devil, here he is. The suspect of the hour."

They'd arrived outside one of the interrogation rooms. The wall closest to them served as a two-way mirror. Connolly withdrew a small key from his pocket and took the cuffs off, allowing Baker to rub circulation back into his numbed wrists.

Dressed in a wool sweater and dark slacks and nursing a Styrofoam cup of coffee, Jasper Heo looked a little tired and shaken, but otherwise completely normal. The real monsters of the world always did. They didn't pop out of the closet with bloodied claws and razor-sharp fangs. They put their pants on one leg at a time just like everybody else.

The only difference was that everybody else didn't go around cutting young women in half and slicing off their tits like your favorite deli counter man. Baker tried to look for obvious signs of guilt—nervous tics like a thumping leg, a chewing of the fingernails, rapid blinking—but couldn't spot any. Not much of a conclusion one way or the other, though if the perp had an obvious tell, it was something a seasoned cop might be able to exploit to their benefit.

For the slightest moment, Baker felt an overwhelming urge to rush inside the room and wring the man's neck until he was dead.

"Gonna let him sweat in there for a bit before I start tightening the screws," said Connolly, cracking his knuckles. "I'll be seeing to this one personally."

"He does look pretty ill," Baker said. Heo was pale and gaunt, as though he'd lost a lot of weight in a very short span of time.

"Could be the flu that's been going around," replied Connolly. "But I never seen anyone vomit up blood while battling the sniffles."

"What do you mean?"

"Soon as we cuffed him, Jasper opened his mouth and let loose. You'd think it was the first plague brought on the Egyptians."

"Jesus," said Baker. "It looks almost like..."

"What?"

"Almost like he was poisoned," answered Baker, who knew the telltale signs of a body fighting off a foreign toxin.

"Maybe he just ate a bad clam or something."

"Could be..."

"You're not convinced?"

"I'm not the one who needs convincing. Any idea of the motive? What would compel a person to do something like this?"

"We've got a pretty solid theory."

Connolly reached into his pocket and pulled out a stack of newspaper clippings within a clear plastic evidence bag. "These were pinned up next to all the murder photographs."

Baker looked at the top one, saw it was an excerpt from Yang's deranged manifesto.

"You think there's some sort of connection?" Baker asked. "That Yang inspired Heo to kill Liz?"

"About the only story that makes sense at the moment," answered Connolly, seeming a bit queasy. "HUAC's gonna have a fuckin' field day when they find out. I'm hoping to have a confession before they whisk him off to the nearest torture dungeon. Anything he tells 'em under duress would be inadmissible. Not that the courts would care much. The public is out for Korean blood, and they don't care how they get it."

"You say Heo wanted to get caught. That doesn't look like a guilty man to me."

"Maybe not consciously, but leaving his trash bins out like that? It's sloppy. Some part of him must have wanted us to know. Or he could just be a shit murderer."

"Or he got swept up in the rantings of Yang's manifesto and came to his senses too late."

"Won't know for sure until I get in there. Wanted to give you a chance to see the guy before HUAC gets their slimy paws on him. You deserve closure, Morris."

"Did Thomas get the results back on that dirt from under Liz's fingernails?"

"You must have a lot of wax in your ear, Jew-boy," Brogan said, jabbing a finger at the two-way glass. "This is our man. The evidence is overwhelming. What is some dirt gonna tell us?"

"Brogan..."

"All right, all right. If you must know, Thomas hasn't heard back yet. The boys in the lab are working their way through the backlog left over from before Christmas."

"What happened to the Connolly I knew?" Baker asked. "The one who exhausted every avenue?"

"Simple," Brogan said. "He lost his partner."

"Flattery will get you nowhere. Have you spoken to Liz's roommate yet? Debbie?"

"We questioned her earlier, but... hang on just a second. How do you know her name?"

"She was the prostitute I slept with the other night."

"I'll be damned. You really do know how to pick 'em. Still doesn't explain how you knew she and Liz lived in the same apartment. I doubt very much there's a lot of small talk in Milner's line of work."

"Would you believe it if I said it was a lucky guess?"

"No, I wouldn't," Connolly said, an angry flush creeping up his meaty neck. "You never can leave well enough alone, can you? I told you I would handle this case personally and you go and stick your big nose in it anyway. I had a feeling Milner's story of working the Boulevard all day was bullshit. I sent patrols out looking for her and none of the girls they spoke to had seen her show up once. I suppose that was *your* doing?"

"Ask me no questions and I'll tell you no lies."

"Fair enough."

"Have you told Debbie about Heo's arrest?" Baker asked.

"No, not yet."

"Mind if I deliver the news?"

"Knock yourself out. Just do me a favor and take the back exit. Mr. Heo and I have some catching up to do."

CHAPTER 31

Back at Liz's old apartment behind the Florentine Gardens nightclub, he gently knocked on the door. "Debbie?" he called out. "It's me, Morris. You there?"

No answer. He knocked again, this time a little louder. Still nothing, not even the quiet pitter-patter of footsteps on carpet as the occupant crept up to the peephole to see who was calling. Baker supposed she might be out working the Boulevard.

Not that she needed the money, of course. He had paid her rather handsomely over the last couple of days. Enough to keep her afloat for a month or two at the very least. But he knew that if Debbie was whoring herself at the moment, it had nothing to do with money. Throwing yourself into work was a way to stave off the moment when delicate emotional fault lines would split open and send you tumbling headfirst into the naked abyss.

He considered leaving, but something, call it an indescribable compulsion, kept him rooted to the spot. As if coming to from an epileptic seizure, Baker realized he was down on one knee, picking the apartment's lock. The door noiselessly swung inward, and he entered. The interior of the apartment felt steamy, and Baker was immediately reminded of Lamotte's greenhouse.

The place was not large: a 300-square-foot box mostly dominated by two full-sized beds and a humble kitchenette. Baker had been here many times while dating Liz, who always kept the apartment neat and tidy. Debbie's residency, however, seemed to have introduced a little more entropy to the living quarters.

Brassieres, stockings, wigs, and boas hung pell-mell over chairs, hooks, drawer handles, and the oven door. An overflowing pile of greasy, unwashed dishes were stacked in the sink, whose basin had become the prime breeding ground for a colony of buzzing fruit flies. Old issues of the *Los Angeles Times* and *Counterattack*, the government's official newspaper, littered the grimy floor.

If Baker didn't know any better, he'd have said he was standing in the middle of his own messy and cluttered home back in Chinatown. He only wished he'd met Debbie sooner. The young prostitute was more of a kindred spirit—at least in terms of household upkeep.

He crossed over to the bed closest to the door, where a framed photo of Debbie and Liz making funny faces at the camera sat atop the nightstand. Baker smiled and made to pick up the picture for a closer look when a large black something jumped out at him, hissing.

"Fuck!" he shouted, fumbling for his gun.

It was nearly out of its holster and cocked when he realized the thing was just a cat with puffed black fur. The animal, which had leapt onto the crumpled bedspread, was thoroughly unbothered by his outburst. It stretched, pawed at the blanket, and curled up into a ball.

"You're one lucky son of a bitch, you know that?" Baker said, bending down to scratch the cat behind the ears, causing the animal to purr in delight. "I nearly cut you in half. Sorry, poor choice of words," he quickly added, catching sight of Liz's face on the nightstand.

"Anyway, what's your name?" The cat continued to purr, looking up at him with eyes the color of dehydrated urine. "Not in the talking mood, eh? Any idea where your owner is? Out working?"

At this, the cat turned its head in the direction of the bathroom and let out a forlorn meow.

"Much appreciated," he said to the cat with a half salute, remembering how Debbie said she'd planned on taking a long bath. Sure enough, he saw wisps of steam tendrilling out from beneath the door, which explained why the apartment felt so muggy.

"Debbie?" he called, lightly rapping his knuckles on the door, whose beige paint was starting to peel off like the skin of a cucumber. "You in there? It's Morris. I have news about Liz. They've arrested someone for the murder."

Still nothing.

"Did you fall asleep in there?"

Silence again. Baker started to worry; could feel a prickly sense of dread expanding inside the pit of his stomach.

"All right," he began, his voice cracking a little as he tested the knob to make sure it wasn't locked. "I hope you're decent because I'm coming in."

The door creaked open and Baker took an involuntary step backward, cupping a hand to his mouth. A scream nearly escaped his throat, but he wrangled it into submission at the last second. Debbie was in the tub, all right, though this would be her last soak. She was dead. Her slit wrists hung over the porcelain on either side, giving off the impression of a female Christ.

And that's exactly what Baker was saying over and over.

"Christ! Christ! Christ!"

When the blaspheming had subsided, he tore his gaze away from the naked Debbie lying in a pool of steamy, crimson water. The razor blade that had clearly done the deed rested on the floor, now just a harmless glint of silver. The initial wave of shock receding, Baker took a step into the bathroom, trying hard not to look directly at Debbie, whose delicate skin—impossibly white from severe blood loss—was beginning to prune and pucker.

He found a piece of paper, wet and fragile, on the sink, weighted down with an empty bottle of sleeping pills. Baker gingerly picked up the note and read the neat message written in deep purple ink, which was starting to bleed in jagged lines down the page:

It's all too much for me.
Empty. I am empty
I'll be with Liz soon.
I'm sorry.
Goodbye.

"Why, Debbie?" said Baker, still clutching the note. The girl's eyes were closed, her lips blue. She looked almost serene. "Why would you do this?"

It wasn't much of a mystery. The note said it all. In Baker's experience, people who contemplated suicide were always on the precipice of going through with the act. All it took was one really bad day to drive them over the edge. Losing Liz—a roommate, friend, and coworker—had been Debbie's tipping point.

Baker had seen it a lot in the camps. Individuals would run headlong into an electrified fence, swallow an entire bottle of poison, and yes, cut their veins wide open, rather than go on living another moment in mental and physical agony.

Something brushed against his leg—the cat. It trotted over to the bathtub, sniffed one of Debbie's limp hands, and uttered another sad meow. The cat looked up, perhaps hoping for Debbie to pop over the lip of the tub with a large, exasperated smile that said, *What are you doing in here, you naughty little thing?*

No such luck. The cat meowed again and began to lick the dead girl's fingers.

"Don't do that," said Baker, stuffing the suicide note into his pocket and rushing over to scoop up the feline. He carried it out of the bathroom, and back to the bed. Looking around at the various debris, he spotted the cat's food bowl, in which there sat a few chunks of lumpy brown fish.

"If you're hungry, then eat this... Mat-a-got," he said, reading out the name etched into the surface of the light blue dish. The cat's ears pricked up at the sound of his name. "Matagot, eh?" Baker said, sitting down on the bed and allowing Matagot to curl up in his lap. "Nice to meet you. My name's Morris. Guess you'll be needing a new place to stay, huh?"

They sat there for a while, Baker scratching Matagot behind the ears, the cat purring contentedly. For the sweetest, briefest moment, it didn't feel like a young girl was lying dead in the other room.

The next logical step would be to call Connolly and let him know about Debbie's grief-driven suicide. He leaned over and grabbed the phone sitting atop a pile of unfolded laundry when something on the floor caught his eye. Baker got off the bed and knelt down, inadvertently displacing Matagot, who did not appreciate being woken up. Hissing again, the cat scampered out of sight through a vine-like curtain of drying pantyhose.

The item on the floor turned out to be the sheet of Baker's monogrammed stationery, the one he'd given to Debbie earlier that day with his home number and address. Underneath his contact information was more writing:

Eggs
Milk
Cheese
Bread
Tuna fish
Apples
Butter
Endive
Potatoes

He then examined the note from the bathroom. The neat and prim handwriting of the suicide note was a far cry from the untidy scrawl of the shopping list.

Not too surprising; shopping lists were often written down in haste. A person took more time and care while penning their own epitaph. Despite those noticeable differences, however, the two styles didn't look terribly dissimilar. Except for the capital *E* on the suicide note, which looked more like a backward *3*. Why compose a shopping list at all? he wondered.

People did strange and irrational things when they weren't thinking clearly. Once that final tether anchoring the mind to reality was wrenched loose, you simply floated away into oblivion. You'd sit in silence, staring at the wall until you died of starvation, or else put your cat in the oven instead of that night's meatloaf. The brain was capable of jumping through any hoop once all reason drained away.

With that said, something felt off here. Call it a hunch, intuition, or fuck it, even God Himself—this depressing tableau of open veins and grocery lists didn't sit well with Baker.

Maybe it was just paranoia. After all, a suspect was already in custody. Connolly was currently tightening the metaphorical screws around Jasper Heo before HUAC swooped in and broke out the literal ones.

Heo had most likely killed Liz, kicking off a butterfly effect that resulted in Debbie's taking her own life. It all fit, and that's why Baker was having trouble swallowing the story. This turn of events was just a little too neat. A macabre present, beautifully wrapped and left under the Christmas tree by Santa for the kids to find the next morning.

If Heo truly was responsible, then a deranged psychopath was off the streets and away from more innocent victims. All the evidence pointed toward that conclusion. But if Heo was some kind of patsy, then Baker owed it to Liz—and now Debbie—to discover the truth.

"*I told you I'd handle it, goddamnit!*" came the reproving voice of his ex-partner. "*You really can't leave well enough alone, can you?*"

This hypothetical Connolly had a point.

"*It couldn't hurt to have another pair of eyes on this*," Baker told the Irish manifestation of his conscience. "*You even said it yourself: You lost some of your edge once I left the force. I know the chances of Heo's innocence are slim, but wouldn't you want to make absolutely sure?*"

"He's guilty, Morris!"

"That sounds like the Hueys talking, Brogan. Guess you're more like them than I thought."

A slight pressure against his leg signaled the return of Matagot; the cat nuzzled his fluffy black head against the cuff of Baker's pants.

"So..." he said. "What's your stance on Chinese food?" The cat purred. "I'll take that as a 'yes.' Now quiet, I've got a call to make."

He dialed the LAPD switchboard and asked for Connolly. His former partner came on the line after what felt like an eternity.

"This is Sergeant Connolly."

"Brogan, it's Morris. Listen, I hope you're able to stop by Debbie's apartment for dinner tonight. She was just telling me the most amusing story about her Aunt Peg."

"Aunt Peg, eh?"

"Yes," Baker said, briefly pulling the phone away from his mouth and addressing the empty apartment. "What did you say her last name was, Debbie? Right, right." He came back on the line. "Peg Entwistle."

"I'll be right over."

CHAPTER 32

"Why," began an exasperated Connolly, standing in Debbie's bathroom forty-five minutes later, "does this kind of shit always fall right into your lap? You got some sort of hidden shit-magnet I need to know about?"

"Believe me," replied Baker—now smoking a Kool—"I've been trying to figure out the answer to that question ever since I stepped out of that cattle car in Poland."

"Christ," a quick cross, then, "what a mess. What an absolute fucking mess."

Both men stared at Debbie's corpse in the cooled water of the tub.

"You know what this means, don't you?" asked Connolly.

"That every woman I sleep with somehow ends up dead?"

"No, wiseass. It means I really won't be able to keep this from HUAC any longer. A pair of women, both roommates, turn up dead within the span of two days? And one of them murdered by a Korean extremist to boot? I'll have to report this tonight. I'm just grateful you had the good sense not to blab about it over the phone."

"Do I look meshugge? Glad you haven't forgotten 'Aunt Peg.'"

"How could I?"

Peg Entwistle was an actress who decided to throw herself off the Hollywood Sign a year before Hitler was appointed chancellor of Germany. Over the years, the LAPD had turned the woman's name into an obscure bit of cop-speak. "Pulling an Entwistle" or "Aunt Peg" became shorthand for a person committing "suicide." The terms quickly fell out of vogue as UAP eroded the history of Old Hollywood.

"And I trust you'll leave my name out of it?" Baker asked. "I bet they'd love to splash 'Jew' next to 'Korean extremist' once the story hits the papers."

"I'll omit that part for now, but it's only a matter of time until they find out you used to go steady with Liz. I can't just cover up the last twelve years. They're bound to unearth something."

"Understood. I promise this'll be the last thing I ask of you, Brogan. Can't thank you enough for sticking your neck out for me."

"More than just my neck," growled Connolly. "Now get out of here."

"How you gonna spin this one?"

"I'll say it was an anonymous tip. The Hueys listen to all the calls that come in through the switchboard. No doubt they heard your message from earlier. I can't promise they won't connect all the dots once I brief them on the case. Leave enough chimps in a room with typewriters and they'll end up writing Shakespeare."

"How poetic," said Baker.

"If we're lucky, your call will have slipped through the cracks. If not, well..." Connolly let the sentence drop off there.

"Don't worry," said Baker. "If they do end up coming for me, you can say I coerced you with my Jewish magic."

"So you people can do magic, then?"

"Get fucked."

Baker turned to leave, found the doorway blocked by Connolly's sizable frame.

"Where is it?" Brogan inquired, holding out his hand.

"Where is what?"

"The note."

"Note?"

"You really do enjoy pushing my buttons, don't you? The suicide note, Morris. I can't let you leave with it. Hand it over."

"How in the world did you know?" Baker said, pulling the note out of his pocket.

"Let's call it an educated guess," said Connolly, daintily lifting it from Baker's fingers. "I know you too well to just assume you'll drop this and walk away. That's not your style. And you know I'll *strongly* advise against it, but I've learned that's about as useful as trying to piss against the wind."

"Something isn't right here, Brogan," Baker said, ignoring Connolly's exaggerated eyeroll. "Look at this..."

Now that Connolly had the note, there was no point in keeping his theories to himself. He handed over the piece of stationery with his contact information and Debbie's shopping list, pointing out the minor discrepancies in handwriting.

"Hmmm," mused Connolly, holding up both pieces of papers, side by side. "I do kind of see what you mean about the *E*'s, but everything else looks pretty much the same to me. I assume she'd take more care with—"

"With the suicide note, yeah," finished Baker.

"Then what's the problem?"

"I don't know. All of it just seems so... convenient," Baker finished lamely. "Heo say anything yet?"

"Still insisting he's innocent. Lawyer's with him now, but none of that will matter once HUAC gets involved."

"What does your gut tell you?"

"That we've had our fair share of sloppy perps. It happens. People aren't perfect. They slip up. Sometimes royally."

"I guess..."

"As for Miss Milner," Connolly pressed on, "this would not be the first time shock and grief drove a person to do something rash. The mind of a whore and nudie actress can't be all that structurally sound to begin with."

"Maybe you're right," said Baker, not believing a word of it.

"Good man. Now get out of here and don't contact me again for a few days at least. If there's anything to report, I'll find you. The only question that remains is what are we gonna do about the cat?"

"Don't worry about that," said Baker, crouching down to beckon Matagot, who was cautiously eyeing Connolly from a pile of boas. "He's coming with me."

"It's either your place or the pound, I suppose."

"Thanks. Say, do Bletchley and Pistone have any updates on the Kissinger case?"

"Kissinger..." Connolly repeated the name distractedly. "Kissinger? Oh, Nixon's man! No, nothing yet. Both of them are still on vacation. Why?"

"Kissinger's 'wife'"—Baker placed air quotes around the second word—"turned out to be a nudie actress who worked with Liz and Debbie."

"No shit."

"Yes, shit. Still think I'm crazy for wondering if there's something else going on here?"

"What? You think it's those Krauts again?"

"I don't know what to think. Something tells me the Black Symphony wouldn't go for the same damsel-in-distress ploy twice."

"I'll admit it's odd, but coincidences do happen," said Connolly. "Want some friendly advice, Morris?"

"Not particularly."

"Well, here's some anyway—on the house. Stop jumping at shadows, or else they'll ship you cross-country to Punxsutawney. First class."

Baker opened his mouth to ask another question but closed it just as quickly. His constant—and somewhat selfish—desire to be absolutely certain of the truth put Connolly in danger. The Hueys were in charge now. A fella, especially one working for the LAPD, needed to be careful these days. Connolly had a wife and two daughters to think about. He didn't need to be roped into the raging shitstorm that was Baker's life.

"Got something else to say? You look like a goddamn fish over there."

"It's nothing. Good night, Brogan."

CHAPTER 33

It was not customary to light the menorah in the total absence of light, but he could not bring himself to switch on the apartment bulbs. Could not bring himself to look upon the tangibleness of the world after so many had left it before their time. Matagot watched curiously from the bed, his yellow eyes flashing.

Baker ignited a match and lit three Hanukkah candles on the menorah left for him the previous night by Rabbi Kahn.

Baruch ata Adonai Eloheinu, melech ha'olam, asher kid'shanu b'mitzvotav v'tzivanu l'hadlik ner shel Hanukkah.

Baruch atah Adonai Eloheinu Melech ha'olam, she'asah nisim la'avoteinu ba'yamim ha'heim ba-z'man ha'zeh.

The brachot came out hollow and Baker wondered why he was even continuing with the tradition.

He thought of his parents; of his brother, Ze'ev; and of his sisters, Magda, Ana, and Ruth. He thought of how he'd never properly mourned their deaths. He had simply adopted a new identity in an effort to escape the past. A rather Sisyphean effort, Baker soon came to learn, once the sun dipped low and his epileptic mind replayed the worst moments of his life over and over again. His brain was a record with deep scratches cut into the smooth vinyl surface.

Maybe it was finally time to grieve for them after all. Lighting candles in honor of deceased loved ones was another tenet of Judaism, was it not? A simple wick was lit every year on the anniversary of an individual's passing, or yahrtzeit.

Maybe he should light two for Liz and Debbie as well. Hell, why not light six million more while he was at it?

Baker leaned in closer to the map of Los Angeles flattened out across his kitchen counter, using the meager candlelight to scan the length of Fairfax Avenue. It would take days, perhaps weeks, to find the Nine-Tailed Fox.

Oy, what are you even doing, Morris? he asked himself, taking a long pull of schnapps. *Just admit it, you have absolutely no idea what you're do—* An intersecting street name caught his attention: Fox Tail Road. He bent forward and blew out the Hanukkah candles. The smoke furled up to the ceiling and disappeared.

Turning to the cat, he said, "Try not to rip up my bed."

Matagot flicked his bushy tail and lowered his head onto the mattress.

"I'll take that as an 'okay.'"

He pulled off Fairfax Avenue and onto Fox Tail Road, driving slowly. This stretch of asphalt, an idyllic collection of mom-and-pop shops straight out of small town USA, seemed completely devoid of life. Most of the empty and darkened storefronts were all closed down for the evening.

The only place that still had its lights on was Fox & Sons Hardware. Another coincidence?

Baker parked the Continental in an empty space down the block and got out. He noticed a silent squad car on the other side of the street, discerning a pair of motionless silhouettes in the front seat.

A shiver crept up Baker's spine. He'd been on many stakeouts with Connolly, and a person always got restless after hours of sitting in a car. You jimmied around in your seat, got out and stretched your legs, sipped coffee, and cracked jokes to pass the time. Baker crossed the pavement and tried to look into the window, opaque from all the frosty condensation.

"Hello?" he said, tapping on the glass. "Anyone home?"

Nothing. Had both officers fallen asleep? Rare, but not unheard of. Baker reached for the driver's seat door, grabbed the handle, and pulled. "Fuck!" The pungently sweet smell of rotting meat shot into his nostrils as the dead body of Officer Alfred Pistone toppled onto the wet asphalt. The man's pudgy throat had been slit, ear to ear, and Baker could already see a few white maggots squirming inside the gash.

Calling on his tenure as a member of the Sonderkommando, he lifted up Pistone from around the armpits and squashed him back into the front seat next to Kelvin Bletchley, who had befallen a similar fate. A maggot wriggled out of Pistone's left nostril, awakened by all the commotion.

"What'd you poor schmucks find out here?" Baker muttered, wondering if his jugular might be next.

He used the sleeve of his trench coat to wipe down all the surfaces he had touched and slammed the door shut. The thought of calling Connolly and reporting the officers' deaths briefly crossed his mind, but his ex-partner had made it abundantly clear not to make contact for a few days at the very least. Baker decided to let sleeping cops lie. Being found in the company of dead cops wasn't a good look for anyone.

Hoping to locate a back entrance to the hardware store, Baker strolled around the perimeter of the building, casually as he could, and found himself in a vacant lot overgrown with ivy and piled high with soggy leaves. A hint of faded yellow showed through the frondescence, and with a little hand-related pruning, he unearthed the rusted sign of a nuclear fallout shelter barely clinging to the brick facade. Kicking away a mound of leaves, he found a neat square of thick concrete where the shelter entrance should have been. There was a plethora of these bunkers scattered throughout the city, but to his knowledge, all of them were active and regularly maintained by the city in case of a surprise Russian strike. So why would this one be filled in?

The sign on the front window said closing time had come and gone three hours before. Nevertheless, Baker tried the door and was surprised when it opened with no resistance. His nose immediately registered the pungent scents of metal, sawdust, and fertilizer. Baker tiptoed inside, creeping past a tall display of mulch sacks on sale for $1.99 a pop. He made it all the way down the gardening aisle when a harsh voice stopped him dead in his tracks.

"What in the hell do you think you're doing?" A towering man in a thick flannel shirt with the sleeves rolled up, lumberjack-style, flounced toward him. "Can't you read? We're closed."

"Yeah, I saw," Baker began. "Are you the cashier?"

"That depends. Who the fuck are you?"

"It's just... uh... well, I need to hang a painting and I'm out of nails."

"At this hour?"

"I've got insomnia."

"Hands up."

"What?"

"You heard me."

"Look—*oof!*" The cashier threw him against a collection of spades and started to roughly pat down his legs and torso. "I can explain."

"Do you usually need a gun to hang paintings in the middle of the night?"

"I said I can expl—"

"Shut it," said the cashier, now sifting through the contents of Baker's pockets. "I want to know what you're doing here and I want to know n—" The cashier trailed off at the sight of the Lamotte Exports business card, his eyes nearly bulging out of their sockets. "Jesus, Mary, and Joseph! I am so sorry, sir. Why didn't you just say you had an invitation?"

Baker gave an awkward shrug. "It's my first time."

"That's quite all right, sir," said the cashier, clumsily smoothing out the ruffles he had created on Baker's pants and jacket. "Follow me." He led the way down an adjoining aisle of differently sized hammers.

"Did you park in the underground lot?" the cashier asked over his shoulder.

"No" said Baker. "My car is just down the block."

"Not a problem, sir. I can have it moved if you like."

"That's all right. I won't be long."

"I'd appreciate it if you didn't mention me giving you a hard time back there."

"The thought didn't even cross my mind."

"Much obliged. Now, kindly step aside."

They had reached the back of the store, where a massive display of wrenches dominated the entire wall. The burly man grabbed a faded pipe wrench at the top and gave it an almighty tug. There was a deep *ka-thunk!* And the wall creaked outward, revealing a gloomy concrete stairwell lined with thick, soundproofing material. The bodyguard leaned into the hollowed-out space and pressed a small white button three times.

"Down you go," he said. "Have that invitation of yours ready."

"Thanks," said Baker.

He started down the steps and the cashier wasted no time in pushing the wall back into place. This cut off most of the light and Baker felt as though he were being sealed into a mausoleum. The ensuing silence was oppressive as claustrophobia gnawed at his insides.

After what felt like hours of descension, he reached the bottom. Just when he thought he could stand it no longer, the wall ahead of him slid open and the sounds of lounge music and drunken revelry poured into the space. A tall and golden-jacketed maître d' stood in the entrance, backlit by an eerie red glow. His white-gloved palm was open and expectant.

"Name?"

"Uh..." said Baker. "Henry Kissinger."

"Invitation, please."

Baker handed over the business card, backside up. The maître d' accepted the cream-colored square of lacquered paper and held it under a nearby black light, which revealed the illustration of a leaping fox stamped atop the letters. He did not hand the invitation back, but produced an ampule of clear liquid and turned it over, allowing two drops to hit the card. At once, the ink began to fade until it was gone completely.

"Very good, sir," said the maître d', tossing the now-ordinary business card into a wastebasket. "Welcome to the Nine-Tailed Fox."

CHAPTER 34

The maître d' stepped aside, and Baker heard himself audibly gasp. The club was immense, its floors a deep black obsidian that reflected a high ceiling full of crimson bulbs.

Waiters decked out in the same golden jackets and white gloves as the maître d' swiftly moved about, carrying silver trays of drinks and cloche-covered entrées.

An ample bar sat against the back wall, overlooking a sea of tables, almost all of which were full. The tables bordered a dance floor, where couples swayed in time to a soothing rendition of Paul Anka's "Put Your Head on My Shoulder," belted out by a pretty singer in a tight, sequined dress. More than a few lone men watched her longingly from their seats.

Even the band members seemed in awe of the singer's beauty, often forgetting to hit certain notes. But it hardly seemed to matter—everyone was having a grand old time, including a number of influential Los Angeles power players such as Mayor C. Norris Poulson and California Governor William Knowland (whose staunch anti-Communist views had helped him win the gubernatorial election against Pat Brown the year before).

"Complimentary soju, sir?" A waiter had appeared at Baker's side, seemingly out of nowhere, cradling a tray full of bamboo shot glasses.

"Uh... what?" Baker asked.

"Soju," repeated the waiter. "A traditional Korean liquor."

"Thanks," said Baker, accepting one of the shot glasses and guzzling the liquid, which tasted like a mixture of vodka and schnapps, in one go. "Mind if I have another?"

"Not at all."

"Thanks," said Baker, throwing back two more in quick succession. "Good stuff."

He drifted over to the bar and was about to signal the head bartender for some proper schnapps when someone called out his name.

"Baker! Hey, Baker! Is that you?" He turned, saw Boaz Friedman striding over, his arms looped around a pair of thin waists. "It is you, you son of a bitch!" exclaimed Boaz, a shit-eating grin on his face. The Ohev Shalom congregant grabbed Baker's hand and pumped it with vigor. "What are you doing here? How'd you get an invite?"

"I'm working a case," Baker muttered, hoping no one had noticed the mention of his actual name. "What are *you* doing here?"

"I work here!"

"I thought you worked at a cannery."

"Oh, that's just a bullshit cover story for the wife."

"You mean the wife you're currently holding hostage over divorce proceedings?"

"Excuse me?"

"Tzipora has asked for the writ of divorce over half-a-dozen times now. What's the holdup?"

"You've got no clue what you're talking about, Baker," said Boaz. "My cunt of a wife—"

Wham! Baker socked Boaz squarely in the mouth and felt the man's two front teeth come loose.

Friedman howled in pain and fell over backward. "Motherfucker!" came the muffled insult as his hands probed the damage.

"You'll be fine, Boaz," Baker said. "Go see Dr. Bagley and he'll fix you right up. The man does good work. And one last thing..." He got down on Friedman's level. "Give your wife that writ of divorce, or I won't be so generous next time. Is that understood?"

Boaz nodded slowly, eyes still alight with shock.

"I need to hear you say it, Boaz."

"I'll give her the fucking get."

"Good man," Baker said, standing back up to address Boaz's female companions. "My sincerest apologies, ladies. Mr. Friedman here just remembered he has an urgent dental appointment."

Boaz staggered to his feet, blood pouring out from between his closed fingers. "Come on, let's get out of here," he said to the women, who didn't look too interested anymore. "Fine, you two dames can pay for your drinks from here on out."

"Well then," said Baker after the emasculated Boaz had stalked off and a pair of waiters came over to hastily clean up the mess, "I'd be happy to purchase a round for you lovely ladi—"

There was a tap on his shoulder, and thinking it was Boaz back for Round 2, he spun around, fists at the ready. It turned out to be the maître d'.

"Excuse me, sir," he said. "You may put your fists down. The owner would like you to join him in the private dining area."

"Not in trouble, am I? Might be some sort of record, I suppose. I just got here."

"No, sir. This way, please."

The maître d' turned heel, strode across the dance floor, past the bandstand, and over to an inconspicuous archway hidden behind a pair of thick velvet curtains. He held them aside for Baker, who stepped into a room similar to the one he had just left.

The only real difference between the two was that the private dining area was virtually empty and did not contain a bar or bandstand. Its only occupants were the heavyset owner, a man with thinning hair and pouted lips, noisily slurping up a plate of raw oysters. To his left sat an extremely beautiful, yet bored-looking, woman admiring her reflection in a compact mirror.

"Ahem," coughed the maître d', clearing his throat.

The owner paused, his two-tined fork in the middle of lifting an oyster from its craggy shell. He wasn't obese, per se, but was well on his way to getting there. The fork fell with a clatter onto the plate, and he clapped his hands together with a guttural exclamation of joy.

"A-ha! Just the man I wanted to see," he said with a clear New York inflection. "Come on in and take a load off, Mr. Kissinger. I'm honored you finally decided to grace my humble establishment with your presence."

Baker did as he was told, taking the chair opposite the bivalve eater, who asked: "What's your poison? Bong here will bring ya anything ya like. Pro bono, of course."

"Peach schnapps," Baker said. "Cold as you can make it."

"Another champagne for me," said the owner, picking up a thin glass flute and shaking it. "Oh, and break out a tin of the Sevruga while you're at it."

"Very good, Mr. Cohen," said Bong. He gave a slight bow and left the room.

"So..." Baker said, but the owner held out a stalling hand.

"Leave us, toots," he grunted to the woman.

She did as instructed, looking only too happy to rejoin the main club. The owner gave her buttocks a firm slap and returned to his plate of oysters with renewed vigor.

"Hungry?" he asked, dousing one of the snot-like sea creatures with blood-red cocktail sauce and guzzling it down with an uncouth *Schluuuup!*

"Think I'll just stick with schnapps for now."

"Suit yourself. If only my ma could see me now—all this treif would probably give her a goddamn heart attack."

Bong returned with their drinks and a large metal tin. The owner crowed with delight and popped it open to reveal a bulging mass of jet-black sturgeon eggs swimming in a pool of vividly yellow fish oil. "Pure Russian caviar," he said, scooping generous clusters of eggs onto each of the remaining oysters. "Nearly impossible to import."

They sat in silence for another minute—Baker sipping his schnapps while his host sucked down caviar-topped oysters like there was no tomorrow.

"So..." Baker said, interrupting the lull. "Your name's Cohen?"

"Mickey," he replied, guzzling half of his latest glass of champagne in one go. "Call me Mickey."

"Nice place you got here, Mickey."

"Glad you like it. This club is my pride and joy."

"How'd you get the city to part with one of its precious fallout shelters?"

"Gas main explosion," Cohen said. "Least that's the story we paid for."

"What can I do for you, Mickey?"

"I'd like ya to have a drink with me, is all. Maybe an oyster, too. It's quite an honor to have you in my establishment, Mr. Kissinger. I was wondering when you might show up."

"Pardon?"

"You reserved a table here for the entire week, flaunted your Nixon connections to get bumped up the waiting list, but only show up tonight. You also just assaulted one of my security people."

"Boaz Friedman is a chazer," said Baker. "A pig."

"To that," Cohen said, "I agree wholeheartedly. But you can't just come in here and assault my men. This is a respectable place of business and I have a reputation to uphold. I'm sure you can understand that. However, I'll let it slide this one time because of who you know. If it happens again, all your fancy government contacts won't be able to protect you."

"I appreciate that, Mickey," said Baker. "I'll be sure to pass along the message to Henry Kissinger when I find him."

"Huh?"

"I'm not Henry Kissinger."

"Then who the hell are you?"

"The PI hired to track him down. My name is Morris Baker."

"The hell you are," replied Cohen with a snort. "Prove it."

"You know me?" asked Baker, handing over his PI license.

"*Know* you?" Cohen leaned over to heartily shake Baker's hand. "I'm an admirer of your work. A *big* admirer. I must've listened to that Liberty Boys broadcast a hundred times. I had my guys press it into a fuckin' record. Hand to God! Always hoped to meet ya, but had no clue what you looked like. Wow, Morris Baker in my club. What an honor. Hey, you wanna take another swing at Friedman? You go ahead and be my guest! Beat his face into a pulp if you like!"

"No, that's okay."

"You're a Yid with balls of brass who doesn't take shit from no one!" Mickey continued. "Showed those Nazi fucks what we're all about last year. Made us Jews proud."

"...Thanks."

"Reminds me of a story," Mickey pressed on. "Must've been"—*Shlorrrrrp!* The oyster-eating frenzy began afresh—"ohhh, '37 or '38. Before the Nips attacked and we got into the war. Those German Bundist shits were causing all sorts of trouble out here. I was serving a stint in County at the time, and one day, they bring in this Kraut-loving prick named Noble with a friend of his, right? I don't know if some paperwork got switched around or what, but the pair ends up in my cell. *My goddamn cell*, can you *believe* it?"

Cohen shrieked with mirth, spraying flecks of chewed-up oyster all over the table. Baker scooted his chair away, but the club owner was too caught up in his own reminiscence to notice.

"I know them, and they know me, right? They try to move to the other side of the cell, like I wouldn't notice, but I grab 'em and start knocking their heads together. With two of them, you'd think they'd put up more of a fight, but they didn't do nothing. Not surprising. Look at the rats they looked up to. Hitler, Goebbels, Himmler. Swallowed poison the minute they realized they weren't on top of the food chain no more. Yemach Shemo!"

Cohen let out another bray of laughter. Fortunately, he had stopped eating for the moment, so there were no oyster projectiles this time.

"So Noble and his buddy—can't remember the name of the other putz just now—they're good and frightened, right? They're trying to squeeze through the bars, both of them, and I'm pulling them back. Now they're screaming and hollering so much, it sounds like a full-on riot. They keep going on and on about their 'rights.' Their *rights*! What a crock of shit! As if you and the rest of our brothers and sisters across the pond were shown any rights under the Huns. Of course, the cops on duty have heard all the ruckus and one of 'em's trying to get the cell open. He's all flustered and can't get the key in the lock while Noble's shouting, 'Why did ya put us in with this *wild animal*?'

"By the time the cop gets the door open, I'm already back in my little corner, pretending to read the newspaper. The cop walks right up and says, 'You son of a bitch, what happened now?' And if ya can believe it, Baker, I put my paper down like I'm at the fuckin' breakfast table and I says to him, I says, 'What are you asking me for? I was just sitting here, minding my own business, when these two got in a fight. I have no idea what happened!'"

Cohen slapped the table, causing his champagne flute to topple over. The fizzing wine spread over the white tablecloth and dripped onto the floor.

Baker certainly shared Cohen's disdain for Nazis—and could admire the man's attempt to strike fear into the hearts of those who supported them—but he didn't think he'd ever fully come to like the blustering and self-absorbed Cohen. People like him cared about only one thing: themselves. They performed what one might call "good deeds" not out of the kindness of their hearts, but so they could have something to gloat about later.

"Yes, sir," Cohen said. "I got quite a reputation as a Jewish defender after that. If someone in this town needed to bust some anti-Semites, they called on ol' Mickey. They knew I'd take care of business."

Without warning, he popped up out of his seat with a surprising amount of speed, which did not match his incredible girth, and began to shadowbox. The bib-like napkin stuffed into his collar gave Cohen the appearance of a large baby.

Baker fought a desire to laugh, surmising that "ol' Mickey" did not take kindly to jests made at his expense. The faux heavyweight bout with no one went on for longer than it should have when Cohen, sweaty and red-faced, sat down and reached for a glass of ice water he had miraculously not knocked over. He sucked it all down, ground the chips of ice between his teeth, and smacked his lips in satisfaction.

"Those were the golden days. Everyone, and I mean *everyone*, knew my name. They knew me or, at the very least, owed me a favor. I was king of the fuckin' world. Then it all came crashing down when the feds decided to send me to Alcatraz on some trumped-up tax charge. I spent four years in the big house, and when I got out in '55, the world I knew was gone. It was supposed to be my big homecoming. I was supposed to be bigger than I ever was, but instead, I find Adolf Jr.'s running the country and my reputation is all but gone. All the great things I'd done for this town no longer mattered. I was no better than dirt—all because I got a clipped prick."

"So how'd this place come about?" Baker asked. "Must've cost a pretty penny."

"Didn't cost me a dime," Cohen replied smugly, now using the bib-like napkin to wipe all the sweat from his brow. "Koreans bankrolled the whole operation. They just needed someone who knew the turf and had a flair for drumming up business. They keep the lights on, and in exchange for reeling in the customers, I keep all the profits."

"And what do the Koreans get in return?"

Cohen leaned over the table and whispered the next word, even though they were completely alone: "Information. After I got out of the slammer, none of my old friends would speak to me. They avoided me like the goddamned plague. My old life in what you might call the 'criminal underworld' was finished. I thought about heading for Lansky's Jewish sanctuary out in Vegas, but a ghetto's still a ghetto, no matter how much you try to gussy it up with girls and gambling. Then the war started to drag on and the Koreans approached me with a proposition I couldn't refuse. I ain't in the crime business no more, Baker...I'm in the spy business."

"So you turned traitor?"

"'Traitor'? No, I don't think so," Mickey said, all the joy gone from his voice. "I got no country left to betray. Not after the US of A turned its back on me. On us! We're nomads, you and me. Just like our ancestors who wandered in that farkakte desert for forty years. We gotta look out for ourselves now and that means teaming up with the highest bidder."

Cohen's face darkened and took on an unpleasant leer.

"I built this club from the ground up, turning it into one of the hottest joints in town. I'm sure you saw the mayor and governor out there. They're regular customers, every last one of 'em. The very bastards who cast us aside. They come here, I pump them full of booze, and they unknowingly piss information like a bucket drilled full of holes. Right into my waiting hands."

"Impressive," said Baker, realizing he could use Cohen's wounded bravado to his advantage. "You're right, we are very alike."

"Damn straight. We're the underdogs."

"To the underdogs," Baker said, raising his glass of schnapps in a toast and Cohen did the same with his empty champagne flute.

"To the underdogs."

"If you are privy to all this information, maybe you can help me out with something."

"Name it," Mickey said without hesitation. "Like I said, we gotta stick together. You ever need anything—and I mean *anything*—you just call. Bong will set you up with my private number. I change it every few weeks so HUAC don't get wise. Ya can't bug what ya can't catch."

"That's very generous of you. Like I said, I came here tonight because I'm looking for Henry Kissinger. You said he had hasn't shown up at all?"

"Nope. And I had to bump some very angry customers out of their usual tables to get him the weeklong reservation. How'd you get his invitation anyway?"

"I found it stamped on the back of a Lamotte Exports business card in the hotel room where Kissinger was last seen. Any idea if Orson Lamotte has ties to the State Department?"

"Lamotte...Lamotte..." Cohen said, scratching his chin. "Don't have much to do with him, to tell you the truth. The shipping required for the club doesn't exactly go through legitimate channels. But I'm sure he's greased some palms over in DC to make them look the other way so he can do business in Commie-run waters. But if it's dirt on Lamotte you're lookin' for, I know some guys who can probably be of more help."

"Oh?"

"Two of the best smugglers on the entire West Coast," Mickey declared. "They're how I get all my contraband, like this caviar, for instance." To get his point across, he guzzled down another oyster topped with black gold.

"Where can I find them?" Baker asked.

"They usually hang out down in San Pedro by the ports with all the other sailors. Look for an out-of-the-way tavern called Charybdis on West Thirty-Seventh Street right off South Anchovy Avenue. It's the last stop before the water. And when you get there, tell 'em Mickey sent ya. If not, you might just be tossed into the Pacific with your hands tied behind your back and your balls stuffed down your throat. Those guys don't fuck around."

"Guess I'll be trying out my sea legs," said Baker. "By the way, there are two dead cops sitting just up the street from your establishment. You didn't have anything to do with that, did you?"

"*Me? Murder cops?*" Cohen said, affronted. "I won't deny there's a bit of blood on my hands, but killing LA's finest? No, sir. That's very bad for business. Thanks for sounding the alarm, though. I'll make sure they're found by the right people."

"Thanks a lot for your time, Mr. Cohen."

"I told you, it's 'Mickey,' and what, you're leavin' already? It's not every day you get to share a few rounds with one of your heroes. Bong?... *Bong!*"

The maître d' came rushing back into the room. "What can I get for you, Mr. Cohen?"

"Another round for myself and Baker here. And while you're at it, bring me two dozen more oysters."

CHAPTER 35

Mickey insisted on having several more drinks—each one more potent than the last—before he let Baker leave the private dining room. In fact, Mickey didn't even give him permission; the club's owner simply started to nod off from the surfeit of booze and caviar-topped mollusks, which gave Baker the perfect opportunity to quietly excuse himself from the gangster's presence.

Thoroughly inebriated himself, he stumbled back into the main area of the Nine-Tailed Fox, nearly toppling a British patron with a pompous grin.

"Blimey!" said the man through the cigarette perched between his lips. "Do watch where you're going, old chap!"

"My apologies, old sport," slurred Baker, suddenly reminded of old Archie Hicks. "God save the Queen and all that! Pip-pip, cheerio!"

"Quite all right, sir," said the Brit. "Look after yourself, then."

"Thank ya kindly. Ta-ta for now," answered Baker, ambling up to the bar. "God save the Queen!" he repeated. The club was much noisier than he remembered and he could barely hear himself order a peach schnapps on the rocks. "Put it on Mickey's tab!" he shouted to the bartender.

"What an unusual drink order..."

This from an extremely pretty Asian woman in a low-cut cocktail dress of green fabric, which left just enough to the imagination. The premature streaks of gray running through her long black hair seemed vaguely familiar.

"Don't knock it 'til you try it, doll," he said.

"This is me knocking it before I try it."

She rapped her knuckles on the polished wood of the bar and Baker guffawed.

"Very clever. I like a dame with a sense of humor."

"Can I buy you a drink?" she asked.

"Already got one," he said, accepting the chilled glass of schnapps.

"I meant when you're done with that one."

"Shouldn't I be the one offering to buy *you* a drink?"

"Ever heard of Sadie Hawkins?"

"Nope."

"Two more orders of peach schnapps on the rocks," she told the bartender.

"I also like a woman who takes charge," said Baker, polishing off his drink.

"Oh?" She leaned in closer to him. "What else do you like in a woman?"

"Say," he said, squinting in an effort to bring his blurred field of vision into focus. "Don't I know you from somewhere?"

"I get that a lot. Guess I've just got one of those faces."

"Not sure I've seen many faces like yours before."

"Maybe you haven't been looking in the right place."

"Clearly."

Their drinks arrived.

"To trying new things," said the woman.

"To looking in the right places," countered Baker.

They drank deeply and Baker felt himself slip into a deeper state of drunkenness that turned all the sounds of the club into a deadened pounding. The woman continued to speak, but he couldn't understand a word of it.

It was nice to simply drift away, to dissociate from everything. But wait—something felt off. His legs were starting to feel weak, his vision darkening. He'd blacked out enough times to know this wasn't what it felt like. The woman's brow furrowed, and she leaned forward to grab his arm. Baker forced himself to actively listen to what she was saying.

"Are you okay?" she asked a little louder than was necessary. "You're not looking too good."

"*Hurmm*," was all he could manage as he slumped over the bar, the only thing keeping him upright. His face fell level with the second glass of schnapps, and at last, he understood. It was too late to rush to the bathroom and force his stomach to regurgitate whatever Mickey—*Ha! How fitting!*—had been slipped into the drink.

"Darling," said the woman, "I do believe you've had enough for tonight. I think it's time we head home. Sorry," she added, turning to the bartender and slipping several bills into his palm. "He always gets like this. Doesn't know his limit, I'm afraid."

Baker was a prisoner in his own body, could only watch helplessly as the bartender chuckled and surreptitiously pocketed the money. "Not a problem, ma'am," he said. "I see it all the time. Do you need some help getting him out of here?"

"If you wouldn't mind helping him to the car, that would be swell."

"Sure thing."

The woman leaned over and whispered in Baker's ear: "I'm very sorry about this, mister... What's that you're saying?"

"*Gu... Gu... Gu...*" slurred Baker, trying to form the word that referred to a striking beauty who lured unsuspecting men to their deaths.

"I'm afraid I don't understand," she said.

Finally, he managed to get it out: "Gumiho."

Then the blackness consumed him.

CHAPTER 36

Debbie had joined the nightmarish troupe at the Griffith Observatory. She led the charge, growling at von Braun, the dead-eyed children, and Liz if they tried to get too close. It was her turn to torment Baker. Her moment to shine. The dripping ribbons of her slit wrists contorted and stretched like octopus tentacles around his neck, choking all the air from his windpipe. He choked and sputtered, trying in vain to pry the torn flesh away from his throat.

But it was no use.

"You deserve this," hissed Debbie, her blue lips parted to reveal a darkened maw from which a pair of bright yellow cat's eyes, Matagot's eyes, stared out at him. "You know you deserve this, don't you? For not saving me. For not saving any of us. You deserve this."

"You deserve this," echoed the crowd roiling behind her. "You deserve this."

"Cast him into the pit!" proclaimed von Braun, pulling out the knife lodged inside his spine and licking the blood off the tip of its blade with a forked tongue.

"Cast him into the pit!" sang the gassed children, joining hands.

"History comes for us all!" crowed the top half of Elizabeth Short.

"You deserve this!" Debbie screeched.

The tendrils of her slit wrists tightened.

"Hey . . . Hey, fella . . . *Hey!*"

Baker's eyes fluttered open, and consciousness came flooding back in a little too fast for his drugged brain. He shut his eyes and murmured, "Fuck."

"Oh, thank goodness, you're alive. You were thrashing around and coughing. I thought you might choke on your own vomit or something."

"Trust me," said Baker, taking slow, deep breaths in an attempt to fight off the dizziness and nausea. "It's nothing new."

"You sure?"

"Quite sure."

"Well, I guess it's a good thing I restrained you, then."

Certain he wouldn't be sick, Baker cautiously opened his eyes and found his legs and wrists tightly bound to the posts of a twin bed in the middle of what could only be a cheap and ratty motel room. The moth-eaten curtains were drawn but could not fully hide the blinking of a red-and-blue neon sign just outside the window.

His captor, the woman who had bought him a drink at the Nine-Tailed Fox, sat in the room's only chair. Now dressed in black slacks and a matching turtleneck sweater, she was more undercover soldier and less promiscuous floozy. The gun—his snub-nosed .44 Magnum—in her hand completed the ensemble.

"You know," said Baker, awkwardly lifting his head up to address her, "I'm not opposed to getting a little weird in the bedroom...but there are better ways to seduce a guy."

"I am sorry about this," she said, and to her credit, there was a note of genuine sorrow. "To be quite frank, I was getting a little desperate."

"You didn't have to slip me a Mickey if you wanted to talk to me alone. I also respond to politeness."

"I wasn't sure who you were working for. When I saw you leaving Kissinger's hotel room yesterday, I thought you might be—"

"Hang on," said Baker, cutting her off. "You're the maid I saw at Chateau Marmont. I knew you looked familiar!"

"I'm not actually a maid," said the woman with a diffident smile. "I stole that uniform and cleaning cart to gain access to Kissinger's room."

"If you're not a maid, then who the hell are you?"

"I don't think you're in any position to be demanding answers. Now talk. Who do you work for? HUAC?"

"*What?* No! Name's Morris Baker—I'm just some PI schmuck who was hired to find the guy. My ID and license are in my wallet in case you don't believe me."

The woman got up, walked over to the bed, and extracted his overstuffed wallet. She flipped it open and began sifting through its jumbled contents.

"I introduced myself," he said. "Now it's your turn."

"My name is Evelyn Yang," she said, holding his PI license up to the room's naked bulb.

"Yang as in—?"

"Yes, my brother was William Yang."

"The guy who blew himself up in the department store?"

Evelyn's face soured. "He didn't blow himself up. At least not willingly."

"What makes you say that?"

"Because my brother was sweet and kind. The William I knew would never do such a thing."

"You'd be surprised what a person will do once a radical ideology takes root inside their head. I'm living proof of that, sweetheart."

"I'm not as forgiving as that girl you met in the club," she said. "You will address me as 'Miss Yang,' or I'll put a bullet right between your eyes."

"All right, Miss Yang, I'm sorry. Let's just take it easy." He tried to hold up his palms in a surrendering motion, which caused the ropes to tighten. "Ouch! You really know your knots."

"Twelve years in the Girl Scouts," she said. "You pick up a few useful skills along the way. Who hired you to find Kissinger?"

"A woman claiming to be his wife came to my office two days ago and asked me to track him down," Baker explained. "He was in town for the Kishi peace tour and vanished. Turns out the woman who hired me wasn't actually his wife. I'm trying to figure out why someone wanted to dupe me. What's your interest in him?"

"Henry Kissinger was my brother's boss at the State Department."

"Your brother worked *for* Kissinger? That wasn't mentioned in any of the papers."

"Of course not. That would just embarrass the government."

"Don't be so sure. I bet McCarthy would love an opportunity to say 'I told you so.'"

"My brother and I were raised right here in Los Angeles. Our loyalty to this country should not be in question, Mr. Baker. William fought in Korea for several years. *On the American side*," she added angrily when Baker opened his mouth to ask a question. "He came back from the war and advocated for peace and nuclear disarmament. That's what got him a job in the State Department in the first place. He and Kissinger were back-channeling, desperate for some kind of diplomatic solution. They masterminded a peace plan that would effectively bisect Korea into two separate countries."

"So what happened?"

"Are you kidding? The president couldn't accept a plan like that. It'd go against his entire image of being hard on Communism. It's either unconditional surrender or nothing. The proposal was scrapped, and William was devastated. The last thing he wanted was more bloodshed on either side and Henry agreed. But the fighting went on and McCarthy started directing animus toward Asian-Americans to deflect attention away from the fact that we were no closer to winning the war than we were to having detente with the Soviets. William was let go from his job because he was Korean."

"That's the classic radical origin story, Evelyn," Baker said. "Sounds like your brother went from optimist to malcontent. Hitting back against the system that failed you seems oh-so-enticing when everything else has gone kaput. 'The best laid plans of mice and men—'"

"'Gang aft a-gley,'" finished Evelyn. "I'm well aware of the poem, Mr. Baker. And maybe I could have believed that, had William not reconnected with Henry about a year ago. He wanted William back for one more go at an off-the-books peace plan."

"I see your point," Baker said, now experiencing a definite lack of sensation in his bound limbs. "Blowing yourself up in a department store does seem a little counterproductive to peace."

"William wrote me regularly every week, but after three months or so, his letters just stopped. Not even a quick phone call to say he was too busy. I tried getting through to Henry's office but was told they had no record of a William Yang. I called his apartment building, only for the super to tell me there was no tenant under that name. It was as though my brother never existed. I didn't see him again until his face was splashed all over the newspapers."

"What are you implying?" Baker asked. "That Kissinger had

something to do with your brother's disappearance? That he somehow *convinced* William to kill all those people?"

"I don't know what I'm saying," said Evelyn, and she plopped back into the chair, tired and defeated. "All I want is the truth about what happened to William. If anyone has that information, it's Henry Kissinger—except he seems to have vanished, too."

"How'd you know he was out here?"

"I traveled down to Washington and did some snooping. I lied my way into his office and purloined a copy of his winter agenda."

"What about the club? How did you know he'd be at the Nine-Tailed Fox?"

"Look at me, Mr. Baker."

"How can I not? You've got a gun pointed at my face."

"That was rhetorical. I'm not an unattractive woman," she said. "It's not all that difficult to coax information out of men. You put on the right outfit, show them an iota of skin, and they're clay in your hands."

"Your bartender accomplice. Pretty resourceful for a Girl Scout, Miss Yang."

"Watch it."

"Noted. Okay, I think it's clear we both have the same goal here. How about untying me and we work together to find Kissinger? I've got a hunch we're not the only ones looking for him."

"How do you figure?"

"The two dead cops I found outside the Nine-Tailed Fox is how I figure. They were also tasked with finding Kissinger from his *actual* wife. They must've gotten wind of him having a reserved table at the club and waited for him to show up. Only someone else caught up to them first. Someone who wants Kissinger dead."

"You're saying…"

"That Kissinger orchestrated his own disappearance? Sure. Maybe he knows something he shouldn't. And he's still a Jew. If he turned up dead, no one would shed a tear. Good riddance to another no-good Hebe. But if the man was smart enough to broker peace with Korea, I'm sure it wouldn't be too hard to turn himself into a ghost. Probably had this little contingency plan in his back pocket for a while on the off chance he became a target."

"You think the people who hired you are the ones who want him dead?"

"Yes. Who better to find a Jew marked for death than another Jew they can also take out once the job is done? Nice and clean, which is why they don't want the LAPD involved. They make too much noise. And you're right, if your brother was set up or coerced into doing what he did, then Kissinger will know how and why."

"You agree he was just a patsy?"

"I don't have all the pieces to say that with absolute certainty, Miss Yang. However, I do know what it's like to be at the center of a frame-up job. I'll help you clear William's name—if he was innocent in all of this."

"You'll really help?"

"Just said I would, didn't I? Can't do shit if I'm tied to this bed, though."

"Oh, right." Evelyn put down the gun and began undoing the ropes around Baker's wrists and ankles.

"Thanks," he said. "How long was I out, by the way?"

"It's five thirty in the morning."

"Best sleep I've had in a while."

Once he was free, Baker sat up, registering a stiffness in his back that would probably make itself at home for several weeks to come.

"You certain we haven't met before?" he asked, now getting his best look at Evelyn's face. "Beyond our little run-in at the hotel, I mean."

"Not that I know of," said Evelyn.

"I could swear I've seen you somewhere else bef—" A coughing fit took hold again. Evelyn took a step forward, but he shooed her away.

"It's nothing."

"You call hacking up blood 'nothing'?"

The fit subsided. Baker looked down to see fresh flecks of blood glistening on the bedspread. He turned to Evelyn, wiping his mouth with a shirtsleeve, staining it red as well.

"I don't think you'll be getting your incidental fee back on this room, Miss Yang. Got a cigarette?"

Dear Valued Service Member:

Your government and fellow citizens thank you for joining the Nuclear Negation Administration (NNA) as a member of our on-the-ground team currently working in South Korea.

In your welcome packet, you will find an anti-radiation suit, a pocket-sized dosimeter, an English-to-Korean dictionary, a box of fancy chocolates (on us!), and a Beretta M1951. Please make sure to wash your suit regularly with soap and warm water, as you will only be given one.

Upon landing at Gimpo International Airport in Seoul, you will meet with a supervisor and be assigned to a specific region and town. As a member of the NNA, you will prove instrumental in reducing collateral damage in the unlikely event of a nuclear strike from Soviet-backed North Korean forces.

Your tasks are as follows:

- Practice evacuation drills with civilians and valued dignitaries
- Offer support to ground troops stationed overseas
- Deliver seminars on the efficacy of the duck-and-cover method
- Quarantine and sanitize potentially irradiated areas
- Extol the virtues of American capitalism and the freedoms that come with it
- Assist in medical care for individuals suffering from radiation sickness
- Compile data on the effects of radiation on the human body

If you hear a member of the Korean population—be they man, woman, or child—espousing pro-Communist sympathies with the North, please report it to a superior immediately. A united front alongside the United States is the only way to ensure total victory in this conflict.

If you yourself become sick from a radioactive incident, you will be afforded the best medical care our great nation has to offer. If, on the off chance, you succumb to your affliction, your next of kin will be awarded with a one-time payment of $5000.

Not only are you doing your country a great service, but you are also ensuring a better and brighter future for Democratic peoples around the globe. We know you will do us proud.

Good luck and Godspeed!

John A. McCone, NNA Chairman

OUR STORY

Since our restructuring from the Atomic Energy Commission in 1955, the Nuclear Negation Administration has dedicated itself to the containment and safe application of fissionable energy. Upon taking office in 1953, President Joseph McCarthy wisely concluded that the devastating power of a split atom should remain firmly in the hands of a select few for the sole protection of America and her citizens.

He feared—as so many of us do—another betrayal from the Semitic population (à la the Rosenberg scandal). But Jewish irresponsibility with our atomic arsenal goes back several years before that treasonous betrayal to 1946 when Louis Slotin's pigheaded mishandling of a plutonium bomb core (known in some circles as the "demon core") resulted in his death. The Hebrews have, time and again, proved themselves unworthy of dabbling in this precarious scientific realm.

Erecting a higher fence around the deadly secrets contained within the very building blocks of life was the only way to ensure that such events—both traitorous and clumsily accidental—would never happen again. Concurrently, the president ingeniously recognized the unlimited potential of nuclear energy, which now powers our homes, businesses, and cars.

Moreover, our commander-in-chief showed his inspiring solidarity with democratic countries abroad by sympathizing with South Korean concerns of an outbreak of nuclear war on the East Asian Peninsula. He agreed that the people of South Korea deserved to be prepared and thus, the NNA—the honorable sixth branch of the US Armed Forces—was born.

Non-US delegations from the United Nations withdrew from

the peninsula in early 1956, allowing American forces to assume full control of the conflict against the North Korean insurgents and their Russian and Chinese masters. Since that time, America's bolstering of South Korean forces under the bold leadership of General Douglas MacArthur has been a rousing success. An unconditional surrender from our enemies is just around the corner!

PART IV

December 28, 1959

I'm waking up, I feel it in my bones
Enough to make my systems blow
Welcome to the new age, to the new age
Whoa, oh, oh, oh, oh, whoa, oh, oh, oh
I'm radioactive... radioactive.

—*Imagine Dragons*

CHAPTER 37

Baker was right about Evelyn's room. It belonged to a condemn-worthy motel with no name (that, or its sign had faded away long ago) on the outskirts of South Gate. His car was still parked on Fox Tail Road, but Evelyn agreed to give him a ride back to his apartment in a rented 1953 Studebaker Commander.

Baker still felt a little groggy and slept for a majority of the ride. His eyes had barely closed when she shook him awake.

"We're here," said Evelyn.

The sky was starting to lighten, bit by bit, and if the sun didn't break free of the clouds in the next hour or two, then Los Angeles would have to swallow another helping of miserable weather.

"Already?" Baker said, yawning and wiping a line of drool from the corner of his mouth. "What time is it?"

"Coming up on seven thirty."

"I need a coffee."

"Want me to take you to a café or something?"

"No, that's all right. What I *really* need is a shower. Listen, go back to your motel room and lay low. I'll call you when I get to my office."

"Sounds like a plan, Morris. I can call you Morris, can't I?"

"Only if I can call you Evelyn instead of 'Miss Yang.'"

She blushed. "Oh, that's just the English teacher in me."

"So you're a teacher, eh?"

"Only part-time."

"Well, Teach, I need a shower, shave, and coffee. In that order."

He trudged across the potholed parking lot and into the musty interior of the Paradise Apartments, managed by Eddie and Marlena Huang. The Huangs weren't exactly the best landlords around, but the building's rundown existence (rotting carpets, chipping masonry, and an out-of-order elevator) had nothing to do with apathy on their part.

It mainly came down to the fact that contractors refused to do work in Chinatown because of anti-Asian sentiment. The tong-employed contractors who did operate in this part of the city were backed up for months.

Climbing up two flights of stairs felt like a chore and he wondered how long it would take for the effects of Evelyn's drug to fully wear off. Devastating hangovers and phenobarbital-induced mental fogs he could live with. But this? This was something else entirely.

It would be a relief to stand beneath the hot stream of the shower. The promise of washing the night off his skin pushed him forward to the scratched wood of 2A.

Reaching into his pocket for the key, Baker heard a strange yowling from within the apartment and remembered with a pang of guilt that he'd left Matagot alone.

"Shit," he hissed, placing the key into the lock. "It's all right, kitty. I'll get you your breakfast in a second." He turned the knob, pushed the door inward, and stepped inside. "Matagot? Here, kitty, kitty, kitty. Pss, pss pss. You hungry?"

The door slammed shut and Baker felt something loop around his throat. For a moment, he assumed he had walked into a stray cobweb. Then his fatigued brain caught up with reality: *No. Air. Stupid.*

Baker's hands jumped to his throat, desperately scrabbling to remove the cord pulled tight around his neck. Snatching a glance from the corners of his bulging eyes, he vaguely registered the towering figure trying to kill him. Fingers dug underneath the cord (*I wonder if it's piano wire...*), prompting the assailant to double their efforts.

If any more force was exerted, Baker would lose the digits, too. Not that it would matter in the long run if he couldn't break free. His vision started to dim. It was like being drugged for the second time in less than twelve hours. He tried to push the assassin backward, but he might as well have been trying to move a boulder for all the good it was doing.

Maybe this is for the best... No! We're not out yet!

While one set of fingers tried to remove the garrote, the other set remained tightly closed around the apartment key. Desperate for even one last breath, Baker struck backward and heard a ghastly squelching noise as the key made contact with something soft.

"Merde!"

Air—glorious fucking air—rushed back into Baker's lungs as the assassin finally loosened their death grip and stumbled backward, repeating the French word for "shit" as if it were going out of style.

Baker doubled over and drew in too much oxygen at once, bringing on another coughing fit, which forced him to his knees.

Wham! Tinkle... tinkle... tinkle... A punch, wild and uncalculated, made contact with the side of Baker's head, knocking him to the ground.

"Fils de pute!" Again, that queer tinkling sound.

Baker rolled over and looked up, taking in one of the strangest sights he'd ever seen: A tall and powerful man in a herringbone overcoat had Baker's key ring dangling out of his left eye socket. Coming to the same realization about the foreign object lodged inside his skull, the Frenchman reached up and yanked it free. The eye came out with it, precariously hanging from the spaghetti-like optic nerve. Blood splattered onto the floor.

"*Fuck!*" the man bellowed in English, dropping the keys and desperately trying to stuff the eyeball back into place.

Something soft brushed against Baker's face. He looked over and saw Matagot curiously pawing at his gun. Baker grabbed it, cocked the hammer back, took aim. The assassin's dislodged eye saw it first (the other peeper was tightly closed against the pain).

"Merde..."

Baker unloaded a round into the Frenchman's forehead right between... well, not the eyes necessarily, but between the space where both eyes had once rested comfortably inside their respective sockets. The towering assassin immediately stopped trying to fix his grievous injury.

His bulging and loping (*sloth-like,* Baker thought) arms fell limp and his good eye rolled up into his head, revealing the ghostly white of the sclera. He toppled forward, his face landing squarely in the dish containing dried tuna remnants from Matagot's last meal. The cat scampered over to the dead man and started licking his dislodged eyeball.

"Said I'd feed you, didn't I?" Baker said hoarsely, massaging his throat.

He sat up, slowly catching his breath. That's when he noticed the noose hanging from the ceiling fan, as well as the small wooden stool lying on its side. Standing up, he circled the apartment, making sure no one else was lying in wait. His inspection of the kitchen yielded another interesting find: a suicide note penned in a style eerily similar to his own:

This world is too cruel a place for me.
The horrors of life are never-ending.
Goodbye.

A bit lazy and vague for his liking, but it would have gotten the job done. "You crafty son of a bitch Frog," he said, turning around to address the corpse lying in an accumulated puddle of blood and processed fish. "Well, Matagot," he said to the cat, "I think we know who killed your previous owner."

CHAPTER 38

Baker tore the suicide note into pieces and began snooping inside the assassin's pockets. His search yielded four items: one large roll of hundred-dollar bills, a French passport in the name of Louis Emele Arnaud (the capital *E* of the signature at the bottom of the document looked more like a backward *3*), a dropper bottle containing a liquid whose scent stung the nostrils, and a crumpled slip of paper with a phone number scribbled upon its surface. Falling onto the bed, stomach first, he grabbed the phone off the floor and dialed the mystery number.

There were two curt rings, then a chipper female voice answered: "*You have reached HUAC, Los Angeles, Echo Park Branch. This is Inspector Lonergan's office, how may I help you this morn—?*"

Baker slammed the phone down.

Ring! Ring! Thinking it was Lonergan's office calling back, Baker picked up the phone, his heart hammering. "Yes...?"

"Morris?" It was Joanna, and she sounded wary.

"Yeah, it's me."

"Do you plan on coming into the office today? You have a delivery."

"What is it?"

"Flowers. Seems you have a secret admirer."

"I doubt that very much. Is there a note?"

"Yeah. It's in a sealed envelope."

"Okay, just leave it for me. Is Hersh there?"

"Not yet. He said he'd be a little late—had to take Mindy for a checkup on the baby. And Rabbi Kahn called to see if you had a moment to talk. I told him I'd ask once you were here. Are you coming in at all today?"

"Yes. I'll be there within the next hour or so. I just have something"—he eyeballed Arnaud's corpse—"to take care of first."

A groggy Mickey Cohen answered his call on the fifth ring.

"What is it?"

"Mickey? Hope I didn't wake you. It's Baker."

"Baker! Not at all. Not all. To what do I owe the pleasure?"

"This line clean?"

"As a whistle."

"I need a favor."

"What kind of favor we talking here?"

"The kind that involves the removal of a dead body."

Mickey laughed. "Well, you called the right guy for the job, Baker. You'll find that getting rid of corpses is my specialty."

CHAPTER 39

I'll send my best guys," Mickey said. "My two golems."

"Golems?"

"You'll see. Just give me your address..."

Baker didn't have to wait long for Mickey to make good on his word. Two burly, yet nondescript, men in dark blue janitorial jumpsuits arrived at his apartment door less than half an hour later, a massive, rolled-up Persian rug held between the pair of them. They asked no questions—in fact, they didn't speak at all—and immediately got to work, wrapping Arnaud's body in a plastic sheet and then into the rug. It was only when they were squashing the body into the middle of the second layer that Baker noticed the dried dirt on Arnaud's scuffed black boots.

"Hold on," Baker said, having a sudden thought. The workers obliged without a word of dissent. He rushed into the kitchen, grabbed a butter knife and plate, and returned to scrape off a sampling of the dirt. "Carry on."

Mickey's golems continued their work, which included a deep scrub of the floor with bleach and horsehair brushes. Baker, meanwhile, had to restrain Matagot from trying to lap up any more of the blood. Once the job was complete, the two men tipped their hats in farewell and left with the stuffed rug.

Baker let go of the cat, which started to sniff around the newly cleaned area. The scent of bleach was pungent and the feline's whiskers stood on end.

"Let's cut your blood intake to once a year," Baker said with a smile. "How about we get you a nice saucer of cream instead?"

Joanna was typing up some client notes when Baker entered the waiting area an hour and a half later (having taken a cab to Fairfax in order to retrieve his car first).

"Morning," she said in a frosty tone.

"Morning," he replied automatically, making his way to the office door.

"That it?" she inquired.

"Is what 'it'?"

"Would you like to talk about yesterday?"

"Not now, Joanna."

"Well, I would like t— Morris! What the hell happened to your neck?"

"A Frog by the name of Arnaud tried to kill me."

Joanna clapped a hand to her mouth in horror. The engagement ring on her finger caught the light, nearly blinding him.

"Oh my goodness!" she exclaimed. "Do you think it could be the Symphony?"

"No, I don't think so."

"What are you going to do?"

"The same thing I always do—figure out why."

"You said his name was 'Arnold'?"

"No, Arnau— Christ!"

"What?"

"I think he worked for Orson Lamotte."

"What makes you say that?"

"Just something his daughter mentioned yesterday."

"Why would Orson Lamotte want you dead?"

"Why, indeed?"

Baker was halfway to his desk, lost in thought, when something else occurred to him. He turned around and leaned back into the waiting room.

"Joanna?"

"Yes?"

"I'm sorry about yesterday and congratulations on the engagement."

She smiled. "Thank you and apology accepted. Who was that man who came to see you?"

"My brother."

"Want to talk ab—?"

"Nope!"

The delivery of flowers turned out to be a magnificent display of freshly picked magnolias standing inside an emerald green vase painted with feeding coy fish. He plucked out the envelope, ripped it open, and read:

Today
Santa Monica Pier Archway
3:30

The phone started to ring just then. Startled by the sudden noise, Baker dropped the note, which fluttered behind his desk and out of sight.

"This is Baker," he said, picking up the receiver.

"Morris, it's Hollis."

Shit!

"Hollis!" Baker exclaimed, thinking fast. "What a coincidence, I was just about to call you."

"Cut the bullshit, Morris. My associates are growing impatient."

"It's my top priority, Hollis. In fact, I've got a strong lead I'll be following up with today. I promise."

"We want results, Morris—not promises."

"And you'll get them. I just need another day or two. These things take time."

"They won't like it, but I'll get you another twenty-four hours. But that's *it*, Morris. After that, I can't stop whatever they decide to set in motion."

Baker considered telling Hollis that the tong could join the long line of people threatening his life. Not wanting to press his luck, he said, "You're the best, Hollis! I won't let you down!"

Click... Baker had never seen Hollis this angry before. He did not want to compromise their friendship, especially since he didn't have many friends to begin with, and he pledged to do better with his investigation into the disappearance of Han Zhao. But first, he called Evelyn.

"Pat?" he said, using the code name they had agreed upon earlier, lest someone was listening in. "This is Ollie. Listen, I had a great time with you last night and was wondering if you might want to go out for a late lunch with me this afternoon...?"

"Ollie!" she cheered, sounding genuinely excited. Her quickness on the uptake reminded him of Sophia. "It's so great to hear from you. Yes, I'd love to grab a late lunch."

"Fantastic! Shall we say a quarter to three? I'll pick you up."

"It's a date."

"See you then."

He pulled out a fresh bottle of schnapps, poured a healthy measure, used it to chase down another tablet of phenobarbital, and sat there wondering.

Wondering why Arnaud would want to kill him before Henry Kissinger was found. There could be little doubt over the Frenchman being the one who had paid Midge to pose as the man's wife. What did Lamotte even want with Kissinger? And why would the hot-tempered robber baron go to all the trouble of hiring Baker, only to order his death two days later? The presence of Lonergan's phone number in Arnaud's pocket hinted at a possible explanation of such discordant behavior: The late assassin served two masters.

He began sorting through a pile of mail left on his desk by Joanna. Bill, bill, junk, bill, bill, junk, junk, bill, bill (the government might hate his guts, but they sure had no problem taking his tax dollars). The last bit of junk mail made its way into the trash bin when the two-way intercom situated in the corner of his desk buzzed to life.

"Morris," Joanna said, her voice crackling over the speaker, "A Mr. Abrams is here to see you."

Baker hid the schnapps and depressed the transmit button: "Send him in."

The office door opened, revealing a handsome young man in his mid-to-late twenties, though the baby face made it hard to gauge how old this boy truly was. The kid removed his tweed cap, unbuttoned a moleskin jacket, and nervously ran a thumb and forefinger across a wispy mustache that screamed, *I'm trying to look older than I really am. It's working, right?* His skin bore the unmistakable signs of a heavy tan fading back into pale white.

"How can I help you, son?" Baker asked.

"You are Morris Baker?" asked the kid, his voice quavering a little. Baker picked up on a strange accent he could not place right away. "*The* Morris Baker?"

"How many Morris Bakers do you know?"

"You killed Wernher von Braun. You stopped the Black Symphony from detonating an atomic bomb. You're a legend."

"Oh, not one of you crazies," Baker groaned, making to push the intercom and ask Joanna if Hersh was around to escort this fanatic off the premises. "I don't need this, not after the morning I've had."

"No, wait!" exclaimed the young man, taking a step forward. "You've got me all wrong. I'm not here for an autograph or anything like that."

Baker removed his finger from the button. "Then what can I do for you, Mr.... Abrams, was it?"

"Yoni, please. Call me Yoni."

"Okay. Please have a seat, Yoni." Abrams sat and his eyes widened. "Keep 'em in your head, kid," Baker said, "or you'll lose them—trust me on that."

"I can't believe I'm actually speaking with you," Yoni mumbled. "I've come a very long way."

"From Israel, perhaps?"

"Yes, sir. How did you know?"

"For one thing, your tan is fading. For another, someone at my shul said a young Israeli came around his dress shop the other day, asking for me. I'd be a little more careful if I were you. Asking certain questions in this town will get you killed, particularly if you bring up my name to the wrong person."

"Yes, sir," said Yoni again. "Wow, you're just as rugged as all the stories say you are."

"Listen, kid, I'm no hero. I was just the poor bastard who happened to fit into the Symphony's messed-up plans. Now, I will ask you again for the third and final time: What the hell do you want from me?"

"It's just that... well, I have a... proposition of sorts for you."

"And what would that be exactly?"

Yoni rolled up the shirtsleeve of his right arm to reveal a string of blue letters tattooed upon the skin. "I'm just like you, see?"

"Where are you from originally?"

"Romania. My parents and I were sent to Auschwitz in 1943. They were gassed as soon as we got there. I was eight at the time."

"I'm sorry."

"I was only able to survive because Mengele took an interest in me. Children were his favorite test subjects. I won't go into heavy detail, Mr. Baker, because I know you already understand, but the fucking Angel of Death rendered me incapable of having kids of my own."

"Christ."

"I made it to Israel once the war was over and never stopped thinking about revenge. My journey led me to Mossad, which was creating profiles on escaped war criminals. Eichmann was going to be the first big bust, but then Wiesenthal turned up dead and the war broke out. The Israeli government had no extra manpower to spare. Months turned into years, and I got tired of waiting for the Nazi bastards to receive their just deserts."

"So you decided to take matters into your own hands?"

"Correct," Yoni said proudly. "I'm headed down to South America to take care of the ODESSA. Cut the head off the snake and every other Nazi outpost lingering around the globe—including the Black Symphony—will fall."

"Ever heard of the hydra, Yoni? Cut off one head and two additional ones grow in its place."

"We won't know that for sure until we try," Yoni said. "That's why I came to see you first, Mr. Baker. We need a leader with firsthand experience."

"What do you mean 'we'?"

"I didn't come alone. I've got several like-minded individuals traveling with me. We call ourselves the Tattoo Trackers."

Baker burst out laughing. "You can't be serious."

"I am, and there's nothing funny about it."

"Look at yourself, Yoni. You're just a child, treating this like it's an innocent game of cops and robbers. These people are extremely dangerous. They know how to hide, and more importantly, they know how to kill. If they get wind of what you're up to—and make no mistake, they will—they won't waste a second in trying to put a bullet in your skull. In fact, they'll relish the opportunity to do so."

Yoni looked mortified. Clearly, the conversation was not going the way he'd hoped. "You took on the Black Symphony single-handedly."

"Not true. I had some help. I also had no choice."

"Well, neither do I. The Nazis stole our futures. Mengele pretty much castrated me! Lang exposed you to intense radiation that should have killed you! Doesn't that make you angry? Doesn't it make you want to *do* something about it? At this very moment they run amok in this country, getting fat off the government, and you sit here, acting like there's nothing to be done about it. Not me. I'm done waiting around for the world to correct itself."

Baker sighed, leaned forward. "A wise woman once told me that bearing witness to evil after the fact is just as important as fighting it head-on. In that way, you help make sure it never happens again. I know it feels like you have to do something, Yoni, but maybe that something is telling your story to as many people as possible. You don't need to go around knocking down hornets' nests. Sooner or later, you're going to get stung—and badly."

"I'd have to respectfully disagree. Look at the state of the world. Would you say that 'telling your story' has done anything to change McCarthy's attitude toward Jews?"

"Go home, Yoni. Try to let go of all that rage swirling inside of you. It's poison. Take it from someone who knows—dwelling on the past never ends well."

"This is your final word?"

"It is."

"You really won't join us?"

"I won't."

"Very well." Yoni shot up and crossed over to the office door. His hand was on the knob when he turned around, his voice full of menace. "The stories were wrong about you. You're nothing but a cowardly drunk."

"Better cowardly than dead."

Yoni Abrams slammed the door on his way out.

CHAPTER 40

"*What happened to your neck?*" Evelyn screamed when Baker picked her up outside the motel. She had changed into a pair of corduroy slacks and a white shirt, whose dainty collar poked out the top of a thick maroon sweater.

"Someone was waiting to off me in my apartment this morning."

"What happened to them?" she asked, prompting Baker to raise his eyebrows. "You didn't..." Evelyn mouthed the words *kill them?*

"If I didn't, I'd be swinging from my ceiling fan at this very moment."

"What'd you do with the body?"

"I called in a favor."

"To whom?"

"What's with all the questions? Bottom line is the guy is dead and I'm not."

"You think it's got something to do with Kissinger?"

"Most likely."

"Where are we going now?"

"Santa Monica Pier. Got a note this morning telling me to show up there at three thirty on the dot. Could be the exact lead we're looking for."

"Do you think it could be some kind of trap?"

"It'd be a piss-poor spot to spring one," said Baker, lighting up a cigarette and violently coughing after a single puff. "Too many people around."

"That's reassuring."

"It ain't the Hueys, Evelyn. If they wanted to take me in, they wouldn't be sending cryptic notes to my office. They'd just show up at my office and arrest me."

Santa Monica had existed as a Spanish encampment seven years before the United States came into being and was not incorporated as a city until one hundred and seventeen years later in 1886. More than twenty years after the bloodbath of the Civil War haphazardly stitched a divided country back together, allowing the gangrene of hate to once again blossom inside the still-exposed wound.

But long before humanity set up shacks and thatched roofs, barber shops and air-conditioning, Santa Monica was simply where the ruggedness of the North American continent met the haunting vastness of the Pacific Ocean. A wild place where the waves slapped against sand and rocks; where shellfish scuttled in tide pools; where pelicans scooped up mouthfuls of fish.

Where peaceful silence reigned for millennia. When humans came along, they conquered everything—including the silence. The screams of their children replaced the sounds of the waves. Their houses replaced the tide pools, the scuttling shellfish, and the diving pelicans.

And when that wasn't enough, they set out to conquer the ocean, too, chopping down trees so they could build a pier that would allow them, in their laughable hubris, to walk on water like Christ himself. Surely all of it would one day succumb to the waves and sink into the sea like the fabled city of Atlantis.

Baker pulled off the Interstate 10 exit leading to Santa Monica twenty minutes later. McCarthy began construction on an interstate highway system in 1956, its purpose being to quickly move troops around in the event of a Russian invasion. And yet, with all the graft in the president's administration, the long stretches of road linking East and West remained largely unfinished. Luckily for Baker, the roads in California had already been completed before the money ran out.

Opened in 1909, the Santa Monica Pier was a collection of wooden planks creaking under the activity of food stands, amusement parks, and games of chance. The place had fallen on hard times during the Depression, but saw a resurgence owing, in large part, to the war's recovering effects on the economy and was now a popular destination for tourists and locals, who could stroll the pier on any given day to fish, eat, play, or just take in the magnificent view of the ocean and the refreshing tang of salty sea air.

Today, however, the drab weather transformed the usually idyllic spot into a miserable focal point of harsh winds and thick fog banks. Had it not been for the sounds of crashing waves through the mist, one might have thought they were standing at the very edge of creation.

Despite all this, the beachside town was packed to the teeth with droves of well-wishers attending the latest stop on Prime Minister Kishi's speaking tour. Japanese flags hung from every lamppost and building leading down to the main stage set up on the pier.

Vendors hawking all sorts of wares—from souvenir flags, shirts, hats, and snow globes to exotic foodstuffs such as sushi, bowls of noodles, fish cakes, uni, and purple yam desserts—had set up shop all along Colorado and Ocean Avenues, using palm trees as cover from the drizzle.

Baker now understood why the meeting had been set for this location. So many spectators in one place meant one thing: enough noise to drown out a secret conversation. The downside: The crowd made it nearly impossible to find parking. He started to get a little nervous when three twenty rolled around and they still couldn't find a viable spot.

"There!" screamed Evelyn, pointing to a red-and-white Nash Metropolitan inching its way out of a tight space on Broadway. While not the best at parallel parking, Baker jerked the steering wheel and incautiously drifted into the spot, almost hitting a family of four.

"*You nuts, pal?*" screamed the father—wearing a shirt that announced the wearer had been a FAN OF JAPAN SINCE AUGUST '45—slapping the hood of the car with a fist.

"Sorry!" called Baker, rolling down the window and checking his watch. Five minutes to go. He shut off the engine, and they leapt out of the car.

"Come on!"

He grabbed Evelyn's hand and starting shoving people out of the way with a lot of *Pardon me*'s and *Excuse me*'s. There were two minutes left until the arranged meeting time when Baker spotted the iconic archway to the pier.

SANTA MONICA
YACHT HARBOR
SPORT FISHING ☆ BOATING
CAFÉS

Just beyond that was the stage where Japanese Prime Minister Nobusuke Kishi chatted animatedly with Vice President Nixon.

"Excuse me, sir! Sir!" A hand closed tightly on Baker's shoulder. He turned around, finding himself face-to-face with a HUAC inspector in a long, Gestapo-like trench coat of black leather.

"What is it?" Baker demanded. "We're in a bit of a hurry here."

"The woman needs to be subjected to a protractor and temperature exam," said the inspector, leveling a finger at Evelyn. He then pointed over to a line of Asian attendees roped off from the rest of the giddy crowd. "Only Japanese with no signs of the Yang Flu will be admitted."

"You can't be serious."

"No exceptions are to be made," said the inspector. "Not after William Yang."

Baker felt Evelyn's nails dig into the soft flesh of his palm.

"I'll escort her to the back of the line, and she'll be with you in no time, so long as everything checks out, of course," said the inspector.

"Go," Evelyn said. "We'll meet back at the car."

Baker nodded and hurried forward, though he was pleased to hear Evelyn tell the HUAC inspector he could take his protractors and thermometers and shove them up his ass.

Kishi got up from his seat and approached the podium wired up with microphones from the major networks. There was a roar of applause and cheering from the crowd.

The Japanese prime minister held up a gloved hand and smiled, forgoing his usual drooping pout for a dignitary's smile that revealed a large overbite.

"Thank you very much," he said in English, his voice amplified throughout the pier. "It is a great honor and privilege to be here with you all in Santa Monica today."

There were more cheers as Baker skidded to a halt under the archway, knocking into a teenage girl with her face covered in geisha makeup.

"Watch it!" she hissed.

"Sorry," he whispered back.

"Moreover," Kishi continued, "I am proud and delighted to be a part of this tour, the purpose of which is to underscore mutual cooperation and security between Japan and the United States. It is truly a historical occasion. The goal, set out by myself and President McCarthy, is to establish an indestructible partnership between our two countries, in which our relations would be based on complete equality and mutual understanding. This agreement likewise reflects the closeness and breadth of our relations in the political and economic as well as security fields..."

"Thank you for meeting me, Mr. Baker."

Baker swiveled around, to find a short stranger in a trench coat and bowler hat. "Don't look at me, you fool," they said. "Keep your eyes forward. We're just two strangers watching the speech. Nothing more."

"Right," Baker said out of the corner of his mouth. "Who are you?"

"A representative of the Korean government."

"Which one?"

"Immaterial," said the stranger. "They are close to being one and the same thanks to the futile efforts of your military. I'm here to discuss Henry Kissinger. I was informed that you used his invitation to gain entry into the Nine-Tailed Fox last night."

"Yeah, I did. I'm trying to find him. What's he got to do with you?"

Kishi said something about eradicating Communism around the globe, and the crowd cheered once more.

"He was supposed to meet with one of our contacts at the club four nights ago but never turned up," replied the stranger. "Our man has been stationed there every night since, waiting for him to show."

"What was the purpose of the meeting?"

"I don't know, but on the evening Kissinger was supposed to make an appearance at the club, I received a call from him. It was full of static and his words were practically unintelligible."

"What did he say?"

"He delivered a vague warning—that Korea, the rest of East Asia, and perhaps the rest of the world were in grave danger."

"Anything else?"

"Just one more thing I could barely understand. Something about gaining his independence."

"You think he skipped town?"

"Either that or he's lying low somewhere here in Los Angeles. He's as good as dead if he's willing to give up national secrets to an enemy government."

"I had the same thought," said Baker. "Why are you telling me all this?"

"Because like it or not, you are a part of this now, Mr. Baker. You found Kissinger's invitation and went digging. You work for us now."

"Hold on just a goddamn second there, fella." He turned to face the stranger, who tipped the brim of their hat to further hide their face. "I only take orders from one person and you're talking to him right now."

"We'll compensate you handsomely, of course," said the stranger. "Find Kissinger and you will be paid two thousand American dollars."

"I don't care if it's a million!" shouted Baker.

Some other spectators looked around with curiosity as Kishi droned on about his favorite California landmarks so far.

"Good God, man—I suggest you lower your voice. For both our sakes," spat the stranger. "My only job is to protect the safety and sanctity of Korea by any means necessary. I need to know what Henry Kissinger knows. It's not exactly easy for my associates and me to move around this city without being rounded up by HUAC. You, on the other hand, are free to do as you please."

"Don't be so sure—Jews are being sent to the internment camps, too."

"Even so, the color of your skin and shape of your eyes raise fewer alarm bells than mine would. I take it you weren't subjected to the indignity of having your eyes measured and your temperature taken when you first arrived?"

"Well... yeah."

"Good, then you understand what we're up against. The shortsighted actions of William Yang have put us all in danger."

"You mean he wasn't an agent of the North?"

"Pyongyang has no record of training anyone by the name of William Yang or 'The Tiger,' as he referred to himself in that manifesto of his. Yang was, as far as we can tell, a lone radical with delusions of grandeur."

"So he was innocent?"

"Don't put words in my mouth. Now, here is a down payment made in good faith."

The stranger slipped a bulging envelope over to Baker, who accepted it begrudgingly.

"Fine. How can I reach you once I have something to report?"

"Call Mickey Cohen and he'll pass along the message."

Baker furtively looked down at the envelope and thumbed through the generous collection of fifty-dollar bills contained within. "And what about—?"

"DEATH TO AMERICA! LONG LIVE KOREA!"

A pair of shots rang out. Kishi clutched his chest and slumped forward onto the podium. Someone screamed in horror. Japanese security forces, led by Akihiro Takagi, rushed forward to tackle the gunman to the ground as the crowd erupted into chaos.

CHAPTER 41

Panic took over, driving the crowd in every direction like a herd of startled buffalo. Baker found himself shoved backward and nearly trampled by the teenager in geisha makeup. He regained his footing and saw Kishi's body carried off the stage, where the assailant was pinned to the ground. Chief HUAC Inspector Lonergan stepped forward, pulled out his gun, and fired a bullet into the man's head without a moment of hesitation.

"Morris!" began Evelyn, "What happened? I heard gunshots and screams." She was leaning against the car, absently picking bright pink fluffs of cotton candy off a paper cone.

"Kishi," Baker replied, unlocking the door. "They assassinated him. We need to get you out of here."

They hopped inside. Baker locked the doors and turned on the radio.

"*I repeat...*" came the voice of Walter Winchell.

> "The Japanese prime minister has been shot. The foreign dignitary was delivering remarks on closer diplomatic ties between the US and Japan in Santa Monica this afternoon. Mr. Kishi is currently being rushed to the UCLA Medical Center. According to early intelligence from HUAC, it is believed that the shots were intended for Vice President Richard Nixon, who was present for the speech. The gunman, a suspected Korean extremist inspired by William Yang, was shot and killed while trying to escape..."

"Bullshit," said Baker. "They had him pinned to the ground. He wasn't going anywhere. It was a cold-blooded execution."

"Oh my God," Evelyn said, hands clasped around her mouth. "Not again."

"You need to keep a low profile," he said, starting the engine. "They're going to crack down worse than ever after this."

"Like I didn't already work that out for myself."

It was painfully slow, trying to navigate around the now-dispersed crowd. The high energy of the hour before was gone and people shambled about in the middle of the road like zombies, unsure of what to do or where to go.

"So...?" Evelyn began once they had pulled back onto the highway half an hour later. "Did the person show up for the meeting? What'd you learn?"

"Yeah, they did. Kissinger knows something, all right," Baker said. "Enough to put him in mortal danger. And it seems like your brother was a lone wolf. The Koreans have no record of him."

"Of course they wouldn't! I told you he was innocent in all of this."

"He killed twenty-six people, Evelyn. I wouldn't exactly call that 'innocent.' All we really know for certain is that he wasn't working on behalf of the North Korean government."

Evelyn didn't look too pleased with this sentiment as Baker recounted the rest of the meeting. "What's this about Kissinger gaining his independence? You think he's being held hostage?"

"Unlikely. He made that call on the twenty-fourth, the day *before* I was hired to find him. If the opposition had him already, we wouldn't be here. Besides, they wouldn't exactly be letting him make phone calls to Korean spies."

"So what's our next move?"

"I don't know about you, but I'm starving. What do you say to an early dinner?"

"You're joking, right?" asked Evelyn. "Who could be hungry at a time like this?"

"I always find my brain works a little better on a full stomach. Any suggestions?"

"Jesus, you *are* serious."

"Might as well get some food in us and wait for the cover of nightfall."

"Fine," Evelyn said. "What do you think of Korean barbecue?"

"Never had it, but I'm willing to learn. We just have to make one quick stop."

"Baker!" LA Medical Examiner Thomas Noguchi was in the middle of slicing open a fresh cadaver when Baker strode into the freezing morgue deep below city hall.

While still creepy and unpleasant down here, the place felt a bit homier thanks to numerous woodblock prints of crashing waves, snow-capped mountains, and fire-breathing dragons.

Noguchi let his scalpel fall with a clatter and quickly switched off the reel-to-reel recorder he was using to capture his visceral findings.

"What are you doing here? Did anyone see you come in?"

"No—don't worry, Thomas. You hear the news about Kishi?"

"How could I not?"

"Any updates?"

"He's still under the knife last I heard. Nothing to do now, except wait."

"You mean wait and let HUAC arrest every Korean-American in Los Angeles."

"What can I do for you?"

"I just wanted to see if you got the results back on the dirt found under Liz's fingernails the other night."

"You know I can't discuss an open murder investigation with civilians. I could lose my job or—"

"Or worse, yeah. I know how it goes, Thomas. I'm asking you as a friend."

Thomas seemed to be experiencing some sort of inner turmoil. He screwed up his face, plunging his gloved hands into the open corpse on the operating table and rooting around for God-knew-what.

"If you must know," he said, "the dirt yielded no significant findings."

"You're sure?"

"Quite sure."

"Would you be able to check again and compare it to another sample?" He produced an empty pill bottle containing the dirt he'd scraped off Arnaud's boots.

"Do you ever think that you ask too much from us, Baker?" Noguchi said, flustered. "The rest of us actually value our lives. I don't want to end up on this slab—at least not anytime soon."

"You're the best, Thomas."

"You really are a son of a bitch, Morris. What am I looking for?"

"Just any similarities between the two."

"Leave it by the pickled brain over there and get the hell out."

"Thanks again, Thom—" The scent coming off the brain in its jar stung his nostrils and gave him pause. "Say, what's this stuff?"

"What?" asked Thomas, still engrossed in his work. "The brain?"

"No, the stuff it's floating in."

"Formaldehyde," answered Thomas, extracting a lesioned gall-bladder.

"Is it easy to get?"

"Not unless you work at a medical supply depot or funeral parlor."

"Thomas . . . ?"

"What is it now, Baker?"

"What would happen if . . . if a person ingested formaldehyde?"

Thomas looked Baker dead in the eyes. "Sorry, what was that you said? I didn't hear you."

"Never mind. Goodbye, Thomas."

CHAPTER 42

Evelyn took him to a nondescript eatery on Normandie Avenue, ten minutes away from his office. The place was called Banchan, which Evelyn explained was a Korean word for small side dishes often served alongside a larger meal. They stepped inside the empty restaurant, where a lone waiter was glued to the radio:

> "Prime Minister Kishi is in critical condition after being shot today by a Korean extremist whose name we can exclusively reveal as Sung-Ho Park. It is believed that Park was part of an anti-American, pro-Communist terror group operating in Los Angeles. Its membership is known to include the suicide bomber William Yang—a close associate of Park's—and newly charged murderer, Jasper Heo, whose gruesome homicide of a young woman earlier this week has shocked the city of Los Angeles to its very core. For this unspeakable act, Heo has been sentenced to public hanging, scheduled to take place in the new year..."

"You're lucky!" the waiter exclaimed, looking both nervous and delighted. "I was about to close up early. Didn't expect any customers after..." The man trailed off when he got a good look at Evelyn. "You," he seethed, raising a finger to the door. "Out! Out now!"

Evelyn turned to go, but Baker held out a hand to stop her. "Why does she have to leave?"

"She's a Yang!" thundered the waiter. "That no-good brother of hers started this mess and now look"—he jabbed a finger at the radio—"just as things start to quiet down, copycats begin to run amok. Out!"

"Come on, Morris," said Evelyn. "Let's just go."

"Hang on just a second," Baker said. "Evelyn's got nothing to do with any of this."

"As far as I'm concerned, she's no better than her piece of shit bro—"

Baker grabbed the man by his collar and slammed him against the wall. "Listen here, asshole. HUAC is the one out there pointing fingers and making wild accusations. What good does it do to stoop to their level? Now, Evelyn and I are hungry, so are you going to serve us or not?"

"Y-y-y-yes..." squeaked the waiter, who looked about ready to piss himself.

"Thank you kindly," said Baker, letting go. "We'll need a minute before we order."

"You didn't have to do that," Evelyn said. "I'm used to it by now."

"Well, you shouldn't have to be. I just hope the food is worth it."

"They've got the best Korean food outside of New York City. At least in my humble opinion," said Evelyn as they removed their shoes and seated themselves on opposite sides of a circular grate above a bed of white-hot coals.

"I'll take your word for it," replied Baker. "They got booze here? Maybe more of that *show-jee* stuff I had at the club last night. It wasn't half bad."

"Soju," Evelyn corrected him. "And sure. Mind if I do the ordering for us?"

"Be my guest," he said, turning the menu this way and that, looking for a single word of English printed upon its surface. "Doubt I'll be speaking fluent Korean by the time we hit dessert."

She nodded and turned to the waiter, who had returned, a mechanical smile stretching his lips. Once Evelyn put in their order, the waiter rushed off to fetch them glasses of ice water and cups of warm soju.

"Geonbae," Evelyn said, holding up her liquor.

"L'chaim," said Baker, lifting his own. "I hope this one's safe to drink."

Evelyn giggled. They clinked their glasses of soju and drank. Baker finished his in one go and signaled the waiter for another.

"You really can put it away, huh?" Evelyn said.

"When you've been through as much shit as I have, it's about the only thing that makes trudging through the muck we call 'life' tolerable."

"You said you're living proof of what happens when a person is brainwashed by a radical ideology. What did you mean by that?"

"That, my dear lady, could fill several volumes. Where to even start . . . ?"

He provided a brief rundown of his experiences during the war. How Stormtroopers had goose-stepped into his shtetl and burned down the synagogue. How he had lured people to their doom in the gas chambers and burned their bodies in the crematoria. How Adolf Lang had chosen him to take part in a twisted science experiment.

"My God," she gasped, absolutely horrified. "That must have been hell."

"Worse," Baker replied, taking a large gulp from his third glass of soju.

Their food arrived just then: bowls of marinated beef, pickled vegetables, lettuce leaves, and a pungent fermented cabbage called kimchi.

"I don't know where to begin," Baker said, breaking apart a pair of wooden chopsticks.

"It's pretty simple," said Evelyn. She grabbed her own chopsticks, lifted a thin piece of beef, and laid it gently over the grate. Soon, the tantalizing smell of sizzling meat filled the air. "We call this meat 'bulgogi,'" she explained. "It literally translates into 'fire meat.'"

"Fitting name," said Baker, following her lead and placing strips of meat on the grate.

"Gochujang?"

"Bless you."

"No," said Evelyn, holding out a tureen of deep red mush. "It's a hot chili paste meant to complement the beef. Smear a little bit on the lettuce before adding the beef, kimchi, and zucchini pickles. Then wrap it all up and enjoy."

She helped him assemble an edible parcel of meat and vegetables. "What's so funny?" she asked, noticing Baker's smile.

"Just a small case of déjà vu," he answered, thinking back to the night he introduced Sophia to Peking duck. "I swear I've seen you before. You're certain we've never met?"

"Like I said, I've just got one of those faces."

"Must be. Wow, this stuff is delicious! Can't believe it's taken me this long to try it."

"I'm surprised. Before you passed out at the bar last night, you mumbled something about 'gumiho,'" Evelyn recalled. "I figured you might be familiar with Korean culture."

"I thought I was being lured to my death by a beautiful woman."

"Where'd you learn about it?"

"A buddy of mine taught it to me. He fought in Korea before a land mine blew his leg off."

"That's awful. William would barely tell me about what he saw over there. Just that some of the men would lose their minds. I imagine it's why he wanted to bring the war to an end. That was William, always certain there was a solution to the most complex problems plaguing humanity."

"Were you ever in Korea?" Baker asked her.

"Not since I was a very little girl. I can hardly remember what it was like. William was eight and I was four when my parents decided to immigrate to Los Angeles in 1932. They had a feeling that things were about to turn ugly with Japan, and they were right. It killed them to pack up and leave everything behind, but they wanted to give my brother and I a better life."

"That's what got me here," said Baker, signaling the waiter for a refill. "I swallowed the lie about the American Dream, too—hook, line, and sinker."

"Are you always this cynical?"

"Most of the time, yeah."

"My parents really did achieve the American Dream. At least for a while. They opened a successful produce market here in LA and saved enough money to give my brother and I a proper education on the East Coast."

"What'd you study?"

"English."

"Bookworm, eh?"

"I suppose you could put it like that," Evelyn said, wrapping a piece of bulgogi around her chopsticks and laying it atop the coals like a shish kabob. "I've always enjoyed reading. Truth be told, I wanted to be a novelist after graduating. Have you ever read Machen?"

"Can't say that I have."

"Jules Verne? H. G. Wells? H. P. Lovecraft?"

Baker shook his head. "Don't do much reading. Never have."

"Ah," Evelyn said. "Well, I love stories about extraordinary and frightening worlds beyond our own."

"What?" Baker said, pulling a piece of fatty gristle from between his teeth. "This one not scary enough for you?"

"It wasn't always. Things only started to go wrong when McCarthy took office. The produce market burned down and the police tried to write it off as an electrical fire caused by my mother's incompetence as a foreigner. But I know it was arson. Several other businesses burned down that day and they were all Korean-owned."

Evelyn's neglected slice of beef was starting to burn on the grill. Baker peeled it off. "You said the police blamed your mother. Your father no longer in the picture?"

"I see you haven't read all the excerpts from my brother's purported manifesto," said Evelyn. "Our father walked out on us years ago."

"Oh..." mumbled Baker. "I'm sorry."

"It's okay. Doesn't really bother me anymore. I've tried to look him up on several occasions, but I guess he changed his name."

"So what happened after the market burned down?"

"The insurance company refused to pay for the damages, so Mom lost the shop. Luckily, she's pretty resourceful. I guess that's where I get it from. She started doing a bunch of odd jobs: sewing dresses, fixing broken radiators—that sort of stuff. Of course, the intermittent income meant she had to move out of Los Feliz and over to Hawthorne. By that point, I had given up on my dream of being a writer and found a part-time teaching position at a private school in upstate New York."

"I take it your mother...?"

"Hasn't shown her face since William's attack? She can't. The community would probably stone her to death if she stepped foot outside her apartment. That's part of why I'm back in town—helping her with groceries and the like."

"I've read *some* of those snippets the papers say came from William's manifesto. Are they accurate?"

"Some of it. All the personal details—like the Korean legends our mother would tell us before bed and our father leaving—are correct, but the rest feels as though it were written by a totally different person. What about you, Morris? Do you have any living family?"

"Until yesterday I didn't." Evelyn raised her eyebrows in a questioning look. "Turns out my older brother, Ze'ev, survived the war," Baker added. "He only just tracked me down yesterday."

"That's incredible!"

"Not really."

"How so?"

"Don't have much need for him anymore."

"What does that even mean?"

Baker shrugged. "It means I've made it this far without him. What's the rest of my life?"

"You won't even entertain the idea of reconnecting with him? I'd give anything to speak with William just one more time."

"I'll be joining your brother pretty soon. Turns out that concentration camp experiment I was lucky enough to be a part of finally caught up with me. I've got lung cancer."

"No!"

"Yep."

"Are you seeking treatment?"

"Nope."

"*Why?*" Evelyn was so indignant that she started to choke on a piece of kimchi.

"I'm not really bothered, and that's the honest-to-goodness truth. The world is so fucked up and doesn't seem to be changing anytime soon. What's the point, really?"

"I have never met someone who has such an ugly outlook on life."

"Call me one of a kind, then."

"You're unbelievable!" Evelyn slammed her hand on the table, shaking the coals and toppling Baker's fourth glass of soju.

"Hey, watch it!"

"With all due respect, Mr. Baker, fuck your drink. Koreans, Chinese, and Jews are being rounded up as we sit here, and you're just waiting for the clock to run out on your life like it's some sort of football match! Most of the country thinks my brother is a homicidal monster and they'll probably go on thinking it, even if I am lucky to find a shred of evidence that says otherwise. But do you see me throwing in the towel?"

"Give it time," said Baker, wiping soju off his pants. "You don't crumple all at once; the fight just slowly leaks out. One day, you turn around and realize there's nothing left."

"You think you're so tough, don't you? Well, you're nothing, but... but... a coward," she said at last. "That's it. You're just a coward."

"Believe it or not, you're not the first person to call me that today."

"It's well deserved then! If you are so craven, why even agree to help me at all?"

"Because a woman by the name of Elizabeth Short was murdered a few days ago. I broke her heart once upon a time and now I'm looking to make amends before I kick the bucket. The world is too far beyond my help, but maybe I can gain a little peace of mind with one last accomplishment that doesn't end with me hating myself."

"Sounds more like helping yourself."

"I've got a nagging hunch that Kissinger is the key to everything. Liz, your brother, the son of a bitch who tried to kill me this morning. The only link I've got to Kissinger right now is Orson Lamotte."

"The businessman? What makes you say that?"

"Liz became Orson Lamotte's mistress after we broke up."

"I still don't—"

"The guy who nearly squeezed the life out of me was named Louis Arnaud. To the American ear, that surname could easily be misconstrued as 'Arnold.' When I went to see Lamotte at his home yesterday, his daughter told me that Daddy lost his temper with a very large Frenchman named 'Arnold.' On Christmas Day, a woman posing as Kissinger's wife hired me to find him. Two days later, this fraud tells me the guy who hired her was—"

"Let me guess," said Evelyn, "a very large Frenchman."

"Glad to see you're keeping up. The other link to Lamotte is what I found in Kissinger's hotel room at Chateau Marmont. It was an invitation to the Nine-Tailed Fox printed on the back of a Lamotte Exports business card."

"Couldn't that just be a—?"

"Coincidence? Sure. That's where my mind went at first, too. I only visited Lamotte to learn more about his affair with Liz in the hopes of finding her killer. But when I mentioned Kissinger's name offhand, the guy lost it and threatened to have me arrested."

"You think Lamotte and Kissinger were partners in... this threat to East Asia?"

"Not only that. I also think Liz got wind of it somehow and Lamotte ordered Arnaud to silence her. Jasper Heo, the Korean perp the cops and HUAC want to pin the murder on, was the perfect fall guy."

"But then you got involved?"

"Correct, and I had the very poor foresight to involve Liz's roommate, who also went the way of a nice and neat suicide. What started as a simple plan to murder a mistress and frame another Korean 'radical' began to snowball. Now, Lamotte needed two more people dead in order to keep the secret from coming out. And then you've got the two dead cops outside of the club, where Kissinger was expected to turn up."

"All of this seems tenuous at best, Morris."

"Like I said, I've got no hard proof yet. Still, if I can expose Liz and Debbie's actual murderers while saving an innocent man from the gallows, it's worth a try. We get to the bottom of the 'Why?' and hopefully prove that William and Jasper were innocent in one fell swoop. Hell, maybe the guy who allegedly opened fire on Kishi earlier is a patsy, too. The Hueys seemed pretty eager to take him off the board, and Winchell conveniently had all the details minutes after it happened."

"That's all well and good," said Evelyn, "but we're still at a dead end."

"I know of two guys who might be able to help us find the connection between Lamotte and Kissinger."

"Who?"

"A pair of salty sea dogs."

CHAPTER 43

It was nearing ten o' clock when they finished dinner. Driving all the way down State Route 11 to the seaside community of San Pedro, where Mickey Cohen's smuggler contacts were said to hang around, would probably take close to an hour. Nevertheless, Baker also saw it as an opportunity to look into Han Zhao for Hollis and the other tong members.

Evelyn offered to drive, but Baker turned her down.

"You must be exhausted," she said.

"I can sleep when I'm dead."

The trip took closer to an hour and a half thanks to a heavy logjam of vehicles on Route 11, just before Carson.

Midnight was fast approaching when they turned onto South Anchovy Avenue—a fitting name, given the community's reliance on a maritime economy. The fog bank was even worse at night, forcing Baker to cruise along at a maddening five miles an hour, so as not to accidentally drive off the road and into the depths of the Pacific Ocean.

"Keep an eye out for West Thirty-Seventh Street," he said to Evelyn, tightening his grip on the wheel and leaning forward in a futile effort to see more than ten feet ahead of the car's headlights.

"There!" Evelyn shouted after fifteen minutes. Baker, who was starting to feel a dull pounding in his temples, hit the brakes and slowly, agonizingly, turned onto the side street thick with a prehistoric chaparral of swaying palms, giant dioons, knotted Bay fig trees, and buttressed roots.

"Okay, now look for a place called Charybdis. I doubt they'll have a sign. Maybe roll down the window and listen for the nightly call of drunken sailors..."

To his amazement, Evelyn actually did it, hanging her head out the open window. He was about to say, "I was only joking," when she shushed him.

"Pull over and stop the engine," she said. "It's so noisy."

Baker obeyed and rolled down his own window, listening intently. His ears immediately picked up the ataractic sound of the nearby ocean, but there was something else, too. Unless he was very much mistaken, Baker could also discern the muffled notes of an accordion and the swell of laughter crashing in tandem with the waves.

"There," Evelyn said, pointing into a dark thicket of drooping palm fronds. "I think I can see a bit of light."

"All right," Baker said, leaning over to pop open the glove compartment and pull out a flashlight. "Take this. I'll be right beside you." He pulled out his gun and made sure it was loaded. Two chambers were now empty after his scuffle with Arnaud and the drunken men outside Ohev Shalom.

They rolled up their windows and quietly got out of the car. Evelyn turned the flashlight on and pointed its beam into the thick vegetation. They crept forward and the cacophony of unbridled revelry became more pronounced; the gloom started to pulsate with an anemic orange glow.

Evelyn moved the light over the ground, where roots, fallen branches, and other obstacles threatened to bring them toppling face forward into the squishy dirt underfoot.

"Damn," she hissed as the torch began to fail, swatting it against her leg.

"It's okay," Baker said. "Look..."

"Oh my."

The path had taken them all the way to the water's edge, where a slanting, rusted shack of corrugated iron rested upon an ancient dock. Wavelets of ice-cold seawater lapped at the rotted support beams covered in barnacles and ropes anchoring a collection of dinghies.

Every gust of wind made the humble sign bearing the tavern's name creak on its chains. A secret pirates' hideaway ripped straight out of the pages of a boys' adventure.

Neutral territory where hardened men of the tide, both those of honor and ill repute—travelers, smugglers, thieves, merchants, and cutthroats—made port to carouse their loneliness away. The shack was ablaze with light and the noise of intoxicated sailors belting out off-tune shanties.

"A rather lively bunch, aren't they?" said Baker, stepping onto the dock, which was slick with blue-green algae. He nearly slipped into the water below when Evelyn caught him at the last second, hanging on to the belt of his trench coat.

"Much appreciated," he said, regaining his balance. He extended a hand and helped Evelyn onto the dock.

They stood outside for another moment, listening to the jocularity.

Baker was reminded of Mickey's warning from the night before: *When you get there, tell 'em Mickey sent ya. If not, you might just be tossed into the Pacific with your hands tied behind your back and your balls stuffed down your throat. Those guys don't fuck around.*

"Time to see if anyone's home," he said, stepping up to a rectangular outline of light he assumed to be the front door and knocking three times.

The debauchery inside faltered for a split second (like a candle flame flickering in a blustery rainstorm) and the door was suddenly wrenched open with a horrible screeching.

Baker and Evelyn instinctively covered their eyes against the expulsion of brilliant illumination spilling onto the dock. Through his fingers, Baker could just make out a stocky figure standing in the entranceway, but it would take another minute until his eyes were fully able to make out any specific features: a tipped sailor's cap imprinted with an anchor, a striped shirt at least two sizes too small, and an impatient sneer.

"The fuck you want?" he rasped, and even from a distance, Baker could detect the rancid fetor of rum and unwashed gums.

"Hello," Baker began, "we're—"

"This ain't the fuckin' Ritz," said the stocky figure.

"I'm well aware of that," answered Baker.

This was obviously the wrong approach because the man was now on his tiptoes, holding a rusted dagger to Baker's throat.

"Talk like that again and I'll turn your guts into chum. Then your pretty lady friend can have a seat at my table." The stocky seaman winked at Evelyn, who slapped him. Again, this was interpreted as poor Charybdis etiquette and the man howled in anger.

"Whoa now," said Baker, stepping between Evelyn and the sailor. "I think we got off on the wrong foot here, pal. Whaddya say I buy you a round or two?"

"Piss off! This ain't some hoity toy nightclub. We don't give a shit how much money your willing ta spend."

"Mickey Cohen sent us," Baker said, which caused the man to look as though he'd been slapped for a second time. "Ah good," Baker added. "I see you've heard of him."

"Course I heard of him. What's your business?"

"Smuggling."

"Really narrows it down," snorted the sailor.

"Duffy! Are you giving these people a hard time?"

Another figure had emerged from the tavern and was leaning against the doorframe. Baker suspected that this might be the most handsome man he had ever seen. Evelyn must have thought so, too, because Baker caught her staring, slack-jawed, at the man's high cheekbones, intense blue eyes, and strong chin indented with a slight dimple. The newcomer smiled, revealing a mouth of straight and dazzlingly white teeth.

There was an indescribable aura of charm and warmth around him that seemed to glow even brighter than the tavern's own radiance.

"Evenin', folks," said the newcomer, grabbing Duffy and tousling his hair in an elderly brother sort of way. "Sorry about ol' Duffy here. I promise his bark is worse than his bite. Welcome to Charybdis. Now, what's this I hear about an interest in smuggling?"

CHAPTER 44

My name's Morris Baker, and this is Evelyn Yang," Baker said. "We're looking for the two guys who handle Mickey Cohen's smuggling operation."

"That's easy," said the man. "You're talking to one of them right now! Name's Issur." He stuck out a hand roughened with healed-over calluses, and Baker shook it. "Come on inside and have a drink with me and my first mate."

"But—but—" bleated Duffy.

"But what, Duffy?" said Issur. "You heard the man. He's got it in with Mickey, and any friend of Mickey's is a friend of ours. Or do you want to piss off the big man?"

Duffy stepped aside, allowing Baker, Evelyn, and Issur to cross the threshold of Charybdis.

The interior of the tavern could not have been more different from the unassuming exterior. It was incredibly warm in here, owing to a collection of once-opulent chandeliers now adorned with hundreds of candles, their waxy runoff forming irregular stalactites.

The ceiling was also covered with old fish nets that hung like cobwebs in an abandoned manor house. The ribbed metal walls were decorated with an eclectic menagerie of mounted trophies: a leaping swordfish, gaping shark jaws, and scuffed brass plaques bearing the names of mariners long since passed.

As for the seating arrangements, Charybdis contained a mismatched collection of driftwood tables and booths, every inch of them packed with inebriated men of the sea. They smoked, sang arm in arm, played cards, rolled dice, argued over women, and clinked steins of ale and bottles of rum. The only other woman besides Evelyn was a harried barmaid, who flitted around the tavern, fulfilling orders nonstop. The live entertainment came courtesy of a brawny seafarer, who fingered the wheezy accordion strapped to his chest.

"Please accept my apologies on Duffy's behalf," Issur called over the din. "He's just a little overprotective of this place. But we sometimes do get the odd character in here. Last week, for instance, some crazy Asian fella runs in, eyes as wide as a porthole, screaming 'Lamb hot! Lamb hot!' at the top of his lungs. One of the strangest sights you ever did see."

Evelyn walked ahead to admire an old diving helmet, but Baker stopped Issur. "Wait," he said. "Did the man look like this?" He pulled out the picture of Han Zhao given to him by the missing tong member's daughter.

Issur studied the photo. "You know, I do believe that was the guy. Mind you, he looked a lot crazier than that. Like he'd lived a thousand lifetimes before he stepped foot in here. He a friend of yours?"

"Not exactly. What happened to him?"

"Duffy sent him on his merry way."

Any idea where he went?"

"Not a clue. I was deep in the bottle that night, to tell the truth. We're just over here!"

He pointed to a darkened corner, where another extremely handsome individual was in the middle of lighting a pipe at a table carved with profanity.

"Paul!" Issur shouted. The man looked up, his eyes the color of a piercing blue sky in the dead of winter. "I'd like ya to meet Morris and Evelyn. They're friends of Mickey's."

"Are they now?" said Paul, shaking out his match and leisurely tipping his chair against the wall.

"This is my first mate, Paul," Issur explained. "You two have a seat and I'll get us all a round of drinks."

Issur made a beeline for the bar. Many patrons shouted with delight as he passed, eager to shake his hand or give him a pat on the back.

Paul smiled and puffed away on his pipe. "That's Captain Danielovitch," he said. "A celebrity no matter where he goes. He'd be the biggest movie star on the planet right now, had it not been for McCarthy."

"He was an actor?" Evelyn asked.

"We both were," Paul said. "I was just starting out myself, but the captain had a pretty good foothold in the industry. But our Jew blood counted against us once UAP started running the show, so"—he shrugged—"we switched career paths, though I guess you could say there is a bit of acting required in what we do. And there ain't no one better at it than Captain Issur Danielovitch of the *Varinia*."

Issur took the notoriety in stride and, upon arriving at the bar, simply reached over, grabbed four cloudy mugs, and started filling them from the tap, which looked as though it had been fashioned out of an old diving tank. He slapped some coins on the counter and made his way back to the table, where he handed out the beers, raising his own in a toast.

"The meek shall inherit the earth. The brave will get the oceans!" he declared.

Foam slopped onto the table as the four steins met in midair. Everyone drank and Baker laughed when Evelyn pulled her mug away to reveal a light foam mustache on her upper lip.

"So how can we humble sailors be of assistance?" the captain asked, placing his own stein down and leaning over the table. He looked even more dapper in the ambient candlelight from above.

"We're here because Mickey said you might be able to tell us about Orson Lamotte."

"Ha!" Paul exclaimed with derision in his voice. "What do you wanna know about that bum?"

"Bum?" inquired Baker.

Issur's perfect lips turned down. "Lamotte's plum broke, or close to it anyway. Made a bunch of bad investments with all that money his daddy left him. Tried to get it back by betting on the ponies and dug himself in deeper. Now he can't even afford to pay his own dock workers—let alone the folks who operate the boats."

"He's on the ropes," added Paul. "Financially speaking."

"How has this not reached the papers yet?" Baker asked.

"Lamotte still holds quite a bit of influence in this town," Issur said. "Friends in high places can lean on the press and keep a story like that under wraps."

"Friends in the government?" Evelyn prompted. "The State Department, for instance?"

"Oh, sure," said Issur, taking another generous swig of ale. "State Department, Department of Commerce, Customs, Border Patrol—the whole kit and caboodle. He ain't that different from us smugglers. The only difference is that when he does it, it's not considered a felony."

" 'Lamb hot,' " Baker said. "You think the man who burst in here the other night was trying to tell you something about Lamotte?"

"Now there's an idea," Issur said. "That never even occurred to me. What do you think, Paul?"

"Could've been one of his people. Lamotte likes to hire immigrants for peanuts," said Paul. "His entire staff comes here after hours—or at least they *did* when the money was still rolling in. They're seriously pissed off. When did they go on strike, Captain?"

"'Bout three weeks ago. Lamotte's side of the port is deader than roadkill at the moment. And who could blame them? That's why Paul and I prefer the freelance life. We sail to the beat of our own drum, following the call of adventure. Traversing forbidden waters."

"I saw the bootleg caviar you get for Mickey," said Baker. "Pretty impressive. What else do you run, besides luxury products from the Soviet Union?"

"A whole manner of things, Mr.... What did you say your last name was again?"

"Baker."

"Baker... Baker..." Issur repeated. "Now, why does that name sound familiar?"

"Didn't we just bring over a passenger who mentioned a Morris Baker?" asked Paul. "Young kid from Is-real."

"Yoni Abrams?" asked Baker.

"That's him," Paul said, gesticulating with his pipe. "Good kid, but he wouldn't shut up about how great you are. Guessing he found you, then?"

"Yeah, I told him to give up his silly quest and go home. *You* smuggled him into the States?"

"Well, sure," said Issur. "Him and his little band of Nazi hunters or whatever they call themselves. They couldn't get in with the strict embargo on Israel, now could they? We don't just ferry cargo, we ferry people, too. Why do you think the Israelis haven't surrendered yet? We supply them with a steady force of able-bodied volunteers from America."

"We're helping 'em cast a giant shadow," Paul offered.

"Ha!" Issur laughed. "I like that."

"Why bother?" said Baker. "You're just postponing the inevitable."

Issur exchanged a troubled look with his first mate. All the warm geniality seemed to drain from their handsome faces. "'Just postponing the inevitable,' you say? You're a fellow Member of the Tribe, are you not, Baker?"

"Yeah."

"Then Israel's the only chance we got. You see a dry piece of desert in the middle of nowhere, but I see the only place on the face of this earth where our people can truly be who they are. Where would the Jews run tomorrow if Ben-Gurion waved the white flag of surrender? The United States? Fat chance! We're a fraction of a fraction of a fraction of the global population, but numbers don't matter. Never have.

"There's always the risk of losing, sure, but giving up before you even try is like saying you don't need to make your bed in the morning because you're just gonna mess it up again later. We need to give a damn because no one else will. Look at what happened the last time we didn't fight back? The last time we bowed to the 'inevitable'? Six million of our people dead."

"And you're trying to make it seven! Or more!" snarled Baker. "You're leading people to the slaughter all over again!" he shouted. "While you sit here in this cozy little bar and sip beer, Jews are being killed! Can you really live with all of that blood on your hands?"

"If it means securing our homeland, then yes, I can. Maybe you should, too."

"I was in one of those goddamn concentration camps for three years, tricking people into the gas chambers and shoveling their bodies in and out of the ovens. Don't you dare try and lecture *me* on what it means to give a shit... *Captain!*"

The boisterous tavern went deathly silent as every eye in the place roved in their direction. Some men started to rise from their own chairs, brandishing pistols and knives, but Issur held up a hand to stop them. Duffy might run security, but Issur was clearly top banana around here.

"I think it's about time you took your leave," said Paul, his dazzling blue eyes clouding over, threatening snow.

"Good, we were just about to go anyway," said Baker, standing up so quickly, his chair fell over with a clatter. "Evelyn, you coming?"

CHAPTER 45

"Do you rub everyone you meet the wrong way?" Evelyn asked once they were back in the car.

"Most people, yeah."

"You really are something else, you know that? We didn't even get a chance to ask about Kissinger."

"Didn't need to."

"'Didn't *need* to'? Why, you... you..."

"*Enough!*" roared Baker, and Evelyn shrank away. "I saw the way you were gaping at Issur. You're free to go back inside and enjoy a romantic evening with him if you like. Me? I'm going to find Kissinger and clear your brother's name like we agreed."

"Morris, how can you—?"

"Are we still united on that front?"

"Yes..." Evelyn whispered.

"I didn't hear you..."

"*Yes!*" screamed Evelyn, her eyes leaking with tears. "The world is falling apart before our very eyes and people are trying their hardest to fix things. But what do you care? You'll be dead soon, right? Well, that day can't come soon enough, if you ask me!"

Her words hung in the air like poison gas.

"Morris?" she said at last. "I—I'm sorry. That was just an awful thing to say."

"Don't apologize," Baker said, turning to face Evelyn. "I deserve that and so much more. I'm the one who should be saying sorry. My... anger has always gotten the best of me since the camps. Please don't judge me by those outbursts."

"That's quite all right," she said, reaching over to grab his hand and give it a squeeze.

"Do me a favor and get the wire cutters in the glove box."

"What do you need wire cutters for?" asked Evelyn, popping open the compartment and shifting its contents around.

"We're going to break into Lamotte's side of the port. You heard what Issur said: Lamotte's deep in debt. I bet most men like him would make a deal with the devil to protect their wallet. Then there's that story about the crazed Asian man screaming Lamotte's name in terror. I wonder what could have spooked him like that."

"Have you ever read Homer's *Odyssey*?"

"Can't say I have," he answered, lighting a cigarette and starting the engine.

"In it, Charybdis was a monster—a massive whirlpool that swallowed ships and men whole."

"Your point...?"

"It's just the name of that tavern felt like... I don't know... an omen or something. I fear we're being sucked into the vortex. What happens if we can't get out?"

"If that happens," he said as he steered back onto South Anchovy Avenue, "then we abandon ship."

CHAPTER 46

The Port of Los Angeles sat dormant in the frenzied aftermath of the Christmas consumer rush, the glorious Free Market in a brief period of hibernation. A lonely foghorn sounded far off in the distance as Baker and Evelyn crept up to the chain-link fence separating Lamotte Exports from the Seaside Freeway.

Evelyn kept a lookout while Baker cut through the links at the bottom in such a way that no one would be any the wiser once they were gone.

"Okay," he said, after fifteen minutes of hard work that left his hands aching from exertion and cold. "This opening should be big enough for the both of us. You first."

He pulled the broken piece of fence back and up, allowing Evelyn to duck under. She then did the same for him on the other side.

The massive shipping containers stamped with the Lamotte Exports logo—arranged in alternating stacks of red and blue—dominated the port, rising hundreds of feet into the air and creating a maze of shadows, dead ends, and intense pockets of swirling mist. The only thing taller than the metal boxes was the powerful crane used to lift them onto the barges that carried them overseas.

"What are we looking for?" asked Evelyn.

"An office or records room of some kind," said Baker. He brought out his gun and cocked it.

"Don't you think they've got a night guard on duty?"

"Not if Lamotte's as broke as they say. Come on..."

He started off into the towering labyrinth of shipping containers, ears pricked for any noises beyond the rippling ocean water, scampering of rats, and isolated foghorns. It was slow going. The narrow avenues created wind tunnels of frosty air, which nipped at every exposed piece of flesh, and the repetitiveness of the path made it impossible to gauge the passage of time.

"Do you think we're getting close?" Evelyn asked after what could have been twenty minutes or two hours.

"I'm not sure—wait!" he hissed. "What's that?" They had just rounded a corner into a particularly dark stretch of concrete, and there, fifty or so feet ahead, sat a crumpled mass. A sleeping bum or something worse? "Get behind me," said Baker, reaching into his pocket and bringing out the pack of matches he'd taken from the Chateau Marmont.

He set one of the matches aflame when a sudden gust of wind blew out the fire and confirmed Baker's worst suspicions. The scent that reached his nostrils was not the sour harshness of poor bodily hygiene, but the fruity sweetness of decomposing flesh.

"Ugh! What is that?" said Evelyn, pinching her nose in disgust.

"One unlucky bastard," answered Baker, who decided to close the gap before lighting another match.

Once they had reached the body, he crouched down and struck another flame into being, revealing the corpse of Han Zhao. The tong leader was completely naked and a wooden sign reading COMMIE hung around his broken neck. Zhao must have been here for a while because his eyes were gone, presumably pecked out by seagulls or eaten by hungry rodents.

"Oh my God!" Evelyn turned away, gagging. "Oh my dear God!"

"Well," said Baker, shaking out the match and plunging Zhao's cadaver back into darkness, "that's another closed account. Evelyn . . . Evelyn?"

Evelyn had retreated several hundred feet away. She vomited and fell to her knees, sobbing uncontrollably.

"Evelyn, it's okay," he said, walking over and crouching down beside her. "I understand—it's hard seeing a dead body for the first time."

"No," she choked. "It's not that. Oh God." She retched again, spitting up the rest of her bulgogi.

"Then what's wrong?"

"That man . . . " She pointed toward Zhao's naked and defiled corpse. "That man . . . is my father."

CHAPTER 47

"Your...father? I think you're mistaken. That man's name is Han Zhao. He's a high-ranking member in the Chinatown tong. He's got a daughter!"

"Me," breathed Evelyn.

"No," Baker said. "Her name is Mingmei and she's younger than you. In her teens, I think."

"So that's what he did," Evelyn said, regaining a bit of composure, though still convulsing from shock. "Changed his name, started a new family—passed himself off as Chinese. No wonder it was so hard to find him all these years."

"Jesus," Baker said, understanding why Evelyn looked so familiar.

"It's fine," she said, now getting shakily to her feet. "I'm fine. It just caught me off guard, is all."

"Would you like to hold a little vigil of sorts? I've got plenty of matches."

"No," she said, a frostiness in her voice as she turned away from Zhao's body. "My father was dead to me long before tonight."

"For the love of Christ, Morris! You ever think about opening your own morgue? You'd make a killing, no pun intended."

"No, thanks. Think I've seen enough corpses for a lifetime," said Baker, lighting up one of his Kools, which he flicked away in disgust after the first puff.

Connolly wasn't too happy about having to drive down to San Pedro in the dead of night. He rubbed his hands together and pulled out a pack of Pall Malls, offering one to Evelyn, who gratefully accepted. She was still wide-eyed and shaking. Despite claims to the contrary, the discovery of her father's gruesome remains had cut deep, slicing open emotional wounds that had only just started to heal.

"It's all right, lass," said Connolly, lighting the smoke for her. "Just try and calm down. That's it. Nice deep breaths." He rounded on Baker. "I thought I told you not to call me for a couple of days at the very least! What the fuck did you think that meant? Do I have to reteach you English or something?"

"Connolly..." he began.

"You gonna tell me what you were doing here?" Connolly asked, cutting him off.

"We were looking for evidence connecting Lamotte to Kissinger."

"And I shouldn't arrest you and your pretty friend here for illegal trespass because...?"

"Orson Lamotte is the one you should be arresting."

Connolly raised an eyebrow. "Why would I do such a thing?"

Baker spent the next few minutes walking Connolly through his theories. To his great surprise, Connolly guffawed once he was finished.

"That all you got, Morris? A few hunches and a dead member of the tong who could barely speak English? You really want me to go after one of the most powerful men in the state on *that*?"

"This isn't a joke, Connolly. Lamotte, Kissinger, even William Yang—they were all involved in something big. It's why Kissinger flew the coop. I'd stake my badge on it if I still had one."

"Forget it, Morris. No one's going to lose sleep over one dead Chinaman."

"That dead Chinaman is lying just over that fence with no eyes, Brogan! He also happens to be Evelyn's late father! Show some goddamned respect!"

"You mean over the fence you destroyed so you could illegally trespass on private property? Even if you found Amelia Earhart cradling the Lindbergh baby in there, it'd be totally inadmissible."

"You're not listening! It's not just Zhao. Liz and Debbie were also a part of it. I'd be dead, too, if it hadn't been for sheer luck. Even Pistone and Bletchley got in the way."

"How do you know about Pistone and Bletchley?"

"I found their bodies on Fox Tail Road, where Kissinger was expected to turn up."

"And you didn't call me?"

"You found them in the end, didn't you? What were they even doing there? You told me they were on vacation."

"They were supposed to be," Connolly said. "Pistone apparently got some sort of tip on Christmas night and went to follow up on it with Bletchley. Their wives just thought they were working overtime. You know what it's like when you get a lead that can break a case wide open: Everything else just sort of melts away. Nobody thought anything was amiss until someone called the station to report two cops rotting in Fairfax."

"Who do you think would run the risk of killing two police officers, Connolly? Some very powerful people looking to hide a secret, wouldn't you say?"

"I'll admit it's a little fishy. Hell, maybe Kissinger was into something dangerous, but I don't see anything connecting him to Lamotte."

"I already told you—"

"That Lamotte got angry when you brought up Kissinger's name? That a Lamotte Exports business card just so happened to be in a room where Kissinger was staying? Another bit of trespassing on your part, I might add. You think any of this will hold up in court, Morris? Come on, you're smarter than that."

"Arnaud, then. Lamotte's daughter—"

"Is a little girl. We both know a child's testimony is worth little more than dog shit, Morris. Did you stop to think that Lamotte's got a business associate actually named Arnold? Hell, the man has connections all over the country. You're grasping at straws."

"Grasping at straws? I was nearly killed this morning, Brogan! Doesn't that concern you in the least *bit*? The guy was going to fake my suicide, note and all! It was going to be a repeat of Debbie if I hadn't killed him."

"Got a body?"

"What?"

"The Frenchman who tried to killed you. This Arnaud. Where's his body?"

"It's not like the guy is just lying dead in my apartment. I had to—"

"I've heard enough, Morris. I can't be implicated in any of this."

"His passport, goddamnit!" Baker shouted, pulling out the document and throwing it at Connolly, who let it fall to the ground. "Look at the way he wrote out the capital *E* in his signature. The same style as Debbie's suicide note. And there's this!" He pulled out the dropper bottle. "Arnaud had this on his person, too—it's full of formaldehyde."

"Meaning...what?"

"Isn't it obvious? Arnaud used it to poison Jasper Heo and keep him out of the way while framing him for Liz's murder. A surreptitious drop or two in the man's morning cup of coffee is all it would take! You can't just buy formaldehyde off the shelf; you need someone who works with the stuff on a regular basis."

"You're not really suggesting..."

"Yes, Arnaud got it from the ME's office. Thomas as good as told me earlier today! The Frog also had Lonergan's office number in his pocket. He must've gotten the formaldehyde with the Hueys backing him up. You said it yourself, they *are* the LAPD now. They don't need to bother with acquisition orders anymore; they take what they want. This dung heap is a mile high."

Connolly took a deep breath and placed a friendly hand on Baker's shoulder. "I get it, I really do," he said calmly. "You want to make sense of Liz's death but—"

"Don't you dare," said Baker, jabbing a finger into Connolly's chest. "Don't you dare try and make me think that I'm the crazy one here."

"Whoa, take it easy now. No one's saying you're crazy. All I'm saying is grief can play tricks on the mind, make you see things that aren't there. The brain is a fragile thing and wants to make sense of every little detail when things spiral out of our control."

"I know Lamotte had Liz and the others killed. If we can just find Kissinger..."

"Liz was killed by Jasper Heo," Connolly said, and now there was a shade of pity in his voice. "I'm sorry, Morris, but that's where all the evidence points."

"You'd really sentence an innocent man to death?"

"I won't be sentencing anyone. I'm sure you heard the reports over the radio. HUAC got wind of the case this morning. They want to make an example of Heo. Public hanging on television sometime after New Year's. They'd do it sooner, but I hear they're hoping to lock down several sponsors first."

"Connolly, you can't—"

"Can't what, Morris? Tell HUAC not to hang the guy? I took your call and came all the way out here because you're my friend. But there are limits to what I can do, and what you're asking of me right now is suicide. Not just for me, but for my family as well."

"So you're just burying your head in the sand, then?"

"Forget about what you saw in there," Connolly said, pointing into the maze of shipping containers. "Forget about Lamotte and Kissinger and Yang and go mourn Liz properly. Her mother is doing a burial at Evergreen. Maybe you can help her with the funeral arrangements. And do me a favor: Next time you find someone without a pulse, leave me out of it."

He tipped his hat in Evelyn's direction, got back into his car, and drove off.

CHAPTER 48

Hollis answered the door to the Golden Fowl in a checkered sleeping coat, his eyes nearly crusted shut with tiredness. "Morris? Is that you? What time is it?"

"Three in the morning, Hollis. Sorry to wake you, but I found Zhao."

"You *did*?" Hollis looked more alert now and eagerly peeked over Baker's shoulder as though expecting Han Zhao to pop out yelling *Surprise!* "How is he?"

"Dead."

"Dead?"

"As dust."

"Where is his body?"

"Propped up against a shipping container in San Pedro. When were you gonna tell me he was the tong's head smuggler?"

"How—?"

"Don't worry, I figured it out on my own. I'm assuming you don't actually brew baijiu in your bathtub. Zhao had an arrangement with Lamotte's people, right?"

"Come inside."

"I can't stay long."

Baker stepped inside. Hollis locked the door and ran off to put on a kettle of tea.

"Yes, you are correct," Hollis said, returning from the kitchen with two steaming cups of Longjing. "Han would pay Lamotte's dock workers to look the other way whenever we needed to take delivery of a shipment from China."

"I take it he went missing on a day he was scheduled to take delivery of a shipment?"

"Yes."

"And Lamotte himself didn't know about the arrangement?"

"Certainly not. His workers often complained of their wages being late or not coming at all. We simply took advantage of those grievances."

"Then Han must have stumbled onto another off-the-books transaction going on that night. Something big."

"How do you mean?"

Baker recounted the story told to him by Captain Issur—of how Han had stormed into Charybdis, screaming Lamotte's name. "They kicked him out of the tavern, and I'm sure someone was waiting out there in the dark to strike."

"Do you think Lamotte showed up unexpectedly at the port that night?" Hollis asked.

"If he did, we have no way of proving it," said Baker. He ran his hands through his hair, feeling weary and drained. Connolly's recent words rang in his head: *The mind is fragile and wants to make sense of every little detail when things start to spiral out of our control.*

"Any reason why you didn't bother to tell me that Zhao was the father of William Yang?"

"The less you knew, the better," Hollis explained. "There's enough heat on us already. If HUAC found out we were working with the man who sired William Yang, I shudder to think of the consequences. Our little slice of Los Angeles might be burnt to the ground. Besides, his past needn't concern you."

"It does now," Baker said. "His firstborn daughter is sitting outside in my car as we speak and she's pretty shaken up about the whole thing."

"How did you—?"

"I'm asking the questions, Hollis." Baker drained his cup of tea, barely minding how hot it was. "I suggest you have someone pick up Han's body before dawn. I cut a small hole in the chain-link fence near the shipping containers just off the Seaside Freeway." He stood up and held out the picture of Han and his daughter. "Just don't let Mingmei see her father like that. Tell her I'm sorry."

Evelyn was lightly snoozing, her face pressed against the window. "Oh! It's just you, Morris," she said, jolting awake after he tapped her on the shoulder. "I was having the most terrible dream. My father...he was...reaching out for me. His eyes..."

"Apologies if I frightened you," he said. "Let's get you back to your motel."

"No," she said, grabbing his arm. "I don't want to be alone tonight. Can I stay with you?"

"You sure?"

She nodded. "I can't bear the thought of being alone."

"Okay," said Baker, who understood the feeling. "Just a fair warning that my apartment is...a little messy."

"Honestly, I'd be more surprised if it wasn't."

CHAPTER 49

Matagot's eyes flashed like two golden coins when Baker unlocked the door to his apartment. He had his gun raised just in case someone was there to finish the job Arnaud had started. The place was deserted.

"Forgot to mention I also have a cat," he said as Matagot cautiously crept out from under the bed.

"I was always more of a dog person," Evelyn said, chuckling weakly. "He's adorable."

"More like a pain in the ass." Baker made to turn on the light, but Evelyn stayed his hand.

"Leave it off," she whispered, moving closer to him.

"Evelyn," he breathed, catching a whiff of rose, honeysuckle, and light perspiration.

She had begun to sob again, and he held her close—fulfilling the terms of a curse that compelled him to stand present for the unending despair of the world. There was nothing he could do except rub her back and murmur hollow promises that everything was going to be okay. When the worst of it had passed, he moved over to the bed and tried to make it look presentable. Matagot stopped swatting at an old Hershey's wrapper and watched.

"You take the mattress," Baker said. "I'll sleep on the floor."

"No," she said, removing her shoes and falling onto the bed, fully clothed. "I'd rather if you stayed beside me."

"All right." He lay down, facing her. "Good night, Evelyn."

"Good night, Morris. Hope I'm not a burden."

"You kidding?" he said, pulling the blanket over her. "If anyone's the burden, it's me. Get some rest. I'll be here if you need anything."

"Thank you. Part of me hopes I'll wake up in the morning and everything—William, the internment camps... my father—was all just a bad dream."

"You do that," Baker said, rolling onto his back, thinking *If horses were wishes...*

Evelyn nodded off, occasionally jerking or quietly yelping in response to some unconscious stimuli Baker could not see. He stayed up for as long as he could, afraid of slipping into his familiar nightmare. It was a losing battle, and at long last, he slipped into uneasy oblivion, but not before his fatigued brain reminded him that he'd forgotten to light the Hanukkah candles.

Baruch ata Adonai Eloheinu, melech ha'olam, asher kid'shanu b'mitzvotav v'tzivanu l'hadlik ner shel Hanukkah.

Baruch atah Adonai Eloheinu Melech ha'olam, she'asah nisim la'avoteinu ba'yamim ha'heim ba-z'man ha'zeh.

The following article appeared in the tabloid known as *Confidential* in early August 1958. The piece in question was written by one Daryl B. Payne (a suspected pen name of Andrew Phillip Sullivan, now a full-time staff writer and editor for the *Los Angeles Times*).

According to unsubstantiated eyewitness accounts, Sullivan once admitted to penning the article out of spite when Morris Baker refused to give him an exclusive interview about what really transpired on the night of July 4, 1958. Sullivan has since refuted these claims, citing his close friendship with Baker, and threatened to bring libel litigation against anyone who attempts to perpetuate the narrative.

NAZIS FROM OUTER SPACE?!

JEWISH COP EXPOSES ALIEN KRAUTS IN LOS ANGELES!

More than a decade after the unconditional surrender of Nazi Germany at the close of the Second World War, the National Socialists have reared their ugly heads once again. Their resurgence raises important questions about what planet they really come from...

Photos by Lee Keyrear
Words by Daryl B. Payne

It's been 13 years since Adolf Hitler put a well-deserved bullet in his brain, allowing Nazi Germany to wave the white flag of unconditional surrender in the face of advancing Allied powers in Europe. For more than a decade, the world has considered the National Socialist menace to be dead and gone—a thing of the bloody past. We were sadly mistaken, however, for the genocidal band of Krauts suddenly cropped up after all this time just a month ago.

And on American soil no less!

What were they doing here? Well, if you happened to catch the Liberty Boys broadcasts that have been on repeat for the last several weeks, you'd learn that this band of Nazis call themselves the "Black Symphony," a fancy name for a bunch of Hitler's former eggheads that our government secretly recruited once the war was over in '45 (either we got them or the Soviets would, went the rationale).

The Symphony's aim? To blow up some sort of novel atomic device in Los Angeles and blame the ensuing devastation on a local Jewish homicide detective working for the LAPD named Morris Baker. You can't make this stuff up, folks! The Huns love messing with the Hebrews... or do they?

It is no secret that once he was done with Europe, Hitler planned to take on the entire world. Why was he so hellbent on conquering all of humanity? *Confidential* can exclusively report that the former chancellor of Germany was not actually a human born in Austria—as he so often professed—but an extra-terrestrial from outer space. That's right, the most deplorable character of this century was not of this planet, and neither were many of his followers.

"The group of individuals we refer to as 'Nazis' are actually a race of lizard-like beings native to a planet in the vicinity of Betelgeuse," an anonymous source close to the matter tells *Confidential*. "They have spent millennia perfecting the art of mind control, which explains how they were able to sway an entire nation to their way of thinking."

That's right, the Second World War was not the work of an unhinged madman and his cronies, but a coordinated invasion planned by a formidable race from beyond the stars. Of course, not all of Germany is made up of these lizard creatures—only Adolf and his leading band of miscreants. When their regime fell, a rescue craft was sent here to pick them up and take them back home.

"The saucer that crashed in Roswell in 1947? That was them," continues our source. "The military captured the pilot and has been experimenting on him ever since at a remote outpost operated out of Edwards Air Force Base. That's why this so-called 'Black Symphony' did what they did. They can't get home and they're looking to even the score with our government."

The Symphony's interest in Baker—and their greater disdain for all Jews—is apparently all just a big misdirection. "They don't love or hate us. We're like scurrying ants to these beings," the source concludes. "Singling out a single group of people is just another part of their mind games; it takes suspicion off of what they really are and what they really want."

This brings much into question and could help shed light on why we sent a man to the moon earlier this year. Were we really trying to beat the Soviet Union to cosmic supremacy or are we sowing the seeds for some kind of militarized space force meant to protect us against the next wave of Nazis looking to take over our world?

The White House press secretary has declined every single one of *Confidential*'s requests for comment thus far. We'll keep submitting inquiries because the American people deserve answers. Keep watching the skies, dear readers!

PART V

December 29, 1959

The Cold War isn't thawing; it is burning with a deadly heat. Communism isn't sleeping; it is, as always, plotting, scheming, working, fighting.

—*Richard Milhous Nixon*

CHAPTER 50

From what Baker could see through the blinds the next morning, the day would once again be gray and forbidding. He allowed Evelyn to continue sleeping as he brewed up some coffee, first scraping out the black sludge at the bottom of the pot left over from the last batch. Filling up a chipped mug, he brought it over to the bed and sat down next to Evelyn.

"Morning," she groaned, her eyes shivering open.

"Morning," he responded, handing her the mug. "How'd you sleep?"

"I've had better." She smiled. "Thank you for letting me stay."

"My pleasure," he said, feeling his own lips curl into a reciprocal grin.

"Can I ask you a question?" he asked, getting up to fill a mug for himself.

"Shoot," Evelyn said with a yawn.

"I hope I'm not being too imprudent here, but how is it that some lucky guy hasn't already locked you down?"

"You mean made an honest woman out of me?"

"Sure, if you wanna put it like that."

"You sound like my mother. Let's just say you aren't my type, Morris Baker."

"Not into Jews?"

"Men," Evelyn replied, laughing.

"Ahhh," he said.

"Gonna call HUAC on me for my deviant ways?"

"Miss Yang, I'm a Jew who once fell head over heels for a Soviet spy not too long ago. I'm in no position to lecture anyone on who they can and can't love. Here's to being who we are—no more and no less."

They clinked mugs together and sipped coffee, listening to the rain patter against the sill.

"What was she like?" Evelyn asked.

"What was 'who' like?"

"The Soviet spy."

"She was... something else."

"Was she the one... who was murdered? Liz?"

"No," Baker said, not eager to elaborate.

Picking up on the melancholy in his voice, Evelyn did not press the matter.

"Your book," Baker said, hoping to change the subject. "The one you said you wanted to write before McCarthy took office. What was it about?"

"Oh," said Evelyn, taken aback. "How familiar are you with the Great Old Ones?"

"Any connection to Oz the Great and Powerful?"

"No," she replied, laughing again. "My novel centers around a brother and sister who run away and join the circus, only to discover that the ringmaster plans to release the fury of ancient gods. But it's really a metaphor for growing up and facing the terrors of adulthood."

"Can't wait to read it someday."

"I wouldn't hold your breath, especially since my last name doesn't engender much goodwill these days. Speaking of, what do we do now, Morris? Last night was a—"

"A literal dead end," he finished. "Don't count us out just yet." He put his mug on the counter, bent down, and started to grope around the mess on the floor for the phone. "I've got one last trick up my sleev—whoops!" He'd accidentally grabbed Matagot's tail, causing the cat to jump three feet into the air and slink away, hissing in displeasure.

Evelyn sat up farther, watching his quest for the phone with interest. "What's the lead?"

"Arnaud," said Baker, who had just located the phone. "I found a number on him yesterday that I really didn't want to call again, but seeing as we're out of options..."

The cheery voice from the day before answered: "You have reached HUAC, Los Angeles, Echo Park Branch. This is Inspector Lonergan's office, how may I help you this morning?"

"This is Morris Baker calling for Inspector Lonergan. Tell him I want to meet about Louis Arnaud."

"One moment, sir..." Lonergan's secretary returned on the line a minute later. "What does your schedule look like for the rest of the day, Mr. Baker?"

CHAPTER 51

The meeting with Lonergan was set for early afternoon, so Baker decided to spend some time at the office. Evelyn remained at his apartment, agreeing to look after Matagot. He promised to call her with an update as soon as he was clear of the HUAC building in Echo Park, where he'd once been tortured.

"There he is!" boomed Hersh, reeling Baker into a crushing side hug after he'd climbed the stairs to the rented office space. "Where have you been?"

"Fucking your pregnant wife," Baker said. "Your unborn child grabbed my dick." Hersh roared with laughter. It was one of the many reasons Baker liked him. The man could take even the most off-color of jokes. "How is Mindy? I heard you had to take her to the doc yesterday."

"Oh, she's fine. Just a few painful contractions, is all. Too many latkes with vanilla ice cream. These strange cravings of hers make my stomach turn. What happened to your throat? You jerking off with a belt around your neck? Risky, but I hear the orgasm is incredible."

"Would you believe a French assassin tried to kill me yesterday?"

"With you? Nothing surprises me."

"You know me, Hersh, never a boring moment."

Smiling, Baker turned toward the open door of the reception area to find Rabbi Kahn waiting there, hat gripped in his only hand, an embarrassed look on his face. Joanna relieved the rabbi of his hat and placed it on the rack next to her desk. Baker's smile faltered and he rounded on Hersh, who shrugged nonchalantly. "He just wants to talk, Morris."

"*We'll discuss this later*," he hissed at the bodyguard, who didn't seem too worried about job security. Turning back to Kahn, he said, "Rabbi, step into my office." Kahn, who had just accepted a mug of coffee from Joanna, followed Baker into the office. "Please, have a seat."

The rabbi sat. "Thank you for agreeing to see me, Morris," he said. "I was curious if you have made any progress on those missing men."

"No," Baker said maliciously. "Their wives seem to have it handled."

"I know I am probably one of the last people you want sitting in your office right now."

Baker said nothing. He could not bring himself to give the rabbi a reprieve when the man had allowed the shul board to ban him following his outburst at the potluck.

Kahn, always sharp as a tack, bowed his head in comprehension.

"I only came to clear the air and apologize for what transpired," he continued. "So long as I am part of any community, no one will be made to feel unwelcome. Our people have endured too many hardships... too much exclusion and animosity. That is why I tendered my resignation with Ohev Shalom the morning after the vote to ban you took place."

"*What?*" Baker's wintry pride melted away in the blazing light of this unexpected news. "Rabbi, you can't do that! The congregation needs you!"

Kahn smiled. "The moment I am no longer needed is the moment I can no longer lead by example."

"Oh, come on!" Baker shouted. "Drop the humble bullshit shtick for once, would you? You can't be blaming yourself for a cunt like Shelly Horowitz... excuse the language."

Kahn stuck a finger into his ear and turned it dramatically. "My sincerest apologies," he said. "Wax buildup makes it hard to hear sometimes. I missed that last part."

"Right... All I'm saying is that we're a stubborn people. We're like children—we never know what's best for us until someone like you comes along to show us the way of righteousness or whatever."

"Oh, I don't presume to—"

"Then I'll presume for you! You're not giving up this job for me. I'm not worth all that. Not by a long shot. *I* blew up at Shira and Kremnitzer. Me! You shouldn't have to pay for my mistakes." He pressed the intercom. "Joanna, send Hersh in here, please."

"You called, boss?" Hersh said, stepping into the office seconds later.

"Yes, block that door. No one gets in or out."

"Roger." He stepped back into the waiting area.

"Morris, what are you doing?" Kahn asked.

"Rabbi, you have done more kindnesses for me than I can put into words. It's about time I returned the favor."

He picked up the phone and asked the operator to connect him with a residence in Pico-Robertson. It rang three-and-a-half times before his quarry answered.

"Hello?" answered Shelly Horowitz.

"Shelly, it's Morris Baker. Just shut up and listen."

"Excuse me?"

"You're excused. I'm sitting here in my office with Rabbi Kahn. He came to ask me about your missing husband, even though he already resigned from his post at Ohev Shalom three days ago. He doesn't owe you jack shit, and yet, here he is. I'm calling to make you a deal. I'll find Netanel and his friends on the condition that you and the rest of the board reinstate the good rabbi. Do that, and I'll never step foot in that shul again as long as I live."

Silence.

"This is a limited-time offer, Shelly. Clock's ticking. Nu?"

It took her so long to respond, he thought she'd hung up.

"Okay," she replied at last. "You've got a deal."

"Good. Happy Hanukkah. My best to the kids." He hung up.

Kahn looked at him, openmouthed. "Morris, I cannot allow you to do that!"

"What's done is done, Rabbi. Ohev Shalom is nothing without you. Hersh!"

"Yeah, boss?"

"Make sure Rabbi Kahn gets to his car safely and that he starts working on his sermon for this Shabbos." Hersh saluted and started to shepherd Kahn—at a genuine loss for words—out of the office. "Oh, and Rabbi?" Kahn turned around. "Thanks for the menorah."

CHAPTER 52

It was ten minutes to noon when Baker pulled up to the wrought-iron gate of HUAC's Echo Park branch, housed within a former library on West Temple Street. The cake-like structure of white and orange bricks looked even more forbidding in this weather—a ghoulish keep where the most heinous of deeds took place.

He pressed the call button outside the gate and waited until a harsh voice squawked over the intercom. The resulting screech of feedback nearly blew out Baker's eardrums.

"State your business," it said.

"Morris Baker to see Chief Inspector Lonergan."

"Do you have an appointment?"

"Yes, I spoke to his secretary this morning."

"One moment."

That moment stretched into an interminable five minutes. To pass the time, he turned on the radio, which informed him that Prime Minister Kishi was "*currently fighting for his life after yesterday's brazen assassination attempt.*" There was a loud mechanical buzz and the gate swung inward. Baker drove through and pulled into a visitor parking spot closest to the exit, wanting to make a quick escape if things went south.

After all, his last visit to the place had not been a pleasant one: He'd walked away with several broken ribs, a fractured jaw, two swollen eyes, a broken nose, and a handful of missing teeth. Still, he supposed he was lucky that was all he'd gotten. Had Edward R. Murrow and his bodyguards not shown up to save him and Sophia, Baker might not be alive to tell the tale.

Leaving his gun and knife—and any other items the Hueys might use as a flimsy excuse to detain him—in the car, Baker walked inside, taking great care to make sure his hands were in plain sight of anyone who might be watching. The last thing he needed was to be accidentally shot if a scratch of the ass was misconstrued as reaching for a hidden firearm.

The place hadn't changed all that much over the last year and a half. A small army of mindless phone operators still answered calls about suspected Communist activity throughout the city, while others listened intently to bugged recordings of alleged subversives.

The same propaganda posters about the dangers of Russia, homosexuality, and the Jewish global influence (JUST SAY NO TO MATZO BALLS) still hung on the walls, now joined by massive prints of William Yang's face. Home sweet home, in other words.

Baker approached the metal detector and was surprised when the on-duty guard gave him a large, unnerving smile that didn't jibe with the dour aura of HUAC's base camp.

"Good afternoon, Mr. Baker," he said. "Could I kindly ask you to empty your pockets into the dish before stepping through?"

"Uh...sure," Baker said, handing over his wallet and a few loose coins.

He stepped through the detector, his eyes automatically roving toward the door he knew led down to soundproofed interrogation/torture rooms. The guard pushed a logbook toward him. "Just sign your name and time of entry. The chief inspector will be down to meet you presently."

As if responding to some prearranged cue, Lonergan suddenly appeared.

"Baker!" boomed the lead Huey—tall, burly, and mean-looking with a pompadour haircut that bobbed with every step. He, too, was smiling a little too much for Baker's liking. The last time they'd met face-to-face, a fuming Lonergan had tried to arrest him. "It's good to see you," he said, though he did not extend his hand for shaking. "Come on in."

"Saw your performance at Kishi's speech yesterday," Baker said.

"The matter required swift action," Lonergan said, running a comb up his hair. "Mr. Park won't be bothering anyone ever again."

Lonergan led him through the desks of operators, who, Baker was horrified to see, had jugs of deep yellow liquid that could only be piss sitting underneath their chairs. He considered asking Lonergan about the bathroom policy here but decided against it.

"Can I get you a cup of coffee?" Lonergan asked. "We just got this puppy in from Italy. Makes the best espresso you ever had in your life." He pointed to a gleaming chrome behemoth sitting in the area once reserved for children's books, which seemed totally unnecessary if no one was allowed to get up and void their bladder.

"No, thanks," Baker said.

"Suit yourself. My office is just up here."

They climbed up a short stairwell near the back wall, taken up by a larger banner depicting the HUAC logo and corny slogan:

FIGHTING FOR WHAT MAKES AMERICA GREAT
SINCE '38!

Situated along the second-floor balcony, from which he could observe his underlings, Lonergan's personal office was a windowless, spartan affair that had no adornments beyond a desk, an ink blotter, two chairs, a metal filing cabinet, and the requisite framed portraits of McCarthy and Nixon. It all reeked of the German efficiency the Hueys were trying so hard to emulate.

Baker took a seat without being asked. Lonergan twitched slightly.

"So," Lonergan said with forced calm, sitting behind the desk and steepling his fingers. "How may I help you today, Baker? My secretary mentioned something about a Lewis Gonad?"

"*Louis Arnaud*," said Baker. "Before we get to that, though, maybe you can explain why you're being so nice to me. I thought you hated my guts?"

"Hate you?" Lonergan asked in a poor imitation of surprise. "My dear, man—what would ever give you that idea?"

"Let's start with the fact that I'm a Jew you couldn't arrest."

Lonergan spread his hands. "Times have . . . changed, Baker. There are bigger fish to fry these days. You are a small guppy in a very, very large pond. Surely you don't want to be arrested?"

"No, I do enjoy my freedom, Lonergan." This elicited another twitch from the Huey, who was probably used to being called "Chief

Inspector" by every bootlicker in the building. "I'm here because I arrived home yesterday morning to find a sizable Frenchman in my apartment, waiting to kill me and frame the murder as a suicide."

"Oh . . . ?" Lonergan steepled his fingers again, an infuriating gesture. "How interesting."

"The interesting part is that your office number was inside his pocket. Now what reason would Louis Arnaud have to call you?"

"I couldn't begin to imagine. Maybe he was given my number by someone else."

"You didn't send the Frog to kill me?"

Lonergan leaned forward, his cloying smile widening. "If I did, Baker, do you really think I would tell you?"

"Then why agree to meet with me at all?"

"I always have time for old . . . acquaintances. Anything else I can do for you today?"

The two men stared at each other, their mutual dislike palpable like a noxious flatulent. Baker opened his mouth, ready to pose a question about Kissinger and Lamotte, when there was an almost imperceptible knock at the door.

"Enter!" Lonergan barked, not taking his eyes off Baker. The door opened and Lonergan's petite secretary nervously popped her head inside. "What is it, Flo?" Lonergan demanded.

"That pamphlet maker you've been after was just brought in by Inspectors Harris and Bailey. Thought you'd want to take a look before they begin . . . interrogation procedures."

Baker took "before they begin interrogation procedures" to mean "before they beat the guy so badly, he can barely remember his own name afterward."

"Very well," said Lonergan. "Wait here, Baker. I'll be right back."

He left the office with Flo. As soon as the door had closed shut, Baker hopped up, made his way around the desk, and pulled open its central drawer. Sifting through the extra pens, pads of paper, and tins of Brylcreem, he unearthed a poorly printed brochure for the "world-renowned" Albus Dens sanitarium and wellness center in Malibu.

Scrawled across the top was a name Baker was only too familiar with: *Hartwell*.

He wanted to inspect the file cabinet but could already hear

Lonergan coming back. He memorized the sanitarium's address, delicately replaced the brochure, closed the drawer, and ran back to his seat with seconds to spare.

Lonergan and his foolish grin returned.

"If that is all, Baker, I really must be getting on with my day," he said. "It was a pleasure to see you again. I trust you can see yourself out."

"Thanks for your time, Lonergan," Baker said, patting the lead Huey on the shoulder. Lonergan flinched in obvious disgust. "If I never see you again, it'll be too soon."

CHAPTER 53

"Who is this 'Hartwell' again?" asked Evelyn as they slowly cruised along the foggy coastal road of California State Route 1 leading to Malibu.

"I already told you," Baker said for what felt like the hundredth time. "He's a Huey. Or *was* one. A friend of mine... well, she shot off his kneecaps."

"The spy?"

"Yes."

"And you think he'll talk to you after *that*?"

"I do not."

"Fine. What makes you think he knows anything about Kissinger?"

"I don't."

"So why are we going to see him?"

"Because we're out of options," Baker said, gnashing his teeth in frustration. Evelyn's repeated questions made it hard for him to concentrate on the road. "Even if Hartwell is no longer part of HUAC, he's only been out of the loop for a little over a year. He might still prove useful."

They arrived at Albus Dens around four o'clock. Located along several acres of the precarious, yet incredibly affluent, Cliffside Drive near the very tip of Malibu, the sanitarium resembled a slanted, rotting tooth jutting out of the cliff's edge.

The palm trees planted all around the entrance looked like chewed-up stalks of broccoli caught in the crevices of unflossed gums, whipping in the vicious gale coming off the sea. Baker pulled off the road and into a small parking lot designated for visiting friends and family.

He figured the place was unimaginably peaceful in better weather but couldn't shake the recurring thought that one good gust of wind might send the entire place toppling into the briny water below. They raced across the lot, collars of their coats barely protecting their cheeks from the polar ocean spray.

It was a relief to enter the hypermodern interior of curved walls painted a sterile, eye-piercing white. Clusters of doctors, orderlies, and nurses—dressed in pristine Nehru uniforms adorned with gold buttons—flitted in and out of the cavernous lobby, discussing patient charts, drug dosages, and what the cafeteria was serving for dinner. The lobby's only piece of furniture, an angular metal desk that looked like a giant staple, sat dead center.

"May I help you?" asked the receptionist, a kindly middle-aged woman sitting in a chair the shape of an egg cup. A pair of horn-rimmed glasses dangled from a chain around her neck and a brass nameplate declared her name: Florence Winbunner.

"Yes, you can, Florence," said Baker. "My name's Randy Hartwell and this is my wife, Regina. I'm here to see my brother, Morton Hartwell."

"Oh, how lovely," said Winbunner. "We haven't had a single visitor all week. Everyone's so busy with their holiday plans." She opened a leather-bound day planner and reached for her glasses. "Hartwell, did you say? Hmmm...Hartwell...Hartwell...I'm not seeing you on the schedule."

"No, you wouldn't," Evelyn said. "It was kind of a last-minute decision." She turned to Baker, feigning exasperation. "I *told* you we needed to call ahead."

"Damnit, Regina! I didn't think I needed an appointment to see my own brother!"

"You never listen to me!" Evelyn shouted back. "You're too damn stubborn for your own good!"

"Oh, here we go again! If you wanted a pushover for a husband, you should've married Frank Beauchamp!"

"Maybe I should have!"

"Excuse me..." quavered Florence.

"*What?*" screamed Baker and Evelyn, turning in Winbunner's direction. The poor old woman cowered in fright.

"Yes... um... well, I can see you really do want to see your brother, Mr. Hartwell. Considering it is the holidays, I think we can bend the rules just this once."

Baker put a hand to his chest and let out a hyperbolic sigh of relief. "You really mean it, Florence? Oh, that'd just mean so much to him."

Florence winked. "Joy to the world, right?" She looked past them, calling out to a slumped orderly with long and powerful arms that were covered in bright orange hair and nearly dragged along the ground like an orangutan's. "Janek!"

Janek slowly turned around, revealing a thick, bushy beard that matched the growth on his arms. "Janek, dear," Winbunner said. "Can you please escort these guests to Mr. Hartwell's room in the East Wing? This is his brother and sister-in-law."

"Uh-yes, ma'am," Janek said in a low, grunting voice. "This way, folks."

"God bless you," Evelyn whispered to Florence, who waved her hand in an *it-was-nothing* gesture.

Baker and Evelyn followed Janek to the far end of the lobby, where the orderly lifted one long finger and punched a lengthy passcode into a keypad set into the wall.

There was a powerful hiss of hydraulics and the wall slid open to reveal a narrow and depressing hallway of scuffed linoleum, humming fluorescents, and thick doors of unvarnished wood. It seemed the forward-thinking design of the sanitarium only extended as far as the lobby.

Janek held his lanky arm against the opening as Baker and Evelyn stepped inside. The orderly followed suit and the door slid seamlessly back into place with another snakelike hiss. Had the orderly not been so slouched, his head might not have cleared the low ceiling.

"Hartwell is all way at end," said Janek, scratching his bearded chin. "Best view in whole place."

The three of them walked down the hallway single-file and Baker caught muffled snatches of sounds from behind each door: cries, screams, maniacal laughter, scratching, and in one instance, a lonely Victrola playing a worn-out pressing of some long-forgotten jazz tune. The warbling music gave the entire place a surrealist, dream-like quality.

"Are any of these people free to roam about the facility?" Evelyn asked as one door shook violently in its frame.

"Some," said Janek. "Here," he added as they reached the very last door at the far end of the hallway. He knocked, but there was no answer. "Mr. Hartwell? Your brother here to see you." Silence prevailed. Janek shrugged. "You go in. Not high-level security guest, so door not locked. I wait down hall once you're ready go."

"Thanks, Janek," said Baker.

"'Tain't nothing," replied Janek, who began to slouch back the way they had come. "Oh, before forget." Janek held out a quarter pint of whiskey. "Give this."

Baker accepted the bottle with a nod. He turned the knob, pushed the door open. The room, which smelled like stale hooch, sweat, and body odor, felt more like a miniature studio apartment—complete with bathroom and kitchenette.

A full-size bed faced a boxy Motorola television set topped with rabbit ears and a generous layer of dust. Nightstand, bookshelf, decorative rug, and diminutive armoire rounded out the modest furnishings, though, like the television, they all carried the same air of neglect.

The most notable thing about the place was the handsome picture window that took up the entire opposite wall. On a clear day, it would—as Janek said—deliver a dynamite view. All it showed today, however, was a grim canvas of swirling mist and rain—a natural television set full of static interference. Baker noted how there were no latches on the window, certain the Albus Dens sanitarium had a hard-and-fast rule against people leaping to their deaths.

Sitting directly in front of the window was a crumpled husk of a man in a rusted wheelchair. His legs were gone—cleanly amputated at the knees—his face a wild thicket of unkempt beard and shoulder-length hair.

Two bloodshot eyes encased in sleepless folds of skin stared unblinkingly out of the bramble while one hand lifted a nearly empty bottle of whiskey to the cracked lips. The mechanical motion reminded Baker of drinking bird toys that bobbed up and down into cups of water.

"I have no brother," croaked the man, and Baker could just hear the ghostly echo of Morton Hartwell's once arrogantly smug tone. "Least not one who would want to see me. The fuck you doing here, Baker?"

CHAPTER 54

How'd you know it was me?" Baker said, moving closer to Hartwell.

"Saw you in the reflection. Had a feeling you'd show up one of these days. You never could keep your big nose clean."

"A gift from Janek," Baker said, holding out the fresh bottle of whiskey.

"'Bout goddamn time." Hartwell drained the last of his current libation and threw it into a nearby graveyard of empty bottles, where it shattered. He accepted the new one without a single word of thanks, immediately twisting off the cap and taking a drawn-out pull. "So what is it you want, Baker? Come to have a laugh at the cripple? You wouldn't be the first."

"No," said Baker, who felt a little sorry for the man sitting in front of the window. His sympathies were limited once he remembered Hartwell was the one who had once beaten him senseless with a Louisville Slugger baseball bat. "How did you end up in this place?"

"How do ya think? Once that Soviet bitch blew my knees off, I didn't have much of a job waiting for me on the other side of a double amputation. Didn't have much of anything left. My bitch of a wife left with the kids, and Lonergan stuck me here to live out the rest of my days. But hey, at least HUAC foots the bill. God bless the US of fuckin' A."

He toasted the empty air and took another swig, most of which dribbled down his beard and onto his matching blue pajamas.

"Listen, Hartwell," Baker continued. "I wanted to ask you a question."

"The whole world is one big question," slurred Hartwell, who might be more pliable than expected, given Janek's steady supply of whiskey. "Question marks everywhere you turn."

"I was wondering if you knew anything about a fella by the name of Louis Arnaud."

"That snail-sucking louse?"

"So you know him?"

"Sure, I do. Works counterintelligence for the SDECE in French Indochina. Targeted political assassinations and the like. Good at his job, but a real self-satisfied asshole."

"Indochina?" Baker repeated. "Then what reason would he have to be in America?"

"He sometimes does a little freelance work for the CIA. They trained him, after all."

"Not anymore," Baker said. "I killed him yesterday."

"His luck was bound to run out sooner or later. Can't say I'll miss the son of a bitch. Here's to you, Louis," Hartwell said, raising the fresh whiskey bottle. "May you rot in Hell."

"Did HUAC ever use him for jobs?"

"All the time."

"But what do HUAC and the CIA have to do with each other?"

Hartwell cackled. It was an ugly high-pitched sound.

"So much you still don't know, Baker. When McCarthy turned a Congressional committee into a secret police force, he alienated the other intelligence agencies. Hoover and Dulles let it happen because the president promised to let them keep their autonomy."

"I'm guessing McCarthy went back on his word?"

"Not immediately. He let the FBI and CIA do most of the heavy lifting as HUAC was just starting out. But once we started to take root all over the country, McCarthy began stripping the other agencies of their power."

"He wanted total control over all intelligence."

Hartwell confirmed this by touching his nose as if they were playing a friendly game of charades. "That way, the president would never be out of the loop, you see? Hoover and Dulles didn't like that one bit. They like their independence too much. Add the bungled shitstorm in Korea to mix, and you end up with a lot of pissed-off people behind the scenes of our government. A lot of folks—like MacArthur, for instance—want us to vacate the area and nuke the Gooks back to the Stone Age."

"Why hasn't McCarthy done it then?"

"The president's a bastard, but he's a lot smarter than any of us give him credit for. He knows that there's no putting the genie back into the bottle once it's been opened. Nuking the Koreans means nuking the Soviets, and there's no way the Reds don't pop off a few of their own bombs before it's all said and done. McCarthy is too addicted to power to risk global nuclear annihilation over a few commies in East Asia. He'd much rather throw countless men into the line of fire before jeopardizing his comfy chair in the Oval Office."

"But that's not working," Evelyn said. Her interjection caused Hartwell to jump.

"Who's the broad?" he asked, jerking a finger in Evelyn's direction.

"Evelyn Yang," she said.

"That name supposed to mean something to me?"

"No," she said, "but maybe you've heard of my brother, William Yang."

Hartwell's bloodshot and puffy eyes swelled with comprehension. Then he cackled again and exclaimed, "Wow! You really know how to pick 'em, Baker!"

"What do you know about my brother's death?" Evelyn said.

"Him going kablooey in that department store was supposed to be the president's ace in the hole. A perfect chance to whip up some much-needed anger at home and justify our continued presence in Korea for a few extra years."

There it was: the admission Baker and Evelyn were looking for. But then Hartwell continued to speak. "At least that's what McCarthy thinks. Yang's suicide was really a distraction meant for the president. A can of snake oil sold to him by Nixon and that smug Hebe."

"Kissinger?" Evelyn asked.

"Yup."

"Nixon's planning a coup?"

"Right on the money there, Baker," Hartwell said, touching his nose again.

"How is he getting HUAC to go along with it?"

"Nixon's a California boy, and the Los Angeles branch is one of the largest in the country. All he had to do was get Lonergan on board and the rest would start to fall in line. It's been a long time coming. Years in the planning."

"So HUAC plans to absorb all the municipal police forces is more for Nixon's benefit than McCarthy's."

"You can't break the law if you control the people who enforce it," said Hartwell. "McCarthy's days are numbered."

"What about the assassination attempt on Kishi?"

"All of it works in Nixon's favor. He's justifying a nuclear strike on the North Koreans."

"Jesus," Baker said to Evelyn. "This is bigger than we could have imagined."

"*It's huge!*" screamed Hartwell. He lunged forward, dropping his whiskey and grabbing Baker around the waist. "The world's gone daffy and the rest of us are *fucked*!" He sang out the last word, turning it into a deranged nursery rhyme. "*Fucked! Fucked! Fucked!*"

"Get offa me!" Baker wrenched himself away from the man's shockingly firm grasp.

"Oh my God, Morris!" Evelyn shrieked. "He has your gun!"

"I'm sorry, Baker. I really am," Hartwell said, tears streaming down into his beard. "For everything."

Morton Hartwell stuck the barrel into his mouth, pulled the trigger, and splattered the contents of his skull all over the picture window.

CHAPTER 55

A piece of Hartwell's brain slid down the fractured glass and dropped to the floor with a nauseating *splat!* The blood coating the window looked like a madman's idea of a Rorschach inkblot test. Hartwell sat flat against the back of the wheelchair. Evelyn's legs failed her, and she sank onto the bed. Baker approached Hartwell's corpse and wrenched his gun out of the stiffening fingers.

The barrel was coated in blood and floppy bits of gray matter. Holding it out in front of him, Baker brought it to the bathroom, giving it a thorough cleaning with a dampened washcloth. As the blood and brains hypnotically swirled down the drain, he chewed over what Hartwell had told them, still wondering how Orson Lamotte fit into the picture. Kissinger's warning, on the other hand, came into sharper focus: Nixon planned to seize the presidency and end the interminable war with an H-bomb or two. If he got away with it, the genie would indeed be out of the bottle. A nuclear strike wouldn't end with East Asia; it would mushroom outward until nothing was left. Would the vice president storm the White House with a personal army of Hueys or was the plan much subtler than that? Would the American people even be aware that a coup had occurred?

"Come on," he said. "We need to get out of here before someone finds out he's dead. I'm guessing Janek didn't hear the gunshot or else he'd already be here."

Evelyn looked up, her eyes red and puffy. "William," she choked. "He trusted Kissinger... believed in peace—wanted an end to all the bloodshed. And they just turned him into another weapon. How do you think they did it? Threatened to hurt my mother and me?"

"Probably," Baker said. He sat down on the bed and put an arm around her. "I've seen it done before. Those in power go right for the balls and squeeze until you're ready to call 'uncle.'"

"He was innocent, Morris. I knew he would be."

"Yeah. Only problem is the one person willing to speak the truth doesn't have much of a head anymore."

They sat for another five minutes until Evelyn was well enough to stand.

"You've been through a lot these past few days," Baker said, ready to catch her if she suddenly fainted. "We'll get you to bed and then figure out what to do next."

Janek was still waiting for them down the hall, and judging by the orderly's blank expression, he was totally unaware of Hartwell's suicide.

"Finished?" the orderly asked dully.

"Yep," Baker said, and Evelyn managed a weak smile. "Thanks for the whiskey, Janek. He was most appreciative. Oh, and Morton said he wanted to take a little nap before dinner. He requested that no one bother him for the next hour or so."

Janek nodded and turned around to punch in another code that would open the door on this side of the wall. He stood aside to let them pass and bade them an enjoyable evening.

"You as well, Janek," said Baker. "Come along now, darling."

They started across the lobby, arm-in-arm, and were a little more than halfway to the exit when Baker felt the floor drop out from under him. There, waiting for them at the reception desk, was Lonergan and a pair of HUAC henchmen. This time, Lonergan's face showed true exhilaration.

"Baker!" exclaimed the chief inspector. "We really need to stop meeting like this!"

CHAPTER 56

Baker had his gun and knife confiscated as he and Evelyn were unceremoniously shoved into the back seat of a Ford Interceptor. One of Lonergan's men held out a pair of black muslin hoods.

"Put them on," he growled.

"Not until you tell us where you're taking us," Evelyn said. The Huey struck her across the face.

"No questions," he said.

"*Hey!*" shouted Baker, leaning over to grab the Huey by his collar. "Do that again, and I'll kill you!" The man shoved him back, laughing.

"Quit your barking, Baker, and do as you're told," said Lonergan, running a comb through his hair in the front seat. "Don't worry, we're not gonna kill you. Not yet anyway. The hoods are just a precaution."

"Against what?"

Lonergan turned, his eyes full of malice.

"Ask another goddamned question and I'll cut one of the girl's ears off." Baker gave the chief inspector one final look of deepest loathing before accepting the hoods and handing one to Evelyn. "That's a good boy," said Lonergan. "I guess you can teach an old Jew new tricks."

Baker couldn't say for sure how long they had been driving. The darkness inside the mask made it impossible to properly gauge the passage of time. After a while, the stale air of his own breathing made him sleepy and he nodded off...

He was back in Hartwell's room at the Albus Dens sanitarium. The dead Huey was rising out of his wheelchair on a number of hairy spider legs sprouting from the amputated stumps. The gaping hole in the back of Hartwell's head pulsated like fresh Jell-O and a voice—deep and rumbling and quite disconnected from tongue and vocal cords—emanated from the crater.

"How does it feel, Baker? All the blood on your hands? Warm and slippery?"

Baker retreated, blindly feeling for the doorknob, but found, to his horror, that it had vanished.

"You will drown in it," boomed the voice coming out of the hole in Hartwell's head. "DrOwN iN iT. DrOwN iN iT. DrOwN iN iT. DrOwN iN iT. DrOwN iN iT. DrOwN iN iT. DrOwN iN iT."

The fatal gunshot wound resolved itself into an image: the porthole of a crematorium oven from which countless pairs of eyes stared out of the flames. It grew wider and wider—big enough to swallow him whole…

"Baker…? Baker…? *Baker!* Do something, Harris, *would* ya?"

A sharp punch to the gut brought him back to a tentative state of consciousness and out of an epileptic seizure.

"Christ, Baker," said Lonergan with a nervous chuckle. "Can't have you shaking like that for the big meeting."

"Wuh—?" Baker said, slowly regaining control of his body. He turned his head this way and that, trying to detect some sort of visual cue through the hood. "What time is it? Where are we?"

"Take him inside."

"Evelyn…" Baker said. "Where is Evelyn?"

"I'm right here," she said, giving his hand a reassuring squeeze.

"Are you coming?"

"She stays in the car," said Lonergan.

"Why?"

"Because I said so, Baker. What did I say about all the questions?"

"Where are we?" Baker asked again.

"Are you two idiots waiting for an embroidered invitation?" Lonergan barked at his subordinates. "Get him inside! The boss is waiting."

The passenger door opened and Baker was forcibly pulled out into the open air. The misty cold felt like a godsend after the stagnant oxygen inside the hood. They led him over a patch of grass, up a number of stone steps, and into the warmth of... what? A house? Apartment? Torture shack in the middle of the desert?

They pushed him into a stiff chair and the hood was whipped off his head. He winced at the sudden influx of light and squinted until his pupils became accustomed to their surroundings.

He was in the middle of a simple, old-fashioned living room, which couldn't have been larger than seventy or eighty square feet. In addition to a moth-eaten rug, chipped wooden China cabinet, and dusty piano, the room also boasted a red-bricked fireplace, in which a number of stacked logs burned down to glowing embers.

Occupying a high-backed armchair by the fire, his fingers lightly scratching behind the ears of a snoozing black-and-white cocker spaniel, was none other than Richard Nixon. He stared at Baker from the end of a long and crooked nose.

"Thank you for coming, Mr. Baker," he said.

"Didn't have much of a choice now, did I?" Baker said, making no effort to hide the contempt in his voice.

"Sorry about Lonergan," said Nixon, his voice deep, clipped, and measured. Every syllable and word carefully weighed on a cunning mental scale. "He takes his job a little too seriously."

"Where am I?" Baker asked.

"They didn't tell you?"

Baker shook his head. "You saw the hood."

Nixon frowned, which deepened the lines around his pinched mouth. "Sounds like I'll have to have a little chat with Chief Inspector Lonergan. You are in Yorba Linda on my family's lemon ranch," he explained. "I was born in this very house and come here from time to time for... certain matters, shall we say."

"Matters concerning a plan to overthrow the president and nuke Korea, you mean?"

"'Overthrow' is such an ugly word. I prefer the term... 'liberation.' Joe has proven himself unworthy of the presidency. The office is sacred, and the people have got to have confidence in the integrity of the men who obtain it."

"And you think you have that integrity?"

"I don't claim to have anything, Mr. Baker. I'm simply fulfilling what our Declaration of Independence states in its opening paragraphs.

When our government can no longer function, it is the people's right to wipe the slate clean and give rise to something new. The American people want the war in Korea over and done with—and I'm going to give them that end. I am going to work toward the cause of peace in the world; toward the cause of prosperity without war and, to the best of my ability, to restore confidence in the White House. It is a big job, but I think it can be done, and I intend to do it."

"You're nothing more than a crook."

Nixon frowned, looking as though he'd been forced to suck on a lemon from his family's ranch. The vice president stopped petting the dog, which looked up, bleary-eyed.

"You have a funny way of pronouncing the word *patriot*, Mr. Baker," said Nixon. "Now, if you are finished insulting me in my own home, I have a very attractive proposition for you."

"What's that?"

"The same thing that lowly tramp masquerading as Ann Kissinger asked of you several days ago. I want you to find Henry Kissinger."

"Very smart of you to hire me through a third party."

"Lonergan said you would refuse if we approached you directly."

"So he's not as stupid as he looks. Why me?"

"Who better?" Nixon replied with a question of his own. "You are a reputable operator, and what's more, you are discreet. My men are loyal and effective, but they lack finesse. I needed someone who could move through... several different circles."

"In other words, you needed a Jew," said Baker.

"Well, the jig, as they say, is up," said Nixon. "But the job remains the same: I want you to find Henry and whatever evidence he might have squirreled away."

"If you want me to find him, why did you send Arnaud to kill me?"

"My apologies for that. Mr. Arnaud had started to act rashly on the orders of... another party."

"Orson Lamotte, you mean?"

"Be careful, Mr. Baker. You are treading on thin ice. You were not brought here today to discuss the minutiae of my political ambitions. You were brought here to give me a simple yes or no answer. Will you find Henry Kissinger for me? I will pay you handsomely, of course."

"I don't want your slush money."

"Very well. Lonergan!" Nixon barked. The Huey came rushing in with a manila folder, his hair bobbing comically. "Take Checkers to his basket, please." Lonergan took the dog and handed Nixon the envelope along with a pair of reading glasses. "Thank you."

Nixon planted the glasses near the tip of his long nose, opened the folder, and began shuffling through the papers within.

"Hmmm, let us see now. Ah yes, two dead police officers. Bletchley and Pistone."

"Guessing that was Arnaud's work?" posited Baker.

"Two dead police officers of LA's Finest. Messy, very messy. An ongoing murder investigation that could be closed today with a Jewish man in handcuffs. Now what'll it be, Mr. Baker? Find Kissinger or go to the gas chamber? I am told you are very familiar with the latter."

"You'd really pin your own dirty work on me?"

"There is nothing I wouldn't do for the safety and security of this nation, Mr. Baker. It says here that the two deceased officers reported to a...Sergeant Brogan Connolly. Would you prefer for him to take the blame in your stead?"

Baker felt his mouth go dry.

"Oh yes," Nixon said. "I know all about your close friendship with Sergeant Connolly. I also know you have involved him a little too much on this case."

"You're a bastard."

"No, Mr. Baker. I am a politician. Do we have a deal?"

"Fine, but I have three stipulations before I agree."

"Name them."

"First, you leave Connolly and his family alone. He doesn't know anything beyond a few of my own wild theories."

"Done."

"Second, the girl sitting in the car outside walks free. There will be no repercussions for her looking into the motivations for her brother's attack."

"You have my word on that as a gentleman. No one will believe her anyway. I must also thank you for providing Hartwell with the means through which he could exit this world. I have been telling Lonergan for a long time that the man was a liability. What is your final stipulation?"

"The release of five Jewish men I believe to be in HUAC custody at Manzanar: Netanel Horowitz, Abner Greenspan, Noah Levinson, Yehuda Mandelbaum, and Eliyahu Margules."

"Is that all?"

"That's all," Baker said.

"Then we have a deal, Mr. Baker. Leave the names of those men with Lonergan and he'll see to it that they are released—on the condition that you hold up your end of the bargain, of course."

"Don't worry," Baker said, "I'll find Kissinger for you."

"Excellent. It is settled then," said Nixon, removing his glasses. "And it goes without saying, Mr. Baker, but this meeting never happened. If you need to relay any updates on the case, call Lonergan directly. I expect swift results. Have a safe trip back to Los Angeles."

Lonergan's men descended on Baker. They started to lead him back through the house and to the front exit when a bathroom door opened and out stepped a perfectly healthy Nobusuke Kishi. The Japanese prime minister looked up from drying his hands and, catching sight of Baker, averted his eyes and hurried away toward the living room.

"Fighting for your life, my ass!" Baker shouted at Kishi's retreating figure.

CHAPTER 57

Baker and Evelyn were not forced to wear hoods on the drive back to Malibu. However, Lonergan did threaten to blow their brains out if so much as a single word was exchanged between them. This suited Baker just fine; it gave him plenty of time to ruminate on his conversation with Nixon. Despite all his deviousness and stratagems, the vice president was scared.

Kissinger held the key to saving or destroying the plot to overthrow McCarthy. Again, the exact details of how Nixon planned to seize power loomed in the background, vague and undefined. There was a piece missing here, and Baker would bet anything that that piece was Orson Lamotte.

But Lamotte wouldn't admit anything to him. And even if Baker could secure another audience with the mogul, Lamotte was clearly in bed with Nixon, HUAC, and CIA-trained killers. The man was untouchable, which meant Baker needed Kissinger.

Night had fallen in earnest when Lonergan and his men dropped them off in front of Baker's car.

"The vice president expects swift results," Lonergan said, leaning out the passenger window and addressing Baker. "You call me with any updates—day or night. I don't give a damn what time it is. Got that?"

"Yes. Just remember the names of those men I wrote down for you."

"Watch your tone, Baker."

"Oh, fuck off. I'll talk to you however I like, Lonergan!" Baker screamed against the yowling ocean wind. "Go ahead and kill me. See how happy Nixon is when you tell him your temper and pride got in the way of the bigger plan!"

Lonergan gritted his teeth. "I've never met a Hebe with more backbone than you."

"Thanks."

"It wasn't a compliment. That mouth of yours is gonna get you killed one day and I so hope I'll be the one pulling the trigger. You fail to find Kissinger, and the vice president won't have a single qualm about me slowly driving an ice pick into your inferior Jew skull."

"And yet Nixon is the one trusting the brain inside this 'inferior Jew skull'"—he tapped a finger against his temple—"to get the job done, not whatever passes for intelligence in you lumbering beheymot."

Lonergan had no retort, probably because he did not understand the Yiddish insult. He simply glared at Baker, rolled up the window, and signaled for his underling to drive away. Once the Interceptor's taillights were nothing more than two specks of red in the foggy distance, Baker unlocked the Continental and got behind the wheel. Evelyn got into the passenger's seat.

"What now?" she asked.

Baker did not answer. He knew what had to be done, but he was certain Evelyn would not agree; would fight him tooth and nail on it. Nevertheless, he peeled out of the sanitarium visitors' lot, and began the trek to downtown Los Angeles.

Evelyn seemed to understand there was much weighing on his mind and remained silent until they pulled up to the red-and-white building at 800 North Alameda Street. The belfry-like clock tower reaching up from the rest of Union Station announced that eleven o' clock was fast approaching.

"Where are we?" Evelyn prompted.

"Come on," he said, cutting the engine and stepping out of the car.

"Are we following up a lead?" Evelyn asked, dutifully following him into the echoey and cavernous interior of the train station.

"Keep your head down," Baker whispered to Evelyn, catching sight of a group of Korean-Americans being herded toward a northbound track. A Huey raised a billy club and brought it down on a child that was lagging behind. The mother's wail reverberated throughout Union Station, but no one dared look in her direction.

Baker approached the central ticket counter, where the clerk peered at him from behind the latest edition of *Counterattack*. The front page teased a story about an alleged Communist plot to poison moviegoing audiences through something called Smell-O-Vision. "When's the next train to New York?" he inquired.

Without putting down his newspaper, the clerk checked his watch and said, "In about forty-five minutes."

"How much for a first-class ticket?"

"Two hundred even."

"One first-class ticket to New York, please."

"Any luggage?"

"No. This should cover it," said Baker, bringing out the down payment given to him by the Korean representative the day before. He slid a few bills over the counter.

Clearly annoyed by the disruption of his leisure time, the clerk slammed his paper down, licked his pointer finger, and began counting the money.

"Morris, what are you doing?" asked Evelyn. The mounting devastation in her voice implied she already knew the answer.

"Sending you home," Baker said, not turning around.

"I don't want to go home."

"I don't doubt that, but you need to get out of town."

"Why? I'm not leaving—not when we're so close. Besides, all my stuff at the motel..."

"Leave it," Baker said, accepting his change and the ticket. "None of that matters anymore. Over here." He led her to a wooden bench, far away from the clerk. "Don't you see? This thing goes all the way to the top, and it's emanating from Los Angeles. It's too dangerous for you here."

"I've proven myself quite capable at protecting myself, haven't I?"

"Of course you have. This isn't a question of your courage, Evelyn. Nixon promised me you wouldn't be harmed, but I don't trust a single assurance coming from a man who plans to overthrow the president of the United States and launch weapons of mass destruction. Nixon plays just as dirty as the Hueys. I'll rest easy knowing you're far away from his immediate sphere of influence. Nixon asked me to find Kissinger. *Me.* He didn't say anything about you. The man is a lawyer and knows how to exploit loopholes."

"This can't be the end," she said quietly. Evelyn blinked, and a single tear ran down her cheek.

"It's not the end," Baker said. "But it could be if you stay here."

"We were so close."

"What do you mean?" He gently lifted her chin up, brought her watery gaze level with his. "You got what you came out here for: confirmation that your brother was innocent in all of this. That weight at least can be lifted from your mind. The rest is up to me—I've got to find a way to prove it to the rest of the world. And I can only do that if I know you're safe back in New York."

Evelyn nodded. "Okay," she said, a begrudging finality to the word. "Okay, I'll go."

She refused to speak to Baker any further—not even when he escorted her onto the train forty-five minutes later to make sure the conductor punched her ticket. The conductor tried to pull out a protractor as well, ready to measure the angle of Evelyn's eyes, when Baker surreptitiously pressed his gun against the conductor's hip.

"You pull that shit, and I'll shoot you right here." Baker pulled out another wad of cash and stuffed it into the man's breast pocket. "There's nothing to see here."

The conductor acquiesced, punching her ticket and moving on to greet other passengers.

"I'll call as soon as it's safe," Baker told Evelyn once she was seated.

"None of us are ever really safe. Not really." It was the first thing she'd uttered since their discussion in the main atrium. "Goodbye, Morris."

"Goodbye, Evelyn."

Baker left the first-class carriage and stepped back onto the train platform to watch the locomotive pull out of the station. Slowly at first and then faster and faster until it was a speeding blur of light and sound. Evelyn had a seat by the window facing him, but when her car passed by, she did not wave.

The following conversation took place in the Oval Office three hours after Joseph McCarthy was sworn in as president of the United States on January 20, 1953. It was secretly recorded by Vice President Richard Nixon for unknown purposes.

15:00:07

JM: Okay, bring him in.

. . .

JM: Roy, thank you for coming on such short notice.

RC: Anything for you, Mr. President.

JM: Don't think I'll ever get tired of folks calling me that.

RC: It'll sink in eventually.

JM: You happen to catch Murrow's segment on me earlier?

RC: A lying, biased product if you ask me.

JM: *{Unintelligible}*

RC: *{Laughter}*

JM: May I offer you a drink?

RC: No, thanks.

JM: You sure?

RC: Yes, Joe. I'm sure. So, what can I do for my favorite client?

JM: Ah, well—this is difficult. *{Unintelligible}*

RC: I must have misunderstood you there, Joe. You're doing what?

JM: I'm making Bobby Attorney General.

RC: You can't be serious. You promised the job to *me*. Bobby's been a lawyer for all of two years. He's a goddamn child, for Christ's sake! After everything we've been through, you give one of the most important offices in the country to a pissant like Kennedy?

JM: I understand your frustration, Roy. I really do. But he's a hard worker and well...

RC: Well, what?

JM: *{Unintelligible}*

RC: You're mumbling again, Joe.

JM: I said Bobby doesn't have... well, he doesn't have the proclivities you do.

RC: Proclivities?

JM: Do I really need to spell it out, Roy?

RC: I think you do.

JM: Bobby is not a homosexual.

RC: Excuse me?

JM: Just as I say. Bobby is not a homosexual. I can't have a lavender lad as my attorney general. Imagine what that would do for my image.

RC: How... how dare you.

JM: *{Unintelligible}*

RC: I am not a homosexual.

JM: Now, Roy. It won't do to insult either of our intelligences. I still consider you a close friend—no matter who you bring into your bedroom at the end of the day. But I can't have someone like that shaping legal policy in my administration.

RC: I... I... you are unbelievable. We had a deal!

JM: Remember to whom you are talking, Roy.

RC: I delivered the Rosenbergs to you on a silver platter! I helped turn that Senate censure into public sympathy when, in any other instance, it would have meant the end of your political career. Do you know how hard that was to pull off? I am the very reason you sit in this office, Joe!

JM: And for those things, I will always remain grateful. But you're not seeing the situation from my point of view, Roy. What if evidence of your... uh... private life fell into the hands of an opponent or a Communist operative? They'd be able to bring this whole administration to its knees with a blackmail scandal of that caliber!

RC: I am not a homosexual, Joe! Who is feeding you these abject lies? Is it that cross-dressing faggot Hoover? Oh, I bet it is, isn't it? *Isn't it?* Are you listening in right now, John? What dress are you wearing today, pray tell?

JM: I'm going to need you and David to clean out your offices effective immediately.

RC: What does David have to do with all of this?

JM: *{Unintelligible}*

RC: *Fuck you, Joe!*

[*sounds of a door slamming, footsteps on carpet*]

RC: It's okay. It's fine. I'll leave of my own accord and send your message along to David. There's no need to have me forcibly removed. Just know this, Joe: You'll come to rue this decision.

JM: I was afraid you'd say something like that. Please take him away.

RC: I swear it on my own mother's grave, Joe! You'll regret this day!

###END OF TRANSCRIPTION###

PART VI

December 30, 1959

I don't see the difference between Nazism and Hitler on the one hand and Communism on the other hand. I think they're both bad and I don't like this double standard where we make heroes out of people who have been exposed for support of Communism.

—*Roy Cohn (chief counsel to Joseph McCarthy)*

CHAPTER 58

The next day dawned as the rest. Baker awoke to find Matagot pawing at the leather straps of the tefillin dangling from the apartment's single chair and onto the floor like whips of black licorice.

Driven by some indescribable compulsion, Baker decided to wrap tefillin. He dressed, found a yarmulke, and rolled up his left sleeve. He grabbed the box labeled של יד and affixed it to his biceps, making sure it pointed inward toward his heart. With the box firmly in place, he began to carefully loop the strap down the length of his arm a total of seven times, taking great care that none of the tight coils overlapped with one another.

Baruch Ato Ado-noy Elo-hay-nu Me-lech Ho-lom A-sher Kidshonu B'mitz-vo-sov V'tzi-vonu L'ho-niach Tefillin...

Reaching the hand, he looped the remaining bit of leather around the palm and turned his attention to the box labeled של ראש. He pulled it around the base of his head, adjusting the knot in the back so that it rested at the very base of the skull where spinal cord met brainstem (the very point where the human soul was said to rest, according to Jewish tradition).

Baruch Ato Ado-noy Elo-hay-nu Me-lech Ho-olom A-sher Kidshonu B'mitz-vo-sov V'tzi-vonu Al Mitz-vas Tefillin...

Matagot watched in naive fascination, his head following each purposeful movement.

For the last step, Baker turned his attention back to the remainder of leather strap on his hand. He unraveled it from the palm and rewrapped it three times up the middle finger and then several more times across the back of the hand and palm until he could make out a rough approximation of the word שד״י—one of the many Hebrew names for God.

The wrapping was complete. All he had to do now was extend thumb and forefinger and cover his eyes for the Shema prayer. In the darkness of his own making, he prayed for Evelyn and Jasper Heo; for Liz and Debbie; for Rabbi Kahn and the safe return of the missing congregants; and for God, in all of His infinite wisdom, to give him a fucking break in the Kissinger case.

The obligatory mist and rain that now defined Los Angeles churned outside Baker's office window, lulling him into an uneasy doze as he sipped schnapps on the Murphy bed and pondered where Kissinger might be hiding. When it became clear that no progress would be made, Baker decided to close up shop for the day, but not before lighting a small copper menorah alongside Hersh and Joanna.

Baruch ata Adonai Eloheinu, melech ha'olam, asher kid'shanu b'mitzvotav v'tzivanu l'hadlik ner shel Hanukkah.

Baruch atah Adonai Eloheinu Melech ha'olam, she'asah nisim la'avoteinu ba'yamim ha'heim ba-z'man ha'zeh.

"Isn't this holiday all about miracles?" he asked Hersh. "I could really use one right about now."

"Unless you're looking for a small amount of oil to last you eight days, I'd say you're shit out of luck, friend."

"When was the last time things were easy for our people?"

"Oh, I'd wager... never."

"That's what I thought."

Baker sent them both home and waited around for the candles to burn down into waxen puddles. Once the flames had gone out, he locked the office and decided to take a stroll by the bubbling tar pits in Hancock Park. He'd barely made it halfway when he saw another group of Korean-Americans being processed for internment. By dawn, they'd be up north, far away from home in...

"Mickey? It's Baker." He was out of breath and coughing, having run back to his office to make the call. "I know where Kissinger is."

Mickey promised to pass along the news, and Baker waited by the phone with bated breath, his heart thumping, until it rang fifteen minutes later.

"Yes? Hello? This is Baker."

"Chateau Marmont," said the husky voice on the other end. "Back entrance. Thirty minutes."

Click...the line went dead.

CHAPTER 59

Baker got to the hotel with five minutes to spare. The only person standing by the back service entrance was old Archie Hicks. The stooped British geezer who had helped him evade Japanese security several days before leaned against the door, smoking a cigarette. Except he wasn't stooped anymore—he stood ramrod straight as though anticipating a military inspection.

"Blimey, you do like to cut things close," said Archie, and Baker noticed his voice was no longer weak and shaky. In fact, it sounded vaguely familiar. Where had he heard that voice before?

"Excuse me?"

"Right then," said Archie, flicking away his cigarette. "Follow me."

He pulled the door open, hunched over, and began to shuffle forward.

"What's this all about?" asked Baker. Archie did not answer, and the door was fast swinging closed. He grabbed it and followed into a dimly lit hallway lined with water boilers. After several hundred feet, they reached a cramped service elevator.

"In you get," Archie said. "No time to waste."

"Uh... I don't do so well with elevators," Baker said.

"Right. Feel free to trounce through the lobby and get picked up by the Japs, especially after the whole Kishi cock-up. Get in the bloody lift, Baker. Now, before someone hears us."

Baker reluctantly stepped into the tight space, trying to keep himself from hyperventilating.

Archie shuffled in and pressed the button for the fifth floor, wrenching the grille shut. The lift shuttered and started its journey upward. Baker closed his eyes, waiting until it was all over.

"Oh, do pull yourself together, man."

"Who are you?" Baker asked. "Really?"

"Save your questions."

The elevator reached the fifth floor with an ominous twanging noise from the high-tension cable that held it in place. Archie pulled back the grate, peered in both directions, and nodded.

"This way," he said, turning to the right. He led Baker to the last door at the end of the carpeted hallway: the Honeymoon Suite. Archie pulled a key from his voluminous trousers and unlocked the door.

"In you go, then."

Much like Hartwell's room at the sanitarium in Malibu, the suite had more in common with a spacious studio apartment than it did with a hotel room.

It contained a large writing desk, several armchairs, a fifteen-inch RCA color television set, an electric fireplace, and a four-post bed so large, it would have dwarfed any man who stood next to it. Sitting on a porcelain column at the end of the hallway was a metal ice bucket in which a bottle of Dom Pérignon champagne rested.

"That should be nice and chilled now," said Archie. "I'm quite parched. This disguise is hotter than hades."

Archie started to claw at his face, pulling off chunks of skin. Baker recoiled until he realized the skin was latex rubber convincingly made to look like the wrinkled and liver-spotted flesh of a senior citizen. The person underneath all the makeup was in his late forties or early fifties. He had thick eyebrows, a sharp nose, and a pompous grin.

"Hang on," said Baker. "I know you. I bumped into you the other night at the Nine-Tailed Fox."

"Guy Burgess, at your service," said the man, already pouring himself a healthy measure of fizzing wine. "Expert in espionage and vintage champagnes."

"What's with the old man getup?"

"I am currently wanted by the American and British governments, both of whom would very much like to hang me for treason. Can't go around town wearing my usual face, now can I?"

"You're a Russian agent?"

"In a manner of speaking..."

"That'll do, Burgess," said another familiar voice from the armchair closest to the window. The seat was occupied by the man with whom Baker had spoken in Santa Monica.

The representative of the Korean government stood up and walked over to join them. Even though he was now facing the agent head-on, Baker found it difficult to hone in on any salient feature. The man was ordinary—almost impossibly so—and could probably blend into any crowd of his choosing. Baker wondered if the man had been born this way or if he had undergone some sort of cosmetic surgery to achieve such a nondescript visage.

"I hear you've found Kissinger?" he asked.

"Yes," Baker said. "That call he made to you the other night about gaining his 'independence'? He wasn't talking about freedom—he was talking about a place. Independence, California. The site of the Manzanar internment camp."

"Bloody brilliant move," said Burgess, taking a dignified sip of champagne (or as dignified as it could be with turkey-like folds of false skin hanging off his neck). "Old Henry's hiding right in plain sight."

"And you're sure about this?" probed the Korean representative.

"Positive," Baker said.

"This does complicate matters. We can't just walk into the place. This will take some planning."

"I'll go."

"What?"

"I'll go," Baker repeated. "I'm a Jew—it'll be easy to get myself onto one of the transports. I can probably be at Manzanar by tomorrow evening. Maybe even by dawn if I leave tonight."

"Are you mad?" said Burgess. "Then we'll have to extract *two* men."

"Kissinger might already be dead. The longer we sit around, the worse our odds become. We need to get into the camp as soon as possible."

"You really are mad," said Burgess. "And how do you plan to get out once you've found him?"

"Nixon," Baker said. "He's planning a coup with HUAC. The whole William Yang affair, the attempt on Kishi's life—all of it was part of a plot to overthrow McCarthy. He and MacArthur plan to end the war with nukes."

"Then the situation is just as dire as we feared," Burgess said.

"No," Baker said. "It's worse. I caught a glimpse of Kishi at Nixon's place all the way out in Yorba Linda yesterday. The prime minister is completely fine. The Santa Monica shooting was another ruse meant to boost sympathy for Nixon before he makes his move. Japan must have something to gain from the coup if the prime minister was willing to go along with it. Kissinger has the answer."

"That's all good and well, but how does any of this help get you out of Manzanar?" Burgess asked, pouring himself more wine.

"Nixon hired me to find Kissinger. If I can strike some sort of deal . . . ?"

"No," said the Korean representative. "You tell that charlatan where Kissinger is and he'll send his men to kill you both. Then we'll know nothing."

"So I don't tell them," Baker said. "You do!"

"Pardon?"

"I'll go up to the camp under an assumed name, find Kissinger, and learn what he knows. After a week or two, you anonymously tip off HUAC about my whereabouts and they come and get me."

"You're barking," Burgess said. "They'll still show up and kill you both."

"We bluff," Baker said. "You tell them we know everything and have the proof to back it up. Say we're ready to take it public if Kissinger and myself aren't brought home safe under the terms of my agreement with Nixon. They'll know what it means."

"And what happens when they find out you don't have anything?"

"We'll cross that bridge when we get to it."

"Think they'll bite?" Burgess asked his superior.

"There's a lot of room for error, but it's the best plan we've got under the circumstances. You're really willing to brave that camp, Baker? From what we've heard, it's not a pretty place."

"I am," he said. "I've been through it all before."

"We'll need to get you some false credentials. Give me a day or two to—"

"It's okay," Baker said, cutting him off. "I know where to find some last-minute credentials. I'll leave tonight."

"Well then," said Burgess, grabbing two more champagne flutes and filling them to the brim. "Let us drink to your safe return home."

CHAPTER 60

Baker returned to the office in order to check an address stored in Joanna's newfangled Rolodex system. It sent him to a nearby boardinghouse in Hancock Park that had seen better days.

The facade was chipped, smog-stained, and coated in a thin layer of what look like dried-up egg yolks. Baker also noticed the remnants of a spray-painted swastika that had not been properly scrubbed away.

He was greeted at the front door by a grumpy landlady pointing a 12-gauge shotgun directly in his face. The comforting smell of freshly made chicken soup wafted out into the cold night air.

"State your business or get the hell off my property," she snarled.

Baker put up his hands and said, "I'm just here to visit your tenant in 3E. Is he around?"

"What do you want with him?"

Baker rolled up his left sleeve to show the landlady his tattoo. "He's my older brother."

The woman lowered her gun at the sight of the string of numbers inked above the crater of scarred flesh. "Why didn't you just say that from the start? I nearly blew your head off."

"Sorry," Baker said, rolling his sleeve back down.

"Come inside, you're letting out all the warmth." She stepped aside to let him pass, her voice now tender and grandmotherly. "Would you like a bowl of chicken soup, maybe? I moved out here for all the sunshine and what do I get for my troubles? More rain and cold!"

"No, thank you, ma'am. I'm good."

"But you're so thin! Please, come—have a bowl of soup."

She wouldn't take no for an answer and practically shoved Baker into the tchotchke museum that was her apartment. Pie birds, Russian nesting dolls, Seder plates, golem statuettes, and several lit menorahs took up every available space.

The overwhelming stench of mothballs and Rolaids mingled with the alluring scent of fresh soup. The landlady sat him down at a small kitchen table and served up a large bowl of broth, egg noodles, matzo balls, vegetables, and pulled chicken breast.

"Eat!" she commanded, and Baker brought a spoonful to his lips, slurping up the golden-brown liquid, which was quite tasty. Realizing he hadn't eaten all day, he dug in with ravenous urgency, drawing a cockled smile from the old broad.

"There's plenty more where that came from," she said. "Now wait here." She shuffled off, leaving him free to guzzle down the entire bowl within a span of three minutes.

"Hungry, are we?" Ze'ev had returned with the landlady, who was now rushing to get him a bowl of soup as well.

"Thank you, Mrs. Heidelbaum," he said, taking a seat opposite Baker.

"Can't believe you actually turned up," Ze'ev said in Yiddish.

"I'm just full of surprises," replied Baker, yielding his bowl to Mrs. Heidelbaum so she could serve him another helping. "Listen, Ze'ev... I wanted to..."

Ze'ev held up a hand to stop him. "No apologies are necessary, Morris. We're brothers."

"You called me 'Morris.'"

Ze'ev shrugged and grabbed his spoon. "If that is what you wish to be called, then I shall respect your wishes. You always were the imaginative one."

They sat in awkward silence, eating their soup as Mrs. Heidelbaum watched over them, beaming with pride.

"It's so nice to have you boys here," she said, now cutting into a loaf of braided challah. "I haven't had much company since my Ruben passed on—zichrono livracha. Sadly, we were never blessed with children of our own."

Both men nodded in deference to the woman. "The pleasure is all ours, Mrs. Heidelbaum," said Ze'ev, making an effort to capture every last drop of soup with his spoon.

"Ze'ev...?" Baker said.

"Yes?"

"It really is good to see you. I've been alone so long, so used to looking out for myself, that I'd forgotten what it was like."

Ze'ev let his spoon fall with a clatter and stood up. Baker did the same and allowed his brother to pull him into a tender embrace. He couldn't stop the tears from falling, but it did not matter—the act of crying was a relief. It felt good to bawl like a child in his brother's arms.

"Please forgive me," hiccupped Baker. "I was a fool to turn you away. What would Mama and Papa say if they saw me doing that?"

"Shush now," said Ze'ev. "There is nothing to apologize for. No one would blame you, sheifale. I'm just glad I found you. You don't have to be alone ever again."

Mrs. Heidelbaum watched their reconciliation with tears of her own, occasionally dabbing at the corners of her eyes with a cloth napkin. The two brothers broke apart and sat back down to finish their meal.

"Ze'ev, I need to ask you for a favor," Baker said once they were both stuffed full of broth, challah, and matzo balls.

"Name it."

"Can I borrow your passport?"

CHAPTER 61

Ze'ev did not think much of Baker's plan to infiltrate Manzanar. "Are you *insane?*" he shouted. "I just got you back and now you want to go on some sort of *suicide* mission?"

"I'll be fine. Nixon and HUAC have no idea I'm going. In fact, they'll be the last ones to know."

"You might never come back."

"Then I'll have at least tried! I'm not the defenseless boy you once knew, Ze'ev. I've come a long way since we parted at the train depot all those years ago."

"You never stop being a big brother, Morris. Those instincts don't just go away. But I see you'll be going with or without my permission. I'll be right back."

He got up from the table and left the apartment, returning moments later with his passport and a tight scroll of yellowing parchment. "It's the mezuzah klaf from our home. I pried it off the doorpost before we left home. It helped keep me safe. Take it for luck."

"Thank you," Baker said, knowing it would be useless. "If something should go wrong..."

"Chas v'sholem," said Ze'ev. "Don't even talk like that."

"We need to prepare for every contingency," said Baker. "If something should go wrong, there's a girl in New York named Evelyn Yang. I don't want her wondering..." He pulled out an envelope filled with cash, a second payment from the Korean representative. Evelyn's address was scribbled upon it. "Give her this and tell her to publish that novel of hers, no matter what it takes."

"I will take care of it."

"Thank you, Ze'ev. Oh, and there's one more thing..." He pulled out his apartment keys and held them out to his brother with a devious smile. "My cat will need feeding while I'm away."

"Anything else, Your Highness?"

"There is one last thing," said Baker. "I need your clothes and your car."

Certain that Lonergan was having him followed, he swapped outfits with Ze'ev and instructed his brother to drive the Continental to his apartment building in Chinatown. Baker thanked Mrs. Heidelbaum for the soup before slipping out the bathroom window and over to Ze'ev's rented Packard Clipper.

A group of Korean-Americans were still being processed at the Wilshire center, even though it was close to one in the morning. Baker pushed his way to the front of the line of weary families—all the while shouting slogans like "Down with McCarthy!" and "Long live Korea!"—and found himself face-to-face with a Huey wearing another one of those ugly trench coats that so recalled the Gestapo. The man opened his mouth to say something, but before he could form a single syllable, Baker socked him in the jaw. Baker barely had a moment to savor the man's resultant yelp of pain and bleeding nose before he was tackled to the ground.

Expanse-less desert
We are human no longer
Home, please wait for me

—Haiku composed from a Japanese internment camp in 1943
(poet is unknown)

PART VII

December 31, 1959

I thought all vacations in the country had armed uniform soldiers at both ends of each car taking us there. And I wondered why the grownups looked so sad. We were going on a vacation!

—*George Takei*

CHAPTER 62

All Baker could remember from the trip were the exhausted and haunted faces of his fellow passengers in the back of the overcrowded military truck. The faces were not too dissimilar from the ones he'd once glimpsed in a crammed cattle car headed for a factory of death.

He tried to stay alert, but the surprising gentleness of the rocking truck lulled him into an agitated sleep. Before the deceased monsters lying in wait for him at the Griffith Observatory could sink their claws into his flesh, Baker was shaken back into wakefulness.

"Get up, kike!" barked a Huey in a thick woolen jacket. "This ain't no pleasure cruise."

It would be laughably easy to grab the pistol resting on the guard's hip and blow the man's brains out right here. But Baker needed to play the good prisoner for as long as possible. It was a role he knew only too well.

He sat up, realizing the back of the truck was almost empty. His fellow passengers were disembarking down a short wooden ramp, their personal effects clutched to their chests like life preservers in a dark and stormy sea.

A song, lazy and ethereal, crackled from speakers somewhere off in the distance. And there was something else: the effluvium of excrement, urine, and poor bodily hygiene. The vulgar perfume of people stripped of their hygienic dignity.

Baker hunched over to avoid hitting his head on the tarpaulin roof. When it was his turn to get off, the Huey forcibly shoved him, sending him toppling down into the dirt. His arms instinctively shot out to soften the blow, but it was too late. He skidded into a sharp pebble, which sliced a shallow, yet painful, gash into his right cheek.

"Maybe that'll teach ya to get up on time!" snarled the Huey.

"Sorry," grumbled Baker, getting to his feet and brushing the dirt off his pants and trench coat. The stench of waste and unwashed bodies was even worse out in the open, carried to his nostrils on the harsh and untamed desert wind.

Looking around, he saw they were at the entrance to the internment camp, a thousand or so feet from the main gate, where a wooden sign strung up between two poles—looking like a man about to be drawn and quartered—read:

MANZANAR
☆ WAR ☆
RELOCATION CENTER

Tacked underneath that was a small addendum: UNDER NEW MANAGEMENT. Baker couldn't tell if that was meant as a joke or not. Either way, it sent a chill up his spine, painfully reminding him of the three German words that evoked a similar incongruence:

ARBEIT MACHT FREI . . .

The camp was nothing more than a collection of guard towers and low barracks erected on several acres of bare sand. A few dark rocks that were probably too heavy and expensive to move broke up the uniform landscape.

Two long flagpoles sat in the middle of the camp, hoisting up the American and HUAC banners, which flapped under a sky slowly turning from inky black to darkest blue shot with subtle hints of yellow and orange. The snow-capped peaks of the Sierra Nevada mountains loomed off in the remote distance, waiting to greet the dawn.

Beyond the rectangle of barbed wire, owls, lizards, tarantulas, and snakes dwelled among the scrub and cacti.

Baker and the rest of the new inmates were slowly shepherded into a building of eroded stone from whose roof a pair of speakers boosted the lethargic tones of Santo & Johnny's "Sleep Walk." Hueys with rifles slung over their shoulders walked down the line, telling people with luggage to leave it just outside the door, where a growing pile of suitcases and trunks sat.

"You will be reunited with your belongings after you have been inducted!" they called out.

Baker felt his stomach clench painfully. He looked in the direction of the barracks, trying to pick out even the slightest movement within.

Was the public wrong about this place? Were "relocation" and "internment" simply euphemisms for "wholesale murder"? He wasn't able to ponder this for long when a commotion broke out halfway down the line. A mother was screeching at the top of her lungs as a Huey attempted to remove the crying toddler from her arms. The guard already had a small gaggle of children standing behind him, all of them wide-eyed and fearful.

Baker ran forward to offer assistance, driving his fist into the Huey's lower back. The guard loosened his grip on the child and doubled over in pain. Baker had no time to process this small victory before the butt of a rifle made contact with the side of his skull.

CHAPTER 63

He woke up completely naked in a large, tiled room filled with dozens of naked men and women. His head ached and felt strangely cold. Placing a hand on his scalp, he discovered that all of his hair had been shorn off.

Turquoise-ringed shower heads lined the space, which echoed with the confused muttering of the other inmates, who were inelegantly trying to cover their breasts and genitals. Baker got to his feet, leaning against the wall for support and forcing himself to focus on a single patch of tile through the double vision of what had to be a minor concussion.

So this was it, then. That shade of blue around the shower heads could only mean one thing: Zyklon B. How many times had he attempted to scrub that very color off the tips of his fingers after reaching into dead mouths to pry out gold fillings? Any minute now all the people in this room would choke to death, banging on the locked doors, clawing at the slippery walls for purchase, climbing over each other for one last desperate gasp of oxygen.

The accumulation of cut hair would then be used to make delayed-action bombs or blankets or pillows, or socks for submarine crews. There was a deep rumbling from within the walls and the shower heads began to shake. Baker closed his eyes, waiting for breathless oblivion.

The intensity behind the shower heads mounted and, with a rushing *pshhhs!* of lowering pressure, dispelled jets of piping hot water. A sickening relief washed over Baker along with the blistering water—as did a flash of insight. It dawned on him that the patches of blue were not the residue of poison gas pellets, but mildew spores thriving in the humid space.

Baker stepped away from the wall and under one of the jets, allowing the scorching moisture to wash away his concussed torpor. He only hoped his newly acquired head injury would not trigger an influx of seizures.

Even if the Hueys did him give his clothes back, the bottle of phenobarbital tablets in the pants pocket was probably in the hands of a Huey looking to have a good time. In fact, it wouldn't have shocked him in the slightest if the guards made a habit out of pocketing whatever valuables entered the gates of the camp. With a jolt of regret, he suddenly remembered his family's old mezuzah scroll was gone, too.

All at once, the jets cut out and the excess water dribbled down through metal grates with an unpleasant sucking noise. Goose bumps broke out on Baker's bare skin. He crossed his arms in an effort to prevent shaking and saw others doing the same. A door at the other side of the room creaked open and a harsh voice barked: "*Everyone out! Now!*"

The freshly washed inmates filed out of the shower and into a room filled with piles of shoes, caps, and striped uniforms. Each costume was marked with different numbers and symbols stitched into the chest: a taegeukgi for Koreans, a yellow Star of David for Jews, upside-down pink triangles for homosexuals, the yellow crescent of a fortune cookie for Chinese, and the hammer and sickle for general Communists.

"Choose the uniform that best fits your person!" called the gorilla-size Huey who had beckoned them out of the shower, a billy club threateningly clutched in one meaty paw. "Anyone found to be wearing a misleading uniform will face dire consequences! Now hurry up and cover your shame!"

Baker chose one of the Jewish uniforms that best fit his physique and was pulling on the slightly-too-big shoes when a young woman approached the Huey.

"Um...excuse me?" she asked timidly. "I'm not able to find anything in my size."

The Huey bent down to get a better look at her and, without warning, brought his club down on the woman's petite neck. She let out an involuntary shriek of pain and fell to her knees.

"Can't find your size, eh?" leered the Huey, raising his bat for another swing. "What do you think this is, you Gook bitch? A fucking

Woolworth's? Now you listen and you listen good. I don't give a flying fuck if you leave this room naked. You've got thirty seconds to pick a rag and put it on. Got that?"

He brought down the billy club several more times—*Whap! Whap! Whap! Whap!*—until the woman was curled up and sobbing, her skin covered in nasty pink welts.

"Anyone else have a problem finding something *in their size?*" he called mockingly to the room at large. "*Huh?*"

There were no more objections as the group hastened to get dressed. Not wanting to endure a similar fate, people pushed one another aside to get their hands on a uniform. Baker pulled on his second shoe and knelt down beside the woman.

"*Get up!*" he hissed at her. "*Get up and get dressed now or he'll kill you.*"

Baker began to help the terrified woman to her feet when the Huey kicked him in the stomach with a steel-toed leather boot, knocking all the wind out of his cancerous lungs.

"Just what in the ever-loving fuck do you think you're doing, kike?"

Baker scrambled to his feet, snatched his hat off his head, and half bowed in the man's direction. "Just making sure the rules are followed accordingly, sir," he said in a sycophantic voice. This pacified the guard's ego and the Huey took a step back.

"Get the bitch to her feet, then. And get her out of my sight."

"Yes, sir. Right away, sir."

He got the woman to stand up and guided her to the pile of Korean uniforms. "*Don't ever do that again*," he whispered. "*Just pick a uniform. You might get a chance to swap it out later.*"

"Th-th-th-thank you," she stuttered back, unable to make eye contact.

Baker helped her pull on an overlarge uniform, tucking the shirt into the waistband of the pants and rolling any extra material up to her ankles. With that done, they made for the exit, a flight of concrete steps leading outside, where the California sun was just starting to peak out over the crest of the mountains—a fiery doubloon that threw the horrors of Manzanar into greater relief.

What Baker had initially taken for large rocks were actually bulging bags of garbage, whose rotting contents lent themselves to the heinous stench of the place.

Buzzing swarms of biting gnats and horseflies congregated around the mounds of decaying refuse. Some of the bags had ruptured, expelling chicken bones, vegetable peelings, and coffee grounds.

"*Dear God!*" Someone pointed. "*The bodies. Look at the bodies...*"

Scattered among the trash were naked corpses, dozens of them, in various states of rot—chunks of flesh missing from arms, legs, and exposed buttocks.

"Move it!" shouted the guards, motioning the herd of inductees forward with raised guns. "You will line up according to your uniform. Anyone found in the wrong group will face dire consequences!"

People started to cluster together, squinting in the semidarkness to see who else shared the symbols over their chests. Baker quickly peered around but didn't see any other yellow stars.

A "Reveille" bugle call sounded and the front door of each barracks opened. One by one, hundreds of inmates came pouring out into the weak morning light, which didn't do much to mitigate the numbing desert cold that cut through the flimsy camp outfits.

Despite their tired, sunken eyes and shambling gaits, the veteran prisoners knew exactly what to do, arranging themselves in orderly lines in front of the flagpoles with mechanical precision. Baker observed a horde of Jewish inmates exiting the nearest dormitory and made his way over to them, keeping an eye out for Kissinger. Before he could get a good look, though, there was a harsh call of "Uh-ten-*chun*!" from the Hueys.

Beneath the pair of metal poles was a small wooden platform. Standing atop it, arms folded tightly behind his back, was a man with neatly parted hair and a long, Nixon-y nose that darted slightly to the right. His lips were curled in a smile of malevolent exuberance.

"Good morning!" the man announced to the inmates.

"Good morning, Director Carto," replied the long haulers.

Director Carto spread his hands wide. "I hear we have some newcomers in the audience this morning. For those of you who don't know me, my name is Willis Carto, and I am the director of this facility. When I wish you a good morning, I expect a response. So, let us try that again. Good morning."

"Good morning," the inmates said again, now joined by the fresh captives.

"Blow it out your ass," murmured someone to Baker's right. He risked a quick glance, catching sight of deep, pouchy eyes, a turnip-like nose, receding hairline, and wide, slack lips. The man noticed the rapid movement and asked him: "You new here, fella?"

"Just got in," Baker whispered back.

"Welcome to Hell. Fix your collar, would ya?"

"Thanks for the tip," said Baker, doing as he was told.

"Very good!" Carto declared. "Very good, indeed! And now to business. I am sure you are all wondering why I asked my men to wake you up a little earlier than usual this morning. Mr. Fredericks, Mr. Delacroix, please bring up the condemned."

A pair of large Hueys came into view, shoving two badly beaten Korean men up to the flagpoles—their eyes swollen shut, cheeks covered in freely bleeding gashes, and hands tied behind their backs.

"The men you see before you," Carto began, "were caught trying to escape late last night. They stole HUAC uniforms from the camp laundry and attempted to walk out the front gate. A nasty trick, but not wholly unexpected from... inferior races and Communists. I woke you up early, so that you may bear witness to how insubordination is punished under my watch."

Carto gave the Hueys a devious nod and Baker watched in horror as nooses, fashioned out of the flagpoles' own thick ropes, were looped around the necks of the barely conscious men.

Carto counted down from 3 and the guards heaved, stringing up the victims. The men jerked about wildly. Even from several hundred feet away, Baker could hear the choking, gurgling sounds of slow asphyxiation.

"Excellent! Excellent!" Carto exclaimed, watching their final death throes with apparent relish. When the two offenders had reached the top of their respective poles, the Hueys hoisting them up secured the ropes around the bottom cleats to keep the dead men in place. "Now, all of you will return to your barracks for the remainder of the week," Carto added. "Outdoor leisure time has been revoked until further notice. Anyone caught outside without authorization will—"

"Let me guess?" Baker whispered facetiously out of the corner of his mouth. "Face dire consequences."

The man to his right snorted. "Now you're gettin' it, friend. Another day in paradise."

CHAPTER 64

"How'd you like the show?" the stranger asked casually as the inmates shuffled back to their respective barracks.

Now that they could speak at regular volume, Baker could hear the man's thick New York intonation, which vaguely reminded him of the late Humphrey Bogart. He also noticed how the man's uniform bore two symbols over the chest: Jewish star and upside-down pink triangle.

"Wish I could say I *haven't* seen something like that before," Baker replied. "How often do they execute people around here?"

"You see the bodies in the trash heap?"

"Yeah."

"There's your answer. I'm Roy, by the way." He held out his hand and Baker shook it, offering up Ze'ev's name in return. "What are you in for, Ze'ev?" Roy inquired.

"Trying to find someone."

"You came here willingly? Damn, you must have quite the pair dangling between your legs."

"Does the name *Henry Kissinger* ring a bell about anyone in the Jewish barracks?"

"Henry Kissinger... Henry Kissinger..." Roy repeated, scratching his chin in thought. "We've got a Henry Goldman. That help?"

Baker shook his head. This news didn't come as too much of a surprise. If Kissinger was smart—and all the evidence pointed in that direction—then he would have entered a camp under a false name just like Baker had done.

"Has anyone mentioned anything about William Yang or Orson Lamotte?"

Roy raised an inquisitive eyebrow. "Haven't heard anything on Lamotte, but I met Yang a few times while he was here," said Roy. "Nice guy. Never would've pegged him as the exploding type."

"He was an *inmate*?"

"Oh yeah, he was here . . . let's see . . . I'd say for close to a year. Him and his old Army buddy, Park. Still can't figure out how they escaped."

There was something oily and almost ferocious lurking behind Roy's tired blue eyes. His blithe callousness to the public hangings and discarded corpses didn't sit right with Baker.

"What are you here for?" Baker asked.

"Me? I helped our prick of a president get elected," Roy answered grimly. "My own fault, really. Should've seen the double cross coming from a mile away. But I guess you could say Joe did help me come to terms with who I am."

The pink triangle on Roy's chest gleamed in the morning sun.

"Wait a moment," said Baker. "How long have you been here?"

"Coming up on three years," Roy said.

"How is that possible? I thought Manzanar was reopened as a response to the Yang incident. There were always rumors about getting it back up and running, but—"

"Ha!" barked Roy. "The propaganda machine's been doing its job, then. Manzanar's been fully operational since '55 and the other camps caught up soon after that. Those 'rumors' you hear about people being deported behind the Iron Curtain are full of shit. Every last 'subversive' is either killed or sent here. Joe offered me the choice personally. His last favor to an old friend."

"You're kidding."

"Not much to kid about in a place like this."

"Where do you get your news from?"

"The guards. Who else?"

"How?"

"Every man has his price. I may not be a practicing lawyer anymore, but I still know how to sway people to my way of thinking. It works better if the mark is already dim-witted, and these HUAC numbskulls fit the bill. Could probably convince them to let me walk out of here if it wasn't for Carto. He's a shrewd one, all right. Ah, here we are. Home sweet home."

Baker got a brief glimpse of the dark barracks' interior when a crowd of people surged forward, calling out Roy's name.

"Roy, where are my cigarettes? I'm dying over here!"

"Roy, did you get that letter from my wife?"

"Roy, where's that magazine you promised?"

"Roy, did that shipment of chocolate bars arrive yet?"

"Roy, my son! Have you seen him? Is he *okay*?"

"Roy! Roy! Roy!"

Roy held out his hands, looking a lot like Director Carto.

"People, people—please!" Roy shouted above the din. And when this didn't work, he bellowed: "*Shut up, all of you!*" The inmates hounding him backed up.

"I'm very sorry, but you're all going to have to wait a little longer," Roy continued. "I was supposed to take delivery of all your items early this morning *before* those two idiots went and got themselves captured. Things are going to get tighter than a nun's crotch around here for a while. I need you all to be patient until things quiet down."

The group dispersed, but the sense of disappointment was palpable in the musty barracks, which contained rows upon rows of stacked wooden bunks that had more in common with catacombs than they did with sleeping quarters. It was almost totally dark in here, but concentrated shafts of morning light leaked through the termite-eaten rafters.

The smell of the overall camp was even worse in here with so many unwashed bodies tightly packed together. Roy flopped onto a bunk nearest the door, sending a plume of sand into the air. He took off his hat and rested it over his forehead, settling in for a nap.

Baker leaned against the frame. "'Every man has his price,' huh?" he asked.

Roy lifted his hat up, looking annoyed. "You still here?"

"How long has your little black market been going on?"

"I see a need and I fill it," Roy said, now lifting himself up by the elbows. "Simple as that. What's it to you anyway?"

"All of these people are already being taken advantage of," Baker said, his voice rising. "They don't need someone else adding to their troubles."

Roy sat up fully now, all exhaustion forgotten, and jabbed a thumb into his chest.

"You want to talk about troubles, pal? I'm a queer kike—shit doesn't get more difficult than that. You've been here all of five minutes and want to judge me? These people depend on me to make their lives a little better in this hellhole. So why don't you just fuck right off?"

Baker grabbed Roy by his uniform and pulled him right out of the bunk. A ring of onlookers started to form around them, but most seemed too wary to do anything about it.

"Wanna say that again?" Baker growled. He made to throw Roy to the ground but was overtaken by another coughing fit, which sprayed Roy with globules of bloody mucus.

"*What the fuck?*" Roy screamed. "Let go of me! Help! *Hel-l-l-l-p-p!* This guy is crazy!"

"Morris...?"

Baker let go of Roy, who fell to the ground in a disheveled heap. Baker turned around, relieved to see Netanel Horowitz, one of the missing Ohev Shalom congregants. Netanel was tall and muscular, and he towered over most of the other inmates.

"*You know this nutcase, Nate?*" Roy shouted at Netanel from the floor.

"I do," Netanel said calmly. "Is there a problem, Roy?"

"Nope," Roy said in an even tone—and Baker realized he was afraid of the hulking Horowitz, who was now flanked by two more missing men: Abner Greenspan and Yehuda Mandelbaum. "No problem at all. In fact, I was just about to go out and have a smoke."

He got up, brushed himself off, stalked off to a different bunk, shimmied underneath it, and vanished from sight.

"Where's he going?" Baker asked.

"There's a loose floorboard under that bunk," Netanel explained. "It takes you out to a small blind spot, where we usually go to smoke."

"That man is a real piece of work."

"Don't pay him any attention. He's nothing more than a no-good shyster. He's promised to get a letter to Shelly for weeks now, but I haven't heard anything. Still, he does pretty well for himself. The guards let him move around the different barracks in exchange for a cut of whatever he makes. You'd be surprised what valuables survive the induction process."

"Son of a bitch."

"Morris, what are you doing here?"

"Well, for one thing, I promised your wife I'd find you and the others."

"So you got yourself captured?" said Abner, incredulous.

He stepped forward to shake Baker's hand and Yehuda did the same.

"Don't worry," said Baker with a weak smile. "I made a deal with Nixon himself to get you out of here."

"Nixon!" Abner exclaimed. "*The* vice president?"

"The very same," replied Baker. "Is everyone okay?"

"Most of us," said Yehuda.

"'Most'?" Baker asked, raising an eyebrow.

"Come," said Netanel.

He took Baker to a section of bunks near the very back, where a dozen men lay motionless—their eyes blank, lips muttering incoherent words. A stooped man moved slowly among them, brushing sweat from their brows and ladling water over their cracked lips.

"Herman," Netanel said to the caregiver. "I'll take over your shift. You get some rest." Herman nodded appreciatively, handing over the rag and bowl of water, and shuffling away. "Come, Morris. See for yourself."

Baker stepped closer and saw Noah Levinson, Eliyahu Margules, and—his stomach did a back flip—Henry Kissinger. Bald, emaciated, and without his thick-framed glasses, the State Department consultant whose disappearance had caused so much trouble looked nothing like the man in the snapshot given to Baker by the woman claiming to be Ann Kissinger. A thick, unkempt beard rounded out Kissinger's altered appearance, making him completely unrecognizable to anyone who wasn't within two feet of the guy.

"What happened to them all?" Baker inquired.

"This place isn't just an internment camp for supposed enemies of the state," Netanel said gravely. "It's also a scientific research facility."

"Research of what kind?"

"Research of the mind," Abner said. "We're not prisoners—"

"We're lab rats," finished Yehuda.

"For what purpose?" Baker asked, though he had an inkling.

"The only people who know the answer to that question are in no state to tell us," Netanel said.

Baker looked back at Kissinger, saw his lips moving, and leaned over, trying to hear what the man was trying to say. "*Pu-pu-pum-pppp-pum-pu-pu-pppp...*" he muttered over and over, sounding like a chainsaw motor refusing to start.

"You're wasting your time," said Netanel. "Alfred's been like that since we got here. We do our best to care for them, but...it's not enough. Without proper medical attention, most of them expire within a couple weeks."

Baker straightened up, resolving to come back after everyone was asleep to see if he could coax some lucidity out of Kissinger. He opened his mouth, on the verge of asking about sleeping arrangements, when the front door of the barracks burst open.

Two rifle-toting Hueys stepped inside, followed by a skeletal man in a white lab coat. He strolled along at a leisurely and unthreatening pace, men quickly moving out of his way. The newcomer reached Baker and pointed a clawlike finger in his direction.

"This one," he said in a luxurious voice.

The Hueys grabbed Baker by the arms and carried him outside. Baker snatched a glimpse over his shoulder at Netanel, Yehuda, and Abner. The helpless expressions on their faces all said the same thing: *It was nice knowing you.*

CHAPTER 65

They carried him far away from the living quarters to a nondescript and windowless building made of thick concrete on the very outskirts of the camp. Down a long hallway, past a cage packed with staring children, and into an examination room containing an upright metal slab.

The Hueys forced him against the cold surface and began pulling thick leather belts—the kind used for restraining the mentally disturbed—over his head, arms, and legs until he couldn't move an inch. One guard propped his eyes open while the other dug small metal hooks into the corners of each eyelid. Their task completed, the Hueys left the room and the bony man closed the door.

"Thank you very much for flying into my web, Herr Baker."

"You know me?"

"My name is Dr. Szell. I oversee all incoming prisoners and select the prime candidates for my research. I noticed you at once, of course. How could I ever forget the face of the Jewish filth that drove a knife into the back of the great Wernher von Braun?"

"He couldn't have been all that great if I was able to lodge a blade into his spinal column that easily," countered Baker.

"Long have I dreamt of this moment. When I would be the one to administer revenge on behalf of Die Schwarze Symphonie."

"How're they doing these days?" said Baker, hoping to stave off Szell's intentions of torture for as long as possible.

"Wernher was the glue that held us together," the doctor said bitterly. "He was so certain his plan would work, and when it did not, our financial backers were not pleased."

"You mean the ODESSA?"

"The various names you had provided to the troublesome Liberty Boys coming out of the radio for weeks on end were the final nails in the coffin. A great many of our number became terrified of exposure, despite there being no proof whatsoever. They felt it easier to keep a low profile than to continue Wernher's dream of cooperation. They preferred to grow complacent rather than see the glory of the Third Reich restored anew. But no matter. No matter at all. For here you are, in the flesh. And now... now we are going to have some fun."

"Depends on how you define 'fun,'" said Baker. "What was your specialty under darling Adolf?"

"Neuroscience," Szell said proudly. "Have you ever held a human brain, Herr Baker? Felt the weight of it in your hands?"

"Can't say that I have."

"Three pounds," said Szell. "That is the exact weight, give or take, of a person's entire being. Love, hunger, hatred, sex, forgiveness... revenge—all of it contained within a single squelching mass lighter than a half gallon of milk. Extraordinary, wouldn't you say? And yet, the human brain is the most complex organ on this planet. Billions upon billions of cells and neural pathways that account for every single nuance of our lives. Three pounds, yes, but also infinite possibilities."

"Get to the point, Fritz."

"I forgot that the Jewish brain lacks the capacity for long attention spans. My point, Herr Baker, is that the mind is a staggeringly complex instrument, but at the end of the day, it is just that: an instrument. One that can be altered and tuned to one's liking."

"You're talking about mind control?"

"Mind control! Bah!" spat Szell. "Such a crude term for it."

"Thanks for confirming," said Baker, adopting a shit-eating grin that was sure to piss off Szell. "I wondered how William Yang was coerced into blowing himself up in that department store."

"Hmmm," purred Szell, squinting at Baker with clinical fascination through his clear-framed glasses. "Perhaps Wernher was a little too foolhardy with his treatment of you. You are an astute one, Baker. *Too* astute. I told those fools Yang wasn't ready. That my research wasn't complete. His conditioning nearly came undone by the end."

"I'm guessing Nixon needed you to move up the timetable?" Szell did not answer, continuing to stare at Baker with a look of detached astonishment. "Not in the talking mood now, Doc? What about Sung-Ho Park? Another rousing success, I take it?"

The ravings of the drunken Army vet who had accosted Baker in Merv's Diner came back to him: *Lizard men straight outta Area 51! They took my friends, abducted them right off the street! Been getting away with it for years! Whoever's left will be brainwashed to do their bidding!*

"How'd you do it anyway? The brainwashing?"

"I grow weary of this conversation. Let us begin."

The doctor moved out of sight for a brief moment, coming back into view with a large black box. "Do you know what this is, Herr Baker?" he cooed.

"Not a clue," said Baker.

"This is a special kind of lamp known as a strobe."

"Lovely," Baker said sarcastically. "I've always been more of chandelier man myself."

"The strobe lamp," Szell continued, "emits an intense, flashing light that has been known to trigger epileptic seizures in photosensitive individuals." Baker's smile faltered and the doctor laughed wickedly. "I can't think of a better way to ring in the New Year, can you?"

Szell pressed a button on the side of the box and the bulb resting within started to flash—slowly at first but growing in intensity until the room resembled the heart of an electrical storm.

Without warning, his brain shut down. He convulsed against the restraints, biting down on his tongue.

Szell cackled madly. "Oh yes!" proclaimed the insane doctor before Baker passed out entirely. "We're going to have some fun!"

CHAPTER 66

Baker was unceremoniously dumped back into the barracks. He had no idea what time it was, and his brain felt as though it had spent the last few hours spinning inside a washing machine. Szell took his sweet time with the strobe torture, eliciting seizures out of him for hours before the doctor grew tired of the sadistic sport.

"Until tomorrow," the doctor called after him in a singsong voice as the Hueys carried away his limp body.

Netanel and Yehuda picked him up and moved him to the bunks where all the men subjected to psychological torment were laid to mutter out their days, trapped within their own bodies. He shut his eyes tight, waiting for all the dizziness and nausea to pass, only vaguely aware that it must now be the first day of 1960.

When the sickening giddiness began to abate, Baker slowly reopened his eyes to find Kissinger staring at him. The man for whom he had been searching no longer had that far-off look. In fact, his eyes were bright and fully aware. He raised a quieting finger to his lips and slipped out of the bunk with barely a rustle.

Baker followed, his movements slow and dissociated after his session with Szell. He made it down to the floor just in time to see Kissinger disappearing beneath the bunk concealing the loose floorboard. Baker crept over, quietly as he could, using the inmates' snores as cover, and got down on his stomach.

It was too dark to distinguish much of anything, but curiosity got the better of him. Propping himself up on his arms like a cadet about to crawl through a muddy obstacle course, he started wriggling under the bunk. He took his time, blindly feeling around for the point of egress, which turned out to be a sudden drop to the cold sand and rocks directly below the barracks.

"*Shit!*" Baker hissed as he belly-flopped onto the fabled loose floor-board, which had been pried away and discarded without ceremony. The resulting hole was well hidden unless a person knew exactly what they were looking for. He blinked, spitting out dirt clots and rubbing dust from his eyes.

A mounting sense of disquiet began to take hold. What if he got trapped down here? Should he just sit tight and wait for Kissinger to come back? Before this anxiety could bloom into full-on panic, he forced himself to close his eyes and take a deep breath. He counted to 3 and opened his eyes, which darted around the crawl space. After a moment of intense concentration, they made out a compressed rect-angle of moon-kissed desert several hundred feet away and he began squirming toward it. The final aperture leading outside was the easiest part as several slats had been torn away to accommodate all different body types.

Baker stood up, sucking in fresh night air and brushing dirt off his raggedy uniform. The blind spot was a narrow strip of land no larger than six feet in length that hugged the fence line around the camp. One wrong move and a person would find themselves entangled in the prickly weave of barbed wire that made escape impossible.

"Don't bother trying to dig under it," Kissinger called out. "The fence is electrified and there are land mines hidden in every direction."

The missing man sat on a small outcrop of rock, staring up at the full moon—a radiant spotlight sewn into an inky quilt of glimmer-ing stars.

"Who are you?" Kissinger asked in a slight German accent. "I saw you looking at me earlier with something like recognition."

"My name is Morris Baker. I'm a private investigator who was hired to find you."

"By whom, I wonder?" Kissinger asked.

"Good question. It started with someone claiming to be your wife, then it was a representative of the Korean government, and after that, it was your pal Nixon. Seems everyone in Southern California is looking for you. Care to tell me why you ran?"

Kissinger stayed silent for another minute before responding with a question of his own. "Have you ever visited the pumpkin patches in Petaluma?"

"What?"

"Petaluma," Kissinger repeated. "It is a city just north of San Francisco. Their pumpkin patches are magnificent. You should pick up a gourd from Manzanetti Farms next time you happen to be passing through."

"Okay...?" Baker said, nonplussed. "Listen, I've come a very long w—"

"Tell me about yourself, Mr. Baker," Kissinger said. "What kind of man are you?"

"What does that have to do with anything?" Baker asked, wondering if Kissinger really had lost all his marbles. "Mr. Kissinger—Henry, I know about Nixon's little coup. What do the Japs stand to gain from it? How does Orson Lamotte fit into the whole thing?"

"If you do not know where you are going, every road will get you nowhere."

"I'm sorry, but I don't have time for th—"

"Good night, Mr. Baker. We'll try again tomorrow evening."

Baker watched, slack-jawed, as Kissinger got up, walked to the gaping hole at the bottom of the barracks, and squeezed himself through it and out of sight.

The individual who provided the following statement, one Yitzak Chabon, immigrated to the United States in 1947. He mysteriously went missing a decade later just before he was set to travel to Berlin and take part in a post-war trial naming Szell as one of the defendants.

Testimony Given to War Crimes Investigators About Dr. Günter Szell in Fall of 1945

He said he wanted my brain and had gone so far as drawing around my bald head with a black marker. I have no doubt in my mind—no joking intended—that he would have gone through with the procedure. I wouldn't be here, speaking with you today, had it not been for the Americans. The doctor ran for it as soon as he heard the artillery fire in the distance.

But the man had an unnatural obsession with the mind.

His entire office had no photographs or any other personal effects—only brains floating in jars. An entire collection of them, all taken from Jews! There was a rumor around the camp that he liked...well...to make love to them. Can you imagine such a thing? He gained a nickname throughout the camp that was...unflattering. They called him "The Skull Fucker."

PART VIII

January 15, 1960

There can't be a crisis next week, my schedule is already full.

—*Henry Kissinger*

CHAPTER 67

The next fortnight passed in a haze of agony. Every morning, the inmates would be summoned to the flagpoles for a sloppily conducted roll call. Numbers were called out in a completely random order, and if a prisoner did not immediately know their designation off the top of their head, they were savagely beaten in front of the others.

Breakfast consisted of a sludge-like gruel and cup of acrid black coffee. Lunch was a watery bowl of soup carrying the faint flavors of carrots and spoiled poultry. Dinner brought a ration of teeth-shattering hardtack and half a sausage link cut with sawdust. The food schedule never wavered in its monotony unless the guard doling it out decided to withhold your allotted portion for their own amusement. Anyone who objected to this was savagely beaten in front of the others.

There were no blankets or pillows, though it was said Roy could get them for the right price. (In fact, it was said he could get you most anything for the right price.) Those who could afford such bedtime luxuries made sure to keep them on their person at all times, and pillows bulging under uniforms like distended beer guts was a common sight around the camp. These lucky individuals were right to jealously guard these items against potential thieves because the barracks provided no insulation whatsoever.

Blighting desert winds blew in through every open crevice each night, causing uncontrollable shivering. You went on shaking until your body simply gave out from exhaustion. If someone tried to lobby for better sleeping conditions, they, too, were savagely beaten in front of the others. Parents were not permitted to visit their children locked away in the depths of Szell's sadistic laboratory, unless, of course, they could afford to engage Roy's services.

There was no rhyme or reason to the place—not even some kind of work detail to break up the tedium. It was, as Yehuda Mandelbaum put it, a rat cage, and a poorly tended one at that.

The eventual test subjects were left to aimlessly wile away the hours within their respective barracks by sleeping, talking, gambling with black market playing cards, taking turns crawling out to the blind spot in pairs so they could smoke, or staring at the ceiling for hours on end.

Personal hygiene was nonexistent. Many inmates could often be found violently scratching themselves until fleas fell off their skin like black flecks of dandruff. The outhouses were ramshackle wooden structures concealing excrement and urine-filled holes in the ground that had never been drained. Spending more than five minutes enveloped in the putrid fumes could cause a person to pass out and fall backward into the craters of human waste.

Some men (including Netanel, Abner, and Yehuda) organized daily minyanim for the three Jewish prayers of Shacharit, Mincha, and Maariv. They took turns saving hardtack so they could make motzi, the blessing on bread, each Shabbos. Baker did not take part in these regular religious gatherings, unable to comprehend how anyone could offer up supplications to a supposedly benevolent deity in a hellish place like this. Manzanar was, like the small space behind the barracks, a divine blind spot: a place where the Lord could not—or would not—see.

Almost every morning, Baker was dragged out of his bunk and taken to Szell's personal torture chamber for more strobe-induced seizures or injections of lysergic acid, which turned reality into a madness-inducing funhouse of unending terrors.

The doctor's goal was to "break" his mind until it could be molded into any shape. "Like clay," Szell said. "What bidding will I send you off to do, I wonder? Would you like to blow up all the picnicking couples of the National Mall in DC? Or perhaps you'd prefer to hijack a passenger airplane and steer it right into the Empire State Building, hmmm...?"

His nightmares clawed their way into the waking world and danced around the room, clutching dirty shovels stained blue. Szell led this festival of torment as a contorted homunculus who shimmered in and out of focus. Whenever Baker seemed on the verge of falling asleep or passing out, the doctor shot adrenaline directly into his heart.

After two weeks of this, he could feel his grip on reality starting to loosen. Soon, he would be no better than the muttering men wasting away in the barracks, prone to any of Szell's fiendish suggestions. Each night, he was dumped back into the Jewish living quarters and, despite his profound exhaustion and fragile state of mind, dragged himself to a rendezvous with Kissinger, who would always be waiting for him without fail.

The man insisted on dictating the terms of the conversation, probing Baker with questions about his life, while offering up nothing of substance beyond bizarre recommendations for pumpkins. Whenever Baker tried to pose a question pertaining to Nixon, Lamotte, Kishi, Yang, Park, or Arnaud, Kissinger would simply bid him good night and head back inside.

Two weeks of these interactions was all Baker could stand. When Kissinger asked him—"What kind of man are you?"—for what felt like the billionth time, he exploded in fury.

"What kind of man am I, Henry? I'm the kind of man who has had enough of your fucking bullshit and wants a few answers!" Kissinger made to leave, but Baker grabbed him and threw him to the ground. "I'm the kind of man who wants Nixon and Lamotte and the rest of them to face justice for what they've done. I didn't come all this way to be tortured by a Nazi psychopath for you to dodge my questions with small talk and non sequiturs. You're not going back inside until you tell me something of value, goddamnit!"

Kissinger looked up at him, stars reflected in his eyes. "You truly mean that?" he asked calmly. "You are only here to see that justice is done?"

"What other reason on earth would get me to come to a place like this?"

"A plethora of unsavory ones," answered Kissinger. "I needed to make sure your mental defenses were down to be absolutely sure."

"So you let Szell torture me just to make sure I wasn't a spy?"

"To be absolutely certain about something, one must know everything about it."

"If I was a spy, wouldn't I have just killed you already?"

"Let's not beat around the bush. Richard wants to know if I confided in anyone else or kept proof of our dealings. I do not fear death. What I do fear, however, is the truth being lost forever."

Kissinger reached into his pocket, bringing out a dull white object sharpened at the end.

"Take this."

"What is it?" asked Baker, accepting the item.

"A chicken bone I carved into a knife in case Richard found me. I always planned to go out on my own terms if worse came to worse."

"You want me to kill you with it then?"

"No," Kissinger said. "Which is your dominant hand?"

"My right."

"Cut off the pointer finger on your right hand. Prove to me how serious you are."

"What will mutilating myself prove?"

"That you value the truth beyond the threat of pain and injury. A man of lesser integrity would probably tell me to take that chicken bone and stick it where the sun doesn't shine."

"This is insanity," Baker whispered. "You really have lost it."

"No," said Kissinger calmly. "This is not insanity, this is a covenant. We are playing a dangerous game here, Mr. Baker. One does not act rashly under circumstances such as these. You strategize and wait until making the next move. Even then, it could be your last. This is why Richard and his men have not found me. They are impulsive and eager to cross the finish line by the easiest route available to them. They play checkers while I play chess, and any move across the board is one of zugzwang. Are you familiar with the term?"

Baker shook his head.

"A position in which any move one makes decreases their chances at ultimate victory," explained Kissinger. "This was never about winning. It was about postponing my defeat. Before I go, I would like to pass on what I know. To do that, I must be sure the next person in line is worthy of carrying on the burden. That person must be capable of overcoming any obstacle, no matter how insurmountable. So, I ask you again, cut off the pointer finger on your right hand. We will forge this deal with a payment of blood and flesh."

"How do I know you'll talk once I do it?"

"You don't. All covenants are based on faith alone. Just as Abraham was instructed to slice off his own foreskin to become the first of a new spiritual breed."

"You saying you're God now?"

"Hardly."

"What if I die of blood loss?"

"If you are smart, then you already have a plan to get out of here once your mission is complete."

"Okay," said Baker, hardly believing what he was about to do. "For the record, I think you've been in here too long. Your mind has gone off the deep end."

"Perhaps, but you must admit that I do drive a hard bargain."

Baker splayed out the fingers of his right hand on the outcrop of rock. "Make yourself useful," he said to Kissinger. "Go grab a piece of wood for me to bite down on."

Kissinger did as he was told, wrenching a meaty hunk of wood out of the splintered opening that led back through the barracks.

"Here goes nothing," Baker said through tightly clenched teeth. His breath was ragged and shallow.

The sharpened chicken bone got to work. Blood oozed out of the wound and pooled on the sand below. He'd hoped to make a clean go of it, but the makeshift knife was duller than it looked and came to a maddening halt anytime a piece of muscle, bone, or sinew got in the way.

The pain was extraordinary and the gruesome sight of self-mutilation forced Baker to close his eyes and pretend he was slicing into an overcooked steak. Surely this was the torment sinners were said to face in the deepest depths of Hell. After what felt like several lifetimes of eternal suffering, the bone reached rock. Baker let it fall and slumped to the ground, exhausted from pain and exertion. Kissinger wrapped the grievous, self-inflicted injury in a piece of fabric torn off his own uniform.

"Hold that tight," he said. "You're going to need antibiotics from the infirmary. Maybe Roy can—"

"Just shut up," Baker wheezed, finding his voice. "I did what you asked. Now it's my turn to speak. Did you suggest to Nixon that William Yang be brainwashed into blowing himself up?"

"The general idea, yes," Kissinger said. "The CIA had already been experimenting on shell-shocked veterans and the homeless for several years. They wanted to create proverbial ghosts—soldiers with implanted memories that could blend into any environment and carry out any task. If they were captured or tortured, their minds would go blank so there was nothing to confess. No one to betray. But never, in my wildest dreams, did I think Richard would use William. I suggested we use any faceless Korean-American male. Richard wanted to use William."

"For maximum PR damage?" asked Baker. "It would prove that everything the president had been saying about Communists and subversives in the government was true. But I didn't see any of his State Department connections mentioned in the papers."

"No, you wouldn't have," Kissinger said. "The risk of blowback was too great. Richard didn't want the public knowing that the government had been working with a Jew and a Korean on matters of global security. I tried my hardest to protect William, but he caught wind of the false flag operation. That's why he was chosen. His alleged terrorist attack gave McCarthy the justification to continue the war he so badly wanted and kept him occupied as we carried out the rest of the plan. The arms deal came next."

"Arms deal?"

"The arms deal with Japan. Richard would sell them a number of nuclear warheads in direct violation of the Japanese constitution, which forbids the production or use of atomic weapons."

"Christ, so the Kishi peace tour was all a front for backdoor negotiations?"

"Yes. We cannot risk a direct confrontation with the Soviets, but Japan is another story. The plan was to have Kishi pressure North Korea into unconditional surrender. Richard has promised them their old empire back if they can end the war once and for all. It was also understood that they would wrestle Mao and China into submission. In return, Japan was to pay a generous sum for the bombs and support Richard's government once he ousted McCarthy."

"And the money from the arms deal?"

"To be used in another deal with the devil. Funneled into the French effort to hold Indochina. France has also promised its support for Richard as president and assured us they would help convince other NATO members to accept the transition."

"That explains Arnaud's participation," Baker said.

"Louis was brought in to keep a tight lid on things and make sure the shipment went smoothly. The warheads have been waiting down at the Port of Los Angeles until the deal is finalized."

"Lamotte," Baker breathed, understanding the man's role at last.

"We needed an inconspicuous way to transport the weapons and he was in financial dire straits. We promised to help Orson settle his debts if he cooperated. He was jumpy about the whole thing from the very start, so Louis was assigned to take care of any worries he might have."

"What made you run?"

"Richard got jumpy and wanted to tie up loose ends. I was against using William from the off. I came out to Los Angeles, going about my scheduling preparations for Kishi's visit. Once I had fallen into a recognizable routine, I set up a meeting with the Koreans, hoping to explain everything in detail, but Richard's people barely let me out of their sight. I knew the order to kill me would be given at any time. So, I left my hotel one morning and never came back, hoping someone like you might discover that business card lodged in the vent."

"Awful big assumption to think that anyone would actually find it."

"My dear Mr. Baker," said Kissinger, "do you really believe that was the only clue I left behind? You are simply the one who made it this far."

"Okay," Baker continued. "Let's say the coup is successful. Nixon just shows up in the Oval Office one day without a single word of explanation?"

"The greatest trick the Devil ever pulled was convincing the world he didn't exist," Kissinger answered cryptically.

"How poetic," said Baker. "You come up with that?"

"The final piece was an upswell of public support for both Richard and the Japanese prime minister. What better way to engender sympathy than by surviving an assassination attempt?"

"Sung-Ho Park."

"Yes. He and William knew each other from their time fighting in

Korea and would meet up regularly once they returned home. Their close friendship would sell the idea of an underground terror group operating in the United States."

Baker allowed these terrible truths to sink into his weary brain. The fabric hugging the amputation site was already soaked through with blood; the pain intensified as his body ran out of adrenaline to keep itself in shock.

"I can see the disgust on your face," Kissinger said. "A natural way to feel. I am indeed a monster—the kind of creature my family and I ran from when we fled Germany all those years ago. I will not deny that I was blinded by power and respect in a time when most people like us receive very little of either. I just hope you know the abhorrence you feel is nothing compared to my shame. Now, let us get you back inside."

CHAPTER 68

It took twice as long on the return trip without the use of his injured hand, but they managed it. Kissinger helped prop Baker up whenever his left arm gave out from overexertion.

"That's it," he kept saying like a patient father training his son to ride a bike for the first time. "Easy now."

"I'm going to sleep like the dead when this is all over," Baker said, pulling himself up through the hole and shimmying under the bunk.

"You can rest once we have your hand looked at," Kissinger said. "I believe there is a doctor in this barracks," he added. "Teddy Peltzman is his name. He should be able to—"

Blam!

The barracks erupted with shouts of fear and astonishment. Kissinger slumped to the ground, a smoking rupture in the middle of his forehead. Lonergan, surrounded by his henchmen and a gathering crowd of curious inmates, had fired the bullet.

"Christ, Baker—what happened to your hand?" Lonergan demanded, almost sounding concerned.

"You . . . you . . . you . . ." stuttered Baker.

"You . . . you . . . you," Lonergan repeated in mock astonishment. "You knew how this would end. Kissinger was never going to leave this place alive."

"I take it you got my message then?"

"What message?"

Baker thought he'd misheard. "The message from my associates."

"Must have missed it," said Lonergan, bringing a comb to his hair. "Got a very interesting call from Director Carto this morning.

It seems two Jewish inmates have been sneaking off every night for the last two weeks to discuss...sensitive topics, shall we say. Well, at least one of them kept rambling on about some sort of conspiracy involving the vice president and Orson Lamotte and a whole host of other absurdities."

"How...?"

In response to his question, Lonergan turned around, beckoned someone over.

That someone turned out to be Roy, who stepped out of the crowd, beaming like a lottery winner about to tell his boss to fuck off.

"I'd like to thank you, Baker," said Roy in a smug tone that made Baker want to lunge at the man. He probably would have, too, had all his fingers still been intact. "You and Kissinger are my ticket out of here. You should really be more discreet next time."

"There won't be a next time," said Lonergan, pointing his gun in Baker's direction. "What I don't understand is how you planned to get out of here."

"If you'd gotten my message," said Baker, trying desperately to maintain a blasé attitude, "then you'd be aware of your obligation to escort me and my friends out of the camp personally."

Lonergan let out a hee-haw of laughter. "And why, pray tell, would I do that?"

"Because of the evidence."

"What evidence?" Lonergan's smile faltered a little.

"The evidence that Kissinger left behind. The evidence that will be made public by my associates if I don't make it home safe and sound."

Lonergan rounded on Roy. "You didn't say anything about evidence," he snarled.

Baker was pleased to see Roy at a loss for words. "I...I...That was never mentioned. I swear!"

"Who are you going to believe, Lonergan?" asked Baker. "Me or the man who swindles prisoners out of basic human necessities? A man who takes to lies like a duck to water? You and I may never be fast friends, but I think you'll agree I always tend to speak my mind. I'm not trying to bullshit you."

"Where's the stash of evidence?"

"Think I'll take that one to my grave."

"That can be arranged."

"You kill me, and Nixon's little arms deal with Kishi will be public knowledge before the week is out."

This lie had the intended affect. Lonergan's face immediately lost its color, and he cleared his throat. "You're... you're bluffing."

"I've got informants of my own, Lonergan. Are you really willing to take such a large risk?"

Roy looked mutinous. "Enough of this. Shoot him and let's go!" thundered the black marketeer.

Blam!

Roy collapsed to his knees, clutching the bullet wound in his chest.

"I don't care much for rats," said Lonergan, reholstering his gun. "All right, Baker. Let's get the hell out of here."

"My friends, too, Lonergan. A deal's a deal."

"You've got five minutes to round them up."

Dear Mr. Lamotte:

I am writing to remind you—once again—of your overdue payment to the Banc of California. Your family's patronage has meant a great deal to us over the years, and it is because of your father's generosity and reputation that the Banc has provided Lamotte Exports with a long leash of debt for such an extended period of time. However, if we do not receive the outstanding amount of $5,000,000 by Feb. 1, 1960, we will be forced to take possession of and foreclose on your various homes, business ventures, and orange groves located throughout Southern California.

This will be your final notice. Wishing you and your family a happy and fruitful new year.

Yours Truly,

Alfred Hart

Banc of California President

PART IX

January 16, 1960

In the councils of government, we must guard against the acquisition of unwarranted influence, whether sought or unsought, by the military-industrial complex. The potential for the disastrous rise of misplaced power exists and will persist.

—*President Dwight D. Eisenhower*

CHAPTER 69

Not trusting Lonergan to refrain from shooting the whole lot of them when he wasn't looking, Baker made sure the other men were dropped off before himself. Noah Levinson and Eliyahu Margules were first on the itinerary, delivered to the offices of Dr. Ehrlich, who could hopefully bring both men back to a functioning state of consciousness.

Abner got out, too, supporting both men and promising to make sure that Noah and Eliyahu were situated before finding his own way home. Netanel Horowitz and Yehuda Mandelbaum were up next, running into the awaiting arms of their spouses. Shelly caught sight of Baker in the back seat and mouthed *Thank you* as overjoyed tears streamed down her face.

"Last stop," Lonergan called when the Ford Interceptor pulled up to the Paradise Apartments in the heart of Chinatown.

"Thanks," Baker muttered, moving to open the passenger door.

"Baker," Lonergan said, stopping him. "I wouldn't get too comfortable if I were you. Just know that you're a dead man the second we find out if you're bluffing about that evidence."

"I don't doubt it," replied Baker. "Now, if you don't mind, kindly fuck off."

Ze'ev was fast asleep on the bed, Matagot at his side, when Baker entered the apartment with the spare key he kept hidden under a loose patch of carpet in the lobby. He closed the door, quietly as he could, but his brother stirred at the faint clicking noise.

"Baruch Hashem," he breathed. "You're okay."

"Don't know if 'okay' is the best word for my appearance," Baker said with a wan smile, sitting on the bed and scratching Matagot behind the ears. "'Like shit' is probably more fitting."

"Our parents taught us not to add insult to injury," called Ze'ev, now stretching and yawning.

"Morris... did you lose a *finger*?"

"Don't ask." Baker got up, walked into the bathroom, and took in the disheveled uniform, shaved head, and dirt-smeared face staring back at him. He was also certain he'd lost around ten to fifteen pounds over the last two weeks.

"Any problems while I was away?"

"Not a one," said Ze'ev. "The only exciting thing around here was an envelope slipped under the door a few days ago. It's over there on the kitchen counter. No name or return address."

Baker stood up, walked over to the counter, and picked up the blank white envelope. Ripping it open, he found a pair of folded lab reports from Los Angeles Chief Medical Examiner Thomas Noguchi.

He read the reports over three times, heart racing. "I need to go," he said to Ze'ev, who was in the middle of pulling on a cream-colored sweater.

"What?" said his brother. "You just got back, and like you say, you look like shit. Come and have a shluf at the very least."

"This can't wait."

Baker rushed out of the apartment without another word.

CHAPTER 70

Orson Lamotte leisurely strolled along the misty lanes of the orange grove planted around his palatial Woodland Hills mansion when he saw a shabby bald man in a striped uniform leaning against one of the trees. And unless he was very much mistaken, this son of a bitch was peeling one of *his* oranges.

"Good day, Mr. Lamotte."

"Baker?" gaped the businessman, recognizing the man's voice. "What did I tell you last time? I'll have you carted away for this!"

"No, I don't think you will," Baker said.

"This is trespass!" Lamotte screamed. "Illegal trespass on my property!"

"The Banc of California's property, you mean?"

"I... I have no idea what you're on about," blustered Lamotte.

"It's over, Lamotte," Baker said, tossing away the orange. "I know that you had Louis Arnaud murder Elizabeth Short and frame Jasper Heo for the crime. Arnaud was also responsible for the deaths of Liz's roommate, Debbie Milner, and two police officers. He would've gotten me, too, had I not shot him dead first."

"Ridiculous!" Lamotte said, his eyes bulging. "You're raving!"

Baker took a few paces forward in the wet soil, brandishing the lab reports. "Elizabeth Short was found with dirt under her fingernails. Louis Arnaud had similar residue on the bottoms of his boots. Both samples were rich in nitrogen and sand—the two optimum elements for cultivating orange trees, as you told me during our first meeting last month."

Lamotte cackled. It was high-pitched and mirthless. "That all you have? A little bit of dirt? Those samples could have come from anywhere!"

"Not likely," said Baker, still advancing. "Given that you own all of the orange groves in this part of the state. Compound that with your affair with Miss Short, which you admitted to me, and I'd say there's a solid basis to convince a jury of conspiracy to commit first-degree murder."

"Preposterous! On what grounds would I have anyone murdered?"

"Your agreement to help ship nuclear arms to Japan for Vice President Nixon."

Lamotte's face went from the angry red of a freshly boiled beet to the whitish gray of processed wood pulp. "There's . . . there's no way you can know that."

"But I do, Mr. Lamotte," said Baker, folding up the lab reports. "It's time to come clean."

Like a child caught in wrongdoing, Lamotte let out a wail of despair and fell to his knees. The pants of his silken pajamas sank into the mud. "I didn't want it to happen!" he said. "She came to surprise me out here and overheard us talking about it. I had no other choice. No one was allowed to know." He stuck out an accusatory finger at Baker. "If you hadn't stuck your nose into it, that Milner girl would still be alive!"

"So all that talk about breaking things off for the sake of your marriage?"

"Lizzie wanted to end it," Lamotte said, still bawling in the soil. "I was the one who convinced her to stay. I would have done anything for her," he added, looking up at Baker. "I loved her. Can you believe that?"

"I can, Mr. Lamotte." Then he called over his shoulder: "You get all of that, Connolly?"

"I sure did, Morris," said Brogan Connolly, stepping out from around a particularly large tree trunk.

"What is this?" Lamotte demanded.

"Justice, you son of a bitch," said Baker, watching as Connolly slapped cuffs around Lamotte's wrists and pulled the man to his feet.

"Sorry I didn't believe you," Connolly said.

"Don't worry about it," Baker said. "For a second there, I thought I'd lost it, too."

"You do know he's just going to walk free, right?" Connolly said, lowering his voice. "Guy like this, with all his fancy connections? He'll literally get away with murder."

"I know," Baker said. "But if Jasper Heo is exonerated, then it'll all be worth it."

"You're a regular Whittaker Chambers," Connolly said. "Blowing the whistle."

Baker stopped dead, two wires sparking together in his brain. "What did you just say?"

"You're a regular Whittaker Chambers...?"

"Connolly, do you have everything under control here?"

"Well, sure, but—"

"Good. I'll call you later. There's one last thing I have to check up on."

"Still not gonna tell me what happened to your finger or why you smell and kind of resemble Satan's anus?" Connolly called after his retreating form.

"It's a riveting tale, Brogan! I'd like to do it justice sometime."

With that, he ran ahead, hopped in his car, and, despite his tiredness, began the long trip upstate.

CHAPTER 71

It was fully dark when he pulled up to the Manzanetti Farms Christmas Trees and Pumpkin Patch in Petaluma eight hours later. The place looked lifeless now that Halloween and Christmas had come and gone. Not wanting his trip to be for nothing, Baker slammed his palms against the glass doors of the adjoining farmer's market.

"Hello?" he called. "*Hello?* Is anyone there?"

Someone was: A portly man in blue overalls and a flannel shirt unlocked the door, eyeing Baker with suspicion. "We're closed," he said. "Come back tomo—"

"Do you sell pumpkins?" Baker asked, knowing that he must look insane.

"Pumpkins? We haven't sold pumpkins for two months."

"I know this may sound strange," Baker pressed on, "but do you have any pumpkins or…I don't know—*something* on hold under the name of *Henry Kissinger*?"

The man's eyes flashed with understanding. "So he actually sent someone to pick it up, eh?"

"There *is* something?"

"We've had it out in the back for almost three months now. Damn thing is rotted to hell, but we were paid a hefty sum to keep it around—no matter what—until someone came looking for it."

Baker's heart leapt. "Can you take me to it?"

"Why, sure." The man led Baker to the other side of the building, which jutted up against the empty pumpkin patch. There, sitting against the wall was a very large and thoroughly rotted pumpkin—deflated and covered in mold and barnacle-like fungi of varying colors.

"Not sure what use anyone could get out of it," said the man. "But there ya are."

"Thank you," Baker said, leaning down to admire the decomposed gourd.

"You're welcome," said the man, pinching his nostrils closed. "Just make sure you take the darned thing off the property when you leave."

"Will do. Have a nice evening."

"You as well."

He waited for the man to leave before plunging his hands into the corroded innards of the rancid pumpkin. His fingers moved around the pulpous meat and seeds until they closed around several solid objects, which turned out to be canisters of microfilm.

"Andy? Yeah, it's Baker. I know it's late, but how would you like to break the story of the century?"

COVER SPLASH: A severe-looking man with a ghoulish scar running across the bottom of his right cheek clutches a miniature model of a rocket ship. He smiles at the camera, but the rest of the face belies a profound hauntedness. You can see it in the pouchy blue eyes. It is the sign of heinous recollections taking their mental toll. But there is something else, too. A pride in those twisted memories. The smug acknowledgment of perpetrating evil and getting away with it.

AMERICAN HAS CONQUERED THE MOON—WHAT'S NEXT FOR OUR COUNTRY'S AMBITIOUS SPACE PROGRAM?

NASA's premiere rocket scientist speaks out for the first time in the wake of Wernher von Braun's tragic murder!

Counterattack speaks with Dr. Kurt H. Debus—current acting director of the Eisenhower Space Center located on Merritt Island, Florida, and the Marshall Space Flight Center in Huntsville, Alabama—in this exclusive interview conducted by editor Francis J. McNamara.

This Q&A has been edited for length and clarity.

[INTERIOR]

FJM: Doctor Debus, how are you?

KD: Very well, danke schoen. How about yourself?

FJM: Glad to hear it! I'm doing just swell myself. Thanks so much for taking the time to speak with me. I really appreciate it.

KD: The pleasure is all mine.

FJM: Now, without further ado, let's just address the elephant in the room, shall we? Wernher von Braun. Please accept my sincerest condolences for the loss of your colleague. The American public owes him a great debt of gratitude.

KD: Ja, he will certainly be missed. But we will, of course, carry on the work that he started. I would not be here if not for Wernher. The best thing I can do to honor his memory is to keep "pushing the envelope," as you Americans like to say. I am excited to announce that construction on a strategic Moonport should reach its completion by the end of next year.

FJM: Let's see the Reds try and land there now.

KD: If they place even one booted toe on the cratered surface, they will be sorry.

FJM: I love it! And what about all those whispers of lunar vacations we keep hearing about? How accurate are they, Dr. Debus?

KD: Tsk. Tsk. I don't know where you get your information, Mr. McNamara, but yes, we've already started taking reservations from a select few. Pan Am will be servicing the flights.

FJM: Any chance of bumping me up to the top of the waitlist?

KD: Not on your life. *{Laughs}*

FJM: With all these projects going on under your purview, I'm sure it couldn't have been easy, inheriting Dr. von Braun's work at the Marshall Space Flight Center on top of all your work down in Florida.

KD: You have hit the nail on the head there. I have barely slept a wink since Wernher's unfortunate passing several months ago, and my wife and daughters aren't too ecstatic about my near-constant trips between Florida and Alabama. Then there's all the worry that I may befall the same fate as Wernher. Still, it is an absolute honor to help the United States reach supremacy amongst the stars before the Soviet Union can gain a foothold. All of the sleepless nights are worth it in my eyes. I must add that President McCarthy could not be more generous in his support of the program.

FJM: I've had the opportunity to interview the president on several occasions. Such a lovely man and leader! What kind of conversations did you have with him?

KD: They pertained to the usual topics: Where do we stand in our race for recognition of our capabilities in the Free World and also in relation to Russia? What is Russia bound to do next? The president asks very interesting questions.

FJM: So, what is our country's follow-up to the moon?

KD: Wernher's dream, of course. A manned mission to Mars!

FJM: Wow.

KD: Indeed.

FJM: And how far along are you on that?

KD: Oh, we still have a ways to go. But if our current timeline remains steady, the United States could annex the Red Planet as early as 1975.

FJM: {*Whistles*} That'd make Hawaii look like a drop in the bucket by comparison, eh?

KD: {*Laughs*} I suppose it would.

FJM: More room to stretch our legs, so to speak.

KD: We Germans like to call it "Lebensraum."

FJM: Getting back to the subject of your late colleague, I was curious if you might be able to speak on the circumstances surrounding his death.

KD: Well, I don't comment on rumors, especially when they are tied to the security of our great nation, but all the evidence points toward Communist sabotage.

FJM: That doesn't surprise me in the slightest.

KD: It all comes down to jealousy. The Soviets are envious of what we have accomplished in such little time, and in an effort to slow us down, they snuffed out one of the greatest scientific minds of this—or any—century. Not even the Jew Einstein held a candle to the great Wernher von Braun.

FJM: You said before that there is some worry about you falling victim to the same saboteurs that took von Braun's life. Have you and the president discussed measures to prevent a similar tragedy in future?

KD: The president has been kind enough to lend out a few of his Secret Service agents to protect my team and me. We have taken to calling them the "Rocket Rangers."

FJM: A very fitting name! And what about those unsavory parties who walk among us, hoping to sow discord and upend our plans for outer space?

KD: More competent men than I are working on it, but I would suggest that more attention be paid to those of a Hebraic background. First, the Rosenbergs give the Soviets the hydrogen bomb and then Wernher turns up dead. A pattern is emerging, wouldn't you say?

FJM: Hear! Hear! Would you say Dr. von Braun's death has impeded your work at all?

KD: If anything, we're working even harder in his absence. Wernher would not have liked us to wallow in grief for too long. He would have wanted us to get the job done, and that's exactly what we're doing.

FJM: Thank you again for taking the time, Dr. Debus. I'll see you on Mars.

KD: Ha! From your lips, Mr. McNamara. From your lips...

PART X

February 1, 1960

All the Dachaus must remain standing. The Dachaus, the Belsens, the Buchenwalds, the Auschwitzes—all of them. They must remain standing because they are a monument to a moment in time when some men decided to turn the Earth into a graveyard. Into it they shoveled all of their reason, their logic, their knowledge, but worst of all, their conscience. And the moment we forget this, the moment we cease to be haunted by its remembrance, then we become the gravediggers.

—*Rod Serling,* "Death's Head Revisited"

CHAPTER 72

This is Danville calling Falcon, come in, Falcon. Over."

. . .

"This is Falcon. Over. Baker, m'boy, is that you?"

"Yes, Edward, it's me. It's good to hear your voice."

"And it's good to hear yours, son. Sorry I've been out of pocket these last few months. From what Joanna tells me, you haven't lost your knack for finding trouble everywhere you go."

"Edward . . . ?"

"Yes?"

"Did you know?"

"Did I know what?"

"About Manzanar. The mind control experiments."

. . .

"I thought we were past all of the secret-keeping, Edward."

"We are, Baker, but are you familiar with the phrase 'Don't keep all your eggs in one basket'? You and Joanna were tasked with building out the Liberty Boys network. There is nothing in that job description about being made privy to every shred of information I come across. You operate on a need-to-know basis—not only for my safety, but for your own."

"What about the American people? Don't they deserve to know?"

"The old methods aren't working, Baker. You of all people know that. Yang changed everything. We knew about the experiments, of course, but never thought there'd be a genuine breakthrough. Think about the implications. Your friends and neighbors, random people on the street—all of them capable of being ticking time bombs with the right conditioning. We don't know who to trust anymore. That's why I'm asking Joanna to leave your office, effective immediately."

"What?"

"She filled me in on your time at Manzanar. I'm sorry, Baker, but you've been compromised."

"I'm fine!"

"How can you be certain? How do you know they didn't manage to implant something that can be exploited down the road? We just can't take that risk. Not in the battle we're fighting. I am sorry. Good night and good luck…"

"Edward…? Edward…EDWARD!"

CHAPTER 73

The cold spell had finally broken over Los Angeles. It was as though the revelation of Nixon's coup attempt—and his subsequent execution—were the prerequisites for annulling some evil curse that had been cast upon the city. The vice president and three of his primary coconspirators had been hanged by the neck until dead, swinging on the very gallows constructed for Jasper Heto, whose date with the executioner was briefly delayed.

All of it reminded Baker of the story told on the Jewish festival of Purim: A wicked son of a bitch by the maligned name of Haman the Agagite attempted to hang a righteous Jew, Mordechai, on a custom gallows, only to find himself swinging from it at the end of the story.

The prospect of seeing Nixon, Hoover, Dulles, and MacArthur killed in real time made it the must-watch television event of the New Year (sponsored by Gillette shaving cream, Halo shampoo, and Grape-Nuts cereal).

Just before the lever was pulled, Nixon had done something very curious. He smiled, extended both arms, and threw up a pair of "V for Victory" signs with middle and forefingers extended. No one had a proper explanation for the reason behind this final salute.

The very next day, US tanks rolled into Tokyo, reestablishing a firm military presence led by MacArthur's replacement, General Matthew Ridgway. North and South Korea, meanwhile, announced their plans for an amicable reunification, with an ultimatum for America to withdraw its forces by the end of the month.

And that's when the first rays of sun broke through the gloom. People and palm trees alike thawed out of their dreary funk. Angelenos walked with a bubbly pep in their step once again, proudly striding into some bright new era. That wasn't true, of course.

The status quo had changed, though not for the better. If anything, the attempted overthrow of McCarthy had only made the man more popular. It would all make for some real nice speeches when the president ran for a third term at the end of the year, assuming Ronald Reagan didn't win the Republican nomination.

There was no evidence linking McCarthy to the Yang Affair. Sullivan had only run the parts vilifying Nixon, and even then, there was no mention of mind control experiments or William Yang's innocence—only the correspondence and financials surrounding the illicit arms deal with Kishi, as well as the specifics of the failed government takeover. Sullivan was no dope; he knew that any mention of the president would have meant a heavily censored article and an early death. Orson Lamotte had been named, of course, but Connolly was right: Regardless of his dire insolvency, the magnate still enjoyed a great deal of political influence, allowing him to escape the proverbial maelstrom as a free, albeit embarrassed, man by crying extortion. His admission to Liz's murder didn't stick either, due to insufficient evidence.

Baker stood at his usual thinking spot, the pit of bubbling tar in Hancock Park, quite deserted this early in the morning. It was nice to bask in the sun again, but he could have done without all the sweating. There were always trade-offs in life.

"Got a light?"

Baker jumped, shocked he wasn't alone. He looked over, beheld a young man with large ears and contemplative green eyes. The newcomer had a cigarette perched between his expectant lips. Baker obliged the man's request, pulling out a box of matches and lighting the smoke.

"Thank you very much," said the stranger.

"Don't mention it," replied Baker, expecting the man to leave. But he didn't. He just stood there, smoking and looking down into the pit.

"Can I offer you one?"

"Excuse me?"

"A cigarette. Would you like one?"

He jiggled the box, and for a moment, Baker felt an irresistible urge to partake. Luckily, he mastered the inclination and besides, he didn't much care for Junos.

"No, thank you," he replied. "Trying to cut back myself. Doctor's orders."

"I see. Probably for the best—I've heard they can kill. You from around here?"

"What?"

"I was simply curious if you come from California."

"Oh, no. I'm from Europe originally."

"Small world. Me, too," replied the man. "I live up in Canada now. Funny how that happens. We never quite end up where we started. New lives, new cities, new faces. A stranger in a strange land. Can be a bit maddening sometimes, no?"

Baker didn't feel much like talking but didn't want to be rude. "I suppose."

"You end up thousands of miles from home in a place infested with the wrong sort."

There was something about the man's eyes. A malicious cunning that didn't sit right with Baker. Instinct told him to move his hand closer to the Magnum holstered at his hip. He did this under the pretense of adjusting his waistband with what felt *like* five fingers on his right hand. Dr. Ehrlich had said the odd sensation of sensing a limb that was no longer attached to the body—"phantom pains," he called them—would take some time to fade. He'd just have to learn to pull the trigger with his middle finger or else switch shooting hands entirely.

"What brings you to town anyway?" Baker asked.

"Just passing through for a small matter of business..." said the stranger, "on behalf of the Black Symphony."

He flicked his cigarette away and lunged at Baker, who already had a hand on his gun. He wasn't quick enough. Just as he was extracting the weapon from its holster, the assassin dove like a hungry bird of prey, swatting the gun to the ground. Baker's mind flashed to the image of his lucky switchblade, which vanished in a burst of pain when the stranger drove a fist straight into his gut. Baker staggered backward, the wind knocked out of him. Again, he thought of the knife and again he was knocked senseless as the assassin landed a sucker punch to the jaw.

"I'm going to enjoy this very much, Jew," crowed the man. "You think you can just kill one of our leaders and get away with it? The ODESSA has a very long memory, especially when it comes to bothersome little shits like you."

"Funny," wheezed Baker. "I always thought you guys were the little shits."

The assassin lashed out wildly but Baker was ready for it this time, dodging the swing and landing a blow of his own.

"You fuck!" screamed the man, attempting to stem the flow of blood now streaming into his mouth. "You'll pay for that!"

The Nazi charged, using all his momentum in a tackle that knocked both of them to the ground. Baker landed directly on his back, felt all the air leave his lungs. This made him easy prey for the attacker, who landed punch after punch before Baker regained enough breath to protect his aching face, now speckled with the man's blood, as well as his own.

Looking over, he saw his gun lying in a patch of dewy grass. There was no way to reach it with the man pinning him down. But he didn't need the gun. He allowed the pummeling of his face to continue and slowly lowered his arms, letting the assassin think he was on the verge of victory. The man smiled, slowing the assault, which gave Baker the window he needed to reach into his pocket and bring out the knife that had already killed one member of the Black Symphony.

He flicked it open, accidentally slicing his finger, but it hardly mattered. He plunged the blade into the attacker's chest until it hit the sternum, the entire handle vibrating horribly.

"When you get to Hell in just a few moments," Baker said, pulling the knife out, "tell von Braun I say hello."

The man had no response. He stood up, eyes wide, and staggered around with no direction. He lost his balance at the edge of the embankment and tumbled into the viscous tar below.

Baker was breathing heavily, his vision starting to narrow a little as his eyes puffed up, when the pool of tar began to bubble and froth. He stood up, grabbing his gun out of the grass, and making sure it was cocked and loaded before aiming it at the disturbance in the pit. The Nazi assailant broke the surface. His lips, a small pucker of pink against the rippling canvas of black, greedily sucked at the air.

The rest of his head, including the eyes, were entirely covered in boiling hot goop, fast hardening in the open air. He blindly reached out, clearly searching for the bank, and Baker felt his stomach violently contract. A sizable chunk of the man's skin sloughed off his scalded arm, leaving behind a nauseating exhibition of muscle, tendon, and bone. The immediate area was thick with the stench of overcooked meat.

The would-be killer continued to blindly grasp at nothing, uncaring that his outstretched appendage was liquefying. A portion of scalp containing a thatch of matted hair came off next, giving way to the nightmarish sight of a blistering eyeball ricocheting around its socket like an oyster cooked over a grate of white-hot charcoals.

This was enough for Baker, who took aim—not for the stranger's sake, but for his own. He fired three well-placed bullets into the struggling mass, which immediately went stiff and sank below the surface. And this time, when the bubbles subsided, no one came up gasping for air.

CHAPTER 74

Lonergan was waiting for him at the entrance to the park on Wilshire, leisurely enjoying a cigar.

"You look like shit," he remarked.

"I'm not in the mood, Lonergan. What do you want?"

"I've been sent to collect you."

"By whom?"

"You'll see."

"And if I refuse?"

"Then you'll go the same way as Nixon."

"You mean your late boss?"

"I don't have a clue what you're talking about."

"None of the shit came raining down on your head. Very clever of you to defect back to Joe once the game was up," Baker said. "How'd you do it? Spin a tail of deception and woe like your buddy Lamotte? Claim you were brainwashed like William Yang? Unless, of course, you were a double agent all along and only pretended to be Nixon's lapdog. Stop me when I've got it right."

Lonergan chucked away his cigar, a murderous look on his face. "Are you going to come willingly," he asked, "or do I need to employ brute force?"

Lonergan took him to the Musso & Frank on Hollywood Boulevard. Baker was frisked and had his gun and blood-coated pocketknife confiscated before being let inside. The restaurant's low-lit interior of wood paneling and fancy white tablecloths was totally empty, save for one food-and-drink-laden table occupied by the president of the United States.

Extremely fat and almost completely bald, Joseph McCarthy held court from a strange recliner-like seat that supported his immense weight via the use of thick, black harnesses. The suit covering his immense body looked as though it had been assembled in different pieces from an elastic fabric capable of accommodating an ever-growing waistline.

Baker and Lonergan watched the president consume several shrimps swimming in garlic butter and discard the tails with impunity before Lonergan cleared his throat to announce their presence.

"Huh?" grumbled McCarthy, jowls quivering like congealed bone broth as he turned his attention away from a rare T-bone steak sweating pink juices. He looked up with a peaky, jaundiced face that betrayed an affinity for whiskey that had permanently damaged his liver.

"Ah, just the man I wanted to see. What's with your face, Baker? Lonergan, you didn't . . . ?"

"He was like that when I found him, Mr. President," Lonergan said.

"Very well. Thank you, Lonergan. Sit, Baker."

He raised a beefy hand and pointed to the chair opposite. Baker took it, noticing the HUAC agents stationed in the shadowy corners of the room.

"Can I get you something to eat or drink?" McCarthy asked, reaching for a crystalline glass of whiskey and taking a noisy slurp from it. "My people can get you almost anything you like," he added, smacking his lips and picking up a serrated steak knife, which disappeared into the chunky palm.

"No, thank you," Baker said, hastily adding "Mr. President" to the end of his refusal.

McCarthy shrugged—or at least attempted to. Two strands of what was left of his wispy hair fell down over his high and greasy forehead.

"I wanted to thank you for saving my bacon," the president said, relieving himself of a deep flatulence at the same time. "I always had a feeling Nixon was a snake in the grass. I was so busy weeding out the Communists and keeping the Koreans under control that I forgot to keep an eye out for traitors in my own backyard. Should've known

Dick would try to take me out sooner or later. Wish I hadn't made him my VP, but there you are."

"You are very welcome, Mr. President," Baker said, thinking how easy it would be to murder the vulnerable McCarthy with his own steak knife. To spill all that thick blood sluggishly pumping through the president's obese veins.

"Speaking of wishes," McCarthy continued, forcing a large piece of beef into his batrachian mouth, "I wanted to know if there was anything I could do for you as a token of my gratitude."

"Mr. President?"

"Joseph McCarthy always repays his debts," the president declared. He picked up the steak bone and began to gnaw on it. "You have done me a great service, Baker, and I am simply wondering if I can do anything to settle our... *account*, as it were." He grabbed a plate of roast chicken legs, tore a chunk out of one of them with his teeth, and asked: "You ever play poker?"

"Yes, although I can probably count the number of times on one hand."

The president laughed, sucking chicken grease off his chunky fingers. "I don't get many chances to play, either," he said, "but I used to be pretty good in my day. The game, as I'm sure you know, isn't just about luck and assembling a winning hand—it's also about deception. Trying to bluff your opponent into folding."

The president stopped eating for a moment and looked across the table with intense, piggy eyes. A sudden and almost telepathic understanding occurred to Baker. The offer to "settle our account" was not born out of gratitude. It was a bribe cleverly hidden under the guise of thanks.

As much as he probably would have liked to, the president could not kill Baker with a wave of his hand like he had done with so many other poor souls. Who was to say that Baker had not tasked someone else with publishing the rest of the damning documents, should he turn up missing one day without explanation? Baker was holding back either a royal flush or a handful of crap.

The president had no way of knowing for certain, but he was starting to sweat. His hand was nothing more than a mismatched collection of colors and suits that couldn't be spun into a last-minute victory. His eyes were darting to the middle of the pot—not a collection of plastic chips or cigarettes or even a few dollars—but all the marbles. The whole enchilada.

McCarthy couldn't stand the fact that he was about to fold to a lowly Jew, and Baker took great pleasure in the thought that such an arrangement must have been eating the man up in the same gluttonous way he was demolishing this very table of food.

"That's very kind of you, sir," Baker began, wondering what rare favor he could ask of the most powerful man in the world. "I don't quite know what to say."

"You will name a price!" McCarthy boomed, slamming a fat fist on the table and causing the cutlery and crystal ware to tinkle.

"May I ask you a question first, Mr. President?"

"If you must."

"Forgive me for my ignorance of the way the American government is structured, but what is a former senator's connection to a *House* committee?"

"Because 'Government Operations Committee' doesn't have the same ring to it," McCarthy said. "It's boring, flat. You start throwing around the phrase *un-American*, and all of a sudden, everyone sits up and pays attention. People start to trip over themselves, hoping to prove the phrase doesn't apply to them. They'll rat out their own mothers to prove they're not a traitor."

The president took a noisy gulp of whiskey and continued, "I am oft accused of anti-Semitism in this country, Mr. Baker, but believe me, no one loves the Jews more than I do. Did you know that it was a Jew who helped me graduate high school?"

"No," Baker said.

"Leo Hershberger," McCarthy said, his eyes taking on a far-off look of nostalgic wistfulness. "The principal of Little Wolf High School back in Manawa, Wisconsin, took a chance on a twenty-year-old boy who just wanted to learn. And you know what? I did it all in a single year. One goddamn year. It's something I am very proud of, but none of it would have happened—none of it!—without Leo's support and encouragement. He even went so far to tell a little white lie in order to get me into college. Since that time, I have judged every Jewish person—man, woman, and child—against the kindness Leo showed to me all those years ago. So, tell me, Baker, are you a Leo Hershberger, or are you the *other* kind of Jew?"

Baker felt anger rise in the back of his throat and resisted the urge to tell the president that he could take his offer of spurious generosity and go fuck himself with it. Instead, he reached over the table—the bodyguards started surging forward, but McCarthy lazily waved them back—grabbed the decanter of whiskey, and poured himself a healthy measure.

"I'm the kind of Jew that can make life very difficult for someone like you," he said.

"Now we're getting somewhere!" McCarthy sang, clapping his greasy hands together. "I do tire of beating around the bush."

"For starters," Baker said, taking a large swig of the president's alcohol, "Orson Lamotte *will* be charged for the murders of Elizabeth Short and Debbie Milner," he said, reflecting on their lonely burials at the Evergreen Cemetery. "I also want him charged for the death of a member of the Chinatown tong by the name of Han Zhao. You can tie him to Nixon or spin whatever bullshit story you want—I just don't want him walking free."

McCarthy briefly bit his lip, but ultimately said: "Fine. It will be d—"

"Secondly," Baker pressed on, "Sergeant Brogan Connolly will not be interrogated or face any repercussions for whatever he may have learned in the course of his investigations into the murders of Miss Short and Miss Milner."

"Done," said McCarthy, sopping up shrimpy garlic butter with a thick sourdough roll.

"Next, you will issue formal pardons to William Yang, Jasper Heo, and Sung Ho-Park—and publicly apologize to their families."

"Outrageous!" screamed McCarthy. "Out of the question! Yang and Park are the only reason I can—"

"Can what?" Baker countered. "Round up American citizens without due process? Keep the public in favor of your pointless war in Korea?"

"You go too far, sir," McCarthy growled.

"I'd say I'm not going far enough," Baker said. "But we all have to start somewhere, don't we, Mr. President?"

"Fine," said the president, looking murderous. The president summoned Lonergan to the table. "Chief Inspector, get in touch with our friends at *Counterattack*. It seems we were gravely mistaken about William Yang and this William Heo. Sung-Ho Park was the sole mastermind behind recent events. Make sure that runs on the front page of the evening edition."

"But—but—" Baker began as Lonergan stalked off to find a phone.

"Do not be greedy, Baker—it is not a good look for Jews," responded McCarthy. "Someone still needs to take the blame. Would you prefer it was Yang instead?"

Baker did not respond.

"Anything else?" asked the president.

"There is one last thing," Baker said. "I've got lung cancer." This came as an obvious shock to McCarthy, whose face twitched with excitement. "Thanks to you, most doctors and hospitals won't treat someone like me. You're not only going to find a doctor who will treat me, you're also going to pay for it."

McCarthy stared at Baker in disbelief, seeing him clearly for the first time. After several moments of stunned silence, he leaned forward, his immense belly causing the table to move forward several inches. The president magnanimously refilled their drinks.

"You drive a hard bargain there, Baker. Very hard, in fact. Still, I think we can make this work."

"Glad you see it that way," Baker replied, lifting his tumbler and downing it in one go.

"You know," said McCarthy, swirling the contents of his tumbler, "when I was a young man, my father lent me a patch of land that I turned into a thriving chicken farm. Then, one day, it all came crashing down because influenza decided to come knocking. Rather than ask my own family for help, I hired some locals who didn't know a single thing about raising chickens. Over the course of several months, they decimated my flock. Who knows? Had I not gotten sick, I might still be shoveling chicken shit to this day."

"Chicken shit... politics," Baker said. "Same thing."

"Very good," McCarthy said, his eyes roving to what looked like half a chocolate cake. "A well-played hand. I just hope your luck holds. We are done here. Influenza can come at any time. Goodbye, Baker."

EPILOGUE

Someday, he thought, I would like to meet a monster
who looked like a monster.
—*Ira Levin,* The Boys from Brazil

February 10, 1960

He'd fallen right back into the Nazi experiment that drove him to the brink of madness during those final dark days at the end of the war. That's how it felt anyway.

His hair, which had only just started to grow back to normal length after his two-week stint at Manzanar, was falling out in alarming clumps and vomit continuously scorched his throat until the delicate tissue felt raw.

He willingly allowed a technician wearing a heavy lead vest to shoot bursts of radiation at his body and was unable to find a suitable level of warmth—owing to horrible paroxysms of chills that kept a proper night's sleep at a safe distance. Baker could only laugh at the irony, laugh at history's sadistic penchant for repeating itself over and over again. He envied his older brother, who was serenely dozing in a chair while an IV bag slowly trickled poison into the needle stuck in Baker's arm. A cocktail of who-knew-what turning his own body against him.

The whole ordeal made his epilepsy look tame by comparison, and the only remedies that might help (schnapps and cigarettes) were forbidden. Quitting both vices cold turkey was one of the hardest things Baker had ever done in his life.

He didn't know how much he had relied on booze and smokes until he was forced to cut them out entirely. In their stead, he'd taken to biting his nails, a habit that yielded its own brand of discomfort as the fingernails were gnawed down to bloody stumps.

The only saving grace was the prescription of heavy-duty painkillers he was meant to take only if the torment became unbearable. So, naturally, Baker swallowed one every hour on the hour.

While the sickness and pain were terribly familiar, the general circumstances were not. There was no German doctor gleefully removing a tumor from his arm without the use of an analgesic. He would not be left on an operating table to slowly die of dehydration and dysentery. There would be a lengthy recovery process, but he would not spend those months regaining his strength at a mass gravesite from which there was no escape.

He felt an indescribable sense of gratitude to Ze'ev as he listened to the hustle and bustle of nurses and doctors moving outside the private room (paid for in full by America's schmuck-in-chief). Ze'ev had accompanied him to every single appointment so far without a word of complaint, obviously making up for lost time.

Morris had been alone and angry for so long that the idea of seeing his family again seemed as impossible as McCarthy attending Shabbos services on a Saturday morning. It was why he had initially turned his own brother away. He was furious not at Ze'ev, but at himself—for walking down a corroded and potholed path of self-destruction while his salvation was out there all along, desperately searching for him.

The time they'd spent together these last few weeks, recalling obscure memories from childhood and laughing until their cheeks hurt, went beyond description. The horrors of the camps—of everything they'd seen and done—melted away in the face of this unspoken bond between brothers.

Despite the discomfort of the radiation and chemotherapy treatments, it was hard to remember when he'd felt this happy and content. Maybe it was that first night he'd spent with Sophia, the phony KGB spy who showed him there was more to life than pain and guilt.

Ze'ev had the same effect. He was the kind of person who could cut through all the bullshit. Someone who knew Morris almost as well as he knew himself.

"You've seen better days, Morris." Baker looked up so fast, he cricked his neck.

Ze'ev jerked awake, looking around and wiping a puddle of drool from his chin. "Who? Wuh?" he wondered aloud. His legs jerked out wildly and hit a side table covered in flowers and greeting cards that wished the recipient to GET WELL SOON!

Several vases of flowers—sent to the hospital by Hollis Li, Maeve Connolly, Rabbi Kahn, and the wives of the missing men Baker had brought home—wobbled and threatened to topple over. The biggest bouquet of them all was from Shelly Horowitz, who had profusely apologized for her behavior and insisted on lifting his ban from the synagogue.

Baker was actually due at the Horowitz household that Friday night for dinner along with Shira and Isaac Kremnitzer. Baker had surprisingly come around to Isaac, now only thinking of him as half the putz he once was.

Evelyn Yang leaned against the doorframe. "What?" she said, clearly in a teasing mood while Morris rubbed the back of his aching neck. "You thought I'd just be a good girl and stay in New York? You obviously don't know me very well, Morris Baker."

With a grin of comprehension, Ze'ev got up, stretched, and said something about grabbing a cup of coffee. He danced out of the room, singing a horrendously off-key rendition of Jackie Wilson's "That's Why (I Love You So)" and clapping his hands at irregular intervals.

"Make it two!" Evelyn called after him, and Ze'ev gave a jerky thumbs-up in response.

"Don't mind him," Baker said. "Just my clown of a brother."

"I bet he's got all sorts of embarrassing stories from when you two were kids."

"That's what I'm afraid of."

Evelyn sank into the free chair. "I just want to thank you for everything. My mother and I couldn't stop crying when the president announced William's innocence."

"When did you get back in town?"

"Yesterday. I actually had lunch with Mingmei Zhao," Evelyn said. "It's a bit odd having a little sister who seems so much older than I am. But since we're now children without a father, I thought it might be nice to be there for each other."

"Getting into the family business of smuggling?"

This drew a laugh from Evelyn. "Not quite. I did quit my teaching job in New York, though. Figured it's probably best to stick around Los Angeles for a while."

"I just lost my secretary if you're in need of a job. Pay's pretty decent, I hear."

"Tempting," said Evelyn. "Did you lose a finger?"

"Would you believe it if I said Kissinger made me cut it off in exchange for information?"

"I'm slowly learning that anything is possible when it comes to your life."

Baker smiled. "How's the novel coming along?"

"You know," said Evelyn, "I'm actually going to put that on the back burner for now. With everything that's happened, I think there are more worthwhile stories to tell. I've got an idea for a biography of sorts. I just hope the subject agrees to take part."

"Who is it?" asked Baker.

"You," said Evelyn.

"Me?"

"Why not? Your story is incredible. I think someone needs to start interviewing survivors of the concentration camps. People should hear their stories."

"I'm not so sure, Evelyn. No one cares about the Jews."

"That's exactly why I want to do it. We have to start holding ourselves accountable. My brother wasn't the first casualty of this administration, and he certainly won't be the last. The world needs to face the truth of what occurs when human beings are treated as roadblocks."

"What'd I miss?" Ze'ev had returned with the coffees.

"My life story, apparently," Baker said.

"So you'll do it?" Evelyn asked eagerly.

"I didn't say that, but it can't hurt to talk. Ze'ev, give the woman her coffee. She's going to need it when I start putting her to sleep."

Evelyn accepted the cup and turned toward Baker, an expectant look on her face.

"You already know the general beats," he said. "I guess it all starts with the shovel. That damned shovel and then the darkness..."

Even from the balcony of his palatial estate, he could not help but feel trapped. He once had the total confidence of a god and now look at him, cowering behind a collection of trees and vines. No matter how much greenery was razed to make way for this lavish compound, nature always beat back, an unrelenting squall blowing against humankind's progress.

A subtle breeze carried the scent of fresh air—one small benefit to living so far away from civilized society. The abundance of so many trees meant the oxygen was pure and uncontaminated by exhaust and other pollutants that choked the modern world. Even in such an unspoiled paradise—a veritable Eden—one could still detect the offending, primal stink of decaying roots, sodden fur, and the accumulated excrement of countless eons.

The jungle was a sanctuary, but it was also a prison—an oppressively humid cage of bloodsucking insects, howling primates, and endless rainfall. Its natural beauty matched only by its primal ferocity.

Everything in the Amazon had evolved to survive the anarchic canopy of thick foliage dripping with moisture and fungi. Frogs, no longer than two centimeters in length, could kill with a single touch; insect larvae could bore into thick trunks of coconut trees with mighty pincers; fish could strip a carcass down the bone; and snakes could crush the life out of a grown man and swallow him whole.

Yes, this was a harsh and unforgiving landscape that had recently added another determined survivor to its diverse ecosystem. Weak and on the verge of extinction, this new species arrived on foreign shores, aided by the kindness of confederates like Father Draganović and the vast stores of emergency wealth gathered during the war: gold and paintings long hidden away in secure bank accounts and hidden mine shafts. An untraceable bounty made possible by the Jewish filth of Europe, their only worthwhile contribution to the Reich's noble cause.

Like everything in this jungle, these remaining SS officers persevered and adapted, placing deep roots into the rich South American soil. In fifteen short years, they had procreated and multiplied, swelling their ranks to sustain a new German society an ocean away from home.

If anything, the new generation of young Aryans raised here was more ferocious than the preceding one. They were taught to think quickly and not to take anything for granted. Survival of the fittest. Hindsight sat at the core of the curriculum for the unspoiled children who went to sleep with a portrait of the Führer hanging over their beds, so that they could always gaze upon his shining countenance.

They knew nothing of the dark days of the Weimar Republic or the bombed-out cities where German women were raped by barbaric Russian soldiers. These children were pure, blank slates fueled by a combination of undying love for the Führer and an all-consuming lust for revenge against the people who had brought about his demise. The Jews, the Soviets, the Communists, the homosexuals, the Gypsies, and all the other lesser races that tainted the world and forced the ODESSA to hide in the shadows like rats on a ship.

But their time was coming. One day soon. Oh, yes. And when that day came, the world would see how ferocious they could be—as merciless and adaptable as any of the creatures found in the Amazon rain forest. A true product of the environment they'd been forced to use as a hiding spot for all these years.

"Sir?"

Martin Bormann turned to face his young adjutant, Dieter, who clicked his heels and saluted. Even down here, they kept up with the old uniforms: polished black boots, iron gray tunic, Death's Head cap.

"What is it?" Bormann asked, sounding annoyed, but inwardly grateful to have his mind distracted from the accursed jungle.

"It's Baker," Dieter said. "The Jew in California."

"Is he dead?"

"Well . . . no."

And this time, Dieter shrank back, imperceptibly pivoting away from the Brown Eminence, who began to swell with anger—an old bullfrog asserting its dominance.

Pushing sixty, he was no longer the specimen of perfect health. The stress of escaping Europe and assuming leadership of the ODESSA had turned him into a gaunt shadow of his former self—an unrecognizable specimen far removed from the paunchy and jovial man who had once served as Adolf Hitler's private secretary. His skin, once filled with ample stores of fat, hung limply in all the wrong places.

The only thing that remained of his youthful days was a death-like gaze that emanated from the intensely brown eyes sunken into his skull like a pair of hot coals melting into a fresh patch of snow. Like the grotesque Candiru of the Amazon Basin, his eyes could find their way into a person's body, whether the victim liked it or not. They bored into the soft tissue of the brain, scanning for treachery while giving nothing of Bormann's own thoughts away.

"What happened to Oberlander?" he asked.

"Dead," Dieter croaked. "It seems Baker...er...pushed him into a pit of hot tar."

Bormann's gnarled hands curled into fists and his assistant took a step back, as though the ODESSA leader was going to explode like a bundle of dynamite with a comedically short fuse. But Martin Bormann was better at controlling his rage than the Führer had been.

If the Führer had been a little better at reining in his emotions and rash decision-making tendencies, Germany might never have lost the war. Not that the war had ever ended for those who remained faithful and devoted to the cause, of course.

"Very well," Bormann said in a level tone. "We will try again, and this time, the Jew will die at our hands. Send a telegram to the good doctor in São Paulo. Tell him that his services are required right away."

"You mean Señor Aspiazu?" asked Dieter, nervous and uneasy.

This pleased Bormann. The doctor's name, even if it was just a pseudonym adopted after the war, still evoked the proper amount of fear in those who had only ever heard of him. Aspiazu's reputation, as the old saying went, preceded the man himself.

"Yes. And while you're at it, send a telegram to Dr. Tarek in Egypt. He'll be needed as well. I want this Baker problem dealt with properly. No foul-ups. And I mean it. The Jew will not thwart us for a third time."

"Yes, sir. However, I regret to inform you that Baker is not the only problem," added Dieter, who was clearly on the verge of soiling his pants with fear. Bormann did not answer, allowing the enraged silence to force his adjutant into speech. "Yes, well…um, our contacts in Buenos Aires have sent word that a small band of Israelis are snooping around the city, asking awkward questions. Right now, they're groping in the dark, but it could become a larger problem down the road."

"Let the Jewish vermin grope around blindly, then," said Bormann. "Aspiazu and Tarek will take care of them *first*."

Dieter saluted again, clicking his heels together. "Yes, sir. Of course, sir. Heil Hitler."

"Heil Hitler," responded Bormann, providing a perfunctory salute back. He was already turning away to face the jungle again, a pained look on his face. *Hitler*, he thought to himself. *Such a weak man he turned out to be. The world deserves a name with more power.* Summer had come to Brazil and the oppressive humidity was wreaking havoc on his arthritis. It seemed that, every day, another part of his body betrayed him.

The thought of the reliable doctors making short work of Baker and the Israelis made him forget about the woes of aging for a blissful moment. Imagining the Jews' pain and agony filled him with an excited vigor that bordered on arousal.

Bormann watched in silence as thunderclouds roiled on the horizon, the rain forest living up to its name. He walked back inside, arthritic fingers laced behind his back in triumph, when the first warm drops began falling on the balcony. Inside his study, he approached a large fish tank containing a school of piranhas fished out of the local river. Their underbites and bulging eyeballs gave them the appearance of immensely stupid creatures, though Bormann knew better. Much like the ODESSA, these animals knew nothing except survival. Survival and hunger.

Next to the tank sat a small wooden table topped with a tea towel stained red. Bormann whipped away the fabric to reveal a bloodied cow's leg severed at the knee—a gory leftover from the compound's cattle ranch and adjoining slaughterhouse. Without hesitation, he picked up the hoofed appendage and dropped it into the tank, where the piranhas moved as one, tearing off large chunks of flesh with their razor-like teeth.

"Your blood is in the water, Baker," Bormann whispered, admiring the ferocity of the feeding frenzy with glee. The leg was almost stripped to the bone, a pearly white already showing through the frothing water and silt. "We can smell it and we're getting close. No more mistakes."

Only when bare bone and hoof sank to the pebbled bottom of the tank did Bormann stand up. He was now feeling mighty peckish himself and headed for the kitchen for a bloody steak.

The first one came out too well done. Bormann shot the chef. He decided to make it himself.

ACKNOWLEDGMENTS

I've said it before and I'll say it again: No one really cares about the acknowledgments at the end of a book. Don't try and deny it, you're going to skip this part, aren't you? It's all right—I'd probably do the same if I were in your position. I hold no ill will against you, dear reader. Just know that a book is a genuine embodiment of that time-honored axiom "It takes a village," and, as such, acknowledgments are a crucial part of the final product you hold in your hand.

An author is only as good as the support system behind them. Parents, siblings, significant others, spouses, early readers, editors, agents, and copyeditors deserve an equal share of the literary pie. It's my name on the cover, yes, but everyone who has supported this book along the way—either directly or indirectly—deserves a special shout-out. If you meet any of the following individuals on the street, shake their hand and congratulate them.

First and foremost, I'd like to pay tribute to the man who made this second adventure with Morris Baker possible: my literary agent, the great Scott Miller of Trident Media Group. When he called me up in late 2019 and said he'd successfully negotiated a two-book deal, I could hardly believe my ears. His continual belief in my writing abilities never ceases to amaze me. Scott, you humble me every day, and, as I've said before, I am forever in your debt.

And then we have the good folks over at Grand Central Publishing, who are forced to put up with my constant flow of neurotic emails on a regular basis. In all seriousness, though, *Beat the Devils* and *Sunset Empire* wouldn't be half as good without the diligence, encouragement, and promotion of the tireless individuals working behind the scenes. They are the ones fixing grammatical errors, addressing narrative gaps, pitching cover art, hawking the finished product for potential media coverage, and performing a whole manner of tasks the human mind can barely fathom.

Well, this human mind at least.

That talented crew includes my uncompromising editor, Wes Miller, who shares my love of James Bond–style interrogations; editorial maven Lauren Bello, sacred purveyor of copyedits and design layouts; marketing manager Alana Spendley and senior publicist Kamrun Nesa, the greatest hype team an author could ever hope for; Bob Castillo, a patient teacher in the mystical arts of editorial and typesetting practices; and GCP senior VP and publisher Ben Sevier, the wonderful man who decided to take a chance on this humbled writer.

As promised, here is an entire section dedicated to my good friend and fellow creative writer Josh Dicristo (or "JD," as he's known in some circles). Hollywood producers, if you're reading this, I'd like you to hire this man to write and/or punch up your screenplays ASAP. Sign him to a multiyear contract if you have to. I promise it'll be worth every penny. If you need proof of his immense talent, go check out his debut feature, "Kings," on YouTube. Josh not only took the time to read *Sunset Empire*, but he also sent along beautifully incisive feedback on a regular basis—all while preparing for a wedding and the move to a new home. Nearly every one of his notes and suggestions made me stop and say to myself: "Why the hell didn't I think of that?!" JD, you are a veritable wellspring of endless humor, warmth, and imagination. Thank you!!

Next up we have Ethan Riback, who should seriously consider a job as a literary editor. Believe me when I tell you this man's thoughtfulness with regards to story and character development (bullet-pointed in neat Google docs for the author's own convenience) is absolutely staggering. Ethan, you gave *Beat the Devils* and *Sunset Empire* more of your time than either deserved, and for that, I am like the little green aliens in the *Toy Story* films: "Eternally grateful." Wishing you and Nick a beautiful life together! (PS: Tell Phoebe I say hello.)

I know the book is already dedicated to her, but my wife deserves a second shout-out. Hi, Roy!! Love you!! **waves vigorously and blows kisses**...She's rolling her eyes, isn't she? Leora, I work hard to make you proud every single day. I'd also like to use this paragraph to draw attention to our adorable Cavapoo: Archie, the cutest little pup you ever did see.

To my family—Mom, Dad, Shani, Rob (who actually came up with the title *Sunset Empire*), Lenny, Ari, Noah, Savta, Uncle Neal, and Uncle Herb—I love you all. And to my new in-laws, the Rychiks—Dr. Jack, Susan, Jordie, Jason, Tali, and Max Hayes—thank you for allowing me into your little club. Believe it or not, Dr. Rychik used a copy of *Beat the Devils* during the toast at my wedding. It was adorable.

And here comes the not-so-humble brag. I cannot tell you how surreal an experience it is when folks like Richard Masur (who played the dog handler, Clark, in John Carpenter's *The Thing*—aka, my favorite movie ever), G Tom Mac (writer/singer of "Cry Little Sister" in 1987's *The Lost Boys*), and Ben Parker (writer/director of the stellar WWII thriller *Burial*) tell you they've ordered your book when you're supposed to be interviewing *them*. Never gets old!

Finally, I doff my cap to those friends, colleagues, peers, and cheerleaders who have supported me on this incredible journey:

J.D. Lifshitz, Mark Greaney, Michael Kronenberg, Ian R. MacLeod, Dr. Eileen Watts, Barry Kirzner, Jordan McClain, Trent Moore, Caitlin Busch, Adam Pockross, Dennis Culver, Alexis Loinaz, Brian Silliman, Matthew Jackson, James Grebey, Marilyn Hassid, Avi and Kayla Pusateri, David Koepp, Ben Wolbransky, Ariel Paz, Steven Yaffe, Ricardo Yanofksy, Peter Fox, David Weil, Liam Shamir, Mike Reyes, Benjamin Schoenfeld, Brendan DuBois, Emily and Mark Appeldorf, Lynn and David Weiss, the Ohayon family, David Klein, Micah Sokolsky, Libby Walker, Jesse Rosenstein, Ryan Graudin, David Dahan, Laizer Mangel, Michael Mellul, Sammy and Dee Blivaiss, Lyssia Katan, Eden Elimelech, David and Sarah Fleishaker, Nathan and Ashley Stritch, Judah Joseph, Kobi Malamud, Nathaniel and Miriam Dahan, Yaniv Dahan, Neal Strauss, David Diamond, Avital Ash, David Tessler, Aaron and Stacie Berk, Talia and Eytan Baratz, Greg and Gabby Bennett, Jake Fischer, Avi Bash, Ben Dalezman, Dawn Gilliam, Becca Tepper, Emily Austin, Jessica and Ben Rosenberg, Richie and Barbara Simon, Steve Kremnitzer, Seth Taratoot, Davida and Matan Ayash, Renee Zwillenberg, Anne Most, Stephen Vanyo, David Weiner, Yaakov Bagley, Greg Longstreet, and Rabbi Chaim and Moussia Goldstein.

If you're looking for more reading material after this one, I highly recommend checking out Robert A. Rockaway's *But He Was Good to His Mother: The Lives and Crimes of Jewish Gangsters* (Gefen Publishing House); David M. Oshinsky's *A Conspiracy So Immense: The World of Joe McCarthy* (Free Press); and Larry Tye's *Demagogue: The Life and Long Shadow of Senator Joe McCarthy* (Mariner Books). Each of these provided me with invaluable historical background for *Sunset Empire*.

My personal favorite is the story of Mickey Cohen's run-in with a pair of Nazi sympathizers in a Los Angeles county jail (see Chapter 34). That actually happened!

Okay, spiel over. Thanks for coming to my TED Talk. You can play me off now…

ABOUT THE AUTHOR

Josh Weiss is an author from South Jersey. Raised in a proud Jewish home, he was instilled with an appreciation for his cultural heritage from a very young age. Today Josh is utterly fascinated with the convergence of Judaism and popular culture in film, television, comics, literature, and other media. After college, he became a freelance entertainment journalist, writing stories for *SYFY WIRE*, *The Hollywood Reporter, Forbes*, and Marvel Entertainment. He currently resides in Philadelphia with his incredible wife, Leora, and their Cavapoo, Archie; as well as an extensive collection of graphic T-shirts, movie posters, vinyl records, and a few books, of course.